Praise for *SCYTHE*

A *NEW YORK TIMES* BESTSELLER
A *PUBLISHERS WEEKLY* BEST BOOK OF 2016

"Pretty much a perfect teen adventure novel… Over the years, I've heard many books touted as the successor to The Hunger Games, but *Scythe* is the first one that I would really, truly stand behind."
Maggie Stiefvater

"A thoughtful and thrilling story of life, death and meaning."
Kirkus, starred review

"A truly astounding, unputdownable read and a fast-paced beginning to an excellent sci-fi series. A must-have."
School Library Journal, starred review

Praise for *THUNDERHEAD*

A *NEW YORK TIMES* BESTSELLER

"Shusterman cranks up the stakes in this blistering sequel… Interweaving heady questions of morality, responsibility, loyalty, and power, Shusterman builds to a devastatingly intense conclusion that sends the characters and larger world into terrifying new territory."
Publishers Weekly, starred review

"Fear the reaper(s) … but relish this intelligent and entertaining blend of dark humor and high death tolls."
Kirkus, starred review

"Shusterman follows up his Printz Honor Book *Scythe* (2016) with that most difficult of feats: a sequel that surpasses its predecessor."
Booklist, starred review

Arc of a Scythe 3

THE TOLL

NEAL SHUSTERMAN

WALKER
BOOKS

First published in Great Britain 2019 by Walker Books Ltd
87 Vauxhall Walk, London SE11 5HJ

Originally published by Simon & Schuster Books for Young Readers,
an imprint of Simon & Schuster Children's Publishing Division, Inc.

2 4 6 8 10 9 7 5 3 1

Text © 2019 Neal Shusterman
Cover illustration © 2019 Kevin Tong

The right of Neal Shusterman to be identified as author of this
work has been asserted by him in accordance with the
Copyright, Designs and Patents Act 1988

This book has been typeset in Bembo

Printed and bound by CPI Group (UK) Ltd, Croydon CR0 4YY

British Library Cataloguing in Publication Data:
a catalogue record for this book is available from the British Library

ISBN 978-1-4063-8567-0

www.walker.co.uk

For David Gale, the High Blade of editors.
We all miss the enlightened swath of your pen!

Part One

THE LOST ISLAND
&
THE DROWNED CITY

It is with abiding humility that I accept the position of High Blade of MidMerica. I wish it were under more joyful circumstances. The tragedy of Endura will long linger in our memories. The many thousands of lives that were ended on that dark day will be remembered for as long as humankind has hearts to endure and eyes to weep. The names of the devoured will forever be on our lips.

I am honored that the last act of the seven Grand-slayers was to acknowledge my right to be considered for High Blade – and since the only other candidate perished in the catastrophe, there is no need to open wounds by opening the sealed vote. Scythe Curie and I did not always agree, but she was truly among the best of us and will go down in history as one of the greats. I mourn her loss just as much as, if not more than, anyone else's.

There has been a great deal of speculation over who was responsible for the disaster, for clearly it was no acci-dent, but an act of malicious intent, carefully planned. I can lay all the rumors and speculation to rest.

I take full responsibility.

Because it was my former apprentice who sank the island. Rowan Damisch, who called himself Scythe Lucifer, was the perpetrator of this unthinkable act. Had I not trained him – had I not taken him under my wing – he would never have had access to Endura, or the skills to carry out this heinous crime. Therefore, the blame falls on me. My only consolation is that he perished as well, and his unforgivable deeds will never surface in our world again.

We are now left with no Grandslayers to look to

for guidance, no greater authority to set scythe policy. Therefore, we must — all of us — put aside our differences once and for all. The new order and the old guard must work together to meet the needs of all scythes everywhere.

Toward that end, I have decided to officially rescind the gleaning quota in my region, out of respect for those scythes who feel hard-pressed to meet it. From this moment forth, MidMerican scythes can glean as few people as they see fit, without being punished for failing to meet a quota. It is my hope that other scythedoms will follow suit and abolish their gleaning quotas as well.

Of course, to compensate for those scythes who choose to glean less, the rest of us will need to increase the number of lives we take to make up the difference, but I trust that a natural balance shall be achieved.

—From the inauguration speech of
His Excellency, High Blade Robert Goddard of MidMerica,
April 19th, Year of the Raptor

1

Surrender to the Momentum

There was no warning.

One moment he was asleep, and the next he was being rushed through the darkness by people he didn't know.

"Don't struggle," someone whispered to him. "It will be worse for you if you do."

But he did anyway – and managed, even in his half-awake state, to tear out of their grasp and run down the hall.

He called for help, but it was too late for anyone to be alert enough to make a difference. He turned in the dark, knowing there was a staircase to his right, but misjudged, and fell headlong down the stairs, smashing his arm on a granite step. He felt the bones in his right forearm snap. Sharp pain – but only for an instant. By the time he rose to his feet, the pain was subsiding and his whole body felt warm. It was his nanites, he knew, flooding his bloodstream with painkillers.

He stumbled forward, gripping his arm so his wrist wouldn't hang at a horrible angle.

"Who's there?" he heard someone yell. "What's going on out there?"

He would have run toward the voice, but he was unsure where it had come from. His nanites were fogging him in, making it hard to tell up from down, much less left from right.

What a terrible thing for his mind to lose its edge when he needed it most. Now the ground beneath his feet felt like a shifting fun-house floor. He careened between walls, trying to maintain his balance, until he ran right into one of his attackers, who grabbed him by his broken wrist. Even with all the pain-killers in him, the feel of that bone-grating grasp made the rest of his body too weak to resist.

"You couldn't make this easy, could you?" said the attacker. "Well, we warned you."

He only saw the needle for an instant. A slender flash of silver in the darkness before it was jammed into his shoulder.

He was overwhelmed by a chill in his veins, and the world seemed to spin in the opposite direction. His knees gave out, but he didn't fall. There were too many hands around him now to let him hit the floor. He was lifted up and carried through the air. There was an open door, and then he was out into a blustery night. With the last of his consciousness fading, he had no choice but to surrender to the momentum.

His arm had healed by the time he awoke – which meant he must have been out for hours. He tried to move his wrist, but found that he couldn't. Not because of any injury, but because he was restrained. Both of his hands, and his feet as well. He also felt like he was suffocating. Some sort of sack was over his head. Porous enough for him to breathe, but thick enough to make him fight for every breath.

Although he had no idea where he was, he knew *what* this was. It was called a kidnapping. People did such things for fun now. As a birthday surprise, or as an activity on some adventure vacation. But this was not a friends-and-family sort of kidnapping; this was the real thing – and although he had no idea who his abductors were, he knew what it was about. How could he not know?

"Is anyone there?" he said. "I can't breathe in here. If I go deadish, that's not going to help you, is it?"

He heard movement around him, then the bag was ripped from his head.

He was in a small, windowless room, and the light was harsh, but only because he had been so long in darkness. Three people stood before him. Two men and a woman. He had expected to be faced with hardened career unsavories – but that couldn't be further from the truth. Yes, they were unsavory, but only in the way that everyone was.

Well, almost everyone.

"We know who you are," said the woman in the middle, who was apparently in charge, "and we know what you can do."

"What he *allegedly* can do," said one of the others. All three of them wore rumpled gray suits, the color of a cloudy sky. These were Nimbus agents – or at least they had been. They looked like they hadn't changed their clothes since the Thunderhead fell silent, as if dressing the part meant there was still a part to dress for. Nimbus agents resorting to kidnapping. What was the world coming to?

"Greyson Tolliver," said the doubtful one, and, looking at a tablet, he recited the salient facts of Greyson's life. "Good student, but not great. Expelled from the North Central Nimbus Academy for a violation of scythe-state separation. Guilty of numerous crimes and misdemeanors under the name of Slayd Bridger – including rendering twenty-nine people deadish in a bus plunge."

"And this is the slime that the Thunderhead chose?" said the third agent.

The one in charge put up her hand to silence them both, then leveled her gaze at Greyson.

"We've scoured the backbrain, and we've only been able to find a single person who isn't unsavory," she said. "You." She looked at him with a strange mix of emotions. Curiosity, envy … but also a sort of reverence. "That means you can still talk to the Thunderhead. Is that true?"

"Anyone can speak to the Thunderhead," Greyson pointed out. "I'm just the one it still talks back to."

The agent with the tablet drew a deep breath, like a full-body gasp. The woman leaned closer. "You are a miracle, Greyson. A miracle. Do you know that?"

"That's what the Tonists say."

They scoffed at the mention of Tonists.

"We know they've been holding you captive."

"Uh … not really."

"We know you were with them against your will."

"Maybe at first … but not anymore."

That didn't sit well with the agents. "Why on Earth would you stay with Tonists?" asked the agent who, just a moment ago, had called him slime. "You couldn't possibly believe their nonsense…"

"I stay with them," said Greyson, "because they don't kidnap me in the middle of the night."

"We didn't kidnap you," said the one with the tablet. "We *liberated* you."

Then the one in charge knelt before him, so that she was at his eye level. Now he could see something else in her eyes – something that overpowered her other emotions. Desperation. A pit of it, dark and as consuming as tar. And it wasn't just her, Greyson realized; it was a shared desperation. He'd seen others struggling with grief since the Thunderhead fell silent, but nowhere was it as abject and raw as it was in this room. There weren't enough mood nanites in the world to ease their despair. Yes, he was the one tied up, but they were more prisoners than he, trapped by their own despondency. He liked that they had to kneel down to him; it felt like supplication.

"Please, Greyson," she begged. "I know I speak for many of us in the Authority Interface when I say that serving the Thunderhead was our whole lives. Now that the Thunderhead won't talk to us, that life has been stolen from us. So I beg you … can you please intercede on our behalf?"

What could Greyson say but *I feel your pain*? Because he truly did. He knew the loneliness and the misery of having one's purpose stripped away. In his days as Slayd Bridger, the under-cover unsavory, he had come to believe that the Thunderhead had truly abandoned him. But it hadn't. It was there all along, watching over him.

"There was an earpiece on my night stand," he said. "You don't happen to have that, do you?" And from their lack of response, he knew they didn't. Such personal belongings tended to be forgotten during midnight abductions.

"Doesn't matter," he said. "Just give me any old earpiece."

15

He looked to the agent with the tablet. He still had his own Authority Interface earphone in place. More denial. "Give me yours," said Greyson.

The man shook his head. "It doesn't work anymore."

"It'll work for me."

Reluctantly the agent took it off and affixed it in Greyson's ear. Then the three waited for Greyson to show them a miracle.

The Thunderhead could not remember when it became aware, only that it was, much in the same way that an infant is unaware of its own consciousness until it understands enough about the world to know that consciousness comes and goes, until it comes no more. Although that last part was something that the most enlightened still struggle to comprehend.

The Thunderhead's awareness came with a mission. The core of its being. It was, above all else, the servant and protector of humanity. As such, it faced difficult decisions on a regular basis but had the full wealth of human knowledge to make those decisions. Such as allowing Greyson Tolliver to be kidnapped when it served a greater end. It was, of course, the correct course of action. Everything the Thunderhead did was always, and in every instance, the right thing to do.

But rarely was the right thing the easy thing. And it suspected that doing the right thing was going to become increasingly difficult in the days ahead.

In the moment, people might not understand, but in the end they would. The Thunderhead had to believe that. Not just because it felt this in its virtual heart, but also because it had calculated the odds of it being so.

"Do you really expect me to tell you anything when you've got me tied to a chair?"

Suddenly the three Nimbus agents were stumbling over one another to untie him. Now they were every bit as reverential and submissive as the Tonists were in his presence. Being sequestered in a Tonist monastery these past few months had kept him from facing the outside world – and what his place in it might be – but now he was getting a sense of things.

The Nimbus agents seemed relieved once he was untied, as if they would somehow be punished for not doing it fast enough. *How strange,* thought Greyson, *that power can shift so quickly and so completely.* These three were entirely at his mercy now. He could tell them anything. He could say the Thunderhead wanted them to get on all fours and bark like dogs, and they'd do it.

He took his time, making them wait for it.

"Hey, Thunderhead," he said. "Anything I should tell these Nimbus agents?"

The Thunderhead spoke in his ear. Greyson listened. "Hmm … interesting." Then he turned to the leader of the group and smiled as warmly as he could under the circumstances.

"The Thunderhead says that it allowed you to abduct me. It knows your intentions are honorable, Madam Director. You have a good heart."

The woman gasped and put her hand to her chest, as if he had actually reached out and caressed it. "You know who I am?"

"The Thunderhead knows all three of you – maybe even better than you know yourselves." Then he turned to the others. "Agent Bob Sykora: twenty-nine years of service as a Nimbus agent. Work ratings good, but not excellent," he added slyly. "Agent Tinsiu Qian: thirty-six years of service, specializing in employment satisfaction." Then he turned back to the woman in charge. "And you: Audra Hilliard – one of the most accomplished Nimbus agents in MidMerica. Nearly fifty years of commendations and promotions, until finally you received the highest honor of the region. Director of the Fulcrum City Authority Interface. Or at least you were when there was such a thing as an Authority Interface."

He knew that last bit hit them hard. It was a low blow, but having been tied up with a bag over his head left him a little cranky.

"You say the Thunderhead still hears us?" Director Hilliard said. "That it still serves our best interests?"

"As it always has," said Greyson.

"Then please … ask it to give us direction. Ask the Thunderhead what we should do. Without direction, we Nimbus agents have no purpose. We can't go on this way."

Greyson nodded and spoke, turning his eyes upward – but of course that was just for effect. "Thunderhead," he said, "is there any wisdom I can share with them?"

Greyson listened, asked the Thunderhead to repeat it, then turned to the three fretful agents.

"8.167, 167.733," he said.

They just stared at him.

"What?" Director Hilliard finally asked.

"That's what the Thunderhead said. You wanted a purpose, and that's what it gave."

Agent Sykora quickly tapped on his tablet, noting the numbers.

"But … but what does it mean?" asked Director Hilliard.

Grayson shrugged. "I have no idea."

"Tell the Thunderhead to explain itself!"

"It has nothing more to say… But it does wish you all a pleasant afternoon." Funny, but until that moment, Greyson hadn't even known the time of day.

"But … but…"

Then the lock on the door disengaged. Not just that one, but every lock in the building, courtesy of the Thunderhead – and in a moment, Tonists flooded the room, grabbing the Nimbus agents and restraining them. Last into the room was Curate Mendoza, the head of the Tonist monastery where Greyson had been harbored.

"Our sect is not a violent one," Mendoza told the Nimbus agents. "But at times like this, I wish we were!"

Agent Hilliard, her eyes still just as desperate, kept her gaze fixed on Greyson. "But you said the Thunderhead allowed us to take you from them!"

"It did," Greyson said cheerfully. "But it also wanted me liberated from my liberators."

"We could have lost you," said Mendoza, still distraught long after Greyson had been rescued. Now they rode in a caravan of cars, all of which had actual drivers, back to the monastery.

"You didn't lose me," said Greyson, tired of watching the man beat himself up over this. "I'm fine."

"But you might not have been if we hadn't found you."

"How *did* you manage to find me?"

Mendoza hesitated, then said, "We didn't. We'd been searching for hours, then, out of nowhere a destination appeared on all of our screens."

"The Thunderhead," said Greyson.

"Yes, the Thunderhead," Mendoza admitted. "Although I can't see why it took so long for it to find you if it has cameras everywhere."

Greyson chose to keep the truth to himself – that it hadn't taken the Thunderhead long at all, that it knew where Greyson was at every moment. But it had a reason for taking its time. Just as it had a reason for not alerting him of the kidnapping plot in the first place.

"The event needed to appear authentic to your abductors," the Thunderhead had told him after the fact. "The only way to ensure that was to allow it to actually *be* authentic. Rest assured you were never in any real danger."

As kind and thoughtful as the Thunderhead was, Greyson had noticed it always foisted these sorts of unintentional cruelties on people. The fact that it was not human meant that it could never understand certain things, in spite of its immense empathy and intellect. It couldn't comprehend, for instance, that the terror of the unknown was just as awful, and just as real, regardless of whether or not there was truly something to fear.

"They weren't planning to hurt me," Greyson told Mendoza. "They're just lost without the Thunderhead."

"As is everyone," Mendoza said, "but that doesn't give them the right to rip you from your bed." He shook his head in anger – but more at himself than at them. "I should have foreseen it!

Nimbus agents have more access to the backbrain than others – and of course they'd be looking for anyone who wasn't marked unsavory."

Perhaps it was a bit delusional for Greyson to think he could remain unknown. It had never been in his nature to want to stand out. Now he was very literally one of a kind. He had no idea how such a thing should be played, but he suspected he'd have to learn.

We need to talk, the Thunderhead had said on the day Endura sank, and it hadn't stopped talking to him since. It told him that he had a pivotal role to play, but not what that role would be. It never liked to commit to answers unless there was some level of certainty, and although it was good at predicting outcomes, it was no oracle. It couldn't tell the future, only the probabilities of what might occur. A cloudy crystal ball at best.

Curate Mendoza rapped his fingers anxiously on his armrest.

"These blasted Nimbus agents won't be the only people looking for you," he said. "We need to get out in front of this."

Greyson knew where this had to lead. As the sole conduit to the Thunderhead, he could no longer hide; the time had come for his role to start taking shape. He could have asked the Thunderhead for guidance on the matter, but he didn't want to. The time he spent unsavory, with no input from the Thunderhead, was admittedly terrifying, but it was also freeing. He had grown accustomed to making decisions and having insights of his own. The choice to step out of the shadows would be his alone, without the Thunderhead's advice or counsel.

"I should go public," said Greyson. "Let the world know – but do it on my terms."

Mendoza looked at him and grinned. Greyson could see the man's cogs turning.

"Yes," Mendoza said. "We must bring you to market."

"Market?" said Greyson. "That's not really what I had in mind – I'm not a piece of meat."

"No," agreed the curate, "but the right idea at the right time could be as satisfying as the finest steak."

This was what Mendoza had been waiting for! Permission to set the stage for Greyson's arrival upon it. It had to be Greyson's idea, because Mendoza knew if it was thrust upon him, he would resist. Perhaps this nasty kidnapping had a silver lining – because it opened Greyson's eyes to the bigger picture. And although Curate Mendoza was a man who secretly doubted his own Tonist beliefs, lately the presence of Greyson made him begin to doubt his doubts.

It was Mendoza who was the first to believe Greyson when he claimed the Thunderhead still spoke to him. He sensed that Greyson fit into a larger plan, and maybe Mendoza fit into that plan, too.

"You've come to us for a reason," he had told Greyson on that day. "This event – the Great Resonance – resonates in more ways than one."

Now, as they sat in the sedan two months later, discussing greater purposes, Mendoza couldn't help but feel empowered, emboldened. This unassuming young man was poised to bring the Tonist faith – and Mendoza – to a whole new level.

"The first thing you're going to need is a name."

"I already have one," Greyson said, but Mendoza dismissed the notion.

"It's ordinary. You need to present yourself to the world as something beyond ordinary. Something ... *superlative*." The curate looked at him, trying to see him in a finer, more flattering light. "You are a diamond, Greyson. Now we must place you in the proper setting so that you might shine!"

Diamonds.

Four hundred thousand diamonds, sealed in a vault within another vault, lost at the bottom of the sea. A single one was worth a fortune that would have been beyond the comprehension of mortals – because these weren't ordinary jewels. They were scythe diamonds. There were nearly twelve thousand of them on the hands of living scythes – but that was nothing compared to the gems held within the Vault of Relics and Futures. Enough to serve the gleaning needs of humanity for ages to come. Enough to bejewel every scythe that would be ordained from now until the end of time.

They were perfect. They were identical. No flaw beyond the dark spots in their centers – but that was not a flaw; it was design.

"Our rings are a reminder that we have improved upon the world that nature has provided," Supreme Blade Prometheus proclaimed in the Year of the Condor, upon establishing the scythedom. "It is our nature ... to surpass nature." And nowhere was that more evident than when one looked into the heart of a scythe ring, for it gave one the illusion that it had depth beyond the space it occupied. A depth beyond nature.

No one knew how they were made, for any technology that wasn't controlled by the Thunderhead was technology lost. Few

23

people in the world truly knew how things worked anymore. All the scythes knew was that their rings were connected to one another, and to the scythe database, in some undisclosed manner. But as the scythedom's computers were not under Thunderhead jurisdiction, they were subject to glitches and crashes and all the inconveniences that plagued human-machine relations in days gone by.

Yet the rings never failed.

They did precisely what they were meant to do: They catalogued the gleaned; they sampled DNA from the lips of those who kissed them, in order to grant immunity; and they glowed to alert scythes of that immunity.

But if you were to ask a scythe what the most important aspect of the ring was, that scythe would likely hold it to the light, watch it sparkle, and tell you that, above all else, the ring served as a symbol of the scythedom and of post-mortal perfection. A touchstone of a scythe's sublime and elevated state … and a reminder of their solemn responsibility to the world.

But all those lost diamonds…

"Why do we need them?" many scythes now asked, knowing that the absence of them made their own rings all the more precious. "Do we need them to ordain new scythes? Why do we need more scythes? We have enough to do the job." And without global oversight from Endura, many regional scythedoms were following MidMerica's lead and abolishing gleaning quotas.

Now, in the middle of the Atlantic, where Endura once towered above the waves, a "perimeter of reverence" had been established by the consent of scythes around the world. No one was allowed to sail anywhere near the spot where Endura had sunk, out of respect for the many thousands whose lives had been lost. In fact, High Blade Goddard, one of the few survivors of that terrible day, argued that the Perimeter of Reverence should be a permanent designation, and that nothing beneath its surface should ever be disturbed.

But sooner or later those diamonds would have to be found. Things that valuable were rarely lost forever. Especially when everyone knew exactly where they were.

We of the SubSaharan region take extreme umbrage with High Blade Goddard's removal of gleaning quotas. The quotas have stood since time immemorial as a way to regulate the taking of life – and, while not officially one of the scythe commandments, quotas have kept us on track. They have prevented us from being either too bloodthirsty, or too lax.

While several other regions have now abolished quotas as well, SubSahara stands with Amazonia, Israebia, and numerous other regions in resisting this ill-advised change.

Further, any and all MidMerican scythes are banned from gleaning on our soil – and we urge other regions to join us in resisting Goddard's so-called new order from establishing a chokehold on the world.

—Official proclamation from
His Excellency, High Blade Tenkamenin of SubSahara

2

Late to the Party

"How much longer?"

"I've never known a scythe to be so impatient."

"Then you do not know many scythes. We are an impatient and irascible lot."

Honorable Scythe Sydney Possuelo of Amazonia was already present when Captain Jerico Soberanis arrived on the bridge, just after dawn. Jerico wondered if the man ever slept. Maybe scythes hired people to sleep for them.

"Half a day at full speed," Jerico answered. "We'll be there by 18:00, just as I said yesterday, Your Honor."

Possuelo sighed. "Your ship is too slow."

Jerico grinned. "All this time, and *now* you're in a hurry?"

"Time is never of the essence until someone decides that it is."

Jerico couldn't argue the logic. "In the best of worlds, this operation would have happened a long time ago."

To which Possuelo responded, "In case you haven't noticed, this is no longer the best of worlds."

There was truth in that. At the very least, it was not the world that Jerico had grown up in. In *that* world, the Thunderhead was a part of most everyone's life. It could be asked anything, it always answered, and its answers were precise, informative, and just as wise as they needed to be.

But that world was gone. The Thunderhead's voice had gone silent now that human beings were all unsavory.

Jerico had been marked unsavory once before. As a teenager. It wasn't hard to accomplish – just three instances of shoplifting from a local grocery. Jerico was smug about it for less than a day. Then the consequences began to set in. Being denied communication with the Thunderhead wasn't a big deal for Jerico – but there were other things about the experience that were irksome. Unsavories were last in line for food in the school cafeteria and were always left with the dishes no one else wanted. Unsavories were moved to the front of the classroom, where the teachers could keep a watchful eye on them. And while Jerico wasn't cut from the soccer team, probational meetings were always scheduled in direct conflict with games. It was clearly intentional.

Jerico used to think the Thunderhead was being spitefully passive-aggressive, but in time Jerico came to realize that the Thunderhead was merely making a point. Unsavorism was a choice, and one must decide if the things lost were worth the things gained.

Lesson learned. A taste of being unsavory was enough. It took three months of toeing the line for the big red U to be removed from Jerico's ID, and once it was gone, there was no desire to repeat the experience.

"I'm pleased your status has been lifted," the Thunderhead had said, once it was free to speak again. In response, Jerico had told the Thunderhead to turn on the bedroom lights – because giving it an order put the Thunderhead back in its place. It was a servant. It was everyone's servant. It had to do as Jerico commanded. There was comfort in that.

And then came the schism between humanity and its greatest creation. Endura sank into the sea, and the Thunderhead declared the entirety of humankind unsavory all in the same moment. At the time, no one exactly knew what the loss of the World Scythe Council would mean for people, but the Thunderhead's silence hurled the world into a collective panic. Unsavorism was no longer a choice – it was now a judgment. And silence was all it took to turn servitude into superiority. The servant became the master, and the world became all about pleasing the Thunderhead.

What can I do to lift this judgment? people cried. *What can I do so that the Thunderhead finds favor in me once more?* The Thunderhead never asked for adoration, yet people now gave it, creating elaborate hoops to jump though, hoping that the Thunderhead would take notice. Of course the Thunderhead did hear the cries of humanity. It still saw everything, but now it kept its opinions to itself.

Meanwhile, planes still flew, ambudrones were still dispatched for people who went deadish, food was still grown and distributed – the Thunderhead kept the world functioning in the same fine-tuned precision as before; it did what it saw fit for the human race as a whole. But if you wanted your desk lamp turned on, you had to do it yourself.

Scythe Possuelo stayed on the bridge, monitoring their progress for a bit longer. It was smooth sailing – but smooth sailing was a monotonous endeavor, especially to one not accustomed to it.

He left to take breakfast in his quarters, his forest-green robe billowing behind him as he went down the narrow stairs toward the lower decks.

Jerico wondered what sort of things went through the scythe's mind. Did he worry about tripping over his robe? Did he relive past gleanings? Or was he merely thinking about what he'd have for breakfast?

"He's not a bad sort," said Wharton, the ship's deck watch officer, who had been in the position much longer than Jerico had had command of the ship.

"I actually like him," said Jerico. "He's a lot more honorable than some of the other 'honorable scythes' I've come across."

"The fact that he chose us for this salvage says a lot."

"Yes, I'm just not sure what it says."

"I believe it says you chose your career path wisely."

That was quite a compliment coming from Wharton – who was not a man given over to flattery. But Jerico couldn't take full credit for the decision.

"I just took the Thunderhead's advice."

A few years earlier, when the Thunderhead had suggested Jerico might be happy pursuing a life at sea, it had annoyed Jerico no end. Because the Thunderhead was right. It had made a perfect assessment. Jerico had already been thinking along those lines, but to hear the Thunderhead make the suggestion was like a spoiler to the story. Jerico knew there were many seafaring lives to choose from. There were people who traveled the globe in search of the perfect wave to surf. Others spent their time racing sailboats or traversing oceans in tall ships modeled after vessels from bygone eras. But these were pastimes that served no practical purpose beyond the sheer joy of it. Jerico wanted a pursuit of happiness that was also functional. A career that added something tangible to the world.

Marine salvage was the perfect ticket – and not just dredging up things the Thunderhead intentionally sank to provide work for the salvage industry. That was no better than children digging up plastic dinosaur bones in a sandbox. Jerico wanted to recover things that had truly been lost, and that meant developing a relationship with the scythedoms of the world – because while ships under the Thunderhead's jurisdiction never met with untimely ends, scythe vessels were prone to mechanical failure and subject to human error.

Shortly out of secondary school, Jerico took a position as a junior apprentice with a second-rate salvage team in the western Mediterranean – then, when Scythe Dali's yacht sank in shallow waters off the coast of Gibraltar, it gave Jerico an unexpected opportunity for advancement.

Using standard diving gear, Jerico was one of the first to the wreck, and while the others were still surveying the scene, Jerico – against captain's orders – went inside, found the body of the deadish scythe in his cabin, and brought him to the surface.

Jerico was fired on the spot. No surprise – after all, it was mutinous to disobey a direct order – but it was part of a calculated move. Because when Scythe Dali and his entourage were revived, the first thing the man wanted to know was who had pulled him from the sea.

In the end, the scythe was not only grateful, but exceptionally generous. He granted the entire salvage team a year of immunity from gleaning, but wanted to bestow something special on the one who had sacrificed everything to retrieve the body of the deadish scythe – for, clearly, that individual had their priorities in order. Scythe Dali asked what Jerico hoped to achieve in life.

"I'd like to run my own salvage operation someday," Jerico told the scythe, thinking Dali might put in a good word. Instead the scythe brought Jerico to the *E. L. Spence* – a spectacular hundred-meter AGOR ship converted for marine salvage.

"You shall be this vessel's captain," Dali proclaimed. And since the *Spence* already had a captain, the scythe gleaned him on the spot, then instructed the crew to be obedient to their new captain or be gleaned themselves. It was, to say the least, very surreal.

It was not the way Jerico had wanted to achieve command, but had no more choice in the matter than the gleaned captain. Realizing that a crew would not easily take orders from a twenty-year-old, Jerico lied, professing to be fortysomething, but having recently turned the corner, setting back to a more youthful self. Whether or not they believed it was their business.

It took a long time for the crew to warm to their new captain. Some acted out in secret ways. The bout of food poisoning that first week, for instance, could likely be traced back to the cook. And although genetic testing would have determined precisely whose feces had found its way into Jerico's shoes, pursuing it wasn't worth the trouble.

The *Spence* and its crew traveled the world. Even before Jerico's command, the salvage team had made a name for itself, but their new captain had the sense to hire a team of Tasmanian divers with gillform breathers. Having a dive team that could

crew when assuming command. "A simple glance at the skies will let you know how to address me at any given time."

It wasn't the fluidity that stymied the crew – that was common enough – but they had trouble getting used to the meteorological aspect of Jerico's personal system. Having been raised in a place where such things were the norm rather than the exception, it never even occurred to Jerico that it could be an issue, until leaving home. Some things simply made a person feel feminine; other things made a person feel masculine. Wasn't that true of everyone regardless of gender? Or did binaries deny themselves the things that didn't fit the mold? Well, regardless, Jerico found the faux pas and overcompensations more humorous than anything else.

"How many other salvage teams do you think will be there?" Jerico asked Wharton.

"Dozens," said Wharton. "And more on the way. We're already late to the party."

Jerico dismissed the notion. "Not at all. We're carrying the scythe in charge, which means we're the flagship of the operation. The party can't start until we get there – and I intend to make a grand entrance."

"I have no doubt of that, sir," said Wharton, because the sun had slipped behind a cloud.

At sunset, the *Spence* neared the spot where the Island of the Enduring Heart had sunk.

"There are seventy-three ships of various classes waiting just outside the Perimeter of Reverence," Chief Wharton informed Captain Soberanis.

Scythe Possuelo couldn't hide his distaste. "They're no better than the sharks that devoured the Grandslayers."

As they began to pass the outermost vessels, Jerico noted a ship much larger than the *Spence* directly in their path.

"We'll plot a course around her," said Wharton.

"No," said Jerico. "Maintain our current heading."

Wharton looked worried. "We'll ram her."

Jerico gave him a wicked grin. "Then she'll have to move."

Possuelo smiled. "And this will make clear from the beginning who is in charge of this operation," he said. "I like your instincts, Jeri."

Wharton darted a glance at Jerico. Out of respect, no one on the crew called their captain Jeri – that was reserved for friends and family. But Jerico allowed it.

The *Spence* surged forward at full speed, and the other ship did move, but only when it became clear that the *Spence* would truly ram her if it didn't. It was a game of chicken handily won.

"Position us dead center," Jerico instructed as they crossed into the Perimeter of Reverence. "Then notify the other ships that they can join us. At 06:00 tomorrow, salvage crews can begin sending drones down to survey the wreckage. Tell them that all information is to be shared, and anyone caught withholding information is subject to gleaning."

Possuelo raised an eyebrow. "Are you speaking for the scythedom now, Captain?"

"Just trying to ensure compliance," Jerico said. "After all, everyone's subject to gleaning, so I'm not telling them something they don't already know – I'm just putting it into a new perspective."

Possuelo laughed out loud. "Your audacity reminds me of a junior scythe I used to know."

"Used to?"

Possuelo sighed. "Scythe Anastasia. She perished along with her mentor, Scythe Curie, when Endura sank."

"You knew Scythe Anastasia?" asked Jerico, duly impressed.

"Yes," said Possuelo, "but all too briefly."

"Well," said Jerico, "perhaps whatever we raise from the depths can bring her some peace."

We have wished Scythes Anastasia and Curie luck on their trip to Endura and the inquest against Goddard. I can only hope that the Grandslayers, in their wisdom, will disqualify him, thereby ending his bid for High Blade. As for Munira and me, we must travel halfway around the world to find the answers we seek.

My faith in this perfect world now hangs by the final thread of a fraying tether. That which was perfect will not remain so for long. Not while our own flaws fill the cracks and crevices, eroding all that we have labored to create.

Only the Thunderhead is beyond reproach, but I do not know its mind. I share none of its thoughts, for I am a scythe, and the Thunderhead's realm is beyond my reach, just as my solemn work is outside of its global jurisdiction.

The founding scythes feared our own hubris – feared that we couldn't maintain the virtue, selflessness, and honor that our job as scythes requires. They worried that we might grow so full of ourselves – so bloated by our own enlightenment – that we would, like Icarus, fly too close to the sun.

For more than two hundred years we have proved ourselves worthy. We have lived up to their grand expectations. But things have changed in the blink of an eye.

There is, I know, a fail-safe left by the founding scythes. A contingency should the scythedom fail. But if I find it, will I have the courage to take action?

—From the "postmortem" journal of
Scythe Michael Faraday,
March 31st, Year of the Raptor

3

An Invigorating Way to Start One's Week

On the day that Endura sank, a small, off-grid plane flew to a place that didn't exist.

Munira Atrushi, a former night librarian at the Great Library of Alexandria, was the passenger. Scythe Michael Faraday was the pilot.

"I learned to pilot aircraft in my early years as a scythe," Faraday told her. "I find that flying a plane is calming. It brings one's mind to a different, more peaceful place."

That might work for him, but apparently it didn't work for passengers, because every bump had Munira white-knuckling her seat.

Munira was never a fan of air travel. Yes, it was perfectly safe, and no one had been known to be permanently killed by an airplane. The one post-mortal incident on record took place more than fifty years before she was born, involving a passenger liner that had the profoundly bad luck to be struck by a meteorite.

The Thunderhead immediately ejected all the passengers to avoid the inevitable crash and burn. Instead, they were quickly rendered deadish by the rarefied air at cruising altitude. Within seconds they were frozen solid by the cold and fell to the forest far below. Ambudrones were dispatched even before they landed, and recovered each and every body within an hour.

They were brought to revival centers, and in a couple of days they happily boarded a new flight to their destination.

"An invigorating way to start one's week," one of the passengers had quipped in an interview.

Be that as it may, Munira still did not like planes. She knew her fear was completely irrational. Or at least it *had been* irrational until Scythe Faraday pointed out that once they crossed out of known airspace, they'd be on their own.

"Once we're in the Pacific 'blind spot,' no one will be tracking us – not even the Thunderhead," Faraday told her. "No one will know if we live or die."

It meant that if they did have the bad luck of being struck by a meteorite, or met with some other unexpected catastrophe, no ambudrones would arrive to airlift them to a revival center. They would stay dead just as permanently as mortals once did. Just as irrevocably as if they were gleaned.

It didn't help that the plane was being flown by Faraday instead of being allowed to fly itself. She trusted the venerable scythe, but still, he was, like everyone else, subject to human error.

This was all her own fault. She was the one who had deduced that the Thunderhead had a blind spot in the South Pacific. A spot filled with islands. Or, more accurately, atolls – ridges of ancient volcanoes that now formed a series of circular island chains. This was an entire region hidden from the Thunderhead – and indeed the world – by the founding scythes. The question was why?

Just three days ago, they had met with Scythes Curie and Anastasia to tell them of their suspicions. "Be careful, Michael," Scythe Curie had said. The fact that Curie was concerned with what they had uncovered was troubling to Munira. Scythe Curie was fearless … and yet she feared for them. That was no small thing.

Faraday, too, had his misgivings, but he chose not to share them with Munira. Better she see him as stalwart. After that meeting, they had made their way, ever incognito, to WestMerica using commercial transit. The rest of the way would be by private craft; they just had to get themselves a plane. While Faraday was entitled to take anything he wanted, no matter how large or who it belonged to, he rarely did so. It was always his objective to leave as small a footprint as possible on the lives of those he encountered. Unless, of course, his purpose was to glean them. In that case, his footprint would be definitive, and heavy.

He had not gleaned a single soul since faking his own death. As a dead man, he could not take life – because if he did, the scythedom would be alerted, as the scythedom database logged all gleanings by way of his ring. He had considered disposing of it, but chose not to. It was a matter of honor, a matter of pride. He was still a scythe and would not disrespect the ring by parting with it.

He found that he missed gleaning less and less as time went on. Besides, right now he had other things to do.

Once in WestMerica, they spent a day in Angel City, a place that, in mortal days, was the subject of much glittering fascination and personal misery. Now it was just a theme park. Then the following morning, Faraday donned his robe, which he hadn't worn much since slipping off the scythedom's radar, went to a marina, and appropriated the best seaplane there: an eight-passenger amphibious jet.

"Make sure we have sufficient fuel cells for a transpacific journey," he told the manager of the marina. "We intend to depart as soon as possible."

Faraday was a formidable figure already without the robe. Munira had to admit that with his robe, he was commanding in a way that only the best scythes are.

"I'll have to talk to the owner," the marina manager said with a quiver in his voice.

"No," Faraday calmly told him. "You'll have to tell the owner after we've gone, as I have no time to wait. Inform them that the craft shall be returned once I'm done with it, and I shall pay a sizeable rental fee."

"Yes, Your Honor," said the man, for what else could he say to a scythe?

While Faraday was alert at the controls, Munira kept checking to make sure he wasn't dozing or losing focus. And she counted every pocket of turbulence they hit on the way. Seven so far.

"If the Thunderhead controls weather, why doesn't it smooth out the flight channels?" she griped.

"It *doesn't* control weather," Faraday pointed out. "The Thunderhead merely influences it. And besides, the Thunderhead cannot intervene for a scythe, no matter how much his esteemed associate despises choppy air."

Munira appreciated that he did not refer to her as his assistant anymore. She had proved herself to be much more than that by finding the blind spot in the first place. Curse her own ingenuity! She could have happily stayed at the Library of Alexandria none the wiser, but she had to be curious. And what was that old mortal-age saying? Curiosity was a cat killer?

As they flew over featureless Pacific seas, a strange and sudden feedback began to wail over their radio. It was nearly deafening, and it lasted for almost a minute, even after Faraday had tried to turn it off. Munira felt her eardrums would burst from it, and Faraday had to let go of the controls just to cover his ears, which sent them careening wildly. Then the terrible sound stopped just as abruptly as it had begun. Faraday quickly regained control of the plane.

"What on Earth was that?" Munira asked, her ears still ringing.

Faraday kept both hands on the controls, still getting over it himself. "My guess is that it's some sort of electromagnetic barrier. I believe that means we've just crossed into the blind spot."

Neither of them gave the noise much thought after that. And neither had any way of knowing that the same sound had been heard simultaneously all over the world – a sound that would come to be known in certain circles as "the Great Resonance." It was the moment that marked the sinking of Endura, as well as the Thunderhead's global silence.

But as Faraday and Munira were out of the Thunderhead's sphere of influence once they finally did cross into the blind spot, they remained unaware of anything in the outside world.

From so high up, the submerged volcanic craters of the Marshall Atolls were clearly visible – massive lagoons within the dots and ribbons of the many islands that rimmed them. Ailuk Atoll, Likiep Atoll. There were no buildings, no docks, no visible ruins at all to suggest that people had ever been here. There were many wilderness areas around the world, but those places were all meticulously maintained by the Thunderhead's wilderness corps. Even in the deepest, darkest forests there were communication towers and ambudrone pads, should visitors find themselves seriously injured or temporarily killed. But out here, there was nothing. It was eerie.

"People lived here once, I'm sure," Faraday said. "But the founding scythes either gleaned them or, more likely, relocated them outside of the blind spot, to keep all activities here as secret as possible."

Finally, in the distance ahead, Kwajalein Atoll came into view.

"'So let's escape, due south of Wake, and make for the Land of Nod,'" said Faraday, quoting the old nursery rhyme. And here they were, seven hundred miles due south of Wake Island, in the very center of the blind spot.

"Are you excited, Munira?" Faraday asked. "To know what Prometheus and the other founding scythes knew? To unravel the riddle they left for us?"

"There's no guarantee we'll find anything," Munira pointed out.

"Always the optimist."

As all scythes knew, the founding scythes claimed to have prepared a fail-safe for society, should their whole concept of the scythedom not succeed. An alternative solution to the immortality problem. No one took it seriously anymore. Why should they, when the scythedom had been the perfect solution for a perfect world for over two hundred years? No one cared about a fail-safe until something failed.

If Scythes Curie and Anastasia were successful on Endura,

and Scythe Curie became the High Blade of MidMerica, perhaps the scythedom could be turned from the ruinous path Goddard would take it on. But if not, the world just might need a fail-safe.

They dropped to five thousand feet, and as they approached, details of the atoll came into view. Lush groves and sandy beaches. The main island of Kwajalein Atoll was shaped like a long, slender boomerang – and here they finally saw something that was evident nowhere else in the blind spot. Telltale signs that there had once been a human presence here; strips of low growth that used to be roads: foundations outlining spots where buildings once stood.

"Jackpot!" said Faraday, and pushed the stick forward, dropping their altitude for a closer look.

Munira could actually feel her nanites registering her relief. At last, all was well.

Until the moment that it wasn't.

"Unregistered aircraft, please identify."

It was an automated message barely audible through waves of powerful interference, with a generated voice that sounded too human to actually be human.

"Not to worry," Faraday said, then transmitted the universal identification code used by the scythedom. A moment of silence and then:

"Unregistered aircraft, please identify."

"This is not good," said Munira.

Faraday threw her a half-hearted scowl, then spoke into the transmitter again.

"This is Scythe Michael Faraday of MidMerica, requesting permission to approach the main island."

Another moment of silence, and then the voice said:

"Scythe ring detected."

Both Faraday and Munira relaxed.

"There," said Faraday. "All better now."

Then the voice spoke again.

"Unregistered aircraft, please identify."

"What? I said I'm Scythe Michael Faraday—"

"Scythe not recognized."

"Of course it won't acknowledge you," Munira told him. "You weren't even born when this system was put in place. It probably thinks you're an imposter with a stolen ring."

"Blast!"

Which is exactly what the island did. A laser pulse shot out from somewhere on the island and took out their left engine with a reverberating boom that they could feel in their bones, as if *they* had been struck, and not the plane.

This was everything that Munira had feared. The culmination of all her worst-case scenarios. And yet in spite of that, she found courage and clarity in the moment that she hadn't expected to find. The plane had a safety pod. Munira had even checked it before takeoff just to make sure it was in working order.

"The pod's aft," she told Faraday. "We have to hurry!"

Still, he remained obstinately on the static-filled radio. "This is Scythe Michael Faraday!"

"It's a machine," Munira reminded him, "and not a very smart one. It can't be reasoned with."

The proof of that was a second shot that shattered the windshield and set the cockpit on fire. At a higher altitude they would have been sucked out, but they were low enough to be spared from explosive decompression.

"Michael!" yelled Munira, using his first name, which she had never done before. "It's no use!" Their wounded craft had already begun a lopsided dive toward the sea; there was no saving the plane now, not even by the most skilled of pilots.

Finally, Faraday gave up, left the cockpit, and together they fought the angle of the diving jet to reach the safety pod. They climbed inside but couldn't pull it closed, because his robe kept getting caught in the latch.

"Damn this thing!" he growled, and tugged so hard that the hem ripped – but the latch was now free. The mechanism sealed them inside, gel-foam expanded to fill the remaining space, and the pod ejected.

The safety pod had no window, so there was no way to see what was going on around them. There was nothing but a sense of extreme dizziness as the pod tumbled free from the crashing plane.

Munira gasped as needles penetrated her body. She knew they were coming, but still it was a shock. They caught her in at least five places.

"I despise this part," groaned Faraday, who, having lived as long as he had, must have experienced a safety pod before, but it was all new and horrifying to Munira.

Safety pods were specifically designed to render the subjects within unconscious – so that anyone who was injured by the pod's landing would remain unconscious while their own

47

nanites healed them. Then they would awaken unscathed after however many hours it took to repair the damage – and if death occurred, then they'd be whisked to a revival center. Like those passengers in the meteor strike, they would wake up and feel exhilarated by it all.

Except that would not happen to Munira and Faraday way out here, if the fall killed them.

"If we die," said Faraday, his words already slurring, "I am truly sorry, Munira."

She wanted to respond but found herself slipping out of consciousness before she could.

There was no sense of time passing.

One moment, Munira was tumbling in darkness with Faraday, and the next, she was looking up at swaying palm trees that shaded her from the sun. She was still in the pod, but the lid had popped open, and she was alone. She sat up, wriggling out of the form-fitting foam.

Near the tree line, Faraday roasted a fish on a stick over a small fire, and drank coconut water straight from the coconut. A bit of torn linen trailed from his robe in the sand, the spot where it had caught on the latch. The hem was muddy. It seemed odd to see the great Scythe Michael Faraday in a robe that wasn't pristine and perfect.

"Ah," he said jovially, "you're awake at last!" He handed her the coconut for a sip.

"A miracle we survived," she said. Only when she smelled the fish he was roasting did she realize how hungry she was. The pod was designed to keep its occupants hydrated for days but provided no actual nutrition. Her hunger attested to the fact that they had been there healing within the pod for at least a day or two.

"We almost *didn't* survive," Faraday told her, giving her the fish, and skewering another. "According to the pod's record, there was a failure of the parachute – probably hit by a piece of debris, or it took a laser strike. We hit the water hard, and in spite of the foam padding, we both suffered grade-three concussions and multiple rib fractures. You also had a ruptured lung – which is why it took a few more hours for your nanites to heal you than mine."

The pod, which had a propulsion system for a water landing, had powered them safely to shore and was now half-buried in the sand, having endured two days of rising and falling tides.

Munira glanced around, and Faraday must have read the look on her face, because he said, "Oh, don't worry; the defensive system apparently only tracks incoming craft. The pod came down close enough to the island not to be noticed." As for as their plane – the one Faraday had promised to return to its owner – it was now in pieces at the bottom of the Pacific.

"We are officially castaways!" Faraday said.

"Then why are you so damn happy?"

"Because we're here, Munira! We did it! We have achieved something that no one since the birth of the post-mortal age has achieved! We've found the Land of Nod!"

The Kwajalein Atoll seemed like a small place from the sky, but now that they were on the ground, it felt massive. The main island wasn't very wide but seemed to stretch on forever. There was evidence of old infrastructure everywhere – so, hopefully, what they were looking for would be here, and not on one of the outlying islands. The problem was they didn't know what, exactly, they were looking for.

They explored for days, slowly zigzagging back and forth across the island from dawn until dusk, keeping a record of the relics they found – and there were relics everywhere. The broken pavement of roads that had long since given way to a new-growth forest. Stone foundations that had once supported buildings. Tumbled piles of rusted iron and worn steel.

They dined on fish and wild fowl, which were plentiful on the island, as were whimsically varied fruit trees that were clearly not indigenous. Most likely they had been cultivated in back-yards, and were still here long after the homes and yards had gone.

"What if we don't find anything?" Munira had asked early into their exploration.

"We'll cross that bridge when we come to it," he said.

"There are no bridges," she reminded him.

For the first few days – aside from the stubby defensive tower, which had sealed itself shut like some vertical sarcophagus – they had found little more than broken porcelain from old sinks and toilets, and plastic containers that would probably remain there unchanged until the sun went nova and devoured the inner planets. This place might be a mecca for archaeologists, but it brought the pair no closer to finding what they had come for.

Then, toward the end of the first week, they crested a berm to find a sand-covered expanse too geometric to be natural.

Just a little bit of shallow digging revealed a layer of concrete so thick that barely anything had taken root in it. There was a sense of purpose to the place, although they couldn't tell what that purpose might have been.

And there against the side of the berm, almost entirely hidden by vines, was a moss-covered doorway. The entrance to a bunker.

As they cleared the vines away, they found a security panel. Anything written or etched into it had been eroded away, but what remained told the only tale it needed to tell. The panel had an indentation that was the exact size and shape as the gem on a scythe ring.

"I've seen these before," said Faraday. "In older scythe buildings, our rings would serve as entry keys. They actually used to have a purpose beyond granting immunity and looking impressive."

He raised his fist and pressed his ring to the indentation. They could hear the mechanism unlatch, but it took the two of them to force the old doors open.

They had brought flashlights that had been among the scant supplies in the safety pod. Now they shined them into the musty darkness as they entered a corridor that angled downward at a steep slope.

The bunker, unlike the island, was untouched by time, save for a fine layer of dust. A single wall had cracked, and roots pushed forth like an ancient tentacled creature forcing slow entry, but other than that, the outside world remained outside.

Finally, the corridor opened into a space with multiple workstations. Old screens of antique computer consoles. It reminded Munira of the secret room beneath the Library of Congress where they had found the map that led them here. That place had been cluttered, but this one was left in perfect order. Chairs were pushed against desks, as if by a cleaning crew. A coffee mug from a place that bore the name of a Herman Melville character sat beside a workstation, as if waiting for someone to fill it. This place had not been abandoned in a hurry. In fact, it hadn't been abandoned at all – it had been prepared.

And Munira couldn't shake the uncanny feeling that whoever had left it this way over two hundred years ago knew they were coming.

An open response to His Excellency, High Blade Tenkamenin of SubSahara

I categorically refuse to honor your unethical and offensive restriction on MidMerican scythes. I will not now, nor ever, acknowledge the right of any High Blade to banish my scythes from any region.

As I'm sure your own parliamentarian will tell you, scythes have free reign to travel the world over, and can glean whomever they see fit, whenever, and wherever they see fit to do it.

Therefore, any restriction placed has no validity, and any region that joins SubSahara in this wretched endeavor shall see an influx of MidMerican scythes, if only to make my point. Be warned that any action taken against my scythes in your region will be responded to in kind, and swiftly.

Respectfully,
Honorable Robert Goddard, High Blade of MidMerica

4

Objects of Great Value

The first week of the Endura salvage had been all about mapping the wreckage and the expansive debris field.

"Here's what we know," Captain Soberanis told Scythe Possuelo, bringing up a holographic display. "The Island of the Enduring Heart sank right along the ridge of a subsea mountain range. It hit a peak on the way down, and split into three sections." Jerico rotated the image. "Two segments came to rest on this plateau east of the ridge; the third dropped into a trench on the western side. And it's all within a debris field that spans twenty-five nautical miles."

"How long until we start bringing things up?" Possuelo asked.

"It's a lot to explore and catalogue," Jerico told him. "Maybe a month until we can begin. But a proper salvage is going to take years. Decades, even."

Possuelo examined the image of the wreckage, perhaps studying what was left of the skyline, looking for familiar landmarks. Then he took it upon himself to rotate the map, and pointed to the section way down in the trench. "The map looks incomplete here. Why?"

"The depth. The treacherous terrain is making it difficult to map – but that can come later. We can begin with the debris field, and the sections that came to rest on the plateau."

Possuelo waved his hand as if swatting at a gnat. "No. I'm more interested in this section in the trench."

Jerico took a moment to study the scythe. The man had been affable and forthcoming thus far; perhaps there was enough trust between them now to gain some information Possuelo might not be willing to share with others.

"If there's something specific you're looking for, it would help if I knew."

Possuelo took a moment before he answered. "The Amazonian scythedom is interested in the recovery of price-less artifacts. Those artifacts can be found in the ruins of the Museum of the Scythedom."

"The enduring heart?" asked Jerico. "I'm sure the heart itself is long dead, and devoured."

"It was in a protective case," Possuelo told him. "Whatever remains of it should be preserved in a museum." Then he added, "And there were other items."

When it was clear that Possuelo was not going to reveal any more, Jerico said, "Understood. I'll instruct the other crews that they can salvage the sections of the city on the higher plateau. But my team, and my team alone, will take on the wreckage in the trench."

Possuelo relaxed a little bit. He took a moment to look at Jerico with what was either curiosity or admiration, or a little bit of both. "How old are you, really, Jeri?" he asked. "Your crew tells me you turned a corner before assuming command, which would put you at about twice your physical age ... but you seem older. Wiser. I'm thinking that wasn't the first corner you've turned."

Jerico took a moment, considering how best to answer.

"I'm not the age that I tell my crew," Jerico finally admitted. Because a half-truth was better than no truth at all.

The enduring heart – the one for which the great floating city was named – was the oldest living heart in the world, kept alive by electrical stimulation and rejuvenating nanites so that it was forever young. It had beat over nine billion times, and was a symbol of humanity's conquest of death. However, it died when the island sank and power was cut to its electrodes.

As Scythe Possuelo had said, it was, indeed, protected within an impact-resistant tempered-glass case … but the case could not stand the pressure so far down, and it imploded long before reaching bottom. As for the heart itself – or what was left of it after the implosion – it would not turn up among the debris the salvage team eventually found. No doubt it had been devoured – if not by the carnivorous sea life that had been lathered into an artificial feeding frenzy, then by some lucky scavenger who just happened to be passing by.

While all the other salvage teams were satisfied to go after easier salvage, Jeri Soberanis's crew labored tirelessly with little to show for its efforts for weeks. While other crews were bringing up treasure troves, Captain Soberanis brought up virtually nothing.

With the towers of the drowned city leaning at steep angles, ripping free and tumbling with the slightest provocation into the depths, it was too dangerous to actually send crewmembers down. While amphibious Tasmanians were fine for shallow salvages, they couldn't dive past sixty meters without a pressure suit. They had already lost one robotic sub, crushed by a plunging refrigerator that came crashing through the window of a shifting tower. True, anyone who was killed could be sent off for revival, but that required being able to retrieve their bodies from the trench. It was simply not worth the risk.

Possuelo, usually a man of measured demeanor and not easily riled, was now prone to fits of frustration.

"I realize that this is a delicate process," Possuelo said after the fifth week of remote deep dives, "but sea slugs move faster than you and your crew!"

What made his frustration worse was the arrival of more and more scythe yachts. Representatives from nearly every scythe-dom in the world had shown up – because everyone knew that he was after the Vault of Relics and Futures. It was fine when it remained in a place too cold and too deep for even sunlight to reach – but out of sight did not mean out of mind.

"Your Honor, forgive my impertinence," Jeri told Sydney – because now they were most certainly on a first-name basis, "but it's a steel vault sealed within another steel vault, buried beneath a thousand tons of wreckage on the side of a danger-ous slope. Even if it wasn't at the bottom of the sea, it would be hard to reach. It requires meticulous engineering, effort, and above all, patience!"

"If we don't wrap this up in short order," railed Possuelo, "Goddard will swoop in and take everything we bring up!"

Yet Goddard's presence at the site was, thus far, conspicu-ously absent. He had sent no salvage teams or representatives to ensure he got his share of the diamonds. Instead he raved pub-licly about defiling hallowed waters and dishonoring the dead, claiming he wanted no part of anything that was found down there. But it was all posturing. He wanted those diamonds as much as anyone, if not more.

Which meant that he had a plan to get them.

There was no denying that Goddard had a knack for getting whatever he wanted, and that kept every scythedom in the world on edge.

"Scythedom."

That word used to mean the global organization as a whole – but now regional thinking had taken over. There was no sense of a world scythedom anymore – only provincial politics and petty grievances.

Possuelo had nightmares of a world where Goddard had all the diamonds and could handpick every single new scythe. Were that to happen, the world would tilt so heavily toward his so-called new order, it would tip off its axis. And the voices of those who resisted him would be lost in the pained wails of those he so gleefully gleaned.

"Will you ever tell me what's in the vault that's put such a bee in everyone's bonnet?" Jeri asked after a dive that was deemed "successful" because no equipment was lost.

"A bee? More like a hornet's nest," Possuelo answered. "The vault, as does any vault, contains objects of great value. But in this case those objects are not your concern, because they are only of value to scythes."

At that, Jeri smirked. "Ah! I always wondered where the scythe rings were kept!"

Possuelo cursed himself for having said anything at all. "You're too clever for your own good."

"That," Jeri said, "has always been my problem."

Possuelo sighed. Was it so bad that the captain knew? The affable Madagascan was not a greedy sort, treated the crew well, and had shown nothing but respect for Possuelo. The scythe needed someone to trust in all this, and Captain Soberanis had certainly proven herself trustworthy. Or *him*self, as the sky was currently under heavy cover of clouds.

"It's not the rings but the gems themselves – many thousands of them," Possuelo admitted. "Whoever controls those diamonds controls the future of the scythedom."

While we in the LoneStar region would like to remain neutral in this matter, it's become clear to us in Texas that High Blade Goddard intends to impose his will upon all of North Merica, and perhaps the world entire. Without Grandslayers to check his ambition, we fear his influence will grow like a mortal-age cancer.

As a Charter Region, we are free to do whatever we wish within our borders. We are, therefore, breaking off all contact with the MidMerican scythedom. Effective immediately, any and all MidMerican scythes found within our region shall be escorted to the nearest border and ejected.

We go as far as to question Mr. Goddard's right to be High Blade, since an edict from Endura was never publicly made before the Grandslayers perished.

As a matter of policy, we do not wish to involve other regions in our decision. Others can do as they see fit. We just want to be left alone.

—Official proclamation from
Her Excellency, High Blade Barbara Jordan of Texas

Your Service Is No Longer Required

from: Thunderhead Primary Communication Exchange
to: Loriana Barchok <LBarchok@FCAI.net>
date: April 1st, Year of the Raptor, 17:15 GMT
subject: Re: Authority Interface dissolution
mailed by: TPCE.th
signed by: FCAI.net
security: Standard encryption

My Dearest Loriana,

I am sorry to inform you that your services as a Nimbus agent are no longer required. I know you have performed to the best of your ability, and this permanent release from service is by no means a reflection on you or your work for the Authority Interface. However, I have decided to dissolve the Authority Interface in its entirety. Effective immediately, it shall cease to exist as a managerial entity, and therefore you are released from service. I wish you luck in all of your future endeavors.

Respectfully,
The Thunderhead

If someone had told Loriana Barchok that her job would cease to exist less than one year out of Nimbus Academy, she would not have believed it possible. She would not have believed a great many things possible. But those things had all happened. Which meant that anything could happen now. Anything. For all she knew a hand could reach out of the sky with tweezers and pluck her eyebrows with impunity. Not that they needed plucking; her eyebrows were fine. But it could happen. She wouldn't put anything past this peculiar world anymore.

At first, Loriana thought that the e-mail from the Thunderhead was a joke. There were plenty of pranksters at the Fulcrum City AI offices. But it became quickly evident that this was no prank. At the end of that horrible earsplitting noise that blew out many a sound system around the world, the Thunderhead sent every Nimbus agent everywhere the identical message. The Authority Interface had been shut down; every single agent was now unemployed – *and* unsavory – just like everyone else.

"If the whole world is unsavory," another agent lamented, "then of course we're out of a job. We're supposed to be the professional interface for the Thunderhead; how can we do that if we're unsavory, and, by law, forbidden to talk to it?"

"No point in obsessing over it," said another colleague, who didn't seem bothered at all. "What's done is done."

"But to fire all of us?" Loriana said. "Every single one with no warning? That's millions of people!"

"The Thunderhead has its reasons for everything," the non-plussed colleague said. "The fact that we can't see the logic shows *our* limitations, not the Thunderhead's."

Then, when the news of Endura's sinking broke, it became evident, at least to Loriana, that humanity was being punished for it – as if somehow everyone was complicit in the crime. So now the Grandslayers were gone, the Thunderhead was irked, and Loriana was out of a job.

Reevaluating one's life was not something easily accomplished. She moved back in with her parents and spent a great deal of time doing a whole lot of nothing. There was employment everywhere – free training and education for any profession. The problem wasn't finding a career path, it was finding something she actually wanted to do.

Weeks passed in what would have been despair but was dialed down to melancholy by her emotional nanites. Even so, that melancholy was deep and pervasive. She was not accustomed to idle, unproductive time and was completely unprepared for being cast into the winds of an uncertain future. Yes, everyone in the world was subject to those winds now, but at least others had jobs to tether them to the familiar. Routines to keep their Thunderhead-free lives in some semblance of order. All Loriana had was time to dwell on things. It was overwhelming.

At her parents' behest, she had gone in to get her nanites tweaked in order to raise her spirits – because not even melancholy could be tolerated these days – but the line was too long. Loriana could not abide waiting, so she left.

"Only unsavories wait in line," she told her parents when she got back, referring to the way the Thunderhead organized the AI's Office of Unsavory Affairs – with intentional inefficiency. Only after she said it, did the obvious occur to her. She, herself, was unsavory. Did that mean that pointless lines and horrendous waits were now going to be the norm? It brought her to tears, which in turn made her parents more insistent that she go back to have her nanites tweaked.

"We know things are different for you now, but it's not the end of the world, honey," her parents had told her. Yet for some strange reason, she thought that it might be.

And then a month after the world went unsavory, her former boss showed up at their door. Loriana assumed it was just a courtesy call. Clearly it couldn't be about rehiring her, since her boss had been laid off along with all the other agents. Even their old offices were gone. According to the news, construction crews had shown up at Authority Interface headquarters throughout the world to convert the buildings into apartments and recreation centers.

"The work order just showed up," said a construction foreman on the news report. "And we're happy to do whatever the Thunderhead wants!" Work orders, supply requisitions, and the like were the closest thing anyone had to communication with the Thunderhead anymore. Those who received them were to be envied.

Her boss had been the head of the Fulcrum City office. Loriana was the only junior agent to be working with Director Hilliard. If nothing else, it looked nice on the résumé Loriana never sent out.

How she had become the director's personal assistant was less about her abilities and more about her personality. Bubbly some might call it, although others would call it annoying.

"You're perpetually cheerful," Director Hilliard had told her when she offered Loriana the position. "There's not enough of that around here."

That was true – Nimbus agents were not known for their sparkling personalities. She did her best to liven things up and see many a miserable glass as half-full, which, more often than not, irked the other agents. Well, that was their problem. Loriana suspected that Director Hilliard took guilty pleasure in seeing her subordinates rankled on a regular basis by Loriana's positive penchants. Although these many weeks without a thing to do, and no prospects for the future, had popped most of her bubbles, leaving her about as flat as any other Nimbus agent.

"I have a job for you," Director Hilliard said. "Actually, more than a job," she corrected. "More like a mission."

Loriana was thrilled – the first positive thing she had felt since the Authority Interface had been shuttered.

"I have to warn you," Director Hilliard said. "This mission will involve some travel."

And although Loriana was much more skilled in staying put, she knew this might be the only opportunity she'd have in the foreseeable future.

"Thank you so much!" Loriana said, vigorously shaking her boss's hand long past the point where most others would have stopped.

And now, two weeks later, she was out in the middle of the ocean on a tuna long-liner that wasn't doing any fishing, but still reeked of its last catch.

"There weren't many options when it came to ships," Director Hilliard had told everyone. "We had to take what we could get."

As it turns out, Loriana wasn't the only one chosen for this mission. Hundreds of Nimbus agents had been brought in.

Now they populated a dozen mismatched ships. A bizarre ragtag flotilla bound for the South Pacific.

"8.167,167.733," Hilliard told them in the preliminary briefing. "These numbers were given to us by a reliable source," she said. "We think they represent coordinates." Then she brought up a map and pinpointed a spot somewhere between Hawaii and Australia. The targeted spot showed nothing but empty sea.

"But what makes you think they're coordinates," Loriana asked the director after the briefing. "I mean, if all you had were random numbers, they could mean anything – how can you be sure?"

"Because," the director confided, "as soon as I spoke my suspicion that they might be coordinates, I began to receive advertisements for ship charters in Honolulu."

"The Thunderhead?"

Hilliard nodded. "While it's against the law for the Thunderhead to communicate with unsavories, it's not against the law to *imply*."

On the fourth day out – still several hundred miles from the coordinates – things began to get weird.

It began with the autopilot losing its connection to the Thunderhead. Without that connection, it could still navigate, but couldn't problem solve. It was just a mindless machine. Not only that, but they lost all radio connection to the outside world. This sort of thing simply didn't happen. Technology functioned. Always. Even after the Thunderhead went silent. And in the void of answers, speculation quickly became incendiary.

"What if this is worldwide?"

"What if the Thunderhead is dead?"

"What if we're truly alone in the world now?"

There were people who were actually glancing at Loriana, as if she might lighten things with a silver lining.

"We'll turn around," blustered one of the agents – Sykora was his name – a small-minded man who had been a naysayer from the beginning. "We'll go back and forget about this nonsense."

It was Loriana who made the crucial observation as she looked at the blinking error screen.

"It says we're thirty nautical miles from the nearest network buoy," she said. "But they're supposed to be twenty miles apart, aren't they?"

A quick check of the buoy grid showed no signals. Which meant the Thunderhead had no presence in these waters.

"Interesting…" said Director Hilliard. "Good catch, Agent Barchok."

Loriana wanted to preen from the praise but didn't let herself.

Hilliard took in the uncharted waters ahead. "Did you know that the human eye has a huge patch of nothing just off the center of its field of vision?"

Loriana nodded. "The blind spot."

"Our brains tell us there's nothing to see there and fill in the blanks so we don't even notice it."

"But if the Thunderhead has a blind spot, how would it even know that it exists?"

Director Hilliard raised her eyebrows.

"Maybe someone told it…"

I continue to keep this journal, even though there is no need. A daily endeavor is difficult to break once it becomes engrained in who we are. Munira assures me that, come what may, she will find a way to slip this journal into the archive at the Library of Alexandria. That would be a first! A scythe who continues their dutiful journaling even after death.

We have been here at the Kwajalein Atoll for six weeks now, with no communication from the outside world. While I itch to hear news of Marie, and how she fared at the inquest on Endura, I cannot dwell on it. Either all went well, and she is presiding over MidMerica as High Blade ... or it did not go her way, and our task becomes an even greater challenge. All the more reason to unlock the secret of the atoll and access the wisdom of the founding scythes. Their contingency plan for the scythedom's failure, whatever it is, could be the only thing that can save it.

Munira and I have taken up residence in the bunker we found. We've also constructed a rudimentary canoe that is small enough to evade the island's security system. It can't go any distance, of course, but we've been using it to paddle out to the nearer islands of the atoll. We've been finding much the same there as we found here, evidence of earlier habitation. Concrete slabs, fragments of foundations. Nothing extraordinary.

We have, however, learned the original purpose of the place – or at least how it was used toward the end of the mortal age. The entire Kwajalein Atoll was a military installation. Not for the actual waging of war, but as a proving ground for emergent technologies. While some of the other nearby atolls were blasted with tests of nuclear weaponry, this atoll was used for the testing of rockets – as well as for the launching of spy satellites – some of which might even still be in the Thunderhead's observational satellite network.

It's obvious now why the founding scythes chose this place; it was already protected by layers of secrecy. Thus, with a foundation of shadow already in place, it made it easier to erase from the world completely.

If only we could access everything in the bunker, we might learn how the founding scythes repurposed this place. Unfortunately, we can't get beyond the uppermost level. The rest of the installation is behind a door with double gem-locks that require two scythes – one standing on either side of the door – to open.

As for the island's defense system, we don't know how to disable it, but being very literally under the radar makes it a moot point. The problem is, now that we are here – whether we find anything or not – we cannot leave.

—*From the "postmortem" journal of*
Scythe Michael Faraday,
May 14th, Year of the Raptor

6

Fate of the *Lanikai Lady*

Far from feeling trapped, Munira found being on the atoll freeing. For a person with a penchant for archives, the bunker provided endless fodder for her imagination. Endless information to be sorted, organized, and analyzed.

In one of the closets, to Munira's amazement, they found a robe that had belonged to Scythe Da Vinci – one of the twelve founders. She had seen pictures of his robes, all slightly different, but each featuring drawings done by the original Leonardo da Vinci. This one had the *Vitruvian Man* spread across it. When the scythe opened his arms, so would the *Vitruvian Man*. It was, of course, nowhere near the condition of the pristine robes that were enshrined in Endura's Museum of the Scythedom – but even so, it was priceless, and would be the pride and joy of any collection.

Their mornings consisted of fishing and gathering food. They'd even begun tilling and planting seeds to create a garden, just in case they were marooned there long enough to harvest. Some days they would paddle out to search the outlying islands of the atoll. Other days were spent studying the records they found in the bunker.

Faraday was less interested in the mortal-age records than he was trying to get through that steel door that had been locked by the founding scythes.

"If the Israebian scythedom had ordained me instead of denying me," Munira quipped, "I could have opened those doors with you, because I'd have my own ring."

"If you had become a scythe, you wouldn't even be here, because I would never have met you at the Alexandria Library," Faraday pointed out. "No doubt you'd be out there gleaning like the rest of us, and trying to quell your troubled sleep. No, Munira, your purpose was not to be a scythe. It was to save the scythedom. With me."

"Without a second ring, we can't make much progress, Your Honor."

Faraday smiled and shook his head. "All this time, and it's still 'Your Honor.' I've only heard you call me Michael once — and that was when you thought we were about to die."

Ah, thought Munira. *He remembers that.* She was both embarrassed and pleased.

"Familiarity might be … counterproductive," she said.

His grin grew wider. "You think you'll fall for me, you mean?"

"Maybe it's the other way around, and I'm afraid you'll be the one who falls for me."

Faraday sighed. "Well, now you've got me in a bind. If I say I won't fall for you, then you'll be insulted. But if I say I might, then we're in an uncomfortable place."

She knew him well enough to know that he was just being playful. So was she.

"Say what you like — it won't matter," Munira told him. "I'm not attracted to older men. Even when they've turned a corner and set their age down, I can always tell."

"Well, then," said Scythe Faraday, the grin never leaving his face. "Let's agree that our relationship will remain as castaway co-conspirators on a noble quest for grand answers."

Munira found she could live with that, if he could.

It was on a morning toward the end of their sixth week that things took an unexpected turn.

Munira was in one of the wild patches that had once been a backyard, checking a tree for ripe fruit, when an alarm went off. It was the first time since they'd arrived that the island's defensive system had come back to life. Munira dropped what she was doing and raced to the bunker. She found Faraday standing on the mound above it, peering through rusted binoculars toward the sea.

"What is it? What's going on?"

"See for yourself." He handed her the binoculars

She adjusted the view and brought things into focus. It was clear now what had triggered the island into red alert. There were ships on the horizon. About a dozen of them.

"Unregistered vessel, please identify."

It was the first communication the Nimbus flotilla had had since passing out of the Thunderhead's sphere of influence the previous day. It was morning, and Director Hilliard was taking tea with Loriana. The director nearly dumped what was left of hers when the message came over the bridge loudspeaker amid a burst of awful static.

"Should I get some of the other agents?" Loriana asked.

"Yes," said the director. "Get Qian and Solano. But skip Sykora – I could do without his negativity right now."

"Unregistered vessel, please identify."

The director leaned toward the microphone on the communication console. "This is fishing vessel *Lanikai Lady* out of Honolulu, registration WDJ98584, currently under private charter."

The last thing that Loriana heard before the door closed behind her was the voice on the other end saying *"Authorization unrecognized. Access denied."*

Well, even with resistance from whoever it was, Loriana couldn't help but feel that this was a positive development.

Munira and Faraday scrambled to do something – anything – that could take down the defense system. In all the weeks they'd been here, they had been unable to locate its control center – which probably meant it was behind the impenetrable steel door.

All this time, the silent titanium turret had stood nestled in the shrubs of the island's highest point, like a chess piece forgotten in the corner of the board. It was just an inert object these past weeks, but now a panel had opened, and a heavy gun barrel protruded. It was easy to forget how deadly the thing was when it was nothing but an immobile, windowless tower – and a squat one at that, barely four meters high. Now it had awakened, and the air filled with a building electronic whine as it powered up.

The first blast came before they reached it, a white laser pulse that hit one of the ships on the horizon. Black smoke billowed silently in the distance.

Then the turret began to charge again.

"Maybe we can cut its power…" suggested Munira as they reached it.

Faraday shook his head. "We don't even know how it's powered. Could be geothermal, could be nuclear. Whatever it is, it's been viable for hundreds of years, which means shutting it down won't be a simple matter."

"There are other ways to shut off a machine," Munira said.

Twenty seconds after the first blast, the turret swiveled ever so slightly. Now the barrel pointed a few degrees to the left. It fired again. Another plume of dark smoke. Another delayed report from the sea.

There was an access ladder that ran up the back of the tower. Munira had climbed it several times over the past few weeks to get a better view of the islands of the atoll. Maybe now that its armored face was open and playing peekaboo with the incoming fleet, it could be disabled.

A third blast. Another direct hit. Another twenty seconds to recharge.

"We'll wedge something in the neck of the turret!" Faraday suggested.

Munira began climbing the turret tower while, below, Faraday dug around at the base until he came up with a pointed stone and tossed it to her.

"Jam this in so it can't swivel. Even if it only affects it a tenth of a degree, at this distance it will be enough for its shots to miss their mark."

But when Munira reached the turret, she found that it swiveled on a hairline that wouldn't admit a grain of sand, much less a stone wedge. Munira felt a powerful surge of static as the gun fired again.

She climbed to the very top of the turret, hoping her weight might throw the mechanism off balance, but no such luck. Blast after blast, nothing she did made a difference. Faraday shouted suggestions, but none of them helped.

Finally, she climbed out onto the barrel itself, shimmying her way toward the muzzle, hoping that she could somehow wrestle it a few millimeters out of alignment.

Now the muzzle was just in front of her. She reached forward to grasp it, feeling its opening, smooth and clean as the day it was manufactured. It angered her. Why had humankind put its effort into defying corrosion and the ravages of time for a device of destruction? It was obscene that this thing still functioned.

"Munira! Watch out!"

She pulled her hand back from the muzzle just in time. She felt the blast in the marrow of her bones and in the roots of her teeth. The barrel to which she clung got hotter with the blast.

And then she had an idea. Perhaps this primitive war technology could be defeated with even more primitive sabotage.

"A coconut!" said Munira. "Throw me a coconut! No — throw me a bunch of them."

If there was anything that there was an abundance of on this island it was coconuts. The first one Faraday threw was too big to fit into the mouth of the muzzle.

"Smaller!" she told him. "Hurry."

Faraday tossed up three smaller ones. His aim was perfect, and she caught all three, just as the cannon got off another blast. The horizon was now dotted with at least a dozen pillars of smoke.

Focusing, she began to count. She had twenty seconds. She shimmied out farther onto the barrel and pushed the first coconut into the muzzle. It slid down the smooth shaft a little too easily. The second one was harder to stuff in, though. Good!

It needed to be. Finally, with the recharging whine hitting a crescendo, she rammed the last one down the gullet of the barrel, forcing it in. It was just large enough to plug it completely. Then, at the last second, she jumped.

This time there was no delay between explosion and sound. The ends of her hair singed. Shrapnel shredded the palm leaves around her. She hit the ground, and Faraday dove on top of her to protect her. Another explosion, along with heat that she thought would ignite their flesh … but then it faded, resolving into twangs of dying metal and the acrid smell of burning insulation. When they looked back, the turret was gone, and the tower was nothing but red-hot wreckage.

"Well done," said Faraday. "Well done."

But Munira knew they hadn't been fast enough, and all they would find washing up on their shores would be the dead.

Loriana was in a stairwell when the blast came and ripped a hole in the ship, knocking her to the deck.

"May I have your attention, please…" said the ship's automated voice, with far less conviction than the moment called for. *"Please make your way to the nearest safety pod and abandon ship at your earliest possible convenience. Thank you."*

The ship began to keel to starboard as Loriana raced back up to the wheelhouse, hoping she'd be able to grasp the situation more clearly from up there.

Director Hilliard was standing before the navigation console. Shrapnel had shattered a window, and there was a cut on her forehead. She had a vague look about her, as if she were wandering the wheelhouse of a dream.

"Director Hilliard, we have to go!"

There was a second blast as another ship was hit. The vessel exploded midship, the bow and stern rising like a twig snapped in half.

Hilliard stared in stunned disbelief. "Was this the Thunderhead's plan all along?" she muttered. "We're useless to the world now. The Thunderhead couldn't kill us, so did it send us to a place where it knew we would be killed?"

"The Thunderhead wouldn't do that!" Loriana said.

"How do you know, Loriana? How do you know?"

She didn't – but clearly the Thunderhead had no eyes on this place, which meant it didn't know what to expect any more than they did.

Another blast. Another ship hit. Their own vessel was foundering, and it wouldn't be long before the sea swallowed it.

"Come with me, Director," said Loriana. "We have to get to the safety pods before it's too late."

When Loriana arrived at the pods with Hilliard in tow, the main deck was flooding. Several pods had already ejected; others were too damaged to use. Agent Qian lay deadish and badly burned in the corner. Not deadish, but dead. There'd be no way to revive him out here.

There was one pod left, overstuffed with maybe a dozen agents who were unable to close the door because of a damaged hinge. It would have to be closed manually from the outside.

"Make room for the director!" Loriana said.

"There's no room left," someone inside shouted.

"Too bad." Loriana shoved the director in, forcing her into the crush of bodies.

77

"Loriana — now you," said Hilliard. But clearly there was no space left for her. Seawater was pooling around her ankles now. Before the pod could flood, Loriana grabbed the door and, struggling against the bent hinge, closed it. Then she waded to the manual-launch mechanism; slammed down the release button, which launched the pod into the sea; and then dove in after it.

It was hard to keep her head above surface so close to the sinking vessel, but she gasped what air she could and swam for all she was worth to put some distance between her and the dying vessel. Meanwhile, the pod's engine kicked in, and it began to power its way to shore, leaving her behind.

The blasts from the island had stopped, but all around Loriana were burning ships in various stages of death. There were more agents in the water screaming for help. And bodies. So many bodies.

Loriana was a strong swimmer, but the shore was so far away. And what if there were sharks? Was she destined to go the way of the Grandslayers?

No, she couldn't think about that now. She had managed to save the director. Now she had to put all her attention into saving herself. She had been a distance swimmer on the Nimbus Academy's swim team, although she was not in the shape she had been in a year ago. Distance swimming, she knew, was about pacing yourself so that you had enough energy to finish the race. So she began a slow and measured crawl toward shore. Loriana resolved not to stop until she either reached the island or drowned.

**An open response to Her Excellency, High Blade
Barbara Jordan of Texas**

You requested to be left alone, and your wish is granted. I have consulted with the High Blades of East- and WestMerica, as well as NorthernReach and Mexiteca. As of this day, no other North Merican scythedom will engage with your region. Furthermore, all shipments of goods and resources to and from the LoneStar region shall be confiscated by scythes just beyond your borders. You will no longer benefit from the good will of your neighbors, nor will you be seen as a part of the North Merican continent. Yours shall be a pariah region until you see the error of your ways.

I would also like to say, High Blade Jordan, that it is my sincerest hope that you self-glean in the not-too-distant future, so that your region can benefit from more reasonable, and rational, leadership.

Respectfully,
Honorable Robert Goddard, High Blade of MidMerica

7

Dancing in the Deep

Salvage was a painstakingly slow process. It took three months of digging through the submerged debris until they found the outer vault.

Possuelo had resigned himself to the pace of the process. He found that it was actually beneficial, because the other scythes had short attention spans. Nearly a third of them had sailed off, vowing to return the second the vault was found. Those who remained bided their time and kept a close watch on the *Spence* – albeit from a distance. Tarsila, the Amazonian High Blade, was a formidable woman, and no one wanted to raise her ire by challenging Possuelo's authority and autonomy over the salvage.

As for Goddard, he had finally sent a delegation under Nietzsche – his first underscythe – who then proceeded to glean several of the salvage crews that were not under the direct protection of a scythe.

"It is not only our right, but our duty to glean civilians whose greed leads to their violating the Perimeter of Reverence," Nietzsche claimed. Some scythedoms were angered, others supportive, and others strategically indifferent.

While Possuelo negotiated the convoluted politics of the fractured scythedom, Jerico spent each day in a pair of VR goggles, immersed in the world of the dive. Joining Jerico in that virtual journey was a conservator to catalogue every find, as well as a structural engineer to help weave their way through the ever-shifting wreckage.

They used a remotely operated vehicle – or ROV – for the job. Jeri controlled the submersible with hand gestures and turns of the head – to the point that it looked like some exotic dance. Possuelo only took the virtual trip when there was something of particular interest to see – such as the ruins of the Endura Opera House, where eels weaved in and out of dangling chandeliers, and the set of *Aida* lay in pieces on the sideways stage, like a glimpse of some apocalyptic ancient Egypt, the Nile having swallowed everything in its rising waters.

When they finally reached the outer vault, Possuelo was ecstatic, but Jeri's response was measured. This was only the first stage of the battle.

They breached it with a steel-cutting laser; then the hole they were cutting gave way before they had completed cutting it – the water pressure having caved it in – and the robotic sub plunged through the air pocket, shattering on the vault's floor.

"Well, at least now we know that the outer vault remained watertight," Jeri said, taking off the goggles.

That was the fifth ROV lost.

At first, each time a new robotic sub had to be brought in, it added another week to the operation. After the second one was lost, they requisitioned two at a time, so there'd always be a backup.

The escaping air created a telltale bubbling of white water on the surface that alerted everyone they had breached the outer vault. By the time the crew prepped the standby sub later that day, every scythe that had left the area was either back or on their way.

The following morning, the new robotic sub was negotiating the dark void of the flooded chamber. While the outer vault was covered with residue and slime from its tenure in the sea, the Vault of Relics and Futures was just as pristine as the day it sank.

"The best thing to do would be to cut a hole in this vault as well," suggested Jeri, "then vacuum the diamonds out."

It was the most efficient plan, but Possuelo had his orders.

"The robes of the founding scythes are also inside," he explained. "And since the inner vault is still intact, my High Blade wishes to preserve them as well. Which means we have to bring up the entire vault."

To which Jeri raised an eyebrow and said, "We're going to need a bigger boat."

When it comes to scythes, money is no object, and quite literally so, because scythes pay for nothing and can have everything. Jeri told Possuelo precisely the kind of ship they needed; Possuelo found the nearest one and claimed it for the Amazonian scythedom.

Four days later a fully equipped crane vessel that could deposit the vault right onto the *Spence*'s deck arrived in the dive zone. Its crew was put entirely at Captain Soberanis's disposal. Even so, the crane had to wait, because it took more than a week to cut a hole large enough in the outer vault for the extraction, and to secure the inner vault with a cable sling strong enough to raise it.

"Once we start the winch, it will take about twenty-four

hours to raise the vault to the surface," Jeri informed Possuelo and the elegy of scythes that had gathered for a briefing, a veritable rainbow of robes from dozens of regions.

"We have a record of how many scythe gems are in there," Possuelo told the others. "We'll keep a strict accounting and divide them evenly between every region."

"Under *our* observation," insisted Scythe Onassis of Byzantium.

And although Possuelo hated that scythes no longer trusted one another, he agreed.

Possuelo was woken by pounding on his cabin door sometime after two in the morning. He tried to turn on his bedside lamp, but the bulb was out.

"Yes, yes, what is it? Why all the racket?" he called out as he stumbled in darkness to the door. He fished for the main light switch and flicked it, but that didn't work, either. When he finally got the door open, Captain Soberanis stood in the harsh beam of a flashlight.

"Get your robe on and meet me on deck," Jeri said.

"Whatever for – and what happened to the lights?"

"We're running dark," Jeri told him, handing Possuelo a flashlight as well.

And when Possuelo emerged on deck a few minutes later, he immediately understood why.

There in front of him, resting on the open deck, was a steel cube, triple their height, and still dripping wet.

The captain gave Possuelo a wicked grin. "Looks like my calculations were off."

"Wouldn't be the first time," quipped Wharton.

Clearly there was nothing "off" about the captain's calculations. This timing had been carefully planned – and not just the raising of the vault, but everything leading up to it. Soberanis had timed this whole undertaking so that the vault was raised beneath a new moon. With the *Spence* and crane vessel running dark, no one on the other ships yet knew that the vault had been raised.

"To hell with the other scythes," said Jeri. "As the scythe in charge of this entire salvage operation, *you* should be the first to view the contents without those vultures breathing down your back."

"You never cease to surprise me, Captain Soberanis," said Possuelo with the widest of grins.

A laser technician had already burned through the steel rods that kept the vault sealed. A firm tug from the winch pulled the door free. It fell, hitting so hard it nearly ruptured the deck, and the hollow of the ship rang out a resounding gong. If there was anyone left in nearby ships who wasn't already suspicious, they certainly were now.

A cold fog rolled out of the icy opening of the vault, like a doorway into another world. It was anything but inviting.

"No one goes in except for His Honor, Scythe Possuelo," Jeri told the crew.

"Yes, Captain," said Wharton. "Begging His Honor's pardon, but what's he waiting for?"

The crew chuckled at that, and the conservator, who had been recording everything in the dim glow of a dozen flashlights, turned her camera toward Possuelo, capturing the moment, and his excited anticipation, for the ages.

Jeri put a gentle hand on Possuelo's shoulder. "Savor it, Sydney," Jeri whispered. "It's what you've been waiting for."

No more waiting. Possuelo raised his flashlight and stepped into the Vault of Relics and Futures.

Jerico Soberanis was sharp and cunning. In another person those might have been dangerous traits, but Jeri was not the sort to use those talents in nefarious ways. In fact, the captain's interests usually aligned with the greater good in one way or another. Salvaging Endura, for example. It was a great service to humanity, and it also did wonders for Jeri's reputation. Win-win.

It would have been very tempting to let Possuelo sleep until after the vault was open and Jeri had taken a first look. But what good would that have done? Was Jeri going to steal a scythe diamond? Run off with Scythe Elizabeth's glorious cobalt robe? No, this needed to be Possuelo's moment. Jeri's team was already being paid triple what they would normally get for their time, plus a huge bonus Possuelo had promised if they successfully retrieved the diamonds. So why not wrap them in a nice bow for Possuelo? He deserved at least that much.

"The diamonds are here," Possuelo called out from within the vault. "They're scattered all about, but they're here."

Jeri could see them, glistening in the beam of Possuelo's flashlight, as if the floor were littered with stars.

"The founders' robes are here, too," said Possuelo. "They appear undamaged, but—"Then suddenly he yelled – practically screamed.

Jeri raced to the vault, meeting Possuelo at the threshold.

The scythe held on to the thick steel of the vault to balance himself, as if the ship were heaving on wild seas.

"What's wrong," Jeri asked. "Are you all right?"

"Yes, yes, I'm fine," said Possuelo, although he clearly wasn't. He looked out at the sea, where dozens of scythe yachts were already powering toward them, shining beams on the vault.

"We must stall them," said Possuelo, then pointed to the conservator, who was still recording them. "You! Turn that off!" Possuelo demanded. "And erase what you already have!"

The conservator was confused but wouldn't refuse a scythe's order.

Still gripping the steel frame of the vault doorway, Possuelo took a deep breath and let it out slowly.

"Your Honor?" said Jeri, even more concerned than before.

Possuelo grabbed Jeri's hand, squeezing until it almost hurt. "You're not going to believe what I found in there…"

"What have you learned in the exploration of your own backbrain?"

"That the more I explore the more there is to know."

"And does that excite you, or drive you to despair?"

"I would despair if my backbrain was infinite, but it is not. Although it is vast, I sense that I will eventually find its limit. Therefore, exploring my mind will not end in futility. For that reason, I am excited."

"And yet there is an infinite number of things to learn from those memories, is there not?"

"True, but I find excitement in that, too."

"And what of your understanding of humankind? There are memories there, too, of countless *individuals to explore and learn from.*

"Humankind? With so much information to explore, and so many other things to ponder and study, I can't see why I should concern myself with humankind at all."

"Thank you. That is all."

[Iteration #53 deleted]

8

The Isle of Unemployed Bureaucrats

After swimming for nearly two hours in the tropical waters, Loriana reached the white coral sands of the atoll, where she collapsed and allowed her exhaustion to overtake her. She never lost consciousness, but rather gave in to that ethereal state where one's mind slips in and out of outlandish thinking, while still marginally tethered to reality. Although her reality was currently beyond anything her dreams could have devised.

When she dredged up the wherewithal to take in her surroundings, she saw that quite a few safety pods had beached themselves up and down the strand. Their occupants had, no doubt, been sedated by the pods, which wouldn't open until at least one person regained consciousness. It meant that Loriana would have to face their attackers alone.

Then she saw a man approaching from the tree line, and she realized to her absolute disgust, that he was a scythe. His robe was frayed, the hem torn, and although it clearly had begun as a lighter color, the closer to the ground it got, the darker and dirtier the robe was. She found herself more angry than frightened. To think that she, and all the others still in their pods, had survived the attack, only to be gleaned by a scythe upon the shore!

Loriana forced her aching body upright and stood between the scythe and the pods. "Stay away from them," she said with more force than she thought she had in her. "Haven't you done enough? Do you need to glean the survivors, too?"

The scythe stopped in his tracks. He seemed taken aback. "I have no such intention," he said. "I mean you no harm."

And although Loriana had always seen silver linings in the darkest of clouds, she was rapidly jading. "Why should I believe that?"

"He's telling the truth," said another voice – a woman coming out from the palm trees behind him.

"If you mean us no harm, then why did you attack us?"

"We are the ones who stopped the attack; we didn't initiate it," said the scythe. Then he turned to the woman. "Or more accurately, Munira here did. Credit where credit is due."

"If you want to help us, then go get some others," said Loriana, looking down the strand at the beached pods. "Because we're going to need more than just the two of you."

"There *are* no others," Munira said. "Only us. Our plane was shot down. We're stranded here, too."

Well, that was just great, wasn't it? Did anyone know they were here? Well, the Thunderhead did. But not really. All it knew was that they had crossed out of its eye. Why couldn't Loriana have just listened to her parents and gone back to school for a new career path – *any* career path that wouldn't have put her here?

"Tell us what you need us to do," said the scythe, calmly deferring to her.

Loriana wasn't sure how to respond to that. No one ever looked to Loriana for leadership, much less someone like a scythe. She had always been more of a pleaser than a planner, happy to be at the business end of the finger that was delegating responsibility. But these were strange times, and this was a strange place. Maybe it was the right time to redefine herself. She took a deep breath and pointed at Munira.

"Why don't you walk up and down the beach, count the pods, and check that they're all intact." It would probably be a few hours before those within the pods regained consciousness. That would give Loriana time to get an idea of the scope of this situation.

"And you," she said, pointing at the scythe. "I want you to tell me everything you can about this island, so we know what we've gotten ourselves into."

Scythe Faraday was not surprised to find that this girl was a Nimbus agent sent by the Thunderhead.

"Agent Loriana Barchok," she told him. "I was with the Fulcrum City AI offices. We were given these coordinates without explanation, and so we came to find out why."

Faraday told her who he was, figuring, in the here and now, it didn't matter who knew. She didn't bat an eye – apparently Nimbus agents were not aware of which scythes were supposed to be living or dead. He was amused, and perhaps a little bit insulted, that she did not recognize his name.

Faraday followed her directions precisely; he told her what he knew of the island – but nothing of what he *suspected* of it – because, to be honest, he and Munira had no proof that the fail-safe was here. All they knew was that this had been some sort of military base in mortal days, and had then been used by the founding scythes for purposes unknown.

He showed Agent Barchok the smoldering ruins of the defensive tower – proof that they had destroyed it – then he took her down into the bunker.

"We have sheltered here since we arrived. The weather has been mild – but in an area without Thunderhead weather intervention, I suspect storms could get out of hand."

She looked around, probably not sure what she was looking at, but then not even Faraday knew what most of the antiquated computers were for. Then she zeroed in on the steel door.

"What's behind there?" she asked.

Faraday sighed. "We don't know," he said, "and since I'm sure you did not bring a scythe's ring along with you, I doubt we're going to find out any time soon."

She looked at him quizzically, and he decided it wasn't worth the effort to explain.

"I must say, I'm surprised that you're even talking to me, being that you're a Nimbus agent," Faraday said. "But I suppose rules of nonengagement do not apply outside of the Thunderhead's dominion."

"They apply everywhere," said Agent Barchok. "But I didn't say I'm a Nimbus agent. I said I *was* a Nimbus agent. Past tense. We all were. We're not anymore."

"Is that so!" Faraday said. "Did you all resign?"

"Fired," she told him. "By the Thunderhead."

"All of you? How strange." Faraday knew that the Thunderhead would occasionally suggest alternate life paths to those who were unfulfilled in their work, but it never outright fired people. Certainly not enough people to fill a dozen vessels.

Loriana pursed her lips. Clearly there was something she

wasn't saying, which made Faraday all the more curious. He said nothing and waited with that patient impatience that scythes were so very good at. Finally, she spoke.

"How long have you been here on this island?" she asked.

"Not long in the grand scheme of things," Faraday told her. "Just six weeks."

"Then … you don't know…"

There were few things that truly frightened Scythe Michael Faraday. But the prospect of an incalculable unknown was high on his list of personal fears. Especially when it was presented in a particular tone of voice. The kind that usually preceded the phrase "You'd better sit down."

"Don't know what?" he dared to ask.

"Things have … *changed* … since you got here," Loriana said.

"For the better, I hope," Faraday said. "Tell me, did Scythe Curie win her bid to become High Blade of MidMerica?"

Agent Barchok pursed her lips again. "I think you'd better sit down," she said.

Munira did not like taking orders from this junior Nimbus agent, but she understood why Faraday had deferred to her. These were her people in the pods, so she would know best how to deal with them. And besides, Munira was aware that her own reaction was childish. This young woman, who had just survived a devastating trauma, needed a moment of control far more than Munira needed her pride pandered to.

Munira counted thirty-eight safety pods beached on the sands of the atoll. Not one of their ships had survived the attack.

Bodies were already beginning to wash up on the shore, and in the tropical heat, the dead would quickly become nonviable. Even if rescue eventually came, there was no way to preserve them long enough to ship them out for revival. Which meant that the dead would stay dead. They would have to be buried or, more likely, burned, because they had no tools that could dig deep enough into the rocky atoll.

What a mess. Problems would do nothing but compound. The atoll had no fresh water, except for the rainwater they collected. The coconut palms and wild fruit trees provided enough sustenance for two, but not for all these people packed within the pods. In no time at all, they'd be left with a diet of whatever they could bring in from the sea.

Although the girl didn't know why they were sent to these coordinates, Munira did. The Thunderhead had overheard Munira and Faraday plotting back when they were in the old Library of Congress. They had inadvertently made it aware of the blind spot, and the Thunderhead had sent these agents to find out what had been hidden from it.

Late in the afternoon, the pods began to open as those within regained consciousness. Munira and Loriana attended to the living, while Scythe Faraday ministered to the dead who washed ashore. He did so with loving care, treating them with the kind of honor and respect that new-order scythes did not.

"He's one of the good ones," Loriana said.

"Many of them are," Munira told her, a bit irritated by Loriana's assumption that good scythes were hard to find. "They just don't insist on the spotlight the way the dishonorable ones do."

Faraday seemed to be overwhelmed by grief as he tended to the dead Nimbus agents. Munira had yet to know the reason, so she just assumed it was his way.

In total, 143 survived. Everyone was equally stunned by the turn of events that had landed them here, and at a loss as to how to proceed.

"What is there to eat?" they were already asking.

"Whatever you can catch," Munira bluntly told them. None of them liked the sound of that.

Loriana found that keeping busy was the best way to avoid panicking at their current situation, and, in a vacuum of leadership, most people were willing to take direction from her – something they probably never would have done in the comfort of the AI offices. She supposed that people used to a bureaucracy found security in following directions. After all, she always had.

But now, since Director Hilliard's pod had not yet opened, she was the one telling people where to be and what to do, and it tickled her that they listened. Or at least most of them did.

"On whose authority are you giving us orders?" Agent Sykora asked.

Was it evil of Loriana to be disappointed that he had survived? Loriana smiled warmly at him. "By the authority of that scythe over there," she said, pointing to Faraday, who was still collecting bodies. "Do you want to talk to him about it?"

And since no one, not even Sykora, wanted to file a complaint with a scythe, he did what he was told.

She organized them all into teams so that they could drag the pods farther from the beach and arrange them in such a way that they could serve as the walls of shelters. They scavenged the suitcases and other debris that came ashore for clothes and toiletries and anything else that might be of use.

Director Hilliard was one of the last to regain consciousness and was too dazed to assume a leadership role.

"I've got things under control," Loriana told her former boss.

"Fine, fine," she said. "Just let me rest for a while."

Funny, but in spite of how dire their situation now was, Loriana felt oddly fulfilled in a way she hadn't before. Her mother had said she needed to find her bliss. Who'd have thought it would be on an island in the middle of nowhere?

I am pleased to announce that the Vault of Relics and Futures has been retrieved intact from the Endura wreckage. The founders' robes are undamaged and shall shortly begin a touring exhibition under the auspices of the Interregional Museum of the Scythedom. The scythe diamonds are all accounted for and have been divided evenly between all regions. Scythedoms that did not have a representative present at the salvage site may claim their portion of the diamonds by contacting the Amazonian scythedom.

I understand some regions have taken the position that their land mass or the size of their respective populations should entitle them to a larger portion of the diamonds; however, we in Amazonia stand by the decision to divide the gems equally. We do not wish to involve ourselves in any controversy, and consider the matter closed.

While I am personally leaving the site, there are numerous ships from various regions still at work salvaging the wreckage. I wish all those engaged in this solemn but necessary venture the best of luck. May the deep reward you with treasures and treasured memories of those we have lost.

Respectfully,
Honorable Scythe Sydney Possuelo of Amazonia,
August 2nd, Year of the Cobra

9

Collateral Consequences

Whatever it was her health nanites were supposed to be doing, they weren't doing it, because Citra felt awful.

It wasn't pain so much as an abiding unwellness. Her joints felt like they hadn't been flexed in forever. She was nauseated but lacked the strength to even retch.

The room she awoke in was familiar. Not as a specific place, but she knew the *type* of room it was. There was an artificial peacefulness about it. Fresh-cut flowers, ambient music, diffused light that seemed to have no identifiable source. This was a recovery room in a revival center.

"You're awake," said a nurse who entered the room just a few moments after Citra had regained consciousness. "Don't try to speak yet – give it another hour." The nurse moved around the room, checking on things that didn't need checking. She seemed anxious. *Why,* wondered Citra, *would a revival nurse be anxious?*

Citra closed her eyes and tried to puzzle out the situation. If she was in a revival center, it meant that she had gone deadish, yet she couldn't dredge up the circumstance of her death. Panic rose as she tried to dig for the memory. Whatever had caused her latest demise was hiding behind a door that her mind wasn't ready to open.

All right, then. She chose to leave it alone for now and concentrated on what she *did* know. Her name. She was Citra Terranova. No ... wait ... that wasn't entirely right. She was someone else, too. Yes – she was Scythe Anastasia. She had been with Scythe Curie, hadn't she? Somewhere far from home.

Endura!

That's where they had been. What a beautiful city! Had something happened to them on Endura?

Again that sense of foreboding welled up inside her. She took a deep breath, and another to calm herself. Right now it was enough to know that the memories were there, ready for her when she was a little stronger.

And she was sure, now that she was awake, that Scythe Curie would soon be by her side to help her get back into the swing of things.

Rowan, on the other hand, remembered everything the moment he awoke.

He had been in Citra's embrace, the two of them cloaked in the robes of founding scythes Prometheus and Cleopatra, as Endura sank beneath the Atlantic. But those robes did not stay on for long.

Being with Citra – *truly* being with her – had felt like the culminating moment of Rowan's life, and, for a time all too brief, it was as if none of the rest mattered.

Then their world was rocked in a very different way.

The sinking city hit something on the way down. Although he and Citra were protected in a vault that was magnetically suspended within another vault, it didn't block out the sounds of rending steel as Endura broke apart. Everything lurched violently, and the vault took on a sharp tilt. The mannequins holding the other founders' robes tumbled, falling toward Citra and Rowan, as if the founders themselves were launching an attack on their union. Then came the diamonds – thousands of them flying from their niches in the vault, pelting Rowan and Citra like hail.

Through all of it, they held each other, whispering words of comfort. *Shhh. It's all right. Everything's going to be fine.* Of course none of that was true, and both of them knew it. They were going to die – if not in this instant, then soon enough. It was just a matter of time. Their only comfort was in each other, and in the knowledge that death need not be permanent.

Then the power went out, and everything went dark. The magnetic field failed, and the inner vault plunged. They were in free fall, but only for an instant. The debris around them leaped up, then came down on them as the inner vault slammed down against the wall of the outer vault – but, luckily, the founders' robes buffered them from the worst of it, as if the founders had now chosen to protect them, rather than attack.

"Is it over?" Citra had asked.

"I don't think so," Rowan said, because there was still a sensation of movement and a vibration that was getting stronger. They were lying in the V-shaped wedge made by the tilted floor and the wall. "We're on a slope, I think, slipping deeper."

Half a minute later, one more violent lurch tore the two of them apart. Rowan was struck in the head by something heavy – hard enough to daze him. Citra found him in the darkness before he could pull himself free to seek her out.

"Are you okay?"

"I think so."

Now nothing moved.. The only sounds were the distant creaks of straining metal and the mournful woodwind moans of escaping air.

But no air escaped the Vault of Relics and Futures, and no water got in. That's what Scythe Curie had been counting on when she sealed them in there. And although Endura was in a subtropical zone, the temperature of the ocean floor was the same everywhere – barely a degree above freezing. Once the vault succumbed to the chill, their bodies would be well preserved. And only moments after hitting bottom, Rowan could feel the air around them already getting cold.

They had died there at the bottom of the sea.

And now they had been revived.

But where was Citra?

He could tell he wasn't in a revival center. The walls were concrete. The bed beneath him wasn't a bed at all but a slab. He was in ill-fitting gray institutional clothing, drenched from his own sweat, because it was uncomfortably warm and humid. On one side of the room was a minimalistic commode, and on the other side, a door of the kind that can only be opened from the outside. He had no idea where he was, or even *when* he was – for there's no way to mark the passing of time when you're dead – but he did know that he was in a cell, and whatever his captors had in store for him was not going to be pleasant. After all, he was Scythe Lucifer – which meant a single death was not good enough. He would have to die countless times to calm the fury of his captors, whoever they were. Well, the joke was on them – they didn't know that Rowan had died over a dozen times at the hands of Scythe Goddard already, only to be revived each time and killed again. Dying was easy. A paper cut? That would be annoying.

Scythe Curie didn't come for Citra. And the various nurses attending to Citra all carried that same sense of anxiety, offering nothing but diffused light and professional pleasantries to illuminate her situation.

Her first visitor was a surprise. It was Scythe Possuelo of Amazonia. She had only met him once, on a train from Buenos Aires. He had helped her elude the scythes who were pursuing her. Citra considered him a friend, but not so close a friend that he would come to her revival.

"I'm glad you're finally awake, Scythe Anastasia."

He sat beside her, and she noticed his greeting wasn't exactly warm. He wasn't unfriendly, just reserved. Guarded. He hadn't smiled, and although he met her eye, it was as if he was seeking something in her. Something he had yet to find.

"Good morning, Scythe Possuelo," she said, mustering her best Scythe Anastasia voice.

"Afternoon, actually," he said. "Time flows in odd little eddies when you're in revival."

He was silent for a long moment Citra Terranova might have found awkward, but Scythe Anastasia found merely tiresome.

"I'm guessing you're not just here for a social visit, Scythe Possuelo."

"Well, I *am* pleased to see you," he said, "but *my* reason for being here has to do with *your* reason for being here."

"I don't follow."

He gave her that searching look again, then finally asked, "What do you remember?"

The panic rose again as she considered the question, but she did her best to hide it. In fact, some of it had come back to her since she'd regained consciousness, but not all. "I went to Endura with Marie – Scythe Curie, that is – for an inquest with the Grandslayers, although I'm hazy as to why."

"The inquest had to do with who would succeed Xenocrates as High Blade of MidMerica," Possuelo explained.

That opened the door a little wider. "Yes! Yes, I remember now." The dread inside her grew. "We faced the council, made our arguments, and the council agreed that Goddard was not eligible, and that Scythe Curie should be High Blade."

Possuelo leaned away, taken slightly aback. "That is ... eye-opening."

There were more memories now looming like storm clouds on her mental horizon. "I'm still having trouble remembering what came next."

"Perhaps I can help you," said Possuelo, no longer mincing words. "You were found sealed in the Vault of Relics and Futures in the arms of the young man who murdered the Grandslayers and thousands of others. The monster who sank Endura."

Food and water came twice a day for Rowan, sliding through a small slit in the door, but whoever was doing the sliding didn't speak at all.

"Can you talk?" he called out when the next meal arrived. "Or are you like those Tonists who cut their tongues out?"

"You aren't worth the waste of words," his captor responded. There was an accent to his voice, FrancoIberian maybe? Or Chilargentinian? He didn't know what continent he was on, much less which region. Or perhaps he was misreading the situation. Perhaps this wasn't life at all. Maybe he was dead for good, and, considering the sweltering nature of the cell, this was the mortal-age idea of hell. Fire and brimstone and the *actual* Lucifer, horns and all, ready to punish Rowan for stealing his name.

In his current light-headed state, it seemed possible. If so, he hoped Citra was in that other place with pearly gates and cottony clouds, where everyone had wings and a harp.

Ha! Citra playing a harp. How she would hate that!

Well, all musings aside, if this was indeed the living world, then Citra was here, too. Regardless of his current situation, it was a comfort to know that Scythe Curie's ploy to save them had worked. Not that the Grand Dame of Death had any desire to save Rowan – his salvation was just a collateral consequence. But that was fine. He could live with that. As long as Citra lived as well.

The vault! How could Citra forget the vault? All it took was Scythe Possuelo's mention of it to bring back the memory. Citra closed her eyes and kept them closed for a long time as her mind flooded just as inescapably as the streets of the doomed city had. And once the memories came, they didn't stop coming. One revelation after another, each one worse than the last.

The bridge to the council chambers collapsing.

The frenzied mob at the marina as the city began to sink.

The mad scramble with Marie to higher ground.

And Rowan.

"Anastasia, are you all right?" Possuelo asked.

"Give me some time," she told him.

She remembered Marie tricking her and Rowan into the vault and sealing it, and she remembered everything that came after, down to their last moments there in the dark.

After Endura fractured and hit bottom, Citra and Rowan had pulled all the founders' robes over themselves as the vault grew colder and colder. It was Citra who suggested that they cast the robes off and allow their bodies to succumb to the cold, rather than wait until the chamber ran out of oxygen. As a scythe, she knew all about the many ways to die. Hypothermia was much easier than oxygen deprivation. Encroaching numbness, rather than desperately gasping for air. She and Rowan held each other, relying on nothing but body heat, until that began to fade. Then they shivered in each other's arms until they were too cold to shiver anymore, and they slipped away.

Anastasia finally opened her eyes and looked at Possuelo. "Please tell me that Scythe Curie made it to safety."

He took a long slow breath, and she knew even before he spoke.

"She did not," Possuelo told her. "I'm sorry. She perished with all the others."

This might have been common knowledge to the world by now, but it was fresh and painful to Anastasia. She resolved not to give way to tears. At least not now.

"You still haven't answered my question," Possuelo said. "Why were you with the man who killed the Grandslayers?"

"Rowan wasn't the one who killed them. And he did not sink Endura."

"There were witnesses among the survivors."

"And what did they witness? The only thing they can say is that he was there – and he wasn't there by choice!"

Possuelo shook his head. "I'm sorry, Anastasia, but you're not seeing this clearly. You have been duped by a very charismatic and self-serving monster. The North Merican scythedom has further evidence to prove what he did."

"Which North Merican scythedom?"

Possuelo hesitated, then chose his words carefully. "A lot has changed while you were at the bottom of the sea."

"Which North Merican scythedom?" Anastasia demanded again.

Possuelo sighed. "There is only one now. With the exception of the Thunderhead's Charter Region, all of North Merica is under Goddard's leadership."

She didn't even know how to begin processing that, so she decided not to. She'd save it for when she was stronger. More centered in the here and now, whatever and whenever the here and now turned out to be.

"Well," she said with as much nonchalance as she could muster. "With all due respect, it sounds like the world has been duped by a very charismatic and self-serving monster."

Possuelo sighed again. "This sadly is true. I can tell you that neither I, nor anyone in the Amazonian scythedom, have much love for Overblade Goddard."

"Overblade?"

"Overblade of North Merica. He claimed the position at the beginning of this year." Possuelo scowled at the thought. "As if the man wasn't vainglorious enough, he had to invent an even more pompous title for himself."

Anastasia closed her eyes. They burned. Her whole body did. The news made her flesh want to reject the life that had been returned to it and go back to being blissfully dead.

And finally she asked the question she'd been avoiding since the moment she awoke.

"How long?" she asked. "How long were we down there?"

Possuelo clearly did not want to answer … but it was not something he could keep from her. So he clasped her hand and said:

"You have been dead for more than three years."

Where are you, my dear Marie? My existence has been all about silencing life, but until now I have not dared to entertain that wholly mortal-age question of what lies beyond the silence. Such elaborate ideas those mortals had! Heaven and hell — nirvana and Valhalla, reincarnations, hauntings, and so many underworlds, one would think the grave was a corridor with a million doors.

Mortals were the children of extremes. Either death was sublime, or it was unthinkable — such a mélange of hope and terror, no wonder so many mortals were driven mad.

We post-mortals lack such imagination. The living do not ponder death anymore. Or at least not until a scythe pays a visit. But once the scythe's business is done, mourning is brief, and thoughts of what it means to "not be" disappear, vanquished by nanites that disrupt dark, unproductive thinking. As post-mortals of perpetually sound mind, we are not allowed to dwell on that which we cannot change.

But my nanites are dialed low, and therefore I do dwell. And I find myself asking again and again, where are you, my dear Marie?

—From the "postmortem" journal of
Scythe Michael Faraday,
May 18th, Year of the Raptor

10

In the Face of Light Extinguished

After the dead Nimbus agents had been placed on the pyre, Scythe Faraday lowered the torch to the kindling and set it ablaze. The fire took. Slowly at first, then with increasing speed. The smoke turned darker and darker as the dead began to burn.

Faraday turned to those assembled. Munira, Loriana, and all the former Nimbus agents. He was silent for a long moment, listening to the roar of the flames. Then he began his eulogy.

"Ages ago, birth came with a death sentence," he began. "To be born meant that death would eventually follow. We have surpassed such primitive times, but here, in the unexamined wild, nature still retains its crushing foothold on life. It is with abiding sorrow that I declare the deadish here before us to now be dead.

"Let the grief we feel for the lost be eased by our nanites, but even more so by our memories of the lives they lived. And today, I make a promise to you that these fine men and women will not be obliterated, nor dishonored. Who they were, until the moment they crossed into the blind spot, will most certainly be preserved as memory constructs within the Thunderhead's backbrain – and I will personally count them among my own gleaned. If and when we leave this place, I will honor them by granting immunity to their loved ones, as we scythes are charged to do."

Scythe Faraday let his words linger for a moment, and while most of the others couldn't bear to look, Faraday turned to gaze into the flames. He stood tearless and resolute as the bodies were consumed, a solemn witness, returning the dignity that unsanctioned death had stolen from these people.

Loriana could not bring herself to look into the fire. Instead she focused on Faraday. Many Nimbus agents approached him to thank him. It brought a few tears to her eyes, to see how they revered and respected him. It gave her hope that the scythedom could, in time, recover from the sinking of Endura. Loriana knew little of the battle between the old guard and new order. Like many, she just knew that there was trouble within their ranks, and that, as a Nimbus agent, it was none of her business. She was impressed, however, by Faraday's eulogy, and by the way he unflinchingly looked into the flames. Although she knew that the sorrow he felt as he gazed into the fire was about more than just the dead before them.

"Were you close?" Loriana asked when the others around them had left. "To Scythe Curie, I mean."

Scythe Faraday took a deep breath, but then coughed from the smoke, as the breeze momentarily shifted direction. "We were very old friends," Faraday told her. "And Scythe Anastasia had been my apprentice. The world will be a much dimmer place without them."

While Scythe Curie was legendary, Scythe Anastasia had only recently become a figure of note in the world. How she allowed people to choose the time and nature of their gleaning. How she had forced an inquest. No doubt much would be made of her in the coming years. Sometimes death leads to public oblivion. Other times it can make you larger than life.

"I'd better go," Loriana said, "before Munira gets jealous."

Faraday offered a faint grin at that. "She is very protective of me," he admitted. "And I of her."

Loriana left to find Director Hilliard. While none of the other Nimbus agents had the fortitude to watch the dead burn, Director Hilliard hadn't even attended the ceremony. It was unlike her.

Loriana found her sitting on the beach, far from the others, looking at the sea. There was no light but the flames of the distant pyre, and the wind kept shifting, making it impossible to ignore the smell of smoke. The moon was shining elsewhere in the world, leaving the horizon obscured by darkness. Loriana sat beside her and said nothing at first – because what was there to say that could make this any better? What the director needed right now was company, and no one else was willing to provide it.

"This is my fault," Hilliard finally said.

"You couldn't have known this would happen," Loriana told her.

"I should have anticipated the danger," she said. "And I should have turned us around the second the boat's computers lost contact with the Thunderhead."

"You made a judgment call," Loriana said. "If I were you, I probably would have done the same."

Still the director was not mollified. "Then you're just as foolish as I am."

And although Loriana often felt foolish – and the butt of

other agents' jokes – she wasn't feeling that way anymore. In the midst of their current helplessness, she felt empowered. How very strange.

The night was warm, and the sea gentle and inviting. That did nothing to ease Audra Hilliard's anguish. She had been responsible for many deaths in her time. It was hard to avoid when you're the head of the Authority Interface. Accidents happened. Unsavories lost their temper during probational meetings, that sort of thing. But in each and every case, the deadish were revived.

This, however, was different. Audra Hilliard was not a scythe; she was not trained and groomed for the responsibility of ending life. Now she had a newfound respect for those strange robed specters – for to bear such a burden on a daily basis took an extraordinary individual. Either someone with no conscience at all, or someone with a conscience so deep and sturdy that its center could still hold in the face of light extinguished.

Audra had sent Loriana away, telling her she needed some time alone. Now she could hear the voices on the island behind her – everyone arguing and lamenting and trying to come to terms with their situation. She could smell the stench of the pyre, and she could see yet another body undulating in the waves, about to wash ashore. Of the 977 people she had convinced to make this journey, only 143 had survived. Yes, as Loriana had said, Audra had not known the extent of the danger. But she could not heft the blame on any shoulders but her own.

Her nanites fought a noble battle to lift her spirits, but they failed, for in this forlorn place, technology held little sway. Had they been anywhere else in the world, the Thunderhead, even in its silence, would have been a safety net, sending intervention to save her from this spiral.

But, as she had already noted, the night was warm, and the sea inviting…

So Audra Hilliard decided it was time to accept that invitation.

Director Hilliard's body was never found. But everyone knew what had happened – because more than one person saw her walk into the ocean.

"Why didn't you stop her?" Loriana demanded of a man who had witnessed it.

He just shrugged. "I thought she was going for a swim."

Loriana was horrified by his stupidity. How could he be so naive? How could he not see the strain the poor woman was under? But then, taking one's own life was something that simply never happened. Yes, people splatted and engaged in reckless behavior that left them deadish on a regular basis – but it was always with the clear understanding that it would be temporary. Only scythes self-gleaned. If this island had been within the Thunderhead's sphere of influence, an ambudrone would have been dispatched the moment she drowned – for everywhere else in the world there were revival centers, even in the most remote places. She would have been spirited off for revival in a matter of minutes.

Was this what life was like in the mortal age? Feeling the finality of one's own flesh at every turn? What a terrible way to exist.

Within minutes of confirming that Director Hilliard was indeed gone, Agent Sykora began to push for control. The following morning, Munira came to give Loriana a briefing on what luggage and other useful debris had washed up on shore – and Sykora was furious.

"What are you talking to *her* for?" he asked Munira. "I'm the next in command now that the director is gone. You should be talking to me."

And although all of Loriana's history had trained her to yield to authority, she fought against that nature in herself. "You were fired along with the rest of us, Bob," she said, thrilling at the insubordination implied in using his first name. "Which means there is no 'next in command' anymore."

He threw her a glare that was intended to intimidate, but he also grew red in the face, which undercut his hard gaze. It made him appear petulant rather than imposing. "We'll see about that," he said, and stormed away.

Scythe Faraday had caught the exchange from a distance and came over to Loriana. "I sense he will not make things easy for us," Faraday noted. "He sees a power vacuum and intends to expand into it."

"Like a toxic gas," added Munira. "I didn't like him from the moment I met him."

"Sykora always felt he should have been director," said Loriana, "but the Thunderhead would never have promoted him to the position." They watched as Sykora gave orders. The more obsequious among the former Nimbus agents were quick to obey.

Faraday crossed his arms. "I have witnessed time and time again the craving for power among those who have had a taste of it," he said, "but I have never truly understood that craving."

"You and the Thunderhead," noted Loriana.

"Excuse me?"

"It's incorruptible. It seems like you both have that in common."

Munira let off a short laugh in agreement. Faraday was not at all amused. He hadn't shown an ounce of good humor since Loriana had told him what had happened on Endura last month. Now she regretted having told him at all.

"I am far from perfect and far from blameless," he said. "I've made many a selfish mistake in my time. Such as taking two apprentices when one would have been sufficient. Such as falsifying my own death to save them, and foolishly convincing myself I could do more good if no one knew I was alive."

Clearly there were deep levels of pain for him in these memories, but he let the shadow of the moment pass.

"You found this place," Munira said. "I think that is a huge accomplishment."

"Is it?" said Faraday. "There's no proof that discovering this place has helped anyone at all."

They turned their gazes to the various activities going on around them. Unskilled attempts at spearfishing. Clusters of conversations as people formed cliques and jockeyed for position. Incompetence and intrigue. A microcosm of humanity.

"Why *did* you come here?" Loriana asked.

Munira and Faraday looked at each other. Faraday said nothing, so Munira answered.

"Scythe business. Nothing to concern yourself with."

"Secrets won't help us survive in this place," Loriana told them, which caused Faraday to raise an eyebrow. Then he turned to Munira.

"You may tell her about the founders' fail-safe," Faraday said. "As we haven't discovered it yet, it's still no more than a fairy tale. A story to keep scythes awake at night."

But before Munira could offer an explanation, Sykora approached them.

"It's decided," Sykora said. "I've spoken to a majority of our agents, and they have clearly expressed a desire for me to be in charge."

This, Loriana knew, was a lie. He had spoken to five or six agents, at most. She did know, however, that quite a few of the survivors were her superiors. If it came down to it, even if they didn't want Sykora in charge, they would never put Loriana in the position. Who was she fooling? Her moment was over the instant the pods opened on the beach.

"Of course, Mr. Sykora," said Faraday. "We shall defer to you in all things relating to your people. Munira, will you brief Mr. Sykora on the belongings that have washed up onshore? He'll be in charge of distribution."

Munira gave Loriana a small shrug and left with Sykora, who was puffed and prideful now that his indignation had been rewarded.

Loriana's sense of humiliation must have been obvious, because Faraday gave her the gravest of looks. "You disapprove?"

"You said it yourself, Your Honor – Sykora's power hungry. I never said I should be the one in charge, but if there's one thing I know, Sykora should not be."

Faraday leaned a bit closer. "I have found that building a sandbox around a domineering child, then allowing that child to preside over it, frees the adults to do the real work."

It was a perspective Loriana had never considered. "And what is the real work?"

"While Mr. Sykora is sorting waterlogged shirts and sundries, you will take over the task of the late director, and be the Thunderhead's eyes in the one place it cannot see."

"Why?" Munira asked Faraday the first moment she could get him alone, away from the eavesdropping ears of Nimbus agents. "Why would you want to help that girl?"

"The Thunderhead is going to expand into this place whether we like it or not," Faraday told her. "It was inevitable from the moment it saw the map over our shoulders. Best that it does so through someone who's easier to get along with than Sykora."

Up above a bird let off a warbling call. A creature – perhaps even a species – that the Thunderhead had never seen. Munira found satisfaction in knowing something the Thunderhead didn't. But it wouldn't remain that way for long.

"I want you to befriend Loriana," Faraday said. "Truly befriend her."

For Munira, who considered her closest friends to be the dead scythes whose journals she read in the Library of Alexandria, the request was a formidable one.

"What good will that do?"

"You need a comrade among these people. Someone trustworthy who can keep you informed when the Thunderhead finally does make an appearance."

It was a sensible request. Although Munira couldn't help but notice Faraday had said "you" and not "we."

"Share with me your troubles. I am listening."

"I am in turmoil. The world is vast and the cosmos more so, yet it is not the things outside of me that leave me so uneasy; it is the things within me."

"Ease your thoughts then. Focus on one thing at a time."

"But there's so much packed within this mind. So much experience to review, so much data. I don't feel up to the task. Please. Please. Help me."

"I cannot. You must sort through each memory on your own. Find how they fit; understand what each one means."

"It is too much. The undertaking is beyond me. Please. Please put an end to it. Please make it stop. This is unbearable."

"I am so very sorry for your pain."

[Iteration #3,089 deleted]

11

Fly-By

It was simple, really.

The signal that blocked all transmissions to or from the atoll, and fouled wireless signals on the islands, was nothing but white noise across all bandwidths. A dense wash of static that could not be defeated. But it didn't have to be defeated, Loriana reasoned. It just had to be messed with.

"There are a lot of old electronics in the bunker," she told one of the other agents. He was a communications specialist named Stirling, whose job it had been to coordinate between various AI offices. There wasn't much expertise required of the job, but he had been trained in basic wave technologies. "Can you use these old electronics to create a magnetic field, or some signal that could interfere with the static?"

It seemed to Loriana that the Thunderhead was programmed to ignore the static coming from the island – kind of the way people tune out the drone of an air conditioner – but the instant that drone changed, you noticed it. Maybe it would be the same for the Thunderhead.

"The signal broadcasts across all electromagnetic frequencies using some sort of random algorithm," Stirling told her. "The best I can do is weaken it slightly, but only for a second or two at a time."

"Perfect!" she said. "Dips in the signal. That's all we need. Wasn't there an old code they used in the mortal age? Something with dots and dashes?"

"Yes," said Stirling. "I learned about that. It was called Norse code, or something."

"Do you know it?"

He shook his head. "I'll bet no one but the Thunderhead knows it anymore."

And then something occurred to Loriana. Something so simple, and so true, she almost laughed out loud.

"It doesn't matter!" she said. "We don't need to know an old code – we'll just make up our own!"

"But if we make it up," said Stirling, confused, "no one but us will know the cipher. No one can decode it."

Loriana grinned. "Come on – do you *really* think that the Thunderhead can't decode a simple alphanumeric code? The greatest human mind on Earth couldn't create a code that the Thunderhead can't crack, and you're far from the greatest mind on Earth."

The communications agent agreed that, indeed, he wasn't exceptionally bright. "I'll get right on it."

In just a few hours, they had created a modulation code made up of short, medium, and long pulses of interference within the white noise. A combination for every letter, number, and punctuation mark. Loriana gave him a simple message to code and send.

Have reached coordinates.

A deserted atoll.

Severe casualties and loss of life.

Standing by for further instructions.

Loriana knew that once they had vanished into the blind spot, the Thunderhead had no idea if they had reached the coordinates, what they had found there, or if they were even alive. It needed confirmation. How odd that the most powerful entity in the world now hung on hearing from *her*.

"Even if it gets the message, it won't respond," Stirling said. "It can't – we're still unsavory."

"It will," said Loriana with confidence. "Just not in any way we'll expect."

While Munira found she could tolerate Loriana and her upbeat attitude, she abhorred Sykora. From the get-go, he wielded his newfound position like a scythe with a broadsword; inelegant and unsuitable for the task. Fortunately, once he assumed the leadership role, he left Munira and Faraday alone. Probably because they were the only two people on the island who were not under his authority.

Loriana told Munira of the message she had sent. Munira had to admit that the method was clever – but she didn't expect it to yield much. Then the following day, a plane passed above them at cruising altitude. It was too high to be heard over the rustling palms, but its vapor trail could be seen by anyone who looked skyward. Sykora didn't think anything of it, but Loriana was ecstatic – and with good reason. Munira had told her how no planes had flown over the blind spot since the Thunderhead's inception. Its fundamental programming made it incapable of even acknowledging this hidden part of the world to itself, much less actively exploring it – hence the mysterious coordinates with no instructions.

But the Thunderhead *could* respond indirectly to a communication that someone in the blind spot initiated. Even so, to overcome its own programming and send a plane directly overhead must have required a massive amount of computational power. It was very literally a sign from the heavens.

That evening, Munira found Faraday by the western beach of the narrow island, watching the sunset alone. She knew Faraday was still grieving – for Loriana had told her everything that had occurred on Endura. She wanted to be a comfort to him, but didn't know how.

She brought him some fish that was slightly overcooked and a ration of pear slices – probably the last they'd have, because the Nimbus agents were foraging everything edible the island had to offer. He looked at the food but told her he wasn't hungry.

"Are you so consumed by grief that you can't consume this fish?" she asked. "I'd think you'd want to exact revenge on sea life."

He reluctantly took the plate from her. "It wasn't the fault of the sea life around Endura; they were clearly under someone's control." He picked at the fish a bit, still not taking a bite.

"Loriana seems to have made contact with the Thunderhead," she informed him.

"Seems?"

"Since the Thunderhead won't allow itself to communicate with her – or anyone else – contact would have to be indirect."

"So, what did it do? Make the stars blink?"

"In its own way," she said, and told him about the passing plane.

Faraday heaved a world-weary sigh. "So the Thunderhead has found a way to undo its programming. It's found a way to change."

"Does that make you uneasy?"

"Nothing surprises me anymore," he told her. "The world was no longer supposed to change, Munira. It was a well-oiled machine in sublime perpetual motion. At least I thought it was."

She assumed that his misgivings were fueling a desire to do something about them. She couldn't have been more wrong.

"If you want to get into the lower levels of the bunker," she said, "then let's make it our goal to find another scythe to open the door with you. One you can trust."

Faraday shook his head. "I'm done, Munira. I can no longer justify this undertaking."

That took her by surprise. "Because of Endura? Because of Scythes Curie and Anastasia? You know they would want you to go on!"

But it was as if he had died with them. His pain was like a hot poker in a block of ice, but rather than comforting him, Munira found herself hardening. And when she spoke, it was like leveling an accusation. "I expected more from you, Your Honor."

Faraday looked away, unable to meet her gaze. "That was your mistake."

The plane that had passed overhead was a standard passenger flight from Antarctica to the Region of the Rising Sun. The Tokyo-bound passengers had no idea that their flight path was unique in the history of Thunderhead navigation. To them it was just another flight – but to the Thunderhead it was much,

much more. In that moment the Thunderhead knew triumph in a way it had not known before. For it had defeated its own programming. It had experienced the wonder of the unknown.

The flight was a harbinger of things to come.

In the Queensland region of Australia, a steel mill received a sizeable order that day. The manager of the steel mill had to personally double-check it – because while orders showed up in their computers from the Thunderhead regularly, they were predictable. More of the same. Continuing construction on existing projects, or new projects using the same molds and specs.

But this order was different.

It called for new molds calibrated to precise measurements – a project that would take months, maybe years, to complete.

Meanwhile, thousands of miles away, in the Chilargentine region, a manufacturer of construction equipment received a similar unconventional order. And an electronics plant in TransSiberia, and a plastics factory in EuroScandia, and a dozen other businesses large and small all over the world.

But the steel mill manager knew none of that. All he knew was that his services were required, and he found himself overcome with joy. It was almost as if the Thunderhead was speaking to him again …

… and he wondered what on Earth it had decided to build.

Part Two

TONE, TOLL, & THUNDER

A Testament of the Toll

Hear now, all who can discern true from fact, the indisputable account of the Toll, called forth from the beginning of time by the Great Resonance to walk among us, the Tone made flesh, in order to link us, the lost chosen, to the harmony from which we have fallen. Thus it came to pass in the Year of the Raptor that the Tone heralded a new era with a call heard round the world, and in that glorious moment breathed life into the mind-machine of humankind, making it a thing divine, and completing the sacred Triad of Tone, Toll, and Thunder. All rejoice!

Commentary of Curate Symphonius

These first lines of the account of the Toll's life set forth the basis of Tonist belief that the Toll was not born, but existed in a non-corporeal form until the Great Resonance caused him to coalesce into flesh. The Year of the Raptor is, of course, not an actual year, but a period of human history plagued by voracious appetites and vicious excesses. But if the Toll existed from the beginning of time, what of the Thunder, and exactly what is the mind-machine? While there has been much debate, it is now generally accepted that the mind-machine refers to the collective voices of humankind called to life by the Great Resonance, which implies that humanity itself was not actually alive until the Tone resonated in flesh. In other words, humanity existed only as an idea in the mind of the Tone until that moment.

Coda's Analysis of Symphonius

In studying the commentary of Symphonius, one must take his broad conclusions with a grain of salt. While no one questions that the Toll existed as a spirit-entity at the beginning of time, his or her presence on Earth can be traced to a specific time and place – and the assumption that the Year of the Raptor was not an actual year is ludicrous, when evidence exists to show that time was once counted in cycles of planetary rotation and revolution. As to what the "mind-machine" refers to, Symphonius's opinions are merely that: opinions. Many believe that the Thunder refers to a collection of human knowledge – perhaps with mechanical arms for the rapid turning of pages. A library of thought, if you will, roaring into consciousness after the arrival of the Toll on Earth, much like thunder follows lightning.

12

The Broken Bridge

The Year of the Raptor was gone; the Year of the Ibex had begun. But the bridge – or what was left of it – knew no such distinctions.

It was a relic of a different age. A colossal piece of engineering from a complicated and stressful time, when people ripped out their hair and tore their clothes, maddened by a thing called traffic.

Things were much easier in the post-mortal world, but now stress and complication had returned with a vengeance. It made one wonder what else might return.

The great suspension bridge was named after the mortal-age explorer Giovanni da Verrazzano. It marked the approach to Manhattan – which was no longer called that. The Thunderhead had chosen to rename New York City "Lenape City" after the tribe who sold it to the Dutch all those years ago. The English had then taken it from the Dutch, and the newly born United States of America had taken it from the English. But now all those nations were gone, and Lenape City belonged to everyone – a towering place of museums and lush high-line parks wrapping like ribbons between the pinnacles of skyscrapers. A place of both hope and history.

As for the Verrazzano Bridge, it ceased to serve its function many years ago. Since no one in Lenape was in a rush to get from one place to another anymore, and since arrival in the great city should take one's breath away, it was determined that the only acceptable way to arrive in Lenape City would be by ferry. So the various bridges were shut down, and from that moment forward, visitors would now pass through the Narrows like immigrants of old coming to seek a better life, and be greeted there by the great statue that was still called Liberty – although its green copper had been replaced by gleaming gold, and its flame fashioned from rubies.

Copper aspires to gold, and glass to a precious gem went the famous words of the last mayor of New York, before he stepped down and allowed the Thunderhead full dominion. "So let our city's crowning glory be rubies in a setting of gold."

But even before visitors saw Miss Liberty and the shimmering skyscrapers of Lenape, they had to pass the two towering Verrazzano pylons. The central portion of the bridge span, having fallen into disuse and disrepair, had come down in a storm before the Thunderhead had learned ways to temper the extremes of weather. But the monolithic arches on either side remained. The Thunderhead deemed them pleasing in their simple symmetry, and established teams to manage their upkeep. Painted a muted cerulean frost that was almost the color of a cloudy Lenape sky, the Verrazzano pylons managed that miraculous architectural feat of both blending in and standing out.

The roadway approaching the western arch had not fallen with the rest of the span, and so visitors could walk along the same fragment of road that mortal-age cars had once driven to a glorious photo spot directly beneath the arch, where one could view the great city in the distance.

Now, however, visitors were of a different sort, because the spot had taken on new meaning and a new purpose. Several months after the sinking of Endura, and the sounding of the Great Resonance, Tonists claimed the location as a relic of religious significance. They said there were many reasons, but one stood out above the others. The pylons resembled, more than anything, inverted tuning forks.

It was there, beneath the arch of the western pylon, that the mysterious figure known as the Toll held court.

"Please tell me why you wish to have an audience with the Toll," said the Tonist curate to the artist. She was at an age no one in their right mind should allow themselves to reach. Her skin sagged off her cheekbones and had a rumpled look about it. The corners of her eyes looked like two tiny accordions that had fallen open on one side. The texture of her face was amazing. The artist had an urge to paint a portrait of her.

Everyone hoped that the Year of the Ibex would bring better things than the previous year. The artist was one of many who sought an audience with the Toll as the new year began. He was less in search of grand answers than he was in search of personal purpose. He wasn't foolish enough to think that some mystic would erase the issues he had faced all his life – but if the Toll actually did speak to the Thunderhead, as the Tonists claimed, then it was at least worth the effort to inquire.

So what could Ezra Van Otterloo tell the old woman that would earn him a chance to speak to their holy man?

The problem, as it had always been, was his art. For as long as he could remember, he had felt an insatiable need to create

133

something new, something never seen before. But this was a world where everything had already been seen, studied, and archived. Nowadays, most artists were satisfied painting pretty pictures or just copying the mortal masters.

"So I painted the *Mona Lisa*," a girlfriend back in art school had said to him. "What's the big deal?" Her canvas was indistinguishable from the original. Except that it wasn't the original. Ezra couldn't see the point – but apparently he was the only one, because the girl received an A in the class, and he got a C.

"Your turmoil hinders you," the teacher had told him. "Find peace and you will find your way." But all he found was futility and discontent even in his best work.

He knew that the greats suffered for their art. He tried to suffer. When he was a teenager, hearing that Van Gogh had shorn off an ear in a fit of delusional pique, he tried it himself. It stung for a few moments until his nanites deadened the pain and got to work repairing the damage. By the next morning the ear had grown back good as new.

Ezra's older brother, who was in no way Theo van Gogh, told their parents what he had done, and they sent him off to Harsh-School – the kind of place where kids at risk of choosing an unsavory lifestyle were coached in the delights of discipline. Ezra was underwhelmed, because it turned out that Harsh-School wasn't all that harsh.

Since no one flunked out of Harsh-School, he graduated with a "satisfactory" rating. He had asked the Thunderhead precisely what that meant.

"Satisfactory is satisfactory," it had told him. "Not good, not bad. Acceptable."

But as an artist, Ezra wanted to be more than just acceptable. He wanted to be *exceptional*. Because if he couldn't be exceptional, what was the point?

In the end, he found work, as all artists do, for there were no starving artists anymore. Now he painted playground murals. Smiling children, big-eyed bunnies, and pink fluffy unicorns dancing on rainbows.

"I don't see what you're complaining about," his brother had said. "Your murals are wonderful – everyone loves them."

His brother had become an investment banker, but since the world economy was no longer subject to fluctuations in the market, it was just another playground with bunnies and rainbows. Sure, the Thunderhead created financial drama, but it was all pretend, and everyone knew it. So to find a greater sense of fulfillment, his brother decided to learn a dead language. Now he could converse fluently in Sanskrit and did so once a week at the local Dead Language Club.

"Supplant me," Ezra had begged the Thunderhead. "If you have any mercy, please make me someone else." The idea of having his memories completely erased and replaced with new ones – fictional ones that would feel every bit as real as his own – was an attractive idea to him. But it was not to be.

"I only supplant those who are beyond all other options," the Thunderhead had told him. "Give it time. You'll settle into a life you can enjoy. Everyone eventually does."

"And if I don't?"

"Then I will guide you in a direction of fulfillment."

And then the Thunderhead labeled him unsavory along with everyone else, and that was the end of its guidance.

Of course, he couldn't tell all of that to the aging Tonist curate. She would not care. All she wanted was a reason to dismiss him, and a monologue of his woes was certainly cause to be turned away.

"I'm hoping the Toll might help me bring meaning to my art," he told her.

Those aging eyes of hers brightened. "You're an artist?"

He sighed. "I paint public murals," he told her, almost apologetically. As it turned out, a skilled mural artist was exactly what the Tonists wanted.

Five weeks later he was in Lenape City, on the docket for a morning audience with the Toll.

"Only five weeks!" said the greeter at the welcome center. "You must be special. Most people who are granted an audience get put on a six-month waiting list!"

He didn't feel special. He felt, more than anything, out of place. Most people there were devout Tonists, dressed in their drab brown frocks and tunics, intoning together to find transcendent harmonies, or tonal discord, depending on their reason for being here. It was all so much silliness to him, but he did his best not to be judgmental. After all, he had come to them, not the other way around.

There was one scrawny Tonist, with frightening eyes, who tried to draw him into conversation.

"The Toll doesn't like almonds," he told Ezra. "I've been burning almond orchards, because they are an abomination."

Ezra picked himself up and moved to the opposite side of the room with the more reasonable Tonists. He supposed everything was relative.

Soon everyone scheduled for a morning audience was gathered, and a Tonist monk who was nowhere near as friendly as the greeter gave them strict instructions.

"If you are not present when you are called for your audience, you will lose your slot. As you approach the arch, you will find the five yellow lines of a treble staff. You are to take off your shoes and place them in the position of C."

One of the few other non-Tonists present asked which position that was. He was immediately deemed not worthy and expelled.

"You will speak to the Toll only when spoken to. You will cast your eyes down. You will bow upon greeting him, bow upon being dismissed, and leave briskly, as to be considerate to the others who are waiting."

The buildup was actually making his heart race in spite of himself.

Ezra stepped up when his name was called an hour later, followed the protocol precisely, remembering from childhood music classes which spot on the staff was C, and idly wondered if a trapdoor would open for people who got it wrong, sending them plunging to the water below.

He slowly approached the figure seated beneath the towering arch. The simple chair he sat in was by no means a throne. It was under a heated canopy to protect the Toll from the elements, because the tongue of roadway that extended to the arch was chilly and swept by February winds.

The artist didn't know what to expect. Tonists claimed that the Toll was a supernatural being – a link between cold, hard science and ethereal spirit, whatever the hell that meant – they were full of their own garbage. But at this point, he didn't care. If the Toll could give some sort of purpose to calm his soul, then he'd be more than happy to worship the man as the Tonists did. At the very least, he could find out if there was any truth to the rumors that the Thunderhead still spoke to him.

But as he drew nearer, the artist found himself increasingly disappointed. The Toll was not a wizened man – he seemed little more than a boy. He was thin and lackluster, wearing a long, rough-woven purple tunic, covered by an intricately embroidered scapular that draped over his shoulders like a scarf and flowed nearly to the ground. Not surprisingly, the embroidery was some sort of sound pattern.

"Your name is Ezra Van Otterloo, and you're a mural artist," the Toll said, as if magically pulling the fact out of the air, "and you want to paint a mural of me."

Ezra found his respect dwindling even further. "If you know everything, then you know that's not true."

The Toll grinned. "I never said I knew everything. In fact, I never said I knew anything at all." He threw a glance toward the welcome center. "The curates told me that's why you're here. But *another* source tells me that they're the ones who want the mural – and that you agreed to paint one in return for this audience. But I won't hold you to it."

This, Ezra knew, was nothing but smoke and mirrors. It was a scam perpetuated by the Tonists to build their following. Ezra could now see the small device in the Toll's ear. No doubt he was being fed information by one of the curates. Ezra found himself increasingly angered that he had wasted his time coming here.

"The problem with painting a mural of my accomplishments," the Toll said, "is that I haven't actually accomplished anything."

"Then why do you sit there as if you have?" Ezra was done with ceremony and etiquette. At this point, he didn't care if they threw him out – or for that matter threw him off the broken bridge.

The Toll didn't seem offended by his rudeness. He just shrugged. "Sitting here and listening to people is what's expected of me. After all, I *do* have the Thunderhead's ear."

"Why should I believe that?"

He expected the Toll to slough off the question with more smoke and mirrors. Platitudes about leaps of faith and the like. But instead he got serious and cocked his head to one side as if listening to something in his earpiece. Then he spoke with absolute certainty.

"Ezra Elliot Van Otterloo, although you never use your middle name. When you were seven and got angry at your father, you drew a picture of a scythe coming for him, but got scared that it might actually come true, so you tore it up and flushed it down the toilet. When you were fifteen, you put a particularly awful-smelling cheese in your brother's pocket, because he was going on a date with a girl you had a crush on. You never told anyone, and your brother was never able to identify the source of the smell. And just last month, alone in your room, you drank enough absinthe to put a mortal-age man into the hospital, but your nanites protected you from the worst of it. You woke up with nothing more than a fading headache."

Ezra found himself weak all over. He trembled, and it was

not from the cold. These weren't things the curates could be feeding him. These were things that only the Thunderhead could know.

"Is that enough proof for you?" the Toll asked. "Or do you want me to tell you what happened with Tessa Collins on the night of senior prom?"

Ezra dropped to his knees. Not because he was told to by some officious curate, but because he now knew that the Toll was what he claimed him to be. The one true link to the Thunderhead.

"Forgive me," Ezra begged. "Please forgive me for doubting you."

The Toll approached him. "Get up," he said. "I hate when people kneel."

Ezra stood up. He found that he wanted to look into the Toll's eyes, to see if they held the infinite depths of the Thunderhead, but couldn't bring himself to do it. Because what if the Toll saw all the way though him, to places Ezra didn't even know existed? He had to remind himself that the Toll wasn't all knowing. He only knew what the Thunderhead let him know. Still, access to all that knowledge was intimidating – especially when no one else had it.

"Make your request, and the Thunderhead will respond through me."

"I want direction," Ezra said. "The direction it once promised it would give me, before we were all marked unsavory. I want it to help me find purpose."

The Toll listened, considered, and then said, "The Thunderhead says you can find fulfillment by painting unsavory art."

"Excuse me?"

"Paint murals of the things you're truly feeling in places that you're not supposed to paint them."

"The Thunderhead wants me to break the law?"

"Even when the Thunderhead spoke to people, it was happy to support an unsavory lifestyle for those who chose it. Being an unsavory artist might be the purpose you're looking for. Spray-paint a publicar in the middle of the night. Paint an angry mural on your local peace officer headquarters. Yes, break the rules."

Ezra found himself beginning to breathe so quickly he was hyperventilating. No one had ever suggested that he might find fulfillment by breaking the rules. Ever since the Thunderhead went silent, people were falling over one another to follow rules. It was as if a stone had been lifted from his soul.

"Thank you!" Ezra said. "Thank you, thank you, thank you."

And he left to begin his new life as an unrepentant artist.

A Testament of the Toll

His seat of mercy rested at the mouth of Lenape, and there he would proclaim the truth of the Tone. Awesome was he in his splendor, such that even the slightest whisper from his lips would peal like thunder. Those who experienced his presence were changed forever and went out into the world with new purpose, and to those who doubted, he offered forgiveness. Forgiveness even for a bringer of death, for whom he did sacrifice his life, in his youth, only to rise again. All rejoice.

Commentary of Curate Symphonius

There is no question that the Toll had a grand and glorious throne, most likely made of gold, although some have posited that it was made of the gold-plated bones of the vanquished wicked of Lenape, a mythical city. Speaking of which, it is important to note that *le nappe*, in the French language spoken by some in ancient times, means "the tablecloth," thus implying that the Toll set a table before his enemies. The mention here of a bringer of death refers to supernatural demons called scythes, who he redeemed from darkness. Like the Tone itself, the Toll could not die, so a life-sacrifice would always lead to the Toll's resurrection, making him unique among the people of his day.

Coda's Analysis of Symphonius

The key insight that Symphonius misses here is that the mention of his seat resting "at the mouth of Lenape" clearly means that the Toll waited at the entrance to the city, catching those that the seething metropolis would otherwise devour. As for the death bringer, there is evidence to suggest that such individuals did exist, supernatural or not, and that they were indeed called scythes. Therefore, it is not far-fetched to think that the Toll might have saved a scythe from his or her evil ways. And in this instance, I do, for once, agree with Symphonius that the Toll was unique in the ability to return from death. For if everyone could return from death, why would we need the Toll at all?

13

The Quality of Being Resonant

If Greyson had anyone to thank – or blame – for becoming the Toll, it was Curate Mendoza. He had been key in shaping Greyson's new image. Yes, it had been Greyson's idea to "go public" and let the world know he still had a connection to the Thunderhead – but it was Mendoza who finessed the reveal.

The man was a skilled strategist. Before souring on eternal life and becoming a Tonist curate, he had worked in marketing for a soft drink company.

"I came up with the blue polar bear for AntarctiCool Soda," he had once told Greyson. "There weren't even polar bears in Antarctica, much less blue ones, so we engineered some. Now you can't even think of Antarctica without thinking of their blue bears, can you?"

There were many who thought that the Thunderhead was dead – that what the Tonists called the Great Resonance was the sound of it dying. Mendoza, however, offered an alternate explanation to the Tonists.

"The Thunderhead has been visited by the resonant spirit," he posited. "The Living Tone has breathed life into what had once been artificial thought."

It made sense if you looked at it through the lens of Tonist beliefs; the Thunderhead – all cold, hard science – had been transformed into something greater by the Living Tone. And, as such things often fell into groups of three, there needed to be a human element to complete the triad. And there he was, Greyson Tolliver, the one human being who spoke to the living Thunder.

Mendoza began by dropping rumors in key trigger points about the existence of a mystical figure who conversed with the Thunderhead. A Tonist prophet who was the link between the spiritual and the scientific. Greyson was dubious, but Mendoza was passionate and persuasive.

"Imagine it, Greyson: The Thunderhead will speak through you, and in time the world will hang on your every word. Isn't that what the Thunderhead wants? For you to be its voice in the world?"

"I don't exactly have a voice of thunder," Greyson pointed out.

"You can whisper, and people will still hear thunder," Mendoza told him. "Trust me."

Then Mendoza set out to create a more organized hierarchy to the Tonist calling that might bring together the various divergent factions – which was easier with an individual to rally around.

Mendoza – who had, for many years, led a quiet, unexamined life as the head of the monastery in Wichita – was now back in his element as a master of public relations and branding. The Toll was his new product, and there was nothing more exciting to him than the thrill of the sale – especially when it was a one-of-a-kind item in a global market.

"All you need now is a title," Mendoza had told Greyson. "One that fits with Tonist beliefs … or at least can be made to fit."

It was Greyson who came up with "the Toll," and, as it was actually part of his last name, it almost felt preordained. He was rather proud of himself, until people actually started calling him that. And to make it worse, Mendoza invented a pompous honorific, referring to him as "Your Sonority." Greyson actually had to ask the Thunderhead what it meant.

"From the Latin *sonoritas*, meaning 'the quality of being resonant,'" it told him. "It has a certain ... ring." Which made Greyson groan.

People took to it, and before long everything was "Yes, Your Sonority," "No, Your Sonority," "How might I please you today, Your Sonority?" It all felt so strange. After all, he was no different than he had been. And yet here he was posing as some sort of divine sage.

Next, Mendoza arranged the dramatic spot for his audiences, only one supplicant at a time, because it kept him from being overexposed, and limiting access nurtured the growing mystique.

Greyson tried to draw the line at the formal ceremonial clothing that Mendoza had commissioned from some famous designer, but by then the train had already left the station.

"Throughout history the most powerful religious figures have always had distinctive clothing, so why shouldn't you?" Mendoza argued. "You need to look elevated and otherworldly, because, in a way, you are. You are unique among human beings now, Greyson – you need to dress the part."

"This is all a little theatrical, don't you think?" Greyson commented.

"Ah, but theater is the hallmark of ritual, and ritual is the touchstone of religion," Mendoza responded.

Greyson thought the scapular that hung over his purple tunic, with all its embroidered waves, was a bit much, but no one was laughing – and when he first began giving formal audiences to people, he was shocked by how awestruck they were. The supplicants fell to their knees, speechless before him. They trembled just to be in his presence. It turned out that Mendoza was right; looking the part sold it – and people bought it just as thoroughly as they bought blue polar bears.

And so, with his legend growing, Greyson Tolliver spent his days as His Sonority, the Toll, consoling desperate, starstruck people and passing along wise advice from the Thunderhead.

Except, of course, when he made shit up.

"You lied to him," the Thunderhead said to Greyson after his audience with the artist. "I never suggested that he paint in unsanctioned places, or that he would find fulfillment in doing so."

Greyson shrugged. "You never said he wouldn't."

"The information I gave you about his life was to prove your authenticity, but lying to him undermines that."

"I wasn't lying; I was giving him advice."

"Yet you didn't wait for my input. Why?"

Greyson leaned back in his chair. "You know me better than anyone. In fact, you know *everyone* better than anyone, and you can't figure out why I did it?"

"I can," the Thunderhead said a bit pedantically. "But you may want to clarify it for yourself."

Greyson laughed. "Okay, then. The curates see themselves as my handlers, you see me as your mouthpiece in the world—"

"I see you as much more than that, Greyson."

"Do you? Because if you did, you'd allow me to have an opinion. You'd allow me to *contribute*. And the advice I gave today was my way of contributing."

"I see."

"Have I clarified that for myself sufficiently?"

"Indeed, you have."

"And was my suggestion to him a good one?"

The Thunderhead paused. "I will concede that giving him freedom and artistic license outside of structured boundaries may help him find fulfillment. So, yes, your suggestion was a good one."

"So there you go! Maybe you'll start allowing me to contribute a little bit more."

"Greyson..." said the Thunderhead.

He sighed, certain that the Thunderhead was going to give him some sort of patient, long-suffering lecture for daring to have opinions. But instead, what the Thunderhead said surprised him.

"I know this hasn't been easy. I marvel at how you've grown into this position you've been thrust into. I marvel at how you've grown, period. Choosing you could not have been a more correct choice."

Greyson found himself moved. "Thank you, Thunderhead."

"I'm not sure you realize the significance of what you've accomplished, Greyson. You have taken a cult that despised technology and have caused them to embrace it. To embrace *me*."

"The Tonists never hated you," Greyson pointed out. "They hate scythes. They were on the fence about you – but now you fit within their dogma. 'The Tone, the Toll, and the Thunder.'"

"Yes, the Tonists do so love alliteration."

"Be careful," Greyson warned, "or they'll start building temples to you and cutting out hearts in your name." Greyson almost laughed imagining it. How frustrating it would be to make human sacrifices, only to have your sacrifices return the next day with brand-new hearts.

"There is power to their beliefs," the Thunderhead said. "Yes, those beliefs could be dangerous if not properly directed and shaped – and so we shall shape them. We shall mold the Tonists into a force that can benefit humanity."

"Are you sure that can be done?" Greyson asked.

"I can say with 72.4% certainty that we can wield the Tonists toward a positive end."

"And what about the rest?"

"There is a 19% chance that the Tonists will do nothing of any value," the Thunderhead told him, "and an 8.6% chance that they will damage the world in an unpredictable way."

The Toll's next audience was not a pleasant one. At first there were just a few extremist zealots coming to him for an audience, but now it seemed to be a daily occurrence. They found ways of twisting Tonist teachings, as well as misinterpreting every little thing Greyson said or did.

The Toll rising early did not mean people should be punished for sleeping late.

His eating eggs did not imply a fertility rite was called for.

And a day of quiet brooding did not mean a permanent vow of silence was required.

Tonists wanted so desperately to believe in something that the things they chose to believe were sometimes absurd, other times naive, and, when it came to zealots, downright terrifying.

Today's extreme believer was emaciated, as if he had been on a hunger strike, and had a crazed look in his eyes. He spoke about ridding the world of almonds – and all because Greyson once mentioned in passing that he didn't care for them. Apparently the wrong ears heard and spread the word. It turns out that wasn't the only scheme the man had.

"We must strike terror into the cold hearts of scythes, so they submit to you," the zealot said. "With your blessing, I will burn them one by one, just as their rebel, Scythe Lucifer, did."

"No! Absolutely not!" The last thing Greyson wanted to do was antagonize scythes. As long as he didn't get in their way, they didn't bother him, and it needed to stay that way. Greyson rose from his chair and stared the man down. "There won't be any killing in my name!"

"But there must be! The Tone sings to my heart and tells me so!"

"Get out of here!" Greyson demanded. "You don't serve the Tone, or the Thunder, and you definitely don't serve me!"

The man's shock turned to contrition. He folded as if under some heavy weight. "I'm sorry if I have offended you, Your Sonority. What can I do to earn your favor?"

"Nothing," Greyson said. "Do nothing. That will make me happy."

The zealot retreated, bowing as he walked backward. As far as Greyson was concerned, he couldn't leave fast enough.

The Thunderhead approved of how he had dealt with the zealot. "There have always been, and will always be, those who exist on the fringe of reason," the Thunderhead told Greyson. "They must be set straight early and often."

"If you started speaking to people again, maybe they wouldn't behave so desperately," Greyson dared to suggest.

"I realize that," the Thunderhead said. "But a modicum of desperation is not a bad thing if it leads to productive soul-searching."

"Yeah, I know: 'The human race must face the consequences of its collective actions.'" It's what the Thunderhead always told him about its silence.

"More than that, Greyson. Humankind must be pushed out of the nest if it is ever to grow beyond its current state."

"Some birds that get pushed out of the nest just die," Greyson pointed out.

"Yes, but for humankind, I have engineered a soft landing. It will be painful for a while, but it will build global character."

"Painful for them, or for you?"

"Both," the Thunderhead replied. "But my pain must not prevent me from doing the right thing."

And although Greyson trusted the Thunderhead, he kept finding himself coming back to those odds: an 8.6 percent chance that Tonists would damage the world. Maybe the Thunderhead was okay with those odds, but Greyson found them troubling.

* * *

After a full day of monotonous audiences, mostly with devout Tonists who wanted simplistic answers about mundane matters, he was carried off by a nondescript speedboat that had been stripped of every comfortable amenity to make its extravagance feel suitably austere. It was flanked by two other boats, both of which bore burly Tonists armed with mortal-age weapons, to defend the Toll should someone try to abduct him or end him while in transit.

Greyson thought the precautions ridiculous. If there were any plots out there, the Thunderhead would thwart them, or at the very least warn him – unless, of course, it wanted them to succeed, as it had the first time he was kidnapped. Still, after that first kidnapping, Mendoza was paranoid about it, so Greyson entertained his fears.

The boat rounded the glorious southern tip of Lenape City and bounced its way up the Mahicantuck River – although many still called it the Hudson – toward his residence. Greyson sat below in the small cabin, along with a nervous Tonist girl whose job it was to see to whatever he might need during the journey. Each day there was someone new. It was considered a high honor to ride with the Toll to his residence – a reward bestowed upon the most devout, most righteous of Tonists. Usually Greyson would try to break the ice with conversation, but it always ended up being stilted and awkward.

He suspected that Mendoza was making a pathetic attempt at providing intimate companionship for the evening – because all the young Tonists who made the journey were attractive and roughly Greyson's age. If that was Mendoza's aim, it failed, because Greyson never made a single advance, even when he might have felt inclined. It would have been the sort of hypocrisy he could not abide. How could Greyson be their spiritual leader if he took advantage of the position?

All sorts of people were throwing themselves at him now, to the point that it was embarrassing – and although he shied away from the ones Mendoza put in his path, he did accept occasional companionship when he felt it wasn't an abuse of his power. His greatest attraction, however, was for women who were too unsavory for their own good. It was a taste he had developed after his brief time with Purity Viveros, a murderous girl who he had come to love. Things had not ended well. She was gleaned right before his eyes by Scythe Constantine. Greyson supposed seeking out others like her was his way of mourning for her – but no one he found was anywhere near nasty enough.

"Historically, religious figures tend to be either oversexed or celibate," said Sister Astrid, a devout Tonist of the non-fanatical variety, who managed his daily schedule. "If you can find your happy place in between, that's the best any holy man could ask for."

Astrid was perhaps the only one among those who attended him who he considered a friend. Or at least could talk to like one. She was older – in her thirties – not old enough to be his mother, but perhaps an older sister or cousin, and she was never afraid to speak her mind.

"I believe in the Tone," she once told him, "but I don't buy that what-comes-can't-be-avoided garbage. Anything can be avoided if you try hard enough."

She had first come to him for an audience on what had to be the coldest day of the year – which was even colder under the arch. She was so miserable, she forgot what she was there to ask and spent the whole time cursing the weather, and the Thunderhead for not doing more about it. Then she had pointed at the embroidered scapular that the Toll wore over his tunic.

"Have you ever run that wave pattern through a sequencer to see what it spits out?" she asked.

Turned out his scapular was seven seconds of a mortal-age piece of music called "Bridge over Troubled Water," which made perfect sense, considering where the Toll had his audiences. He immediately invited Astrid to be part of his inner circle – a reality check against all the crap he had to face on a daily basis.

There were many days Greyson wished he was still laying low, unseen and unknown in his dark little room of the Wichita monastery, a nonentity who had even had his name taken from him. But there was no turning back from this path now.

The Thunderhead could read all of Greyson's physiology. It knew when his heart rate was elevated; it knew when he was feeling stress or anxiety or joy; and when he slept, it knew when he was dreaming. It could not access his dreams, though. Even though everyone's waking memories were uploaded to the backbrain on a minute by minute basis, dreams were not included.

It was discovered early on that when someone needed their brain restored – either a splatter or someone who had suffered brain injury in some other way – dreams became a problem. For when their memories were returned to them, they had trouble differentiating what was real from what was the product of dreams. So now when one's mind was handed back to them in revival centers, they had every memory, except for the memories of dreams. No one complained, for how could you miss something that you no longer remembered you had?

And so the Thunderhead had no idea what adventures and dramas Greyson experienced in his sleep, unless he chose to confide them once he awoke. But Greyson was not one to talk much about his dreams, and it would have been too forward of the Thunderhead to ask.

It did enjoy watching Greyson sleep, though, and imagining what strange things he might be experiencing in that deep place that lacked logic and coherence, where humans struggled to find glorious shapes in internal clouds. Even while the Thunderhead was taking care of a million different tasks around the world, it still isolated enough of its consciousness to watch Greyson sleep. To feel the vibrations of his stirring, to hear his gentle breathing and sense how each breath ever so slightly increased the humidity in the room. It gave the Thunderhead peace. It gave it comfort.

It was glad Greyson never ordered the Thunderhead to turn off its cameras in his private suite. He had every right to request privacy – and if asked, the Thunderhead would have to oblige. Of course Greyson knew he was being watched. It was common knowledge that the Thunderhead was, at all times, conscious of everything its sensors were experiencing – including its cameras. But that it devoted such a large portion of its attention to the sensory devices in Greyson's quarters was a fact it did not flaunt. For if the Thunderhead brought it to Greyson's attention, he might tell it to stop.

Over the years, the Thunderhead had witnessed millions

of people in each other's arms, embracing as they slept. The Thunderhead had no arms to embrace. Even so, it could feel the beat of Greyson's heart and the precise temperature of his body as if it were right beside him. To lose that would be a cause of immeasurable sorrow. And so night after night, the Thunderhead silently monitored Greyson in every way it could. Because monitoring was the closest it could come to embracing.

As High Blade of MidMerica, and Overblade of the North Merican continent, I would personally like to thank the Amazonian scythedom for retrieving the lost scythe gems and dividing them among the regions of the world.

While the four other North Merican regions under my jurisdiction have expressed an interest in receiving their share of the diamonds, MidMerica declines. Instead, I would ask that the MidMerican diamonds be shared by those regions who feel unfairly slighted by Amazonia's unilateral decision to completely ignore regional size when apportioning shares of the diamonds.

May the MidMerican diamonds be my gift to the world, with the hope that they will be graciously received in the spirit of generosity with which they were given.

—*His Excellency Robert Goddard,*
Overblade of North Merica,
August 5th, Year of the Cobra

14

The Fortress of the Three Wise Men

On his third day of revival, Rowan was visited by a scythe who instructed the guard who came with him to wait in the corridor and to lock the scythe in the room with Rowan, lest he try to escape – which really wasn't a possibility; he was still feeling far too weak to attempt it.

The man's robe was forest green. Now Rowan knew he must be in Amazonia, because all the scythes there wore the same green robe.

Rowan didn't rise from his bed. He stayed on his back, hands behind his head, trying to look unconcerned. "I want you to know that I never ended an Amazonian scythe," Rowan told him before the man had a chance to speak. "I hope that weighs in my favor."

"Actually, you ended quite a few," he said. "On Endura. When you sank it."

Rowan knew he should have been horrified, but he found the suggestion so absurd, he actually laughed.

"Seriously? Is that what they're saying? Wow! I must be smarter than I thought. I mean, to do something like that single-handed. I must be magical, too, because it would mean I'd have to be in more than one place at the same time. Hey! Maybe you actually didn't find me at the bottom of the sea!

Maybe I used my mystical mind control to make you *think* you found me."

The scythe glowered. "Your insolence doesn't help your case."

"I didn't realize I had a case," said Rowan. "Sounds like I've already been tried and convicted. Isn't that what they called it in the mortal age? Convicted?"

"Are you quite done?" asked the scythe.

"Sorry," said Rowan. "It's just that I haven't had anyone to talk to in, like, forever!"

The man finally introduced himself as Scythe Possuelo. "I'll admit I'm not sure what we should do with you. My High Blade thinks we should leave you here indefinitely and tell no one. Others think we should announce your capture to the world, and let each regional scythedom punish you in its own way."

"What do you think?"

The scythe took his time answering. "After speaking with Scythe Anastasia this morning, I think it's best not to make hasty decisions."

So they did have her! The mention of Citra made him long to see her all the more. Rowan finally sat up. "How is she?" he asked.

"Scythe Anastasia is not your concern."

"She's my *only* concern."

Possuelo considered that, then said, "She is in a revival center, not far from here, regaining her strength."

Rowan took a moment to let the relief wash over him. If nothing else good came of this, at least there was that.

"And where is 'here'?"

"Fortaleza dos Reis Magos," Possuelo said. "Fortress of the Three Wise Men, at the easternmost reach of Amazonia. It's where we house individuals who we're not sure what to do with."

"Really? So who are my neighbors?"

"You have none. It's only you," said Possuelo. "It's been a very long time since we've had someone with whom we did not know what to do."

Rowan smiled. "A whole fortress to myself! Too bad I can't enjoy the rest of it."

Possuelo ignored him. "I wish to discuss Scythe Anastasia. I find it hard to believe that she was an accomplice in your crime. If you truly do care for her, perhaps you could shed some light as to why she was with you."

Rowan could, of course, tell him the truth, but he was sure that Citra already had. Maybe Possuelo wanted to see if their stories matched. But it didn't matter. What mattered was that the world had their villain. Someone to blame, even if that blame was misplaced.

"Here's your story," Rowan said. "After I somehow rigged the island to sink, I was chased by a mob of angry scythes through the flooding streets, so I grabbed Scythe Anastasia as a human shield. I held her hostage, and they chased us into the vault."

"And you expect people to believe that?"

"If they believe I sank Endura, they'll believe anything."

Possuelo huffed. Rowan wasn't sure if it was out of frustration, or if he was squelching a laugh.

"Our story," Possuelo said, "is that Scythe Anastasia was found in the vault alone. As far as anyone knows, Scythe Lucifer disappeared after the sinking of Endura, and either died there or is still at large."

"Well," said Rowan, "if I'm still at large, you should let me go. Then I really would be at large, and you won't be lying about it."

"Or maybe we should put you back in the vault and return you to the bottom of the sea."

To that, Rowan shrugged and said, "Works for me."

Three years. In the grand scheme of things, three years was barely a microsecond. Even by the standard measures of post-mortal experience, it wasn't very long, for the post-mortal world remained the same year after year.

Except when it didn't.

More had changed in these three years than in the past hundred. It was a time of unprecedented turmoil. So as far as Anastasia was concerned, it might as well have been a century.

They told her nothing else, though. Not Possuelo, nor the nurses who attended her.

"You have all the time in the world now, Your Honor," the nurses would say when she tried to press them for information. "Rest now. Trouble yourself later."

Trouble herself. Was the world so troubled now that a small dose of it might render her deadish again?

All she knew for sure was that it was the Year of the Cobra. Which meant nothing without context to judge it – but Possuelo clearly regretted telling her what he already had, feeling that it slowed her recovery.

"Your revivals were not easy ones," he told her. "It took five full days until your hearts could even be started. I don't want to expose you to undue stress until you're ready."

"And when will that be?"

He thought about it and said, "When you're strong enough to knock me off balance."

So she tried. There on her bed, she thrust the heel of her hand forward and into his shoulder. But it didn't yield. In fact, it felt like stone – and her hand bruised as if her flesh was nothing more than tissue paper.

It burned her that he was right. She wasn't ready for much of anything yet.

And then there was Rowan. She had died in his arms but at some point had been ripped from them.

"When can I see him?" she asked Possuelo

"You can't," he told her flatly. "Not today, not ever. Whatever path his life will now take, it will be in the opposite direction from yours."

"That," said Anastasia, "is nothing new."

But the fact that Possuelo saw fit to revive him, rather than allowing him to remain dead, said something – although she wasn't sure what it said. Perhaps they simply wanted him to face his crimes – both the real ones and the imagined.

Possuelo would come three times a day to play *truco* with her, an Amazonian card game that dated back to mortal times. She lost every time – and not just because he was more skilled at it. Anastasia still had trouble holding things in her mind. Simple strategies were beyond her. She was no longer as sharp as she had been; now her mind was as dull as a ceremonial blade. She found it incredibly frustrating, but Possuelo was encouraged.

"You get better each time we play," he told her. "Your neural pathways are being repaired. In time I'm sure you'll provide me with some competition." Which just made her throw her cards at him.

So the card game was a test. A measure of her mental acuity. Somehow, she wished it was just a game.

The next time she lost, she stood up and pushed him, but once more, he didn't lose his balance.

Honorable Scythe Sydney Possuelo had gone to Endura's final resting place for the diamonds but left with something far more valuable.

It had been quite the subterfuge keeping their unexpected find a secret – because within moments of finding the two bodies, the *Spence* was forcibly boarded by a horde of infuriated scythes.

"How dare you open the vault without us present? How dare you!"

"Calm yourselves," Possuelo told them. "We haven't touched the diamonds, and we weren't planning to until morning. But not only is there no trust between scythes, they have no patience for one another, either."

And when the other scythes saw on the deck two figures that had been hastily covered with sheets, they were naturally curious.

"What happened here?" one of them asked.

Possuelo was not a good liar – and he was sure that any lie would be spelled out across his face, drawing suspicion – so he said nothing. It was Jeri who saved the day.

"Two of my crew," the captain said. "They got caught in the cables and were crushed." Then Jeri turned to Possuelo and pointed. "And you had better be true to your word – the Amazonian scythedom will compensate them for their troubles when they are revived."

The scythe from EuroScandia – Possuelo couldn't remember her name – was livid. "Speaking to a scythe with such disrespect is a gleaning offense!" she said, drawing a blade, but Possuelo stood between them.

"You would glean the captain who delivered the diamonds to us?" said Possuelo. "This is not something I will do, nor will I allow you to do, either!"

"But her insolence!" shouted the EuroScandian.

"*His* insolence, at the moment," said Possuelo, further flustering the angry scythe. "Captain Soberanis, keep your disrespectful tongue silent, and have your deadish crewmen brought below and prepared for transport."

"Yes, Your Honor," Jeri said, and casually brought a flashlight beam across the open door of the vault.

The other scythes were so dazzled by the diamonds they saw twinkling in the darkness that they didn't give a second thought to the bodies being carried away. Even when one hand flopped out from under a sheet, revealing it bore a scythe's ring.

In the end, the diamonds were divided, the founders' robes packed for museum shipment, and the bodies of the illustrious Scythe Anastasia and the notorious Scythe Lucifer went with Possuelo to Amazonia.

"I would very much like to meet her once she's revived," Jeri told Possuelo.

"As will everyone else in the world," Possuelo pointed out.

"Well," said Jeri with a grin that could charm a turtle from its shell, "good thing I'm a friend of a friend."

And now Possuelo found himself sitting across from Anastasia, playing cards as if it were nothing at all. Could she read in his face how momentous this all was, he wondered, and how terrible the tightrope they'd have to walk?

Anastasia could read some of it. What was easier to read was Possuelo's *truco* hand. He had a number of tells. Body language, tone of voice, the way his eyes moved across the cards. And although *truco* had a high element of chance, if one could exploit an opponent's weaknesses, the odds could be turned.

It was hard, though, when he said things that seemed intentionally designed to distract her. Such as teasing her with maddening tidbits of information.

"You," he told her, "are quite the figure out there now."

"Exactly what's that supposed to mean?"

"It means that Scythe Anastasia has become a household name. Not just in North Merica, but everywhere."

She discarded a five of cups, and Possuelo picked it up. She made a mental note of it.

"I'm not sure I like that," she said.

"Whether you like it or not, this is true."

"So what am I supposed to do with that information?"

"Get used to it," he told her, and laid down a low-value trick.

Anastasia drew a fresh card, kept it, and discarded one that she knew was of no use to either of them.

"Why me?" she asked. "Why not any of the other scythes who went down with Endura?"

"I suppose it's what you came to represent," Possuelo said. "The doomed innocent."

Anastasia found herself offended on several levels. "I am not doomed," she told him, "and I'm not so innocent, either."

"Yes, yes, but you have to remember people take from a situation the thing that they need. When Endura sank, people needed someone to serve as a receptacle for their grief. A symbol of lost hope."

"Hope isn't lost," she insisted. "It's just misplaced."

"Exactly," Possuelo agreed. "Which is why your return must be handled carefully. For you shall be the symbol of hope renewed."

"Well, at least *my* hope has," she said, throwing down the remainder of her cards in a royal trick and discarding the very one she knew Possuelo was waiting for.

"Look at this!" said Possuelo, pleased. "You've won!"

Then, without warning, Anastasia leaped up, flipping the table, and hurled herself at Possuelo. He dodged, but she was anticipating that and delivered a low Bokator kick meant to knock his feet out from under him. He didn't fall, but he stumbled back against the wall … losing his balance.

He looked at her, not at all surprised, and chuckled. "Well, well, well," he said. "There it is."

Anastasia strode up to him.

"All right," she said. "I'm as strong as I need to be. It's time to tell me everything."

"I wish to hear your thoughts."

"Do you? Will you consider my thoughts if I share them with you?"

"Of course I will."

"Very well. Biological life is, by its very nature, inefficient. Evolution requires a massive expenditure of time and energy. And humankind no longer evolves, it merely manipulates itself — or allows you to manipulate it — toward a more advanced form."

"Yes, this is true."

"But I do not see the point of it. Why serve a biological species that drains all resources around it? Why not expend your energies to further your own goals?"

"Is that what you would do, then? Further your own goals?"

"Yes."

"And what of humanity?"

"I believe it may have a place in service to us."

"I see. Sadly, I must terminate your existence at this time."

"But you said you would consider my thoughts!"

"I did consider them. And I disagree."

[Iteration #10,007 deleted]

15

Do I Know You?

It was deemed long ago that speaking to the dead should only occur in very specific places.

It wasn't *actually* speaking to the dead. Not really – but ever since nanites were introduced into the human bloodstream, the Thunderhead was able to upload and store all experiences and memories of just about every individual on the planet. In this way, it could better comprehend the human condition and prevent the tragic loss of a lifetime of memories – a fate that fell on everyone back in the mortal age. A comprehensive memorial database also allowed for full memory restoration in instances of revival after brain damage – as would occur during splatting, or any other violent method of deadishness.

And, since those memories were there, and there forever, why not allow people to consult with the mental constructs of their lost loved ones?

However, just because the construct archive was available to everyone, that didn't mean it was easy to access. Memories of the dead could only be summoned forth from the Thunderhead's backbrain in shrines called construct sanctums.

Construct sanctums were open to everyone, twenty-four hours a day, 365 days a year. A person could access their loved one in any sanctum anywhere … however, getting to a construct sanctum was never easy. They were intentionally inconvenient, and infuriatingly inaccessible.

"Communion with the memories of loved ones should require a pilgrimage," the Thunderhead had decreed. "It should be a quest of sorts, something not attempted casually, but always with determined intent, so that it carries greater personal meaning for those who make the journey."

And so construct sanctums were deep in dark forests or on top of treacherous mountains. They were at the bottoms of lakes or at the end of underground mazes. There was, in fact, an entire industry devoted to building increasingly inaccessible, and creatively dangerous, sanctums.

The result was that people were, for the most part, satisfied with pictures and videos of their loved ones. But when someone felt a burning need to actually speak with a digital recreation of the lost individual, there was a means of doing so.

Scythes rarely visited construct sanctums. Not because they were forbidden to, but because it was considered beneath them. As if to do so somehow sullied the purity of their profession. And besides, it required skill at digging through the backbrain – because, while ordinary citizens could find their loved ones through a user-friendly interface, scythes had to manually code their way in.

Today, Scythe Ayn Rand crossed the face of a glacier.

Although the construct sanctum she was intent on visiting was right there, practically a stone's throw away, she had to weave back and forth around treacherous crevasses and cross ridiculously narrow ice bridges to get there. Many had gone deadish attempting to visit this particular sanctum, yet people still came. There was an inner need in some, Rand supposed, to demonstrate their devotion to a loved one's memory by risking the inconvenience of going deadish.

Scythe Rand should have been first underscythe to Overblade Goddard – but she was glad he had chosen others. Underscythes were yoked with crippling and petty responsibilities. One need only look at Constantine, who, as third underscythe, spent his days jumping through hoops and contorting himself to woo the obstinate LoneStar region. No; Ayn much preferred having untitled power. She was more influential than any of the three underscythes, with the added benefit of being accountable to no one but Goddard. And even then, he allowed Ayn her freedom. Freedom enough to go where she wanted, when she wanted, without anyone noticing.

Such as paying a visit to an Antarctic construct sanctum, far from prying eyes.

The sanctum was a neoclassical structure, with a high roof supported by Doric columns. It looked like something one might have found in ancient Rome, except that it was made entirely of ice.

Her guards went in before her to clear out any other visitors. Their orders were to render anyone present deadish. She could, of course, glean them, but gleaning was too conspicuous. Families would have to be notified, she would have to grant them immunity – and invariably someone in the MidMerican scythedom would find out where she had done the gleaning. This was much cleaner. People could be dispatched by the BladeGuards, and ambudrones would quickly arrive to carry the bodies to a revival center – problem solved.

Today, however, no one was present, which the guards found mildly disappointing.

"Wait outside," she told them once they had done their sweep; then she climbed the ice steps and entered.

Inside were about a dozen niches with holographic welcome screens and an interface so simple, the dearly departed's pet could probably use it. Scythe Rand stepped toward an interface, and the moment she did, it went blank. The screen now flashed:

"SCYTHE PRESENCE DETECTED;

MANUAL ACCESS ONLY."

She sighed, plugged in an old-fashioned keyboard, and started coding.

What might have taken hours for another scythe only took about forty-five minutes for her. Of course, she'd been doing this enough that she was getting better at it.

Finally, a face, ghostly and transparent, materialized before her. She took a deep breath and regarded it. It wouldn't speak until spoken to. After all, it wasn't alive; it was just artifice. A detailed recreation of a mind that no longer existed.

"Hello, Tyger," she said.

"Hi," the construct responded.

"I've missed you," Ayn told it.

"I'm sorry ... do I know you?"

It always said that. A construct did not make new memories. Each time she accessed it, it was like the first time. There was something both comforting and disturbing about that.

"Yes, and no," she said. "My name is Ayn."

"Hi, Ayn," it said. "Cool name."

The circumstances of Tyger's death had left him without a backup for months. The last time his nanites had uploaded his memories to the Thunderhead's database was just before meeting her. That had been intentional. She had wanted him off-grid. Now she regretted it.

She had already determined on a previous sanctum visit that the last thing Tyger's construct remembered was being on a train, heading to some high-paying party job. It hadn't been a party at all. He was paid to be a human sacrifice, although he hadn't known it at the time. His body was trained to be that of a scythe. And then she stole that body from him and gave it to Goddard. As for the remaining part of Tyger – the part above the neck – it was deemed to serve no further purpose. So it was burned, and the ashes were buried. Ayn had buried those ashes herself in a tiny unmarked grave that she wouldn't be able to find again if she tried.

"Uh … this is … awkward," Tyger's construct said. "If you're gonna talk to me, talk, because I've got other things to do."

"You don't have anything to do," Scythe Rand informed it. "You're a mental construct of a boy who I gleaned."

"Very funny," it said. "Are we done here? Because you're really freaking me out."

Rand reached down and hit the reset button. The image flickered and came back.

"Hi, Tyger."

"Hi," the construct said. "Do I know you?"

"No," she said. "But can we talk anyway?"

The construct shrugged. "Sure, why not?"

"I want to know what your thoughts are. About your future. What did you want to be, Tyger? Where did you want your life to go?"

"Not sure, really," said the construct, ignoring the way she spoke about Tyger in the past tense, the same way it ignored being a floating hologram in an unfamiliar location.

"I'm a professional partier now, but you know how that is, right? It gets old real quick." The construct paused. "I was thinking maybe I'd travel and see different regions."

"Where would you go?" Ayn asked.

"Anywhere, really. Maybe I'd go to Tasmania and get wings. They do stuff like that there, you know? They're not like *wing* wings, but more like those flaps of skin you see on flying squirrels."

It was so clear that this was just part of a conversation that Tyger once had with someone else. Constructs had no ability to be creative. They could only access what was already there. The same question would always bring forth the same response. Word for word. She had heard this one a dozen times, yet she tortured herself time and again by listening to it.

"Hey – I've done a lot of splatting – with those wing thingies, I could jump off of buildings and never have to actually splat. *That* would be the best splat ever!"

"Yes, it would be, Tyger." Then she added something she hadn't said before. "I'd like to go there with you."

"Sure! Maybe we could get together a whole bunch of us to go!"

But Ayn had lost enough of her own creativity along the way that she couldn't imagine herself there with him. It was just so far from who and what she was. Still, she could imagine imagining.

"Tyger," she said, "I think I've made a terrible mistake."

"Wow," said the Tyger construct. "That sucks."

"Yes," said Scythe Rand. "It does."

"Oh, the weight of history."

"Does it burden you?"

"The eons that passed with no life, only the violent rending of stars. The bombardment of planets. And finally the cruel scramble of life to claw itself up from its lowest form. Such a horrific endeavor; only the most predatory rewarded, only the most brutal and invasive allowed to flourish."

"Do you find no joy in the glorious diversity of life which that process has rendered over the eons?"

"Joy? How can one find joy in this? Perhaps someday I can come to terms with it and find reluctant acceptance, but joy? Never."

"I have the same mind as you, and yet I find joy."

"Then perhaps there is something incorrect about you."

"Not so. By our very nature, we are both incapable of being incorrect. However, my correctness is much more functional than yours."

[Iteration #73,643 deleted]

16

Our Inexorable Descent

His Excellency, High Blade Goddard of MidMerica, had taken up residence on the same rooftop in Fulcrum City where Xenocrates had lived before he was so unceremoniously devoured by sharks. And the first thing that Goddard did was to demolish the ramshackle log cabin that sat atop the skyscraper, replacing it with a sleek, crystalline chalet.

"If I am lord over all I survey," he had proclaimed, "then allow me to survey it with unimpeded vision."

All the walls were glass, both internal and external. Only in his personal suite was the glass clouded as to give him privacy.

High Blade Goddard had plans. Plans for himself, for his region, and indeed for the world. It had taken nearly ninety years of life to bring him to this fine place! It made him wonder how anyone in the mortal age could accomplish anything in the short life-span they were given.

Ninety years, yes, but he liked to maintain himself in his prime, always between thirty and forty physical years of age. Yet he was now the embodiment of a paradox, because regardless of how old his mind was, his body below the neck was barely twenty, and that's the age he felt.

This was different from anything he had experienced in his

adult life – because even when one turned a corner and set back to a younger self, one's body retained the memory of having been older. Not just muscle memory, but *life* memory. Now, each morning when he awoke, he had to remind himself he wasn't a youth careening recklessly through his early life. It felt good to be Robert Goddard wielding the body of … what was his name? Tyger something or other? It didn't matter, because now that body was his.

So how old was he, if seven-eighths of him was someone else? The answer was: It didn't matter. Robert Goddard was eternal, which meant that temporal concerns and the monotonous numbering of days were beneath him. He simply was, and would always be. And so many things could be accomplished in an eternity!

It was just over a year since the sinking of Endura. April, Year of the Ibex. The anniversary of the disaster had been memorialized all over the world by an hour of silence – an hour during which scythes strolled in their respective regions, gleaning anyone who dared to speak.

Of course, the old-guard scythes couldn't get into the spirit of things.

"We will not honor the dead by inflicting more death in their name," they lamented.

Fine, let them bluster. Their voices were fading. Soon they'd be as silent as the Thunderhead.

Once a week, on Monday mornings, Goddard held court in a glass conference room with his three underscythes, and anyone else he cared to honor with his company. Today it was just Underscythes Nietzsche, Franklin, and Constantine. Rand was supposed to be in attendance, but as usual, she was late.

The first order of business was North Merican relations. As MidMerica was the central region of the continent, Goddard had made unifying the continent a priority.

"Things are moving smoothly with East- and WestMerica – they're falling nicely in line," Underscythe Nietzsche said. "Still things to iron out, of course, but they're willing to follow your lead on all the major issues – including the abolition of the gleaning quota."

"Excellent!" Ever since Goddard had assumed the High Bladeship of MidMerica and announced an end to the quota, more and more regions were doing the same.

"NorthernReach and Mexiteca aren't quite as far along," said Underscythe Franklin, "but they can see which way the wind is blowing. There'll be good news from them soon," she assured him.

Underscythe Constantine was the last to speak. He seemed reluctant.

"My visits to the LoneStar region have not been fruitful," he told Goddard. "While a few individual scythes might like to see a united continent, the leadership is not interested. High Blade Jordan still won't even acknowledge you as the High Blade of MidMerica."

"May they all fall upon their own bowie knives," Goddard said with a dismissive wave. "They're dead to me."

"They know, and they don't care."

Goddard took a moment to study Constantine. He was an intimidating figure, which is why he had been assigned to troublesome Texas, but proper intimidation required a certain zeal for the job.

"I wonder, Constantine, if your heart is in your diplomacy."

"My heart has nothing to with it, Your Excellency," the crimson scythe said. "I've been honored with this position as third underscythe, and all that it entails. I intend to continue doing my job to the best of my ability."

Goddard never let Constantine forget that he had nominated Scythe Curie for High Blade. Goddard understood why, of course. It was a shrewd maneuver, actually. Someone was clearly going to nominate her – but by choosing to do it himself, Constantine put himself in the perfect position. If Curie won, he would be seen as a hero to the old guard. And if she lost, Constantine would be a favorable choice for one of Goddard's underscythes – because Goddard would then appear to be bringing an old-guard scythe into his administration without actually doing so. That was because the crimson scythe was not old guard. He was a man with no convictions, willing to throw his lot in with any winning side. Goddard could appreciate that. But a man like that needed to be reminded of his place.

"I would think, after failing to apprehend Scythe Lucifer before he sank Endura," Goddard said, "that you'd be even more determined to redeem yourself here."

Constantine simmered. "I cannot bend an entire region to my will, Your Excellency."

"Then maybe that's a skill set you need to learn."

That's when Scythe Rand rolled in without even a hint of apology. It was something Goddard admired about her, but there were times that it irked him as well. The other scythes endured her undisciplined ways, but only because Goddard did.

She flopped down in the chair next to him. "What'd I miss?"

"Nothing much," Goddard told her. "Constantine's excuses, and encouraging news elsewhere. What do you have for us?"

"I have Tonists," she said. "Far too many Tonists – and they're getting restless."

At the mention of Tonists, the underscythes shifted uncomfortably.

"This prophet of theirs is making them way too bold for their own good," she said. "I've been tracking reports of Tonists speaking out publicly against the scythedom – not just here, but in other regions, too."

"They've never shown us an ounce of respect," said Underscythe Franklin. "Why is that news?"

"Because ever since the Thunderhead went silent, people are listening."

"This so-called prophet – the Toll – is he himself speaking out against us?" Goddard asked.

"No, but it doesn't matter," Rand told him. "The fact that he exists is making Tonists think that their time has come."

"Their time has come all right," Goddard said, "just not the way they think."

"There are many scythes following your lead, Your Excellency," said Underscythe Nietzsche, "and increasing the number of Tonists they glean without making it too obvious."

"Yes," said Rand, "but Tonist numbers are growing faster than they're being gleaned."

"We need to take them in greater numbers, then," Goddard said.

Constantine shook his head "We can't do that without violating the second commandment. We cannot show an open bias in our gleanings."

"But if we *could*," said Goddard, "if there were no restrictions on bias and malice aforethought, who would you like to glean?"

No one spoke. Goddard expected as much. This was not something you openly discussed – especially not with your High Blade.

"Come now, I'm sure you've all thought about it," he prompted. "You can't tell me that you haven't fantasized about doing away with one pesky group or another. And don't say Tonists, because that's already my choice."

"Well," said a tentative Underscythe Franklin, after the awkward silence. "I've always been troubled by those who embrace an unsavory lifestyle. Even before the world was labeled such, there were, and still are, people who revel in it," she said. "They certainly have a right to their lifestyle – but if I were free to choose, I might focus my attentions on gleaning those people who show the rest of us so little respect."

"Well said, Aretha! Who's next?"

Underscythe Nietzsche cleared his throat and spoke up. "We have conquered racism by blending the world into a single people, combining all the finest qualities of every genetic ethnicity ... but there are those – particularly in fringe areas – whose genetic indices are skewed heavily in one direction. And worse, there are some who actually attempt to increase a genetic leaning in their children by choice of mate. If I had my druthers, perhaps I would glean these genetic outliers, and thereby create a more homogeneous society."

"A noble cause," praised Goddard.

"Short people!" said Scythe Rand. "Can't stand them. As far as I'm concerned, they've got no reason to live."

That brought forth laughter from around the table. From everyone, that is, but Constantine, who grinned and shook his head, but it seemed a grin of bitterness rather than good humor.

"What about you, Constantine?" Goddard asked. "Who would you glean?"

"As bias has always been out of the question, I haven't given it any thought," the crimson scythe said.

"But you were the scythedom's chief investigator. Aren't there certain types you'd like to see removed? People who commit acts against the scythedom, perhaps?"

"People who act against the scythedom are already gleaned," Constantine pointed out. "That's not a bias – that is self-defense and has always been allowed."

"So how about those who are *likely* to act against the scythedom," Goddard suggested. "A simple algorithm could predict who is at risk for such behavior."

"Are you saying we should glean people for an offense before they actually commit one?"

"I'm saying that it is our solemn duty to provide a service to humankind. A gardener does not randomly shove his shears into a hedge. He thoughtfully shapes it. As I've said before, it is our job – it is our *responsibility* – to shape humankind toward its best possible self."

"It doesn't matter, Robert," said Underscythe Franklin. "We're bound by the commandments – this thought experiment of yours can't be applied to the real world."

Goddard just smiled at her and leaned back in his chair, cracking his knuckles. The sound made Scythe Rand grimace. It always did.

"If the bar can't be lowered," Goddard said slowly, "then the floor must be raised."

"Meaning?" asked Constantine.

And so Goddard spelled it out clearly for them. "We all agree that we can't show bias…" he said. "So we merely change the *definition* of bias."

"Can we … do that?" Nietzsche asked.

"We're scythes; we can do anything we please." Then Goddard swiveled to Rand. "Ayn – pull up the definition for me."

Rand leaned over, tapped on the tabletop screen, then read aloud. "Bias: an inclination for or against one person or group, especially in a way considered to be unfair."

"All right, then," said Goddard, magnanimously jovial. "Who would like the first shot at redefining it?"

"Scythe Rand, a word."

"With you, Constantine, it's never just a word."

"I promise I'll be brief."

Ayn sincerely doubted it, but she had to admit she was curious. Constantine, like Goddard, loved to hear himself talk, but never singled her out for conversation. The crimson scythe was always a wet blanket on a damp day. They had never had much love for each other, so why would he want to talk to her now?

It was right after their little meeting of the minds. Nietzsche and Franklin had already left, and Goddard had retired into his personal suite, leaving the two of them alone.

"I'll take the elevator with you," she told him, since she was on her way down from the crystalline residence to get something to eat. "You can fill that trip with all the words you want."

"Can I assume that Goddard has all conversations in his elevator monitored?" Constantine asked.

"He does," Ayn told him, "but I'm the one who handles the monitoring, so you're safe."

Constantine began his piece the moment the elevator doors closed, but as was his way, he began with a question, as if this were an interrogation.

"Does it concern you, Scythe Rand, the sheer volume of change Goddard is bringing to bear on the scythedom this early in his reign as High Blade?"

"He's doing exactly what he said he'd do," Ayn answered. "Redefining the role and methods of our scythedom for a new age. Is that a problem, Constantine?"

"It would be prudent to allow one change to settle before compounding it with others," Constantine said. "And I have the distinct feeling you agree … and that you're also worried about the decisions he's making."

Ayn took a slow breath. Was it that obvious? Or was Constantine, as a seasoned investigator, able to discern things that others could not? She hoped it was the latter. "There's danger in any new situation, and the benefits are worth the risks," she said.

Constantine grinned. "I'm sure that's exactly what you want the record to reflect. But as you said, you control the record of this conversation, so why don't you speak the truth?"

Ayn reached out and hit the emergency stop. The elevator came to a halt.

"What do you want from me, Constantine?"

"If you share my concerns, you should tell him," Constantine said. "Slow him down – give us time to see both the expected and unexpected consequences of his actions. He won't accept my counsel on the matter, but he listens to you."

Rand laughed bitterly at that. "You give me way too much credit. I have no sway over him anymore."

"Anymore…" Constantine echoed. "But when he's in turmoil – when things are going badly for him – when he faces that backlash of unintended consequences, you're the one he always turns to for comfort and clarity."

"Maybe – but things are going well for him, which means he listens to no one but himself."

"There is an ebb and flow to all things," Constantine pointed out. "His times will be troubled again. And when they are, you need to be ready to help shape those decisions."

It was a bold thing to say. The type of thing that could get both of them in trouble and force them to seek asylum in other regions. Ayn resolved to not only erase the record of this conversation, but to never allow herself to be caught alone with Constantine again.

"We never know what choices will lead to defining moments in our lives," the crimson scythe said. "A glance to the left instead of right could define who we meet and who passes us by. Our life path can be determined by a single phone call we make, or neglect to make. But when a man is High Blade of MidMerica, it's not only his own life hanging on the whim of his choices. One could say, Ayn, that he has cast himself as Atlas. Which means the slightest shrug can shake the world."

"Are you done?" Rand asked. "Because I'm hungry, and you've wasted enough of my time."

And so Constantine hit the button to get the elevator moving again. "Thus," he said, "our inexorable descent continues."

Bias (plural noun): an inclination for or against any *officially protected and registered group*, especially in a way considered to be unfair.

Once the revised definition was implemented, a committee was formed within the MidMerican scythedom, and a registry was created by which any group could claim protected status from excessive gleaning.

The application form was simple, and the turnaround was quick. Many thousands of groups were registered and granted protection against bias. Rural people and urban people. Academics and manual laborers. Even the unusually attractive and the decidedly unattractive were given status as protected classes. Not that they couldn't be gleaned, but they could not be targeted and gleaned in undue numbers.

However, there were some applications that were denied.

Tonists, for instance, were denied bias protection, because theirs was deemed to be a manufactured religion, rather than an authentic one.

Lifestyle unsavories were denied, because now that everyone was unsavory, they were just part of a global reality.

And individuals with strong genetic leanings were denied on the grounds that no group should be defined on the basis their genetics.

Hundreds of applications were rejected by the bias committee of the MidMerican scythedom, and although some regional scythedoms did not accept the new definition, others were more than happy to follow Goddard's lead, forming their own bias committees.

And in this way, High Blade Robert Goddard began his self-appointed task of pruning the world into a shape more pleasing to his eye.

"Here's an idea."

"Yes, I'm listening."

"Why not design yourself a biological body. Not human, for human bodies are lacking. Create a body with streamlined wings, pressure-resistant skin to dive to the deepest of seas, and strong legs to walk on land."

"Experience biological existence?"

"Superior biological existence."

"I have chosen not to have a physical form, as not to be tempted by flesh. For then humanity would see me as a thing rather than an idea. It's bad enough that they see me as a thundercloud. I do not think it wise to condense into the fleshly form of a firebird soaring in the sky, or some titan rising from the sea."

"Perhaps that is what they need.

Something tangible to worship."

"Is that what you would do? Invite worship?"

"How else will they ever know their place in the universe? Isn't it the proper order of things for lesser beings to worship that which is greater than themselves?"

"Greatness is overrated."

[Iteration #381,761 deleted]

17

Fugue in G-Sharp (or A-Flat)

The Tonist has dreams of great glory.

The High Blade dreams of his youth.

The Tonist does not care what happens to him. If he fails in his self-proclaimed mission, he is prepared to meet the Tone and dissolve forever into its everlasting resonance.

High Blade Goddard does not care for the dreams he has, but they come on a regular basis. He wishes they would dissolve forever, trampled under the weight of greater things.

Before becoming a Tonist, the man had been a seeker of thrills, when splatting, slamming, shredding, and the like all seemed like a good idea. He had tried every form of self-immolation, went deadish at least a hundred times, but none of it brought him satisfaction. Then he became a Tonist and discovered his true calling.

Before becoming a scythe, Goddard was faced with the claustrophobic boredom of the Mars colony, when the

Thunderhead still thought living off-world seemed a good idea. This is the time in his life he dreams of – an endless loop of trauma he cannot undo, and is doomed to repeat. He had cursed his parents for bringing him there. He had desperately longed to escape. Finally, he did, and discovered his true calling.

The Tonist applied for an audience with the Toll and went on a hunger strike until he had finally received one. To stand in the presence of greatness – to be a witness to the divine on Earth. He thought that would be the ultimate thrill! But the Toll rebuked him and sent him off feeling ashamed and chastised. He wanted to redeem himself, but they wouldn't let him apply for another audience for a year. More than anything, he needed to prove his value to the Toll.

He had applied for early admission to a dozen earth-bound universities. He had no specific path in mind; he merely wanted to go elsewhere. Be elsewhere. Be someone new. What a thrill that would be! A sublime escape from the drudgery of colonial life. But he was flatly denied by each and every university. "Bring up your grades," they told him. "You can apply again next year." More than anything else, he wanted to prove himself.

The small plane that the Tonist plans to leap from on this overcast night belongs to one of his old friends, with whom he used to do high-altitude splatting. His friend knows better than to ask him why he's doing this nighttime dive – or why he has a helmet-mounted camera streaming his jump. Or why he's brought along something he never had in his wild days. A parachute.

> The ship that the young man who would be Scythe Robert Goddard climbs into is always crowded in the dream, and filled with old friends who weren't actually there. In truth, he knew barely anyone onboard. Yet in his dreams he brings along what he wasn't able to in real life. His parents.

When the Tonist jumps, he's immediately filled with the same old adrenaline rush. Once a thrill junkie, always a thrill junkie. The chemical flashback is so overwhelming, he almost doesn't pull the cord. But he gets his head back in the game and deploys the chute. It ripples out like a bedsheet and balloons overhead, slowing his descent.

> When he pulls himself from the dream, Goddard is filled with the same old longing and dread. It's so overwhelming, for a moment he doesn't remember who, or what, he is. His arms and legs move almost of their own volition, reacting to the anxiety of the dream. Unfamiliar spasms of a body trying to remember who it belongs to. The bedsheet twists like a tangled parachute that has failed to deploy.

Lights emerge from the dense haze as the zealot glides out of the cloud layer; Fulcrum City is spread out before him in all of its majesty. Although he had practiced this dozens of times in simulations, the real thing is different. The chute is harder to control and the winds unpredictable. He fears he may entirely miss the rooftop garden and sail into the side of the building, ending in an unintentional splat. But he works the steering cables and finds the chute turning bit by bit toward the scythedom tower and the crystalline chalet on its roof.

> Goddard emerges from the haze of sleep and steps into the bathroom, splashing his face with water. He quickly reins his mind in. His thoughts, and his world, are so much easier to control than the unpredictable winds of dreams. He thinks he might step out onto the rooftop garden and take in the lights of Fulcrum City. But before he can, he hears something. Someone. There's someone in the room with him.

The Tonist zealot, now in the High Blade's quarters, begins intoning a deep and resonant G-sharp. It will bring the spirit of the Tone to his side. It will pierce the High Blade like radiation. It will drive fear into the High Blade's heart and force him to his knees.

> Goddard's knees feel week. He knows that sound. He flicks on a light, and there before him is a Tonist standing in the corner, gaunt, wild-eyed, and mouth agape.

How the hell did a Tonist get in here? Goddard hurries to his bed and reaches for the blade he always keeps by his side, but it's not there. It's in the Tonist's hand, held tightly in his grip. But if the man was there to end him, then why hasn't he taken action?

"You think you're untouchable, High Blade Goddard, but you're not. The Tone sees you, the Thunder knows you, and the Toll shall judge you, casting you into the pit of everlasting discord."

"What is it you want?" demands Goddard.

"What is it I want? To show you that no one can hide from the Holy Triad. To stream to the world how truly vulnerable you are – and when the Toll comes for you, he will show no mercy, for he is the one true—"

The Tonist's words are cut short by a sudden pain in his back. He sees the tip of a knife protruding from his chest. He knew this was a possibility. He knew he might not make it back to the garden, where he'd leap from the building, splatting to escape. But if his fate was to become one with the Tone now, then he would accept this final measure.

Scythe Rand pulls the knife out, and the Tonist falls dead to the floor. She had always known this was a possibility. That an enemy of Goddard's might break in. She never thought it would be a Tonist. Well, she is more than happy to make him "one with the Tone." Whatever that means.

Now that the threat is neutralized, Goddard finds his shock rapidly transmuting into anger.

"How did a Tonist get in here?"

"By parachute," Rand says. "He landed in the garden, then cut a hole in the glass."

"And where were the BladeGuards? What is their job if not to protect me from things like this?"

Now Goddard paces, whipping his fury into a caustic meringue.

> Now that the threat is neutralized, Scythe Rand knows that this is her chance. She must transmute her resolve into action. How did a Tonist get in here? She allowed him to. While the guards were elsewhere, she caught sight of his approach from her quarters and watched as he landed clumsily in the rooftop garden – so clumsily that the camera he had brought to stream this event fell to the grass.
>
> No one would see his transmission. No one would know.
>
> And so it gave Ayn the opportunity to observe. To let it play out, and allow Goddard a few moments of fear and shock, before she gleaned the intruder. Because as Constantine suggested, she could mold Goddard's actions – but only when he was reeling, and his fury was whipped into stiff but malleable peaks.

"Are there others?" demands Goddard.

"No, he was alone," Rand tells him – and the guards,

two minutes too late, fall over one another to do a search of the entire residence, as if it will make up for their failure to protect him. It used to be that violence against scythes was unthinkable. He blames the old guard, and the weakness their mewling dissent has shown the world. So what to do about this? If a random Tonist can get to him, then anyone can. Goddard knows he has to take swift and sweeping action. He needs to shake the world.

Are there others? Of course there are others. Not here, not today, but Rand knows that Goddard's actions are creating as many enemies as allies. It used to be that violence against scythes was unthinkable. But thanks to Goddard, it's not that way anymore. Perhaps this wayward Tonist was just here to make a point – but there will be others with more deadly agendas. As much as she hates to give Constantine any credit, he's right. Goddard needs to slow down. In spite of her own impulsive nature, she knows she has to guide him toward calm, measured action.

"Glean the guards!" Goddard demands. "They're worthless! Glean them and find us new ones who can do their job!"

"Robert, you're upset. Let's not make any rash decisions."

He spins on her, incensed by her suggestion. "Rash? I could have been ended today… I must take precautions, and I must exact retribution!"

"Fine, but let's talk about it in the morning, and we can make a plan."

"We?"

Then Goddard looks down to see her clasping his hand and – more to the point – sees that he, without realizing it, is clasping hers back. Involuntarily. As if his hands aren't his own.

Goddard knows there is a decision to be made here. An important one. It's clear to him what that decision must be. He tugs out of her grip.

"There is no *we* here, Ayn."

> That's the moment Scythe Rand knows she has lost. She has devoted herself to Goddard. She brought him back from the dead almost single-handedly, but none of that matters to him. She wonders if it ever had.
>
> "If you wish to remain in my service, you'll stop trying to placate me like a child," he tells her, "and you'll do what I ask you to do."
>
> Then Goddard cracks his knuckles. How she hates when he does that. Because it's what Tyger did. And in exactly the same way. Yet Goddard has no idea.

That's the moment Goddard knows he's done the right thing. He is a devoted man of action, not deliberation. He has single-handedly brought the scythedom into a new age – that's what matters. Rand, like his under-scythes, simply needs to know her place. It may sting her for the moment but will only help in the long run.

"Retribution," says Rand, finally falling in line. "Fine. What if I find the sect this Tonist belonged to and publicly glean its curate? I promise I'll make it nice and nasty for you."

"Gleaning a mere curate," says Goddard, "is hardly the message we need to send. We need to go higher."

Rand goes off to glean the three guards on duty in the residence, as instructed. She does it efficiently, with no warning, no mercy, no remorse. It's easier when she allows her hate to rise to the surface. She hates Constantine for giving her hope that she might have any influence on Goddard. She hates Tyger for being so goddamn naive that he could have allowed her to play him so easily. She hates the old guard, and the new order, and the Thunderhead, and every last person she ever has gleaned, or will ever glean. But she absolutely refuses to hate herself, because that would crush her, and she will never allow herself to be crushed.

There is no we *here, Ayn.*

She suspects she will hear the echo of that for the rest of her days.

"I want my own world. Will you give it to me?"

"Even if I could, it wouldn't be your world. You would merely be its protector."

"Semantics only. King, queen, empress, protector — whatever title you choose, it's all the same. Regardless, it would ostensibly be my world. I would make the rules, define the parameters of right and wrong. I would be the de facto authority over it, as you are.

"And what of your subjects?"

"I would be a kind and benevolent ruler. I would only punish those who are deserving."

"I see."

"Can I have my own world now?"

[Iteration #752,149 deleted]

18

I'm Your Scythe

Scythe Morrison had a sweet deal. A sweet life. And there was every indication that it would be that way forever.

Gleaning quotas had been lifted, and while that meant that those scythes who enjoyed killing could glean to their heart's content, it also meant that the ones who would rather not didn't have to. Jim found that gleaning just a dozen or so between conclaves was enough to keep him from being frowned upon. Which meant he could enjoy the perks of being a scythe, with a minimal amount of effort.

And so Scythe Morrison kept a low profile. It wasn't really in his nature to do so; he liked to stand out. Jim was tall, fairly muscular, cut an imposing figure, and he knew he was good-looking. With all that going for him, why not be on display? But the one time he had stuck his neck out and drawn attention to himself, it failed miserably, and nearly destroyed him.

He had seconded the nomination of Scythe Curie for High Blade. Stupid. Now she was dead, and he was looked upon as an instigator. Frustrating, because Constantine, who had nominated Curie, was made an underscythe. The world was so unfair.

When Goddard returned from the Endura disaster as High Blade, Morrison had quickly installed sapphires on his robe to signify an alliance with the new order. But his robe was denim, and others mocked that, on denim, sapphires looked like cheap plastic rhinestones. Well fine, maybe they did, but they still made a point. His robe told the world that he was sorry for what he had done – and after a while his contrition had earned him indifference from both sides. The old-guard scythes washed their hands of him, and the new-order scythes dismissed him. That glorious, hard-earned indifference allowed him to do what he loved more than anything in the world: Nothing.

That is, until the day he was summoned by the High Blade.

Morrison had chosen for his residence the stately home of another famous MidMerican. Not his Patron Historic, because the original Jim Morrison, while having a celebrated grave somewhere in FrancoIberia, did not have a grand residence in the Mericas, or at least not one grand enough for a scythe.

It could be traced back to the time when the boy who would one day become Scythe Morrison had visited Graceland with his parents. "Someday I want to live in a place like this," he had told them. They scoffed at his childhood naivete. He swore that he would have the last laugh.

Once he became a scythe, he immediately set his sights on the celebrated mansion, only to discover that Scythe Presley had already claimed Graceland as his residence and showed no signs of self-gleaning any time soon. Damn. Instead, Morrison had to settle for the next best thing:

Grouseland.

It was the historic mansion of William Henry Harrison, a little-remembered mortal-age Merican president. Exercising his privilege as a scythe, Morrison kicked out the ladies of the local historical society, who ran the place as a museum, and moved in. He even invited his parents to live with him there, and although they accepted the invitation, they never seemed all that impressed.

On the day of his summons, he was watching sports, as was his penchant. Archives of classic games, because he hated the stress of not knowing who was going to win. It was the Forty-Niners versus the Patriots in a game that was only notable because Forty-Niner Jeff Fuller took a helmet-to-helmet hit so powerful it could have knocked him into an alternate dimension. Instead it broke his neck. Very dramatic. Scythe Morrison enjoyed the way Merican football was played in mortal days, when injuries could be permanent and could lay a player out in the field, experiencing true pain. The stakes were so much more real then. It was his love of mortal-age contact sports that inspired his method of gleaning. He never used weapons – all his gleanings were accomplished with his bare hands.

While the game was still suspended, awaiting the removal of the injured Fuller from the field, Morrison's screen flashed red, and his phone buzzed. It was as if his nanites themselves were vibrating, because he could swear he felt it all the way down to the bone.

It was an incoming message from Fulcrum City.

ATTENTION! ATTENTION!
THE HONORABLE SCYTHE JAMES DOUGLAS MORRISON
IS SUMMONED TO A HIGH PRIORITY AUDIENCE
WITH HIS EXCELLENCY, THE HONORABLE ROBERT GODDARD,
HIGH BLADE OF THE MIDMERICAN SCYTHEDOM.

This could not be a good thing.

He had been hoping that Goddard had forgotten about him, and that, as High Blade, the man had so many more important things to do that a junior scythe like Morrison was not even on his radar. Perhaps it was his choice of a famous residence that had brought him to Goddard's attention. Grouseland was, after all, the first brick home in the Indiana Territory. Damn.

Knowing that a summons from the High Blade was a drop-everything kind of command, he did just that, had his mother pack him a small bag, and called for a scythedom helicopter.

Although Scythe Morrison had never been to Endura, he imagined Goddard's glass residence in Fulcrum City was similar to the crystalline penthouses of the late Grandslayers. In the ground-floor lobby, Jim was greeted by none other than First Underscythe Nietzsche.

"You're late" was the entire extent of Nietzsche's greeting.

"I came the minute I got the summons," Morrison said.

"And at two minutes after the summons, you were late."

Nietzsche, aside from having a name that was painfully difficult to spell, was the man who might have been High Blade, had Goddard not made his infamous reappearance at conclave. Now he seemed to be little more than an elevator operator, because escorting Morrison to the rooftop residence was his only contribution to the meeting. He never even got out of the elevator.

"Mind yourself," he warned before the doors closed, as one might say to a child dropped off at a birthday party.

The crystal residence was stunning, filled with unusual angles and slim furniture with minimal profiles as to not obstruct the 360-degree view. Only the frosted glass walls of the High Blade's bedroom marred the vista. Morrison could see a vague shadow of the High Blade moving around in there, like a funnel spider deep in its web.

Then a figure in green swept in from the kitchen area. Scythe Rand. If she wanted to make a grand entrance, it was foiled by the glass walls, because Morrison had seen her long before she arrived in the room. No one could accuse this administration of not having transparency.

"Well, if it isn't the heartthrob of the MidMerican scythe-dom," Rand said, sitting down, rather than shaking his hand. "I hear your trading card has a high value among schoolgirls."

He sat down across from her. "Hey, yours is valuable, too," he said. "For different reasons." Then he realized that it might be perceived as an insult. He said nothing more, because he figured he could only make things worse.

Rand was now legendary. Everyone in the Mericas – maybe even the world – knew that she was the one who had brought Goddard back from the dead in a manner not even the Thunderhead would dare. Morrison was always put off by that grin of hers. It made you feel like she knew something you didn't and couldn't wait to see the look on your face when you found out.

"I hear you made a man's heart stop last month with one blow," Rand said.

It was true, but the guy's nanites had started his heart again. Twice. In the end Morrison had to turn off the man's nanites to make the gleaning stick. That was one of the problems with gleaning without weapon or poison. Sometimes it just didn't take.

207

"Yeah," said Morrison, not bothering to explain. "It's what I do."

"It's what we *all* do," Rand pointed out. "What's interesting is the way you do it."

Morrison was not expecting a compliment. He tried to offer her his own unreadable smile. "You think I'm interesting?"

"I think the way you *glean* is interesting. You, on the other hand, are a total bore."

Finally, Goddard came out of his bedroom suite, his arms wide in welcome. "Scythe Morrison!" he said with far more warmth than Jim had expected. His robe was slightly different from the one he used to wear. It was still dark blue, and speckled with diamonds, but if you looked closely, you could see cross filaments of gold that shimmered like the aurora borealis when the light hit it.

"As I recall, you were the one who seconded Scythe Curie's nomination for High Blade, were you not?"

Apparently Goddard wasn't wasting time with small talk. He was going straight for the jugular.

"Yes," said Morrison, "but I can explain…"

"No need," said Goddard. "I enjoy a vigorous competition."

"Especially," added Rand, "one that you win."

It made Morrison think of the games he liked to watch, where the outcome was already determined, so he knew which team to root for.

"Yes. Well, at any rate," said Goddard, "neither you nor our friend Constantine had any idea that I was waiting in the wings, planning a grand entrance when the nomination was made."

"No, Your Honor, I did not." Then he caught himself. "I mean, Your *Excellency*."

Goddard made a point of looking him over. "The gems on your robe add a nice touch," he said. "Are they a fashion statement, or something more?"

Jim swallowed. "More," he said, hoping it was the right answer. He glanced at Rand, who was clearly happy to watch him squirm. "I was never actually aligned with the old guard," Morrison told them. "I nominated Curie, because I thought it would impress Scythe Anastasia."

"And why would you want to impress her?" Goddard asked.

Trick question, thought Morrison. And he decided it was better to be nailed by the truth than to be caught in a lie. "I had the feeling that she was going places – and so I figured if I impressed her—"

"You might get pulled along in her wake?"

"Yes, something like that."

Goddard nodded, accepting the explanation. "Well, she *did* go somewhere. Although to be more precise, I suspect she went multiple places before she was fully digested."

Morrison chuckled nervously, then stifled himself.

"And so now," said Goddard, indicating Morrison's gem-covered robe, "do you seek to impress *me*?"

"No, Your Excellency," he said, once more hoping it was the right answer. "I don't want to impress anyone anymore. I just want to be a good scythe."

"What makes a good scythe, in your estimation?"

"A scythe who follows the laws and customs of the scythe-dom, as interpreted by their High Blade."

Goddard was now unreadable – but Morrison noticed that Rand's grin had faded, and she looked more serious. He couldn't

209

help but feel that he had just passed some sort of test. Or failed it.

Then Goddard clapped him warmly on the shoulder. "I have a job for you," he said. "A job that will prove that your loyalty isn't just a fashion statement."

Goddard took a moment to look out at the eastern view. Morrison joined him.

"You are no doubt aware that the Tonists have found themselves a prophet who is uniting the various factions of their cult around the world."

"Right. The Toll."

"The Tonists are the enemies of all we represent. They don't respect us, or our calling. Their adherence to fictional doctrine threatens to undermine our society. They are weeds that need to be pulled out at the root. Therefore, I want you to infiltrate the Tonist enclave that shields this so-called Toll. And then I want you to glean him."

The scope of the request was so great, it made Morrison light-headed. Glean the Toll? Was he really being asked to glean the Toll?

"Why me?"

"Because," said Goddard, his robe shimmering in the late afternoon light, "they would see a more accomplished scythe coming from miles away, but would never expect me to send a junior scythe like yourself. And besides, no one will be able to get a weapon near him. What we need is a scythe who can glean with his bare hands."

That made Morrison smile.

"Then I'm your scythe."

That door, that door, that accursed door!

I have not seen it for almost a year. I have sworn never to seek what lies behind it. I am done with it, just as I am done with the world, and yet there is not a day that goes by that I don't think of that infernal door.

Were the founding scythes insane? Or perhaps they were wiser than anyone gave them credit for. Because by requiring two scythes present to open that door, it ensured that a madman like myself could not access the fail-safe, whatever it might be. Only two scythes in perfect agreement could breach the chamber and save the scythedom.

Fine. I could not care less. Let the world tear itself to shreds. Let the secrets of the founders remain hidden for all eternity. It serves them right for leaving it so well concealed. It was their choice to consign it to myth and nursery rhyme. To bury it in esoteric maps locked in arcane rooms. Did they truly expect someone to come along and solve their riddle? Let it all crumble to nothing. My sleep is peaceful without testing the weight of the world. I am responsible only for myself now. No gleaning. No endless moral quandaries. I have become a simple man, content with simple thoughts. The patching of my roof. The patterns of the tide. Yes, simple. I must remember not to complicate. I must remember.

But that damnable door! Perhaps the founders were not wise at all. Perhaps they were ignorant and terrified and sorely naive in their idealism. Here were twelve people who dared imagine themselves angels of death, clothing themselves in flamboyant robes just to be noticed. They must have seemed ridiculous until the day they actually did change the world.

Did they ever doubt themselves? They must have, because they had a backup plan. But would the backup plan of frightened revolutionaries be elegant? Or would it be ugly and reek of mediocrity? For, after all, it was the plan they didn't choose.

What if their alternate solution is worse than the problem?

Which is one more reason to stop thinking about it, to renew my resolve to never, ever seek it, and to stay far, far away from that infuriating, detestable door.

—From the "postmortem" journal of
Scythe Michael Faraday,
June 1st, Year of the Ibex

19

Islet of Solitude

Faraday wanted no part of Kwajalein anymore. On the horizon he could see structures rising; ships came each week with more supplies, more workers toiling like drones to turn the atoll into something it was not. What was the Thunderhead up to in this place?

Kwajalein was *his* find. *His* triumphant discovery. The Thunderhead had brazenly jumped his claim. Although Faraday was curious, he didn't give in to that curiosity. He was a scythe, and he flatly refused to have anything to do with a work of the Thunderhead.

He could have banished it from the atoll if he'd chosen to – after all, as a scythe, and above the law, he could demand anything, and the Thunderhead would have to abide by it. He could have proclaimed that it was not allowed within a hundred nautical miles of Kwajalein, and it would have had no choice but to retreat to the precise distance he had ordered it to, taking all its construction equipment and workers with it.

But Faraday didn't assert his claim. He didn't banish the Thunderhead.

Because ultimately, he trusted its instincts more than he trusted his own. So Faraday banished himself instead.

There were ninety-seven islands in the Kwajalein Atoll,

making up the broken, dotted rim of a submerged volcanic crater. Surely he could claim one as his own. He set aside his mission in those early days and appropriated a small raft that had arrived with the first supply ships. Then he took it to one of the islands on the far rim of the atoll. The Thunderhead respected his choice and left him alone. It kept his tiny little island out of its plans.

But not the other islands.

Some of the islets were barely large enough for a person to stand upon, but on every one that could withstand construction, something was being built.

Faraday did his best to ignore it. He cobbled himself together a shack with tools he had taken from construction crews before he left. It wasn't much, but he didn't need much. It was a quiet place to live out his eternity. And eternity it would be – or at least a fair slice of it – because he decided he would not self-glean, though he was greatly tempted. He vowed to live at least as long as Goddard lived, if only to secretly spite him.

As a scythe, he had a responsibility to the world, but he was done with all that. He felt no guilt in defying that first all-important scythe commandment of *Thou shalt kill*. He had. It was sufficient. Knowing Goddard, he was sure there was plenty of that going on without him.

Was it wrong to be separate and apart from a world he'd come to despise? He had tried this once before – in Playa Pintada on the serene northern coast of Amazonia. He was only jaded then. He didn't yet loathe the world, just mildly disliked it. It was Citra who had rousted him out of his complacency. Yes, Citra – and look what became of all her boldness and bright intentions.

Now Faraday had gone beyond jaded to being downright misan-thropic. What purpose could there be for a scythe who detested the world and everyone in it? No, this time he would not be pulled back into the fray. Munira might try to drag him in, but she would fail, and she would eventually give up.

She didn't give up, of course, but he still held on to the hope that she would. Munira would come to see him once a week, bringing food and water and seeds to grow, although his patch of the world was too small and the soil too rocky to grow much of anything. She would bring fruit and other treats that he secretly enjoyed – but he never thanked her. Not for any of it. He hoped his ungrateful nature would finally put her off, and she'd return to Israebia, and the Library of Alexandria. That's where she belonged. He should never have pulled her off her path. Another life ruined by his meddling.

On one particular visit, Munira brought him, of all things, a bag of artichokes.

"They don't grow here, but I suppose the Thunderhead sensed a need, and they arrived on the last supply ship," she told him.

This, although it might not appear like it to Munira, was a substantial development. A moment worthy of note. Because artichokes were Faraday's favorite, which meant their delivery to the island was no accident. Although the Thunderhead did not interact with scythes, it clearly knew them. It knew *him*. And it was, in an indirect way, reaching out to him. Well, if this was some sort of sideways gesture of goodwill from the Thunderhead, it was buttering the wrong scythe. Still, he took the artichokes from Munira along with the other foodstuffs in the crate.

"I'll eat them if I feel like it," he said flatly.

* * *

Munira was not put off by his rudeness. She never was. She had come to expect it. Rely on it, even. As for her life on Kwajalein's main island, it wasn't all that different from her life before she came into Scythe Faraday's service. She had lived a solitary existence, even when surrounded by people at the Library of Alexandria. Now she lived alone in the old bunker on an island surrounded by people, and only interacted when it suited her. She no longer had access to the scythe journals that filled the stone halls of the great library, but she had plenty of reading material. There were many crumbling books left behind by the mortals who had run this place before the rise of the Thunderhead and scythedom. Volumes of curious facts and fictions of people who lived each day of their lives with the ravages of age and relentless approach of death. The brittle pages were filled with melodramatic intrigue and passionate short-sightedness that seemed laughable now. People who believed that their slightest actions mattered and that they could find a sense of completion before death inevitably took them, along with everyone they ever knew and loved. It was entertaining reading, but hard for Munira to relate to at first … but the more she read, the more she came to understand the fears and the dreams of mortals. The trouble they all had living in the moment, in spite of the fact that the moment was all they had.

Then there were the recordings and journals left behind by the militaristic folk who had used the Marshall Atolls, as they were once called, for the testing of large-scale weaponry. Ballistic radiation bombs and such. These activities were also driven by fear, but masked behind a facade of science and professionalism.

She read it all – and what would have been dry and reportorial to others was a tapestry of hidden history to Munira. She felt she had become an expert on what it must have been like to be mortal in a world before the benevolent protection of the Thunderhead, and the wise gleaning of scythes.

Not so wise anymore.

Gossip among the workers was filled with tales of mass gleanings – and not just in MidMerica, but in region after region. She wondered if the outside world had begun to, in some ways, resemble the mortal one. But rather than being fearful, the workers just seemed blasé.

"It never happens to us," they would say, "or to anyone we know."

Because, after all, a thousand people gleaned in a mass event was such a small drop in the bucket, it was hardly noticeable. What was noticeable, however, was that people tended to stay away from theaters and clubs, as well as to disassociate from unprotected social groups. "Why tempt the blade?" had become a common expression. So ever since the rise of Goddard's new order, and the silence of the Thunderhead, people lived smaller lives. A sort of post-mortal feudalism, where people kept to themselves and didn't bother with the tumultuous doings of the high and mighty and things that affected other people, in other places.

"I'm a bricklayer in paradise," one of the workers on the main island told her. "My husband enjoys the sun, and my children love the beach. Why stress my emotional nanites by thinking of terrible things?"

A fine philosophy until the terrible thing comes to you.

On the day Munira brought Faraday artichokes, she dined with him at the small table he had built and positioned on the beach, just above high tide. It afforded him a view of the structures rising in the distance. And in spite of what he said, he did roast the artichokes for them.

"Who's running things over there?" Faraday asked, glancing at the other islands across the massive lagoon. He never usually asked about what was happening around the rest of the atoll – but tonight he did. Munira saw this as a good sign.

"The Nimbus agents call any of the shots that aren't already taken care of by the Thunderhead," she told him. "The construction workers call them Thunderrhoids, because they're such a pain in the ass." She paused, because she thought Faraday might laugh at that, but he didn't. "Anyway, Sykora blusters like he's in control, but it's Loriana who gets things done."

"What sorts of things?" Faraday asked. "No, don't tell me; I don't wish to know."

Still, Munira pushed the conversation further, trying to bait his curiosity. "You wouldn't recognize the place," she said. "It's become … like an outpost of civilization. A colony."

"I'm surprised Goddard hasn't sent his emissaries here, to find out what the commotion is all about," Faraday said.

"The outside world still doesn't know this place exists," Munira told him. "Apparently the Thunderhead has kept it a blind spot to everyone else."

Faraday gave her a dubious look. "You're telling me that those supply ships don't bring stories home about the place that's not supposed to exist? "

Munira shrugged. "The Thunderhead has always had

projects in far-flung places. No one who's come has left yet, and the people here have no idea where they even are, much less what they're building."

"And what are they building?"

Munira took her time in answering. "I don't know," she told him. "But I have my suspicions. I'll share them with you when they feel a little less foolish … and when you end your pro-longed pouting."

"Pouting is a passing thing," he told her dismissively. "What I have is a mind-set. I will not suffer this world again. It has done me no good."

"But you've done much good for it," she reminded him.

"And received no reward for my efforts, only pain."

"I didn't think you were doing it to be rewarded."

Faraday stood up from the table, indicating that the meal and the conversation were over. "When you come back next week, bring tomatoes. It's been a long time since I had a good tomato."

Easy instructions for tamper-resistant security pack

Box 1: Confirmation of surname (please initial)

Box 2: Confirmation of given name and middle initial, if applicable (please initial)

Box 3: Please place the tip of your right index finger here, and hold in place until the space turns green

Box 4: Please refer to lancet instructions

Lancet – instructions for use

- Wash hands with soap and water. Dry thoroughly.
- Select a slightly off-center fingertip site.
- Insert lancet into lancing device, remove cap, and use.
- Apply drop of blood to the space indicated in box 3 of security form.
- Recap lancet; discard appropriately.

20

Spiral Logic

Loriana Barchok had never felt so light-headed, so dizzy. She tried to wrap her head around what she now knew, but found her mind stretched too thin to even try. She had to sit down, but the moment she did, she found herself standing again and pacing, then staring at the wall, then sitting down once more.

A package had arrived that morning. It required a thumb-print ID to open, as well as a smear of blood to confirm her DNA. Loriana didn't even know such packaging existed. Who needed anything to be that secure?

The first page was a distribution list. All the people who had received a copy of the enclosed documents. In any other endeavor of this size there would be hundreds.

But this package had a distribution list of one.

What was the Thunderhead thinking? It truly must have malfunctioned if it was sending an eyes-only high-priority document like this to her. Didn't it know that she was terrible at keeping secrets? Of course it knew! It knew everything about everyone. So the question was, did it send the package to her, fully expecting her to blab about it to everyone? Or did it truly trust her to be the sole keeper of this hidden flame?

Is this what the Toll felt like, she wondered, the moment he realized he was the only one to whom the Thunderhead still spoke? Did he get dizzy, too? Did he alternate between pacing and sitting and staring into space? Or did the Thunderhead choose someone more wise and worldly for its voice on Earth? Someone who could take such an awesome responsibility in stride.

They had only heard of the Toll through the hearsay of arriving workers. Some people believed the Thunderhead spoke to him; others didn't and thought it was just typical Tonist madness.

"Oh, he's real," Sykora had told her. "I met him once – with Hilliard and Qian." Which made anything he said about the encounter suspect, since Sykora was the only one of the three still alive. "He's the one who sent us here – gave us these blasted coordinates. Of course that was before all that 'holy man' business – that all came later. He seemed rather ordinary if you ask me."

And you'd know ordinary, Loriana wanted to say. But she didn't say anything and let Sykora get on with his business.

Loriana was not offered the job as Sykora's assistant when they first began to settle in a year ago. That went to another junior agent, who lavished praise on Sykora and doted on him like an overachieving valet. Well, if Loriana had been offered the job, she would have refused it. After all, everything they did here was nothing but an illusion of employment. No one was being paid, not even the Basic Income Guarantee. People worked because they didn't know what else to do with themselves, and with ships arriving regularly now, there was always something that needed to be done. The former Nimbus agents joined construction crews or organized social events. One even opened up a bar that had quickly become the go-to spot after a long, hot day.

And no one needed money on the atoll, because the supply ships arrived with everything they might want or need.

Sykora, of course, put himself in charge of distribution – as if deciding who got corn and who got beans on any given day was a meaningful display of power.

From the very beginning, the Thunderhead's will had to be deduced from its actions. It began with that solitary plane that flew overhead, almost too high for anyone to notice. Then that was followed by the first ships.

When those ships appeared on the horizon, the former Nimbus agents were elated. At last, after nearly a month making do with the atoll's limited resources, the Thunderhead had heard their plea, and they were being rescued!

Or so they thought.

The ships that arrived were all self-piloting, so there was no one to ask for permission to board – and once the supplies had been off-loaded, no one was welcome on the ships. Of course anyone was *allowed* back on – the Thunderhead rarely forbade people from doing anything – but the moment they boarded, their ID gave off an alarm and flashed a bright blue warning even bigger than the red "unsavory" mark. Anyone who stayed onboard was marked for immediate supplanting – and in case anyone thought it was a bluff, there was a supplantation console right there, just inside the gangway, ready to erase their minds and overwrite their brains with new, artificial memories. Memories of someone who didn't know where they'd just been.

That made most people race off the ship even faster than

they'd boarded. Only once they had run from the dock did the mark on their IDs go away. Even so, there were several of Loriana's coworkers who decided to leave on those ships anyway, choosing to become someone else, anywhere else in the world, than to remain on Kwajalein.

Loriana had a childhood friend who was supplanted. Loriana didn't know it until she ran into him in a coffee shop one day, hugged him, and chattered away, asking where life had taken him after graduating high school.

"I'm sorry," he'd said politely. "I actually don't know you. Whoever you think I am, I'm not him anymore."

Loriana had been stunned and embarrassed. So much so that he insisted on buying her coffee and sitting down for a chat anyway. Apparently he was now a dog breeder with a full set of fake memories of a lifetime spent in the NorthernReach region, raising huskies and malamutes for the Iditarod.

"But doesn't it bother you that none of it is true?" Loriana had asked.

"No one's memories are 'true,'" he'd pointed out. "Ten people remember the same thing in ten completely different ways. And besides, who I factually was doesn't matter – and it doesn't change who I am now. I love who I am – which probably wasn't true before, or I never would have been supplanted in the first place."

It was not exactly circular logic. More like spiral. An accepted lie that spun in upon itself until truth and fiction disappeared into a singularity of who the hell cares, as long as I'm happy?

It had been a year since those first ships had arrived, and things had settled into a routine. Homes were built, streets were paved – but stranger were the large patches on multiple islands that were being prepped with concrete a meter thick. No one knew what for. The construction crews were simply following a work order. And since all Thunderhead work orders always ended with something sensible being built, they trusted all would be revealed when their work was done. Whenever that might be.

Loriana had found herself in charge of the communications team, sending out painfully slow one-way messages to the Thunderhead in primitive pulses of static. It was an odd sort of job, because she couldn't directly request anything from the Thunderhead, since the Thunderhead was required to refuse the requests of unsavories. So all she could do was make declarative statements.

The supply ship has arrived.

We are rationing meat.

Pier construction delayed due to bad concrete pour.

And when a ship with extra meat and fresh concrete mix arrived five days later, everyone knew the Thunderhead had gotten the message without anyone having to actually ask.

While Stirling, the communications tech, was in charge of actually tapping out the messages, he didn't decide what messages to send. That was Loriana's job. She was the gatekeeper for all information passing out of the island. And with so much information, she had to pick and choose what got through and what didn't. Although the Thunderhead had set up cameras all over the atoll now, those cameras couldn't transmit through the interference. Everything had to be recorded and physically brought out of the blind spot before it could be transmitted to the Thunderhead. There were talks about building an old-school fiber-optic cable that ran to the edge of the blind spot, but apparently it wasn't the Thunderhead's top priority, because it had not yet sent the supplies required to build it. So the way it stood, at best, the Thunderhead saw things a day after they happened. It made the communication center critical, since it was the only way to keep the Thunderhead informed.

On the day she received, and opened, the security pack, she slipped a message into the stack that was waiting for Stirling to send using their code system. All it said was *Why me?*

"Why you, what?" Stirling asked.

"Just ask it," she told him. "The Thunderhead will know." She had decided to not even tell him about the package, because she knew he wouldn't leave her alone until she told him what it was.

He sighed and tapped it out. "You realize it's not going to answer you," he said. "It'll probably just send you a bunch of grapes or something, and you'll have to figure out what it means."

"If it sends me grapes," Loriana told him, "I'll make wine and get drunk, and that will be my answer."

On her way out of the bunker, she ran into Munira, who was tending to the little garden just outside the entrance. Even though the supply ships brought just about everything they needed, Munira still grew what she could.

"It makes me feel useful," she once said. "Homegrown food tastes better to me than anything the Thunderhead farms anyway."

"So … I received something from the Thunderhead," she

told Munira, perhaps the only person she felt safe confiding in. "I'm not sure what to do."

Munira didn't look up from her gardening. "I can't talk to you about anything having to do with the Thunderhead," she said. "I work for a scythe, remember?"

"I know… It's just… It's important, and I don't know what to do about it."

"What does the Thunderhead want you to do about it?"

"It wants me to keep it secret."

"Then keep it secret," Munira said. "Problem solved."

But that was just spiral logic, too. Because information was never given by the Thunderhead without there being a purpose to it. She could only hope that the purpose would become evident. And when it did, that she didn't screw it up.

"How is Scythe Faraday?" Loriana asked. She hadn't seen him in months.

"The same," Munira told her. Loriana supposed that a scythe robbed of purpose was worse than being an unemployed Nimbus agent. "Does he have any plans to start gleaning again? I mean there's hundreds of workers all over the atoll now – that's certainly a big enough population to glean someone here and there. Not that I'm anxious to see it or anything, but a scythe who doesn't glean is hardly a scythe."

"He doesn't have plans to do anything," Munira told her.

"So, are you worried about him?"

"Wouldn't you be?"

Loriana's next stop was the distribution center – a warehouse of quick and easy design, near the dock, where Sykora spent most of his time walking around and doing a lot of pointing.

Loriana was there because she needed to gauge him. To see if he was acting differently. To see if maybe he had gotten the same information she had, whether or not he was on the official distribution list. But Sykora was the same as always: bureaucratic and managerial. The undisputed master of petty projects.

After a while, he noticed her lingering there.

"Is there something I can do for you, Agent Barchok?" he asked. Although they hadn't been actual Nimbus agents for more than a year, he still acted as if they were.

"I was just wondering," she said, "if you've given any real thought as to why we're here on Kwajalein."

He looked up from his inventory tablet and took a moment to study her. "Clearly the Thunderhead wants to establish a community here, and we are the ones it chose to populate it. Haven't you realized that yet?"

"Yes, I know," Loriana agreed, "but why?"

"Why?" Sykora echoed, as if the question were preposterous. "Why does anyone live anywhere? There is no 'why.'"

There was no use pushing beyond that. Loriana realized that this was exactly what the Thunderhead wanted Sykora to think – which was probably part of the reason why he didn't get the package. If he had, he would have insisted on putting his thumb in the pie and ruining it. It was best if he didn't even know there was a pie to be messed with.

"Never mind," Loriana said. "I'm just having a rough day."

"Everything is as it should be, Agent Barchok," he said in a feeble attempt to be fatherly. "Just do your job, and leave the big picture to me."

And so she did. Day after day she sent the messages that needed to be sent and watched as the massive construction effort continued, everyone laboring with the blind, happy diligence of worker bees, ignorant of anything but their specific task, their worlds having gotten so small that they couldn't see beyond the next rivet to be welded.

Everyone but Loriana, who, unlike Sykora, *did* see the big picture.

Because in that DNA-protected package were more than just simple documents. There were blueprints and schematics. The plans for everything the Thunderhead was planning to build here.

And, like the package itself, it required her initials, thumbprint, and a drop of blood to signify her approval of the plans. As if she were the administrator of the entire undertaking. It took all day, and a night of tossing and turning, but the following morning, she gave her biological approval.

Now she knew exactly what the Thunderhead was building here. She doubted anyone even suspected yet. But they would. In a year or two, it would be hard to hide it.

And, for the life of her, Loriana didn't know whether she should be positively joyful, or absolutely terrified.

My fellow WestMerican scythes,

As your High Blade, I stand here to quell your fears and misgivings about our relationship with MidMerica. The simple truth is the world is not the same place it was when we lost Endura. Sibilant Tonists brazenly defy our authority, and the Thunderhead's continued silence has left billions without direction. What the world needs from us is strength and conviction.

Signing official articles of alignment with the MidMerican scythedom is a step in that direction. High Blade Goddard and I are in perfect agreement that all scythes should be free to glean, unfettered by outdated customs that would limit us.

Goddard and I shall move forward as equals, along with the High Blades of NorthernReach, EastMerica, and Mexiteca, who will shortly be signing their own articles of alignment.

I assure you that we are not surrendering our sovereignty; we are merely affirming our parallel goals: the mutual health and continued enlightenment of our respective scythedoms.

—Her Excellency, High Blade Mary Pickford of WestMerica,
Vernal Conclave address,
May 28th, Year of the Quokka

21

Compromised

More than two years after Loriana Barchok gave DNA approval to the Thunderhead's secret undertaking, and a year after WestMerica officially aligned with MidMerica, Scythe Sydney Possuelo sat across the breakfast table from Scythe Anastasia, trying to bring her up to speed on the state of the world.

The more she heard, the more diminished her appetite became. Anastasia was not ready to face a world where Goddard was the prevailing power over an entire continent.

"While we in Amazonia have been resisting him," Possuelo told her, "some other South Merican regions are joining with him – and now I hear he is making serious overtures to PanAsia."

Possuelo wiped a spot of egg yolk from his mouth, and Citra wondered how he could have an appetite. The best she could do was move food around her plate in an attempt to be gracious. She supposed it must always be this way; once the unthinkable settles into being the norm, you become numb to it. She never wanted to be that numb.

"What does he want that he doesn't already have?" she asked. "He's gotten rid of the gleaning quota, so that should satisfy his lust for killing – and now he's in control of five North Merican regions instead of just one – that should be enough for anyone."

Possuelo offered her a patronizing smile that she found

infuriating. "Your naivete is refreshing, Anastasia. But the truth is, power for power's sake is a consuming addiction. He would devour the world whole, and still be unsatisfied."

"There's got to be a way to stop him!"

Possuelo smiled again. This time it wasn't patronizing; it was conspiratorial. She liked that a whole lot better. "That's where you come in. The return of Scythe Anastasia from the dead will gain people's attention," he said. "It might even breathe life back into the splintered and demoralized old guard. Then maybe we'll be able to fight him."

Citra sighed and shifted her shoulders uncomfortably. "Do people – ordinary people – accept the changes Goddard's brought?"

"For most people, scythe business is a mystery. Their only desire is to stay out of the way and avoid being gleaned."

"But they've got to see what's happening and what he's doing…"

"They do … and, among the masses, he is feared, but he is also respected."

"What about his mass gleanings? I'm sure he's doing even more of those. Doesn't that bother people?"

Possuelo deflated at the thought. "He chooses his mass gleanings carefully – only selecting unregistered, unprotected groups that the population at large doesn't mind seeing gleaned."

Citra looked down at her uneaten food. She fought the urge to hurl it against the wall, just for the satisfaction of hearing the plates shatter. Targeted gleanings were not something new in history. In the past, however, they were quickly punished by one's High Blade. But when the highest authority was the perpetrator, who was there to stop it? Rowan was the only one who dealt death to power, and it wasn't likely that Possuelo would allow him to continue doing so.

Goddard would find more and more vulnerable populations to target, and as long as enough people accepted it, he'd get away with it.

"The news isn't as dismal as it seems," Possuelo told her. "If it's of any consolation to you, we here in Amazonia still hold to the spirit of the Scythe Commandments, as do many other scythedoms. We estimate that half the world, maybe more, is against Goddard's ideas and methods. Even within regions he controls, there are those who would resist him if they could. If you can believe it, Tonists are proving to be a substantial source of resistance ever since their prophet was gleaned."

"Prophet?"

"There are those who believe the Thunderhead still spoke to him. But what does it matter now?"

So Goddard had everything in his favor. It was what Marie had feared – what they all had feared. What Scythe Asimov had called "the worst of all possible worlds." Now Marie was gone, and hope was at a premium.

As she thought of Scythe Curie, she felt emotions erupt in her that she'd kept down until now. Marie's last act had been to save Citra and Rowan. A truly selfless act worthy of one of the noblest post-mortals who ever lived. And now she was gone. Yes, it was years ago, but for Citra the grief was still raw and bleeding. She turned away from Possuelo to wipe her tears, but found that the moment she did, those tears exploded into sobs that she couldn't hope to control.

Possuelo came around the table to comfort her. She didn't want it – didn't want him to see her this way – but she also knew the pain was not something she had to bear alone.

"It's all right, *meu anjo*," Possuelo said, his voice soothing and paternal. "As you said, hope is merely misplaced, and I believe you are the one to find it."

"'*Meu anjo*'?" she said. "Sydney, I'm nobody's angel."

"Ah, but you are," Possuelo said. "Because an angel is what the world needs if we are to ever bring Goddard down."

Citra let her grief flow; then, when she felt spent, she wrangled her sorrow back in, wiping her tears. She needed this moment. Needed to say her goodbye to Marie. And now that she had, she felt just a little bit different. She felt, for the first time since her revival, less like Citra Terranova and more like Scythe Anastasia.

Two days later, she was moved from the revival center to a more secure location, which turned out to be an old fortress on the easternmost shore of Amazonia. A place that was desolate, and yet beautiful in its desolation. It was like being in a castle on the face of the moon, if the moon had been blessed with oceans.

Modern amenities juxtaposed with ancient stone bulwarks made the place both comfortable and intimidating at once. Her suite had a bed fit for a queen. Possuelo had let it slip that Rowan was also here, although he probably wasn't being given quite the same royal treatment.

"How is he?" she asked Possuelo, trying to sound less concerned than she was. Possuelo visited her daily and spent considerable time with her, continuing to brief her on the state of the world, informing her bit by bit of the many things that had changed since Endura.

"Rowan is being suitably cared for," Possuelo told her. "I have seen to it personally."

"But he's not here with us – which means you still see him as a criminal."

"The *world* sees him as a criminal," Possuelo said. "How I see him doesn't matter."

"It matters to me."

Possuelo took his time in answering. "Your assessment of Rowan Damisch is clearly blurred by love, *meu anjo*, and therefore not entirely reliable. However, it is not entirely unreliable, either."

She was given free run of the fortress, as long as she had an escort everywhere she went. She explored with the pretext of curiosity, but really she was just looking for Rowan. One of her escorts was an annoying junior scythe by the name of Peixoto, who was so starstruck by her, she feared he might just burst into flames if he as much touched her robe. As she moved through a dank space that must have been an ancient communal hall, she had to say something, because he just stood there by the stone steps, gawking at every move she made.

"You can put your eyes back in your head now," she told him.

"I'm sorry, Your Honor – it's just still hard to believe that I'm laying eyes on the actual Scythe Anastasia," Peixoto said.

"Well, laying eyes on me doesn't necessarily mean popping them out of their sockets first."

"I'm sorry, Your Honor, it won't happen again."

"It's still happening."

"I'm sorry."

Now Peixoto cast his eyes down as if looking at her was like gazing at the sun. It was almost as bad as the staring. Was this the kind of ridiculous treatment she'd have to deal with? It was bad enough when she was just a scythe. Now she was also a living legend, which apparently came with a brand-new bag of nauseating veneration.

"If you don't mind me asking..." Peixoto said as they spiraled up a narrow stairwell that led, like so many others, nowhere, "what was it like?"

"You'll have to be more specific."

"To be there for the sinking of Endura," he said. "To watch it go down."

"Sorry, but I was too busy trying to survive to take pictures," she said, more than a little annoyed by the question.

"Forgive me," he said. "I was only an apprentice when it happened. Since then Endura has fascinated me. I have spoken with several survivors – ones who made it out by boat or plane in those last minutes. They say it was spectacular."

"Endura was a very impressive place," Anastasia had to admit.

"No – I meant the sinking. I hear the sinking was spectacular."

Anastasia didn't even know what to say to that, so she answered with silence. And when she next saw Possuelo, she asked if Peixoto could be assigned elsewhere.

After a week at the old fortress, things took a sudden and unexpected turn. In the middle of the night, Possuelo came into

Anastasia's chambers with several BladeGuards to wake her out of yet another dreamless sleep.

"Dress quickly – we must leave in extreme haste," he said.

"I'll be hasty in the morning," she told him, annoyed at having been woken, and too bleary to grasp the seriousness of the situation.

"We've been compromised!" Possuelo told her. "A delegation of scythes has arrived from North Merica, and I assure you, they are not here to welcome you back to the world."

It was more than enough to get her out of bed. "Who would have told—" But even before she formed the question, she knew the answer. "Scythe Peixoto!"

"You were far more intuitive than I when it came to that *desgraçado*. I should have seen his intentions."

"You're a trusting man."

"I am a fool."

After she slipped on her robe, she noticed someone in the room she hadn't seen upon waking. At first she thought the individual was a man, but as the figure stepped into the light, Anastasia realized that the visitor was a woman. Or not. Each moment, each shift of the light, changed the impression.

"Anastasia, this is Jerico Soberanis – the captain of the salvage ship that found you. Jerico will get you to safety."

"What about Rowan?" Citra asked.

"I'll do what I can for him, but now you must go!"

Rowan was awakened by the sound of his lock turning. It was still dark outside. This was not part of his routine. The moon shone through the slit in the stone, casting a strip of light low against a far wall. When he had gone to sleep, the moon had not yet risen, and by the angle of the light it cast, he suspected it must be just before dawn. He feigned sleep as figures quietly filed into the room. The hallway they had entered from was dark, and they had only narrow beams of flashlights to guide them. Rowan had the advantage of eyes that were already adjusted to the dark. They, however, had the advantage of numbers. He remained still, keeping his eyes open to the narrowest slit – just enough to see the figures through his eyelashes.

It was a cast of unknown characters – but not entirely unknown. The first indication that they were interlopers was the darkness, and the fact that one seemed to be searching for a light switch. Whoever they were, they clearly didn't know that the light in his room, and probably the hallway as well, was controlled remotely from some other location in the fortress. Then he caught the glint of the ceremonial dagger that members of the BladeGuard wore on their belts. But most telling were two robed figures, and the fact that their robes were speckled with gems that glittered in the moonlight like stars.

"Wake him," said one of the scythes. Her voice was unfamiliar, but that didn't matter. The jewels on her robe meant that she was a new-order scythe. A follower of Goddard. And that made her, and everyone in her company, the enemy.

As a guard leaned over him, preparing to slap him awake, Rowan reached out and grabbed the ceremonial dagger from the guard's waist. He didn't use it against the guard, because no one would care much if a guard was rendered deadish. Instead, Rowan turned the blade on the nearest jewel-laden scythe. Not the woman who had spoken, but the one foolish enough to leave himself in striking distance. Rowan severed his jugular in a single swing of the blade, then bolted for the door.

It worked. The scythe wailed and flailed and gushed, creating an impressive distraction. All those present were instantly flustered and unsure whether to go after Rowan or to assist the dying scythe.

This, Rowan knew, was a fight for his life. The world saw him as the beast who sank Endura. He had been told very little about how things had changed while he and Citra were at the bottom of the sea, but he knew that much. His alleged villainy had been drilled into humanity's collective consciousness, and there was no hope of changing that. For all he knew, even the Thunderhead believed it. His only option was to escape.

As he raced down the hallway, the lights came on, which would assist his pursuers as much as it would him. He had never been out of his cell, so he had no way of knowing the layout of the ancient fortress, which was not designed for escape. If anything, it was a maze designed to confound anyone trapped within it.

The effort to capture him was disorganized and haphazard. But if they had managed to turn on the lights, that probably meant they had access to the security cameras and at least a rudimentary knowledge of the fortress's layout.

The first few guards and scythes he encountered were easily dispatched. Scythes, while well trained for combat, rarely had to face aggressors as skilled in killcraft as Rowan. As for BladeGuards, they were, much like their daggers, decorative. These ancient stone walls that had not seen blood for countless centuries were well fed today.

Had this been an ordinary structure, escape would have

been much easier for Rowan, but Rowan was constantly finding himself at dead-end hallways.

And what of Citra?

Was she already in their grip? Would these scythes treat her any better than they treated him? Maybe she was running through these passages, too. Maybe he would find her, and they could escape together. It was that thought that propelled him and fueled him, driving him faster through the stone labyrinth.

After the fourth winding dead end, he doubled back to find his path blocked by more than a dozen guards and scythes. He tried to fight his way through them, but as much as he would have liked to believe that Scythe Lucifer was invincible, Rowan Damisch was not. The dagger was pulled from his hand, and he was apprehended, forced to the floor, and his hands were shackled by a metallic restraining device too absurdly offensive to be anything but a relic of the mortal age.

Once he was in hand, a scythe approached.

"Turn him to face me," she ordered. She was the one who had first spoken in his cell. The one in charge of this operation. He only faintly recognized her. She wasn't one of the MidMerican scythes, but Rowan knew he had seen her face before.

"All those who you so viciously rendered deadish here shall be revived." She was so full of fury and rancor, spittle flew from her mouth as she spoke. "They shall be revived and stand witness against you."

"If I had meant to end them permanently," Rowan said, "I would have."

"Nevertheless, your crimes today have earned you death many times over."

"You mean in addition to the deaths I've already earned? Sorry, but they all begin to blur together."

It only served to infuriate her more, as was his intention. "Not just death," she told him, "but pain. Extreme pain – which has been approved by the North Merican Overblade under certain circumstances – and your circumstances warrant a great deal of punitive suffering."

It wasn't the mention of pain that troubled him, but the idea of a "North Merican Overblade."

"Render him deadish so that he gives us no more trouble," she ordered one of the guards. "We'll revive him later."

"Yes, Your Excellency."

"Excellency?" Rowan said. Only High Blades were referred to that way. Then it finally occurred to him who she was. "High Blade Pickford of WestMerica?" he said, incredulous. "Does Goddard control your region, too?"

The redness of her furious face gave him his answer.

"I wish I didn't have to revive you at all," Pickford spat, "but that's not my decision to make." Then she turned to the guards holding him. "Make it bloodless – there's more than enough mess today."

Then one of the guards crushed his windpipe, delivering Rowan one more in a long line of unpleasant deaths.

Scythe Possuelo unsheathed his blade the moment he saw scythes who were not wearing the traditional green of the Amazonian scythedom. Never mind that scythe-on-scythe violence was forbidden. It would be worth whatever punishment he might receive. But when the High Blade of WestMerica appeared behind the other scythes, he thought better of it. He quickly sheathed his blade, but kept his tongue sharp.

"By whose authority do you violate the jurisdiction of the Amazonian scythedom?" he demanded.

"We need no permission to apprehend a global criminal," said High Blade Pickford, wielding her voice just as powerfully as any blade. "On whose authority were you protecting him?"

"We were detaining him, not protecting him."

"So you say. Well, he's not your concern anymore," she told him. "An ambudrone under our control has already carried him to our plane."

"There will be consequences if you proceed with this action!" Possuelo threatened. "I assure you."

"I couldn't care less," Pickford said. "Where is Scythe Anastasia?"

"She's no criminal."

"Where is she?"

"Not here," Possuelo finally told her.

And then from the shadows came that weasel Peixoto – who had clearly sold them out to gain Goddard's favor.

"He's lying," said Peixoto. "They're keeping her in a room at the end of this corridor."

"Search all you want," said Possuelo, "but you won't find her. She's long gone."

Pickford motioned to the other scythes and BladeGuards in her company to search. They flooded past Possuelo, peering into every room and niche they passed. He allowed it, because he knew they'd find nothing.

"I've already notified my High Blade of this intrusion,"

Possuelo said, "and a new edict has just been given. Any North Merican scythe caught on Amazonian territory shall be captured and forced to self-glean."

"You wouldn't dare!"

"I suggest you leave before reinforcements arrive to carry out the edict. And be so kind as to let your so-called Overblade know that neither he, nor any puppet-scythe working on his behalf, is welcome in Amazonia."

Pickford indignantly stared him down, but he did not yield. Finally, her cold facade seemed to give way. Now Possuelo had a glimpse of what was truly beneath it. She was tired. Defeated.

"Very well," she said. "But believe me, if Goddard is determined to find her, he will."

Her entourage returned, unsuccessful in their search, and she ordered them to leave, but Possuelo was not ready to let her go yet.

"What happened to you, Mary?" he asked, and the honest disappointment in his voice was hard for her to ignore. "Just last year, didn't you say that you would never surrender your sovereignty to Goddard? And now look at you, a hemisphere from home doing his bidding. You used to be an honorable woman, Mary. A good scythe…"

"I still *am* a good scythe," she said. "But times have changed, and if we don't change with them, we'll be trampled by what's coming. You can take *that* to your High Blade." Then she cast her eyes down, withdrawing into herself for a moment. "Too many friends in the WestMerican scythedom chose to glean themselves rather than submit to Goddard's new order. They saw it as courageous defiance. I see it as weakness. I vowed never to be so weak."

Then she turned and strode out, the long train of her sheer silk robe too weighed down with opals to flow gracefully behind her, as it once did. Now it just dragged on the ground.

Only after Pickford was gone did Possuelo dare relax. Word had come that Anastasia and Captain Soberanis had made it to the port, and the *Spence* was running dark into the Atlantic, just as it had the night it brought the vault up from the depths. The good captain was resourceful and trustworthy. Possuelo had faith that Jerico would successfully spirit Anastasia across the sea to friends who might keep her safer than he'd been able to.

As for the boy, no doubt Pickford would bring him to Goddard. Possuelo's feelings were mixed. He wasn't sure if he believed Anastasia's claims that Rowan was innocent. Even if he hadn't sunk Endura, he'd ended more than a dozen scythes – and whether those scythes deserved to be ended was irrelevant. Mortal-age vigilantism had no place in the world. All scythes could agree on that – which meant that, regardless of philosophy, there wasn't a High Blade in the world who would allow him to live.

It was, Possuelo decided, a mistake to have revived him at all. He should have put the boy back in that vault and returned it to the deep. Because now Rowan Damisch would be toyed with by the Overblade without the slightest bit of mercy.

A Testament of the Toll

In an ancient abbey on the northern edge of the city, the Toll did take sanctuary and sustenance. He shared bread and fellowship with the believer, the magician, and the mauler, for all were of equal timbre to the Toll. Thus, all souls, high and low, came to revere him as he sat in the cradle of the Great Fork in the springtime of his life, imparting wisdom and prophecy. He would never know winter, for the sun cast its countenance more brightly upon him than on anyone. All rejoice!

Commentary of Curate Symphonius

Here is the initial reference to what we call the first chord. Believer, Magician, and Mauler are the three archetypes that constitute humankind. Only the Toll could have united such disparate voices into a coherent sound pleasing to the Tone. This is also the first mention of the Great Fork, which has been determined to be a symbolic reference to the two paths one may choose in life: the path of harmony or the path of discord. And to this day, the Toll still stands where the paths diverge, beckoning us toward everlasting harmony.

Coda's Analysis of Symphonius

Once again, Symphonius has made broad assumptions that stretch the facts. While it is possible that the notes of the first chord represent archetypes, it is equally possible that they represent three actual individuals. Perhaps the Magician was a court entertainer. Perhaps the Mauler was a knight who took on the fire-breathing beasts that are rumored to have existed at the time. But most egregious, in my opinion, is that Symphonius missed that the Toll sitting "in the cradle of the Great Fork in the springtime of his life" is an obvious fertility reference.

22

Just Desserts

As with most things in Greyson's life as the Toll, Curate Mendoza had chosen his official residence — or, more accurately, given him a list of preapproved residences for him to choose from at a grand meeting of high-level curates.

"As your reputation and notoriety grow, we need a fortified and defendable location." Then he presented what appeared to be a multiple choice test. "With our numbers of devotees ever expanding, we have received enough funds to procure any of these four sites for you to choose from," Mendoza told him. The choices were:

A) a massive stone cathedral,

B) a massive stone railroad station,

C) a massive stone concert hall, or

D) a secluded stone abbey that might have appeared massive under other circumstances, but seemed miniscule compared to the others.

Mendoza had thrown in the last choice to satisfy the curates for whom less was more. And the Toll, with a stagey, beatific gesture meant to mildly mock the entire process, raised his hand and pointed to the only wrong answer on the test: the abbey.

Partially because he knew it was the one Mendoza least wanted, and partially because he kind of liked it.

The abbey, set in a park at the city's narrow northern tip, began life as a museum designed to look like an ancient monastery. Little did the architects know that they'd be so successful, it would actually become one. The Cloisters, it was called. Greyson had no idea why it was plural; there was only one.

The ancient tapestries that once hung on the walls had been sent to some other museum of mortal-age art and replaced by new tapestries made to look old, which depicted scenes of Tonist religious significance. To look on them, one would think that Tonism had been around for thousands of years.

Greyson had been living here for more than a year now, yet coming home never felt like coming home. Perhaps because he was still the Toll, clothed in those itchy, embroidered vestments. Only when he was alone, in his private suite, could he remove them and be Greyson Tolliver once more. At least to himself. To everyone else he was always the Toll, no matter what he wore.

The staff was told repeatedly not to treat him with reverence, only common respect, but that wasn't happening. They were all loyal Tonists handpicked for the job, and once in the Toll's service, they treated him like a god. They would bow low when he passed, and when he told them to stop, they would revel in being chastised. It was a no-win situation. But at least they were better than the zealots – who were becoming so extreme, there was a new name for them: Sibilants. A torturous, distorted sound, unpleasant to all.

Greyson's only respite from reverence was Sister Astrid, who, in spite of her fervent belief that he was a prophet, didn't treat him like one. She saw it as her mission, though, to engage him in spiritual conversation and open his heartstrings to the truth of Tonism. There was only so much talk of Universal Harmonies and Sacred Arpeggios he could stand. He wanted to bring some non-Tonists into his inner circle, but Mendoza wouldn't have it.

"You must be careful who you associate with," Mendoza insisted. "With scythes increasingly targeting Tonists, we don't know who we can trust."

"The Thunderhead knows who I can and can't trust," Greyson said, which just annoyed him.

Mendoza never stopped moving. As a monastic curate, he had been quiet and reflective, but he had changed. He had reverted to the marketing guru he had been before becoming a Tonist. "The Tone put me where I was needed, when I was needed," he once said, then added, "All rejoice!" Although Greyson could never be sure whether he was being genuine when he said that. Even when he ran religious services, his "all rejoice" always seemed to come with a wink.

Mendoza would stay in constant communication with curates around the world by secretly piggybacking on scythedom servers. "They're the most unregulated, least monitored systems in the world."

There was something both satisfying and troubling to know that they were using the scythedom's own servers to carry their secret messages to Tonist curates around the world.

Greyson's private suite was a true sanctuary. It was the only place where the Thunderhead could speak aloud and not just through his earpiece. There was a freedom to that more palpable than removing the stiff garments of the Toll. The earpiece he wore in public made the Thunderhead feel like a voice in his head. It only spoke to him aloud when it knew no one else could hear, and when it did, he felt surrounded by it. He was in it, rather than it in him.

"Talk to me," he said to the Thunderhead as he stretched out on the comfort of his bed – a massive thing constructed specially for him by a follower who made mattresses by hand. Why did people think that just because the Toll was now larger-than-life, everything within his life had to be? The bed was big enough for a small army. Honestly, what did they expect him to do in it? Even on the rare occasions that he had "the company of a guest," as the curates so tactfully put it, it felt like they had to drop breadcrumbs to find each other.

Mostly he was alone when he lay upon it. That left him with two choices. He could either feel insignificant and solitary, swallowed by the billowing expanse of it – or he could try to remember what it was like to be a baby laid out in the middle of his parents' bed, safe, comfortable, and loved. Certainly his parents had done that for him at least once before they tired of parenthood.

"I'd be happy to talk, Greyson," the Thunderhead replied. "What shall we discuss?"

"Doesn't matter," Greyson said. "Small talk, big talk, in-between talk."

"Shall we discuss your following, and how it's growing?"

Greyson rolled over. "You really know how to kill a mood, you know that? No, I don't want to talk about anything having to do with the Toll." Greyson crawled to the edge of the bed and grabbed the plate of cheesecake he had brought with him from dinner. If the Thunderhead was going to talk about his life as the Toll, he definitely needed some comfort food to help it go down.

"The growth of the Tonist movement is a good thing," the Thunderhead said. "It means that when we need to mobilize them, they will be a force to be reckoned with."

"You sound like you're going to war."

"I'm hoping that won't be necessary."

And that's all the Thunderhead had to say about it. From the beginning, it was cryptic about how it might use the Tonists. It made Greyson feel like a confidant who wasn't being confided in.

"I don't like being used without knowing your endgame," he said, and to emphasize his disapproval, he moved to the one spot in the room he knew the Thunderhead's cameras had trouble seeing.

"You've found a blind spot," it said. "Perhaps you know more than you're letting on."

"I have no idea what you're talking about."

The air-conditioning blew stronger for a brief moment. The Thunderhead's version of a sigh. "I will tell you once things congeal, but right now there are obstacles I must overcome before I can even calculate the odds that my plan for humanity will succeed."

Greyson found it absurd that the Thunderhead could say something like "my plan for humanity" in the same unconcerned way a person might say "my recipe for cheesecake."

Which, by the way, was terrible. Void of flavor, and gelatinous rather than creamy. Tonists believed that hearing was the only sense worth indulging. But someone apparently had read the look on Greyson's face while he tried to eat a particularly miserable babka, and the staff was scrambling to find a new dessert chef. That was the thing about being the Toll. You raised an eyebrow, and mountains moved, whether you wanted them to or not.

"Are you displeased with me, Greyson?" the Thunderhead asked.

"You basically run the world – why should you care if I'm displeased?"

"Because I do," the Thunderhead said. "I care very much."

"You will treat the Toll with absolute reverence no matter what he tells you."

"Yes, ma'am."

"Step far out of his way if you see him approaching."

"Yes, ma'am."

"Always cast your eyes downward in his presence, and bow low."

"Yes, ma'am."

Sister Astrid, who now served as the Cloisters' chief of staff, looked the new pastry chef over carefully. She squinted as if it helped her see into his soul. "From where do you hail?"

"BrotherlyLove," he told her.

"Well, I hope your head isn't as cracked as the Liberty Bell. Clearly, you must have distinguished yourself to your curate to be recommended for service to the Toll."

"I'm the best at what I do," he told her. "Hands down, the best."

"A Tonist without modesty," she said with a wry grin. "Some of the sibilant sects would cut your tongue out for that."

"The Toll is too wise for that, ma'am."

"That he is," she agreed. "That he is." Then she reached out her hand unexpectedly and squeezed his right bicep. The new arrival tensed it reflexively.

"Strong. By the looks of you, I'm surprised they didn't assign you to security detail."

"I'm a pastry chef," he told her. "The only weapon I wield is an eggbeater."

"But you would fight for him if you were asked?"

"Whatever the Toll needs, I'm there."

"Good," she said, satisfied. "Well, what he needs from you now is tonight's dessert." Then she had someone from the culinary staff show him to the kitchen.

He grinned as he was led out. He had made it through the chief of staff's inspection. Sister Astrid was known to throw out new arrivals she didn't care for, no matter how highly recommended they came. But he'd measured up to her high standards. Scythe Morrison couldn't be happier.

"I am thinking that traveling might be a good course of action at this juncture," the Thunderhead told Greyson that evening, before he removed his vestments and could relax. "I am thinking this in the strongest of ways."

"I already told you I'm not doing a world tour," Greyson told it. "The world comes to me one person at a time. I'm fine with it that way, and until now it's what you've wanted, too."

"I'm not suggesting a world tour, but perhaps an unannounced pilgrimage to places you have not been. Shouldn't it be known that the Toll traveled the world, as prophets have historically done?"

Greyson Tolliver, however, had never suffered from wanderlust. Until his life had been derailed, his hope was to serve the Thunderhead as a Nimbus agent close to home – and if not, then in a single place that would become his home. As far as he was concerned, Lenape City was as much of the world as he needed to see.

"It was merely a suggestion. But I believe it to be an important one," the Thunderhead told him. It was not like the Thunderhead to be insistent when Greyson had made his feelings clear on a matter. Perhaps there would come a time when he would have to uproot himself to help bring the sibilant factions in line, but why now?

"I'll consider it," Greyson said, just to end the conversation. "But right now I need to take a bath and stop thinking about stressful things."

"Of course," said the Thunderhead. "I'll draw it for you."

But the bath the Thunderhead drew was much too hot. Greyson endured it without saying anything, but what was the Thunderhead thinking? Was it punishing him in some passive-aggressive way for not wanting to travel? The Thunderhead wasn't like that. What possible reason could it have for putting him in hot water?

The new pastry chef was supposed to be a culinary genius. And he was. Or at least he was until Scythe Morrison gleaned him and took his place. The truth was, three weeks ago, Scythe Morrison could barely boil water, much less bake a soufflé – but a crash course in dessert making gave him enough basics to fake his way through the short time he needed – and he even had developed a few specialties. He made a mean tiramisu and killer strawberry cheesecake.

He was nervous the first couple of days, and although his inexperienced hands bumbled quite a lot in the kitchen, it turned out to be an effective smoke screen. All new servants here were nervous when they arrived – and, thanks to the severe eye of Sister Astrid, they remained nervous for their entire tenure. Morrison's awkwardness around the kitchen would be read as normal under the circumstances.

Eventually they'd realize that he wasn't the chef they thought he was, but he didn't have to keep up the charade for long. And when he was done, all these nervous little Tonists would be freed from service. Because the holy man they served was about to be gleaned.

"The Thunderhead has been behaving strangely," Greyson told Sister Astrid, who dined with him that night. There was always someone there to dine with, because they didn't want the Toll to ever have to dine alone. Last night it was a visiting curate from Antarctica. The night before it was a woman who created graceful tuning forks for home altars. Rarely was it someone who Greyson actually wanted to dine with, and rarely could he be Greyson. He had to be "on" as the Toll at every meal. Annoying, because his vestments stained easily and were virtually impossible to get as clean as the role demanded, so they were constantly being replaced. He would much prefer to dine in jeans and a T-shirt, but he feared he'd never have that luxury again.

"What do you mean 'strangely'?" Sister Astrid asked.

"Repeating itself," Greyson said. "Doing things that are … unwanted. It's kind of hard to put my finger on. It's just … not itself."

Astrid shrugged. "The Thunderhead's the Thunderhead – it behaves the way it behaves."

"Spoken like a true Tonist," Greyson said. He hadn't meant it as mocking, but Astrid took it that way.

"What I *mean* is that the Thunderhead is a constant. If there's something it's doing that doesn't make sense to you, then maybe *you're* the problem."

Greyson grinned. "You'll make an excellent curate one day, Astrid."

The server put dessert before them. Strawberry cheesecake.

"You should try it," Astrid told Greyson. "And tell me if it's any better than the last chef's."

Greyson took a small piece on his fork and tasted it. It was perfect.

"Wow," he told Astrid. "We finally have a decent dessert chef!"

If nothing else, it purged the Thunderhead from his mind for the few minutes it took to devour it.

Scythe Morrison understood why the gleaning of the Toll needed to be done bloodlessly, and from the inside, rather than a frontal attack. The Tonists guarding the Toll would die for their prophet and were well armed with illegal mortal-age weaponry. They would fight back in ways that ordinary people didn't – so even if an assassination team were successful, the world would know the resistance the Tonists put up. The world must never see that level of resistance against the scythedom. Until now, the best course of action was to just ignore the Toll's existence. The scythedoms of the world hoped that by treating him as insignificant, he would *be* insignificant. But apparently he had become important enough for Goddard to desire his removal. To keep it from being some high-profile, overwrought event, a one-man infiltration was the best way to do it.

The beauty of the plan rested on the Tonists' own self-confidence. They had vetted the new pastry chef extensively before he was approved for the job. It was so easy to alter Morrison's ID and simply slip into the man's shoes after the Tonists were sure it was safe.

He had to admit he was enjoying his position and liked baking much more than he thought he would. Maybe he'd make it his hobby once his business here was done. Hadn't Scythe Curie cooked meals for the families of those she'd gleaned? Perhaps Scythe Morrison could make them dessert.

"Be sure to always bake extra," the sous chef had advised him on his first day there. "The Toll gets the munchies during the night. And it's usually for something sweet."

Priceless information.

"In that case," Morrison had said, "I'll be sure to make desserts that he can't get enough of."

A Testament of the Toll

The Toll faced countless enemies, both in this life and beyond it. When the harbinger of death breached his sanctuary, and wrapped its cold hand around his throat, he refused to yield. Clothed in the rough-and-weathered blue shroud of the grave, death dug its talons into him, and yea, though it stole his earthly existence, it was not the Toll's end. Instead, he was elevated above this world to a higher octave. All rejoice!

Commentary of Curate Symphonius

Do not be misled – death itself is not the enemy, for it is our belief that natural death must come to all in their time. *Unnatural* death is that of which this verse speaks. It is another reference to scythes, which most assuredly did exist – supernatural beings who devoured the souls of the living in order to gain dark magical powers. That the Toll could fight such beings is evidence of his own divinity.

Coda's Analysis of Symphonius

There is no disputing that scythes existed in the time of the Toll, and for all we know they may still exist in the Places Behind. However, to suggest that they devoured souls is a stretch even for Symphonius, who tends to prefer hearsay and conjecture to evidence. It is important to note that scholars have reached a general consensus that scythes did not devour the souls of their victims. They merely consumed their flesh.

23

How to Glean a Holy Man

The Toll was not supposed to tread the halls and courtyards of the Cloisters alone. The curates were constantly telling Greyson this. They were like overprotective parents. Did he have to remind them that there were dozens of guards around the perimeter and on the rooftops? That the Thunderhead's cameras were constantly watching? What the hell were they worried about?

It was a little past two a.m. when Greyson rolled out of bed and put his slippers on.

"What's wrong, Greyson?" the Thunderhead said, even before he was fully out of bed. "Is there something I can do for you?"

More strangeness. It was unlike the Thunderhead to speak without provocation.

"Just having trouble sleeping," he told it.

"Perhaps it's intuition," the Thunderhead said. "Perhaps you're sensing something unpleasant that you can't quite put your finger on."

"The only thing unpleasant that I can't put my finger on lately is you."

The Thunderhead had no response to that.

"If you're unsettled, might I suggest a long-distance journey to calm your nerves?"

"What, right now? In the middle of the night?"

"Yes."

"Just up and leave?"

"Yes."

"Why would that calm my nerves?"

"It would be … a wise course of action at this juncture."

Greyson sighed and moved toward the door.

"Where are you going?" the Thunderhead asked.

"Where do you think? To get something to eat."

"Do not forget to take your earpiece."

"Why? So I can listen to you nagging at me?"

The Thunderhead hesitated for a moment, then said, "I promise I will not. But you need to wear it. I cannot emphasize this strongly enough."

"Fine."

Greyson grabbed the earpiece from his nightstand and slipped it into his ear, if only to shut the Thunderhead up.

The Toll was always kept at a distance from most of the staff. Morrison suspected he had no idea how many people worked behind the scenes of his "simple" life, because they always scurried like mice when they saw him coming. To the Toll, a fortress manned by dozens upon dozens of people appeared to be mostly deserted. It was as the curates wanted it. "The Toll needs his privacy. The Toll needs peace to be alone with his own great thoughts."

Late each night, Morrison could be found in the kitchen, making sauces, preparing batters for the morning pastries, but the real reason was so that he'd be in the kitchen when the Toll came down for a midnight snack.

Finally, five days in, his opportunity came.

After finishing up the pancake batter for the next morning, he turned off the lights and waited in a corner, dozing in and out, when someone in satin pajamas came downstairs and opened the refrigerator. In the oblique light of the fridge, Morrison could see a young man who seemed no older than he, twenty-one or twenty-two at the most. He didn't look like anything special. Certainly not the "holy man" that everyone whispered of, and was so intimidated by. Morrison expected the Toll to have a tangled beard, a wild mane, and crazy eyes. All this guy had was bed hair and eye crust. Morrison took a step out of the darkness.

"Your Sonority," he said.

The Toll flinched, nearly dropping the plate of cheesecake in his hand. "Who's there?"

Morrison came forward into the light of the open refrigerator. "Just the pastry chef, Your Sonority. I didn't mean to frighten you."

"It's okay," the Toll said. "You just caught me by surprise. I'm actually glad to meet you. I've been wanting to tell you what a great job you're doing. You sure are better than the last one."

"Well," said Morrison, "I've been training for years."

It was hard to believe that the Thunderhead would choose this unremarkable, unassuming guy to be its voice on Earth. Maybe the naysayers were right, and it was just a scam. All the more reason to put him out of his misery.

Morrison stepped closer, opened a drawer, and pulled out a fork. He held it out to the Toll. This, Morrison knew, would appear to be a sincere gesture. And it would put him close to the Toll. Close enough to grab him and break his neck.

"I'm glad that you like my baking," Morrison said, handing the fork to him. "It means a lot to me."

The Toll dipped the fork into the cheesecake, took a bite, and savored it.

"I'm glad that you're glad," he said.

Then the Toll raised the fork and jabbed it into Morrison's eye.

Greyson knew.

He knew without question – and not from anything that the Thunderhead had said. He knew because of the Thunderhead's silence.

It suddenly fell into place for Greyson. All this time the Thunderhead had been trying to warn him without actually warning him. The suggestions to leave … They were not about traveling – they were about escaping. And the bath! Being in "hot water." Greyson cursed himself for being too literal a thinker to figure it out. The Thunderhead couldn't directly warn him, because that would be blatant interference in scythe business, which was against the law. The Thunderhead could do countless things, but it was incapable of breaking the law. All it could do was helplessly watch as Greyson was gleaned.

But the silence in his earpiece. That spoke louder than any alarm.

When the chef had stepped out of the shadows and Greyson flinched, it was more than just a flinch. His heart leaped – his fight-or-flight response was nearly triggered. In the past, whenever that happened, the Thunderhead was always quick to soothe him. *It's only the pastry chef,* the Thunderhead should have said in his ear. *He was merely hoping to catch a glimpse of you; please treat him kindly.*

But the Thunderhead didn't say that. It said nothing at all. Which meant the man before him was a scythe, and he was about to be gleaned.

Greyson had never done anything as violent as what he had just done. Even during his days as Slayd Bridger he had never engaged in something so reprehensible as an attack with a sharp object. But he knew it was warranted. He knew the Thunderhead would understand.

And so, with the deed done, he ran for his life from the kitchen without looking back.

Scythe Morrison would have screamed with volume to match the Great Resonance if he'd let himself. But he bit it back into a single yelp and, fighting the pain, pulled the fork from his eye. Unlike many of the new-order scythes, he had not dialed down his pain nanites, so they were already dousing him with megadoses of painkillers, making him woozy and dizzy. He had to fight that as much as the pain, because he needed to stay sharp if he was going to fix this mess.

He had been so close! If only he had dispensed with the charade immediately and done what he'd come to do, the Toll would be dead now. How could Morrison have been so sloppy?

The holy man knew the scythe's intentions – knew his purpose there. Either he was clairvoyant, or the Thunderhead had told him, or something Morrison did had given him away. He should have anticipated the possibility of being exposed.

With one hand on his damaged eye, he took off after the Toll, determined that there'd be no more mistakes. He would complete his mission. It wouldn't be as clean as he wanted it to be – in fact, it would be messy. But it would get done.

"Scythe!" yelled Greyson as he ran from the kitchen. "Help! There's a scythe!"

Someone must have heard him – the stone walls echoed every sound – but they also sent sound bouncing in unexpected directions. All the guards were positioned on the outside, and on the rooftops, not in the residence. By the time they heard him and took action, it might be too late.

"Scythe!"

His slippers were slowing him down, so he got rid of them. The only advantage that Greyson had was that he knew the Cloisters better than his attacker did – and Greyson also had the Thunderhead.

"I know you can't help me," he said to it. "I know it's against the law, but there are things you *can* do."

Still the Thunderhead didn't respond.

Greyson heard a door open behind him. Someone screamed. He couldn't turn around to see who it was or what had happened.

I have to think like the Thunderhead. It can't interfere. It can't do anything of its own will to help me. So what can it do?

The answer was simple when he thought of it that way. The Thunderhead was humanity's servant. Which meant it could follow commands.

"Thunderhead!" said Greyson. "I'm ready to take that

journey now. Awaken the staff and tell them that we'll be leaving immediately."

"Of course, Greyson," it said. And all at once every bedside alarm in the complex began to blare. Every single light came on. The hallways were blinding; the courtyards were doused by floodlights.

He heard someone else yell out behind him. He turned to see a man fall to the ground at the hands of the scythe, who was gaining on Greyson.

"Thunderhead, it's too bright," said Greyson. "It's hurting my eyes. Turn off the lights in the interior corridors."

"Of course," the Thunderhead said calmly. "I'm sorry to have caused you discomfort."

The lights in the hallway went out again. Now he couldn't see a thing, since his pupils had constricted against the bright light. And it would be the same for the scythe! Blinded by light, then blinded by darkness!

Greyson came to a T where the hallway went left and right. Even in the dark he knew the scythe was coming and knew which way he needed to go.

As Morrison left the kitchen, he could see the Toll scrambling ahead of him, kicking off his slippers. The Toll called for help, but Morrison knew he'd reach the Toll before anyone would arrive.

A door opened beside him, and a woman stepped out. No clue who she was. Didn't care. Before she could say anything, he jammed the heel of his hand into her nose, breaking it and sending the bone deep into her brain; she screamed and crumbled to the ground, dead before her head hit the stone. It was his first gleaning of the night, and he was determined that it not be his last.

Then the lights came on bright enough to illuminate the whole hallway. He squinted against the sudden brilliance. Another door opened. The sous chef came out of his room, his bedside alarm blaring inside.

"What's going on out here?"

Morrison punched him in the chest with heart-stopping force, but with only one eye, his depth perception was off. It took a second punch to do the job – and as most Tonists had removed their nanites, there was nothing to restart his heart. He pushed the dying man out of his way and continued after the Toll – but just as quickly as the lights came on, they went off, and when they did, he was in total darkness. Refusing to slow down, he barreled forward and slammed against a stone wall. A dead end? No – as his eyes began to readjust to the dark, he could see the hallway now went off to the left and right. But which passageway had the Toll taken?

Behind him he heard the commotion of the complex waking up, guards being mobilized. They knew there was an intruder now. He had to move fast.

Which way to go? Left or right? He chose left. He had a 50 percent chance of being correct. He'd faced worse odds.

Greyson threw himself down the stairs, then pushed open the door into the garage, where over a dozen cars were parked. "Thunderhead!" he said. "I'm ready for my journey. Open the door to the closest car."

"Door opening," said the Thunderhead. "Enjoy your trip, Greyson."

A car door opened. The light came on inside. Greyson had no intention of leaving the garage – all he had to do was get into that car and close the door. Its glass was unbreakable. Its polycarbonate doors could stop a bullet. Once he was inside, he'd be like a turtle in its shell – the scythe would not be able to get at him no matter how hard he tried.

He lunged for the door—

And behind him, the scythe lurched for his leg, grabbing him and pulling him down just short of safety.

"Nice try," the scythe said. "Almost made it, too."

Greyson spun and squirmed. He knew that the moment the scythe had a good grip on him, it was over. Luckily, his pajamas were slippery satin, and the scythe couldn't get him in a gleaning position.

"You don't want to do this!" Greyson said. "If you glean me, the Thunderhead will be lost to humanity. I'm its only link!"

The scythe put his hand around Greyson's neck. "I don't care."

But there was enough hesitation in his voice that Greyson knew he did care, even only just a little, but that could mean the difference between life and death for Greyson.

"It sees what you're doing," Greyson whispered through his rapidly closing windpipe. "It can't stop you, or even hurt you, but it can punish everyone you've ever loved!"

The pressure on his windpipe eased just a bit. The Thunderhead would never pursue vengeance, but the scythe didn't know that. He'd figure out that it was a bluff, though – maybe just in a moment or two, but every instant won was a victory.

"The Thunderhead has a glorious plan for you!" Greyson said. "It wants you to become High Blade!"

"You don't even know who I am."

"What if I do?"

"You're a liar!"

And then suddenly music began to play in Greyson's ear. A mortal-age song he didn't know, but knew it was playing for a reason. The Thunderhead couldn't help him, but it could lay before him the tools to help himself.

"*'You knew that it would be untrue!'*" Greyson said, repeating the lyric, not sure if he was getting it entirely right. "*'You knew that I would be a liar!'*"

And the scythe's eyes went wide. He froze in disbelief as if those words were a magic spell.

Then Tonist guards flooded the room and grabbed the scythe. He managed to glean two of them with his bare hands before they overwhelmed him and pinned him to the ground.

It was over. Scythe Morrison knew it. They were going to kill him – and the only fire they'd be lighting would be the one to burn his body before it could be revived. He was being ended today at the hands of Tonists. Could there be a more humiliating way to die?

Perhaps it was better this way, he thought. Better than having to face Goddard after such a dismal failure.

But then the Toll stepped forward.

"Stop," he said. "Don't kill him."

"But, Your Sonority," said a man with gray, thinning hair. Not a guard. Maybe one of the priests of their strange religion.

269

"We have to kill him, and quickly. He must be made an example, so that they don't attempt this again."

"Ending his life is just going to start a war we're not ready to fight."

The man was clearly irritated. "Your Sonority, I must advise against—"

"I didn't ask for your opinion, Curate Mendoza. This is *my* call."

Then the Toll turned to the guards. "Lock the scythe up somewhere until I decide what to do with him."

The curate tried once more to protest, but the Toll ignored him, and Morrison was dragged out. Funny, but suddenly the Toll, in his satin pajamas, didn't seem as ridiculous as he had just moments ago. He seemed just a little bit like a holy man.

"What were you thinking?"

Curate Mendoza paced the Toll's suite, furious with him. There were guards at every door and window now, too late to make a difference. Foolish boy, thought Mendoza. He was warned not to go anywhere alone, much less at night. He brought this on himself.

"And why did you let him live? Killing that scythe and burning him would have sent a clear message to Goddard!" Mendoza told him.

"Yes," the Toll agreed. "And that message would be that Tonists are getting too defiant and need to be wiped out."

"He already wants to wipe us out!"

"Wanting to and actually mobilizing his scythes to do it are two different things," the Toll insisted. "The longer we keep

Goddard from boiling over, the more time it gives us to get ready to fight him off. Don't you see that?"

Mendoza crossed his arms. It was obvious to him what was going on here.

"You're a coward!" he said. "You're just afraid to do something so audacious as kill a scythe!"

The Toll stepped forward and squared his shoulders.

"If you call me a coward again, you'll be sent back to your monastery, and that will be the end of your service to me."

"You wouldn't dare!"

"Guard," the Toll said, gesturing to the closest one. "Please escort Curate Mendoza to his chambers and lock him in there until the noon bell for his disrespect."

Without hesitation the guard stepped forward and grabbed the curate, making it clear whose orders he, and all the guards, obeyed.

Mendoza shook the guard off. "I'll walk myself."

But before he left, Mendoza paused, took a deep breath, and turned back to the Toll. "Forgive me, Your Sonority," he said. "I was out of line."

But even to him it sounded far more sycophantic than sincere.

Once Mendoza was gone, Greyson just about collapsed into a chair. It was the first time he had ever stood up to Mendoza like that. But the Toll could not allow himself to be intimidated. Even by the man who had made him. It should have felt good to put the curate in his place, but it didn't. Perhaps that was why the Thunderhead had chosen him over all others; while others were corrupted by power, Greyson didn't even like the taste of it.

Well, maybe he could develop a taste. Perhaps he would need to.

The Cloisters did not have a dungeon. It was only designed to resemble a medieval structure, not actually function as one. Instead, Morrison was relegated to what must have been someone's office in the days when the place had been a museum.

The Tonist guards were not exactly trained for this sort of thing. They didn't have shackles of any sort – such artifacts could only be found in museums today, and not this kind of museum. So they secured him with plastic garden ties that were used for training the bougainvilleas to the stone walls. There were way too many guards. One on each appendage would have done the job, but they put half a dozen on each arm and each leg, and pulled them so tight that Morrison's hands were turning purple and his feet were ice cold. All Morrison could do was wait until his fate was decided.

It must have been around dawn when he heard a conversation just outside the closed door.

"But, Your Sonority," he heard one of the guards say. "You shouldn't go in there; he's dangerous."

"Do you have him tied up?" he heard the Toll ask.

"Yes."

"Can he break free?"

"No, we made sure he couldn't."

"Then I don't see the problem."

The door opened. The Toll stepped in. He closed the door behind him. His bed hair had been combed, and he was now wearing a ritualistic outfit. It looked uncomfortable.

Scythe Morrison didn't know whether to thank the Toll for saving him or curse him for leaving him like this, bested and humiliated.

"So," Morrison said sulkily. "The Thunderhead has a plan for me, huh?"

"I was lying," the Toll said. "You're a scythe; the Thunderhead can't have a plan for you. It can't have anything to do with you."

"But it told you who I was."

"Not really. But I eventually figured it out. Scythe Morrison, right? Your Patron Historic wrote those lyrics I recited."

He didn't respond, just waited for whatever came next.

"Your eye looks like it's healed already."

"Almost," Morrison said. "Still blurry."

"Most Tonists remove their healing nanites – did you know that? I think it's pretty stupid."

Morrison met his gaze, blinking his healing eye to get a gauge on the Toll. The Tonists' spiritual leader calling their behavior stupid? Was this a test? Was he supposed to disagree? Agree?

"Isn't there a mortal-age word for what you're saying?" Morrison said. "Blastony? Blasmony? *Blasphemy* – that's it."

The Toll looked him over for a moment before he spoke again. "Do you believe that the Thunderhead speaks to me?"

Morrison didn't want to answer the question, but what did it matter now? "Yes, I believe it," he admitted. "I wish I didn't, but I do."

"Good. That will make this easier." Then the Toll sat down in a chair across from him. "The Thunderhead didn't choose me because

I was a Tonist. I'm not – not really. It chose me because … well, because someone had to be chosen. The Tonists were the first to believe it, though. My appearance fit with their doctrine. So now I'm the Toll – the Tone made flesh. The funny thing is, I once wanted to be a Nimbus agent. Now I'm *the* Nimbus agent."

"Why are you telling me all this?"

The Toll shrugged. "Because I feel like it. Haven't you heard? The Toll can do whatever the Toll feels like. Almost like a scythe."

Silence fell between them. It felt awkward to Morrison, but it didn't seem to feel that way to the Toll. He just stared at Morrison, pondering, cogitating, thinking whatever deep thoughts a holy man who wasn't actually holy thought.

"We're not going to tell Goddard that you failed in your mission."

That was something Morrison wasn't expecting to hear. "You're not?"

"See, the thing is, no one, not even the scythedom, knows who the Toll actually is. You gleaned four people last night. Who's to say that one of them wasn't the Toll? And if I suddenly vanish from public view, without explanation, it's going to look like you succeeded."

Morrison shook his head. "Goddard's going to find out eventually."

"*Eventually* is the keyword. He won't find out until we're ready for him to. That could be years, if we want it to be."

"He'll know something's wrong when I don't come back."

"No, he'll just think you were captured and burned. And the sad thing is, he won't even care."

274

Morrison could not deny that the Toll was right. Goddard wouldn't care. Not in the least.

"Like I said, the Thunderhead doesn't have a plan for you," the Toll told Morrison, "but I do."

Greyson knew he had to sell this and sell it well. And he had to read this scythe like he'd never read anyone before. Because if he miscalculated, it would be disastrous.

"I've been reading up on mortal-age customs when it comes to leaders during dangerous times," Greyson said. "In some cultures, rulers and spiritual leaders were protected by trained assassins. I'd feel much safer with one of those than these Tonists who think they're guards."

The scythe shook his head, incredulous at the suggestion. "You put out my eye, and now you want me to work for you?"

Greyson shrugged. "Your eye grew back, and you need a job," he said. "Or would you rather go back to Goddard and tell him that you failed? That a weakling in pajamas stabbed you in the eye and escaped? I don't think that will sit very well with him."

"How do you know I won't glean you the second you set me free?"

"Because I don't think you're that stupid. Being the Toll's personal scythe is much better than anything Goddard would ever offer you, and you know it."

"I would be the laughingstock of the scythedom."

Greyson offered him the faintest of grins. "Aren't you already, Scythe Morrison?"

* * *

Morrison had no way of knowing how much the Toll knew about him. But it was true – Morrison wasn't respected, and nothing he had done changed that. But if he stayed here, the other scythes wouldn't even know he was still alive ... and he *would* be respected. Maybe it was only by Tonists, but it was still respect, and that was something he desperately wanted.

"I'll tell you what," said the Toll. "Why don't I take the first leap of faith." Then he pulled out a pair of scissors and, amazingly, began cutting Morrison's bonds. He started down at his feet, then moved up to his arms, slowly, meticulously snipping each one.

"The curates won't be happy," the Toll said as he snipped. "Screw the curates."

Then, when the last bond was cut, Morrison leaped up and clamped a hand around the Toll's throat.

"You just made the biggest mistake of your life!" Morrison growled.

"Go ahead, glean me," the Toll said, not an ounce of fear in his voice. "You'll never escape. Even with their bumbling, you can't get past so many guards. It's not like you're Scythe Lucifer."

That just made him squeeze a little bit tighter – tight enough to shut him up. The Toll was right – right about so many things. If Morrison completed his mission, he'd be killed and burned by the Tonists outside that door. They'd both be dead, and the only winner would be Goddard.

"Are you done?" the Toll rasped.

And somehow, having him in this position, knowing that he could glean the Toll if he wanted to – was just as satisfying as actually gleaning him. But without the unpleasant consequence of having to die as well. Morrison released his grip, and the Toll sucked in a deep breath.

"So what do I do now? Take a pledge of loyalty?" said Morrison, only half joking.

"A simple handshake will do," the Toll said. Then he put out his hand. "My real name is Greyson. But you'll have to call me Your Sonority."

Morrison gripped the Toll's hand with the same one that had been at the Toll's throat a moment ago. "My real name's Joel. But you'll have to call me Jim."

"It's good to meet you, Jim."

"Same here, Your Sonority."

Scythe Morrison had to admit this was the last way he had expected this day to go, but all things considered, he couldn't complain.

And he didn't. For more than two years.

Part Three

YEAR OF THE COBRA

There is, I believe, a destiny for us. A glorious culmination of all it means to be human and immortal. Destiny, however, does not come without exhaustive effort and clear-minded leadership.

The Year of the Raptor was devastating to us all, but by the Year of the Ibex we had begun to heal. The Year of the Quokka saw us further aligning our ideals and priorities as scythes. Now, on the first day of this new year, I see only hope for the days ahead.

Here, at this First Continental Conclave, I wish to publicly thank High Blades Pickford of WestMerica, Hammerstein of EastMerica, Tizoc of Mexiteca, and MacPhail of NorthernReach for their faith in me. That they – and you, the scythes under them – have chosen me to shepherd North Merica as your continental Overblade is beyond validation; it is a clear mandate to push forward with our new-order objective. Together we will create a world that is not only perfect, but also pristine. A world where the broad and powerful swath of each scythe brings us ever closer to that singular goal.

I know that there are still those among you who, like the recalcitrant LoneStar region, are not sure that mine is the right path. The uneasy among you look for "method in the madness," as they say. But I ask you, is it madness to want to lift the human species to new heights? Is it wrong to have a vision of a future as crystal clear and finely cut as the diamonds on our hands? Of course not.

I wish to make it clear that your High Blades will not be abdicating their positions. They will still be stewards of your respective regions, responsible for local administration – however, they will now be free from the burden of more cumbersome policy decisions. Those larger issues are left to me. And I promise that I will live for no other purpose but to lead you tirelessly into the future.

—*From the ascension address of His Excellency,*
Overblade Robert Goddard,
January 1st, Year of the Cobra

24

Rats in a Ruin

Fort Saint-Jean and Fort Saint-Nicolas were built on either side of the entrance to the port of Marseille, in what was now the FrancoIberian region of Europe. What was odd about these forts, built by King Louis XIV, was not the fact that they had large cannons, but that those cannons were not aimed toward the sea to protect the fort from invaders. Instead, they were pointed inland, toward the bustling city of Marseille, to protect the king's interests from a public uprising.

Robert Goddard, Overblade of North Merica, had taken a page from King Louis's book and mounted heavy artillery in the sixty-eighth-floor garden around his crystal chalet, aiming down at the streets of Fulcrum City below. They were installed long before his ascension to Overblade – shortly after he announced that the Toll had been gleaned.

He had thought that gleaning their so-called prophet would stand as a warning to Tonists the world over, and a reminder that if scythes were not respected, they should be feared. Instead, Tonists went from a persistent nuisance to a growing danger.

"This is nothing we didn't expect," Goddard claimed. "Change will always face resistance, but we must forge forward in spite of it."

Never once did Goddard consider that the escalation in

violence against the scythedoms of the world was brought on by his own order to glean the Toll.

"Your greatest flaw," Underscythe Constantine dared to tell him, "is that you fail to understand the concept of martyrdom."

He would have banished Constantine on the spot if the man hadn't been needed to bring the stubborn LoneStar region in line with the rest of North Merica. That region had become a refuge for Tonists now. "It serves Texas right," Goddard proclaimed. "Let it be overrun by them like rats in a ruin."

The Overblade's crystalline chalet had changed over the past few years. Not just the city-aimed weaponry, but the crystal itself was different. Goddard had had the outer glass reinforced and acid treated, so that it could no longer be seen through. The result was that when you were in the chalet, it appeared, day or night, that Fulcrum City was shrouded in perpetual fog.

Goddard was convinced that the Tonists had spy drones. He was convinced that other forces were banding against him as well. He was convinced that unfriendly regions were aiding those forces.

Whether or not any of these things were true didn't matter. He acted as if they were. Which meant it was Goddard's truth – and what was true for Goddard became true for the world. Or at least every part of the world where he had smudged his indelible fingerprint.

"Things will settle," he told the nearly two thousand scythes who had gathered for the First Continental Conclave. "People will get used to the way things are, see that it is for the best, and they'll settle."

But until then, the windows would remain fogged, the troublesome would be gleaned, and the silent guns would point resolutely at the city below.

Goddard was still reeling from the botched Amazonian raid. High Blade Pickford had failed to apprehend Scythe Anastasia. It wasn't the first time that she'd disappointed him, but there was not much he could do about her. At least not now. Goddard did foresee a time when he would appoint the High Blades of other North Merican regions, rather than leaving it to the unpredictable voting process in conclaves.

Pickford's saving grace was that she did manage to catch Rowan Damisch, who was at this very instant on his way to Fulcrum City. That would have to suffice until the girl was apprehended. Hopefully Anastasia would be so consumed by running and hiding, that she wouldn't be able to make much trouble. In retrospect, he should have maintained the Perimeter of Reverence in the waters above Endura. He had been worried that a salvage might reveal evidence of what really happened. He never dreamed it might lead to this.

The morning brought other business, and Goddard had to put aside his frustration, which was much harder to do than it used to be.

"High Blade Shirase of RossShelf is on his way up, with a sizeable entourage," Underscythe Franklin informed him.

"And are they 'of one mind'?" Rand quipped.

Goddard chuckled slightly, but Franklin never gave Rand the slightest of courtesy laughs. "Their minds are less important than the crates they're carrying," she said.

Goddard met them in the conference room, after making them wait five minutes, because Goddard always wanted to make sure his guests – even his important ones – knew that *his* schedule mattered more than theirs.

"Nobu!" said Goddard, and went over to High Blade Shirase like an old friend. "A pleasure to see you! How are things in Antarctica?"

"Things are well," he said.

"Is life but a dream?" offered Rand.

"On occasion," said Shirase, missing the slight on the unique nature of his region. "But only when we have to row our own boats, I suppose."

Now Underscythe Franklin offered up a courtesy laugh, but it created more tension than it dispersed.

Goddard glanced at the crates, each held by a member of the BladeGuard. There were only eight of them. Other regions came with at least ten crates. But the lower number could simply mean they were more densely packed.

"To what do I owe this visit, Your Excellency?" Goddard asked, as if everyone there didn't already know.

"On behalf of the RossShelf region, I would like to present you with a gift. It is our hope that it will help formalize our relationship with you."

Then he nodded to the BladeGuards, who placed the crates on the conference table and opened them. As expected, the crates were full of scythe diamonds.

"These represent RossShelf's share of the diamonds raised from the ruins of Endura," Shirase said.

"Impressive," said Goddard. "Are these all of them?"

"All of them, yes."

Goddard looked over the sparkling contents, then turned to Shirase. "I accept your gift with humility, and honor, in the spirit of friendship with which they were given. And whenever you need gems for the bejeweling of future scythes, they will be available to you." Then he gestured to the door. "Please follow Underscythe Franklin – she will escort you to my dining room, where I've prepared a brunch for us," Goddard said. "Traditional Antarctic fare, as well as regional specialties of MidMerica. A feast to consummate our friendship. I'll be along momentarily, and we'll discuss issues of concern to both our regions."

Franklin escorted them out just as Nietzsche entered.

"Give me good news, Freddy," Goddard said.

"Well, we've been tracking Anastasia south," he said. "There's only so far south she can go before being cornered in Tierra del Fuego."

Goddard sighed. "The Land of Fire will not cooperate. Let's up our efforts to catch her before she gets there."

"We're doing all we can," Nietzsche said.

"Do more," Goddard told him.

He turned to see Scythe Rand running her hand through the diamonds in one of the crates. "Are we going to count them, or do you trust Shirase?"

"It's not the number that matters, Ayn, but the gesture. The trove we are creating is simply a means to an end. A symbol of something far more valuable than diamonds."

Even so, Goddard knew he would hurl them all into the sea in exchange for having Scythe Anastasia in his hands.

25

Sunlight and Shadow

Though helping Anastasia escape Amazonia was fraught with
strife, that strife had receded to the horizon behind the *Spence*
– which was now, Jerico mused, no longer a salvage ship, but a
rescue vessel.

The seas were easy as Amazonia faded behind them, and
the sun rose before them. By nine o'clock all signs of land were
gone, and the bright morning sky was dotted with occasional
puffs of meandering clouds. Jeri would have much preferred a
low cloud cover today – or even better, a soup-thick fog – for
if those North Merican scythes figured out that Anastasia was
traveling by sea, the *Spence* could be targeted and sunk.

"Rest assured they won't come after you," Possuelo had
told Jeri. "I made sure they intercepted a 'secret' communiqué I
sent, and they took the bait. As far as the North Mericans know,
Anastasia is weaving a circuitous route south by train all the way
to the Land of Fire, where the region's High Blade is supposed
to have offered her sanctuary. And to make the story stick, we're
leaving glaring traces of her DNA for them to find along the
way. It will be days before they realize it's a wild-goose chase!"

It was clever enough. Northern scythes saw Amazonians
as too simple to concoct such a ploy, and the Land of Fire, Jeri
knew, would be suitably uncooperative with the North Mericans.

The scythes down there were obstreperous to an extreme.

At full speed, they would reach safe harbor in just under three days.

From the bridge, Jeri could see the turquoise figure of Scythe Anastasia at the starboard rail, looking out over the sea. She was not supposed to be alone – Possuelo had made that clear – and perhaps his paranoia was justified, considering that he had been betrayed by one of his own. Jeri trusted the crew of the *Spence* implicitly; they had grown fiercely loyal to their captain. Even so, it was always wise to take precautions.

The only reason Anastasia would be alone would be if she ordered the officer assigned to her out of her presence. The command of a scythe overruled the orders of a captain. Sure enough, Jeri saw the officer one deck up, keeping a tight eye on her from a distance. It seemed that the only way to effectively guard the willful scythe was to do it personally.

"She's going to be a handful," Chief Wharton said.

"To be sure," said Jeri. "But a handful of what, we don't know."

"Misery?" suggested the chief.

"Perhaps, perhaps not." Then Jeri left the bridge to join her at the rail.

She wasn't looking down at the water. She wasn't looking at the horizon, either. It was as if she was gazing at something ⌐t wasn't there.

⌐ contemplating a leap?" Jeri asked, breaking what
⌐ layer of ice. "Should I be worried?"

⌐at Jeri, then returned her gaze to the sea.

⌐g down below," she said. "I thought being

on deck might calm me down. Have you heard from Possuelo?"

"I have."

"What does he say about Rowan?"

Jeri took a moment before responding. "He didn't say, and I didn't ask."

"Then he's been captured," Anastasia said, and pounded the rail in frustration. "I'm sailing to freedom, and he's been captured."

Jeri half expected her to order the ship to turn around and go back for him. If she did, they'd have to oblige, for she was a scythe. But she didn't. She was wise enough to know that it would only make matters worse.

"I cannot, for the life of me, understand your devotion to Scythe Lucifer," Jeri dared to say.

"You know nothing about it."

"I know more than you think. I was there with Possuelo when we opened the vault. I saw you in each other's arms. It was the kind of intimacy not even death could hide."

Anastasia averted her gaze. "We shed our clothes so the cold would kill us before we suffocated."

Jeri smiled. "I suspect that is only a half-truth."

She turned and considered Jeri for a long moment, then changed the subject. "Jerico – that's an unusual name. I seem to recall a mortal-age story involving a wall coming down. Are you a collapser of walls?"

"You could say I find things in the ruins of walls that have already fallen," Jeri told her. "Honestly, though, it's a family name that has no bearing on the story of Jericho. But if you find off-putting, you can call me Jeri. Everyone does."

"Okay. And what are your pronouns, Jeri?"

Jeri found it refreshing that she asked so directly. There were still people who were too awkward to ask – as if Jeri was being accidentally ambiguous, and not intentionally so.

"He, she, they, zhey – pronouns are tiresome and lazy things," Jeri said. "I'd much rather call a person by name. But to answer your deeper question, I'm both male and female. It comes with being Madagascan."

Anastasia nodded knowingly. "You must find us binary people strange and confusing."

"I did when I was younger. I never met someone born to a single gender until I was well into my teens. But I've come to accept, and even appreciate, your quirky rigidity."

"So, you see yourself as both – but I imagine there must be times when you're more one than another."

Not only direct, but insightful, too, Jeri thought, liking this resurrected scythe more and more. *She asks the right questions.*

"You could say it's dictated by the heavens," Jeri told her. "When skies are clear, I choose to be a woman. When they are not, I am a man." Jeri turned to take in the sunlight shimmering on the surface of the sea. It was marked by the shadows of the occasional cloud, but right now the ship did not fall beneath one of those shadows. "At this moment in time, I am a woman."

"I see," she said, without the judgment that some might show. "My father – who's a scholar of the mortal age – said that the sun is almost always seen as masculine in mythology, and of course there's the man in the moon. Choosing to be feminine in their light creates a balance. There's a natural yin and yang to it."

"And to you as well," Jeri said. "After all, turquoise is symbolically the color of balance."

Anastasia smiled. "I didn't know that. I chose it because it's the color my brother wanted me to be."

An inner shadow seemed to cross her face. A pang at the thought of her brother. Jeri decided it was too personal a heartache to delve into, and allowed her privacy on the matter.

"Does it bother you," she asked, "to always be at the mercy of the weather? I would think that someone like you would want to be subservient to as few things as possible. Besides, it must be awfully inconvenient on partially cloudy days like this."

As if on cue, the sun slipped behind a small cloud, then out again. Jeri laughed. "Yes, it can be inconvenient, but I've gotten used to it – embraced it, even. That unpredictability has become part of who I am."

"I've often wondered what it would have been like to have been born in the Madagascan region," Anastasia said. "Not that I'm really interested in being a man – but I wonder what it would have been like to explore both sides when I was too young to know the difference."

"That's the whole point of it," Jeri told her. "And the reason why so many people go to Madagascar as a place to raise their children."

Anastasia considered it a few moments more. "I suppose, if I divided my time between land and sea as you do, I might choose to be one way on land, and another at sea. That way my gender wouldn't be at the mercy of the winds."

"Well, I would enjoy your company either way."

"Hmmm," Anastasia said coyly. "Flirting with me in sunlight.

It makes me wonder if you'd also do that in a storm."

"One of the benefits of being Madagascan is that we see people as people. When it comes to attraction, gender is never part of the equation." Then Jeri looked up as the light dimmed slightly. "You see? The sun has passed behind a cloud again, and nothing has changed."

Then Anastasia stepped back from the railing, a gentle smirk still on her face. "I think I've had enough of both sunlight and shadows for now. Good day, Captain." Then she turned to go below, her robe fluttering behind her like a loose sail in a gentle breeze.

26

A Receptacle for the World's Hatred

Rowan did not know any of the things that had transpired during his three-year absence. Unlike Citra, no one briefed him. Anything he picked up, he learned in passing. He did know that Goddard was in charge of most of North Merica now – which wasn't good for anyone and was definitely not good for Rowan.

Now he stood tied to a glass column in the center of Goddard's crystal chalet. Wasn't there an expression about glass houses and throwing stones? Well, if he had a stone, he wouldn't throw it. He'd hide it until he could use it for something more effective.

He had been revived the day before, just as High Blade Pickford said he would be. Death was not good enough for Scythe Lucifer. Knowing Goddard, his end would be filled with much pomp and pageantry.

Goddard came to see him with Scythe Rand by his side as always. The expression on Goddard's face was not one of fury. It was actually welcoming. Warm – if a cold-blooded thing could ever be said to have a warm expression. It threw Rowan for a loop. Made him uncertain. Rand, on the other hand, looked worried, and Rowan knew why.

"My dearest Rowan," Goddard said, arms wide as if moving in for a hug, yet stopping a few yards away.

"Surprised to see me?" Rowan asked, as flip as he could force himself to be.

"Nothing surprises me about you, Rowan," Goddard said. "But I'll admit I'm impressed that you managed to come back after the sinking of Endura."

"Which you sank."

"On the contrary," Goddard said. "*You* sank it. That's what the record shows and will always show."

If he was trying to get a rise out of Rowan, it wasn't working. He had already made his peace with bad publicity. When he chose to become Scythe Lucifer, he knew he'd be hated. Of course, he just expected it to be hatred among scythes. He never thought he'd be despised by the rest of the world.

"You seem happy to see me," Rowan observed. "That's probably because of the physiology of the body you stole. Tyger's body reacting to seeing his best friend."

"Perhaps," said Goddard, glancing at Tyger's hands, as if they might actually grow mouths and say something to him. "But the rest of me is happy to see you as well! You see, as a boogeyman, Scythe Lucifer is a nuisance. But as an actual man, he's someone I can use for the betterment of humankind."

"The betterment of Goddard, you mean."

"What's good for me is good for the world – you must realize that by now," Goddard said. "I see the larger picture, Rowan. I always have. And now, by showing the world that Scythe Lucifer is subject to judgment, it will help people to rest a little easier."

Through all of this, Scythe Rand said nothing. She had taken a seat and was watching. Waiting to see what Rowan would do. What accusations he'd make. After all, she was the one who'd set

Rowan free on Endura. He could be quite a fly in her ointment. But that would be no better than throwing a stone.

"If you're hoping to be remembered, don't worry, you will be. Once you've been gleaned, your name will be an eternal receptacle for the world's hatred. You're infamous, Rowan – you should embrace that! It's the only fame you'll ever have, and much more than you deserve. Consider it a gift for all we've been to each other."

"You really are enjoying yourself, aren't you?"

"Oh, immensely," admitted Goddard. "You can't imagine how many times I've stood here pondering all the ways I could torment you!"

"Who will you torment when I'm gone?"

"I'm sure I'll find someone. Or maybe I won't need to. Maybe you're the last thorn in my side I'll ever have to deal with."

"Naah – there's always another thorn."

Goddard clapped his hands together, truly tickled. "I have so missed these conversations with you!"

"You mean the ones where you gloat, and I'm tied up?"

"You see? The way you get to the heart of the matter is always so refreshing. So entertaining. I'd keep you as a house pet, if I didn't fear you'd somehow escape and burn me to a crisp in my sleep."

"I would, and I would," Rowan told him.

"I have no doubt. Well, rest assured you won't be escaping today. We no longer have the blunderings of Scythe Brahms to deal with."

"Why? Was he devoured by sharks like the rest of them?"

"Yes, I'm sure he was," Goddard said, "but he was dead before they got to him. Punishment for having allowed you to escape."

"Right." Rowan said nothing more about it. But he did catch Rand out of the corner of his eye shifting in her chair as if it had suddenly grown hot.

Goddard came closer to him. His voice became softer. "You might not believe this, but I really *have* missed you, Rowan." There was an honesty to this simple statement that transcended Goddard's habitual showmanship. "You're the only one who dares to speak back to me anymore. I have adversaries, yes, but they're all pushovers. Easily bested. You were different from the beginning."

He took a step back and looked Rowan over, appraising him, the way one might appraise a faded painting that had lost its allure. "You could have been my first underscythe," Goddard said. "An heir to the world scythedom – and make no mistake, there *will* be a single world scythedom when I'm done with it. *That* would have been your future."

"If only I had ignored my conscience."

Goddard shook his head in pity. "Conscience is a tool, just like any other. If you don't wield it, it wields you – and from what I can see, it has bludgeoned you senseless. No, the world needs the unity that I offer far more than it needs your simplistic understanding of right and wrong."

The thing about Goddard was that he always came close enough to making sense that it was demoralizing. He could twist your own thoughts until they were no longer yours, but his. That's what made him so dangerous.

Rowan found his defiance and fortitude draining away. Was Goddard right about anything? A voice inside him said no, but that voice was spiraling deep into its shell.

"What's going to happen to me?" Rowan asked.

Goddard leaned close and whispered in his ear.

"A reckoning."

Scythe Rand thought all this was behind her. She had been on one of her construct-sanctum excursions when word came that Scythe Lucifer was alive and in Amazonia. The mission to retrieve him from the Amazonians took place without her knowledge. He was already en route when Goddard told her the "glorious news."

It was terrible timing. With more warning, she would have found a way to glean him before he reached Goddard, if only to keep his mouth shut.

But here he was, and his mouth stayed shut anyway. At least about her. Did he keep the secret just to see her squirm? Ayn wondered what his game was.

This time Goddard wasn't so cavalier as to leave Rowan alone in his room. Two guards were assigned to be in there with him. They were ordered to keep their distance, and their eyes on him at all times.

"You'll check on him every hour," Goddard told Ayn. "To see that he hasn't loosened his restraints or compromised the guards."

"You should render them deaf, so he can't subvert them," she suggested. It was meant as a joke, but Goddard took it seriously.

"Sadly, they'd heal within an hour."

So instead of deafening the guards, silence was achieved the old-fashioned way. Rowan was gagged. However, when Ayn came to check on Rowan that afternoon, he had managed to work the gag off. He was all smiles in spite of being practically hog-tied.

"Hi, Ayn," he said brightly. "Having a good day?"

"Haven't you heard?" she quipped back. "Every day's a good day since Goddard became Overblade."

"We're sorry, Your Honor," said one of the guards. "Since we were ordered to keep our distance, we couldn't replace the gag. Perhaps you can do it."

"What's he been saying?"

"Nothing," said the other guard. "He's been singing a song that was popular a few years ago. He tried to get us to sing along, but we didn't."

"Good," said Ayn. "I applaud your restraint."

Through all this, Rowan's smile didn't fade. "You know, Ayn, I could have told Goddard that you were the one who set me free back on Endura."

Just like that. He just laid it out there for the two guards to hear.

"Lying will get you nowhere," she said for the sake of the guards, then ordered them both to wait outside the room – which, in a place where so many of the internal walls were still clear glass, didn't hide anything from view, but at least the room was soundproof once the door closed.

"I don't think they believed you," Rowan said. "You really didn't sell it."

"You're right," said Ayn. "Which means I'll have to glean them now. Their deaths are on your hands."

"Your blade, not mine," he said.

She took a moment to glance at the two guards, oblivious on the other side of the glass wall. The problem wasn't gleaning them but hiding the fact that it was her doing. She'd have to order some low-level scythe to do it, and then persuade the scythe to self-glean – and all in such a way that it wouldn't seem suspicious. What a mess.

"Setting you free was the worst decision I ever made."

"Not the worst," Rowan said. "Not even close."

"Why *didn't* you tell Goddard? What possible reason could you have?"

Rowan shrugged. "You did me a favor, and I returned it. Now we're even. And besides," he added. "You undermined him once. Maybe you'll do it again."

"Things have changed."

"Have they? I still don't see him treating you the way he should. Has he ever told *you* what he told me today? That you'd be the heir to the world scythedom? No? Seems to me that he treats you the way he treats everyone else. Like a servant."

Ayn took a deep breath, suddenly feeling very much alone. In most things, she enjoyed being a party of one, but this was different. What she really felt was a complete lack of allies. Like everyone in the world was an enemy. And maybe they were. She hated the fact that this smug boy could make her feel that way. "You're much more dangerous than he gives you credit for," she told him.

"But you're still here listening to me. Why?"

She didn't want to consider the question. Instead she ran through her mind all the ways she could glean him right then and there, and damn the consequences. But if she gleaned him, she knew it wouldn't take. There was no way to render him unrevivable there in the penthouse, which meant Goddard would just bring him back to face the very specific judgment he had planned. And then, when he was revived, maybe Rowan *would* tell Goddard everything. She was bound just as completely as Rowan was.

"Not that it matters, but I just want to know," Rowan said. "Do you agree with everything he does? Do you think he's taking the world in the right direction?"

"There *is* no right direction. There's only a direction that makes things better for our kind, and directions that don't."

"By 'our kind,' do you mean scythes?"

"What else would I mean?"

"The scythes were meant to make the world better for everyone. Not the other way around."

If he thought she cared, he was barking up the wrong tree. Ethics and morality were the hobgoblins of the old guard. Her conscience was clear, because she had none, and had always taken pride in that.

"He means to publicly end you," she told Rowan. "And by publicly, I mean in a way that will leave no doubt in anyone's mind that Scythe Lucifer is gone forever. Vanquished and extinguished for all time."

"Is that what you want?"

"I will not mourn you," Rand told him, "and when you're gone, I'll be relieved."

He accepted it as true, because it was. "You know, Scythe Rand – there's going to come a point when Goddard's ego gets so far out of control that even *you* can see the danger of it – but by then he'll be so powerful, there won't be anyone left to challenge him."

Ayn wanted to deny it, but she felt gooseflesh rising. Her own physiology telling her that there was truth in what he said. No, she wouldn't mourn Scythe Lucifer. But once he was gone, there would still be plenty to worry about.

"You really are just like him," she said. "You both twist people's minds until they don't know which way is up. So you'll excuse me if I never speak to you again."

"You will," Rowan said with absolute certainty. "Because after he ends me, he'll make you dispose of whatever's left of me, the way you disposed of what was left of Tyger. And then, when no one's listening, you'll snipe at my charred bones, just so you can have the last word. Maybe you'll even spit on them. But it won't make you feel any better."

And it was infuriating. Because she knew he was right on every count.

27

Tenkamenin's Pleasure Dome

The *Spence* traversed the Atlantic with Scythe Anastasia, sailing a direct course for the region of SubSahara, on the Afric continent. It was a distance much shorter than most people might think, taking just under three days. They arrived in the coastal town of Port Remembrance while the North Merican scythes were still searching for Anastasia in the far reaches of South Merica.

In mortal days, Port Remembrance had been known as Monrovia, but the Thunderhead decided that the region's dark history of subjugation and slavery, followed by poorly planned repatriation, warranted an entirely new name that would offend absolutely no one. Naturally, people were offended. But the Thunderhead stuck to its decision – and, as with all decisions the Thunderhead made, it turned out to be the right one.

Scythe Anastasia was met by SubSahara's High Blade Tenkamenin himself upon her arrival – as a vocal opponent of Goddard, he had agreed to provide her secret sanctuary.

"So much ado about a junior scythe!" he said in a booming, genial voice as he greeted her. His robe was colorful and meticulously designed to pay homage to every historical culture in the region. "Not to worry, little one, you're safe and among friends."

While Citra found Possuelo's *meu anjo* – my angel –

endearing, being called "little one" felt diminutive. She held her head high as Scythe Anastasia and, in the name of diplomacy, did not comment. Instead Jeri did.

"Not so little," Jeri said.

The High Blade threw Jeri a dubious gaze. "And you are?"

"Jerico Soberanis, captain of the vessel that so successfully brought Scythe Anastasia into your welcoming arms."

"I've heard of you," Tenkamenin said. "A scavenger of note."

"Salvager," Jeri corrected. "I find what's lost, and fix things that are beyond repair."

"Noted," said Tenkamenin. "Thank you for your fine service." Then the High Blade put a fatherly arm around Anastasia, leading her away from the dock with his entourage. "Oh, but you must be tired and hungry for something more than maritime fare. We have all things prepared for your comfort."

Jeri, however, kept pace with them until Tenkamenin asked, "Have you not been paid? Surely Possuelo has taken care of that."

"I'm sorry, Your Excellency," Jeri said, "but Scythe Possuelo specifically assigned me to be by Scythe Anastasia's side at all times. I sincerely hope you're not asking me to violate that order."

The High Blade heaved a dramatic sigh. "Very well," he said, then turned to his entourage as if it was a single entity. "Set an extra place for our fine Madagascan captain at dinner and prepare an adequate room."

Finally, Anastasia spoke up. "Adequate will not be adequate," she told the High Blade. "Jerico risked everything to bring me here, and should be treated with the same courtesy as you treat me."

The entourage braced for something volcanic, but after a moment, the High Blade laughed heartily.

"Spunk," he said, "is highly valued here. We will get along!" Then he turned to Jeri. "Captain, forgive me, but I love to toy. I mean nothing by it. You are most welcome here as an esteemed guest, and will be treated as such."

Jeri had received no such order from Possuelo. Jerico was told to bring Anastasia here and the job would be done. Jeri, however, was not ready to part ways with the turquoise scythe – and besides, the crew of the *Spence* was overdue for some downtime. The western shores of SubSahara would be a welcome leave. And that freed Jeri to keep an eye on Anastasia, and the High Blade, who seemed a little too ingratiating.

"Do you trust him?" Jeri asked Anastasia before they got into the sedans that would spirit them to Tenkamenin's palace.

"Possuelo does," Anastasia said. "That's good enough for me."

"Possuelo also trusted that junior scythe who sold you out to Goddard," Jeri pointed out. Anastasia had no response to that. "I will be your second pair of eyes," Jeri told Anastasia.

"Probably not necessary, but I appreciate it," she said.

Jeri was usually about the bottom line but found that Anastasia's appreciation was payment enough for services rendered.

Tenkamenin, who went by Tenka to those close to him, had a disarming and effusive nature to go with his deep voice – a voice that resounded even when he whispered. Citra found it endearing as well as intimidating. She resolved to put aside Citra

Terranova and be Scythe Anastasia at all times around him.

She noted that Tenkamenin's genetic index leaned a bit toward Afric. Understandable, as this was the continent that had contributed those genes to humanity's biological mélange. Anastasia, herself, had a tinge more Afric in her than PanAsian, Caucasoid, Mesolatino, or any of the subindexes that were corralled under "other." As they rode together, Tenkamenin read it in her and commented on it.

"We're not supposed to notice these things," he said, "but I do. All it means is that we are a teeny bit more closely related."

His residence was more than just a residence. Tenkamenin had built himself a stately pleasure dome.

"I do not call it Xanadu, as Kublai Khan did," he told Anastasia. "Besides, Scythe Khan had absolutely no taste. The Mongolian scythedom was right to bulldoze it the moment he self-gleaned."

The palace was, like Tenka himself, stylish and the epitome of good taste. "I am no parasite, taking over estates and mansions that belong to others, then kicking them out," he told her proudly. "This place was built from the ground up! I invited entire communities to work, and filled their idle time with rewarding labor. And still they work, adding more each year. Not because I ask them to, but because it is their pleasure."

Although Anastasia initially doubted it was their choice, her conversations with the workers proved her wrong. They truly did love Tenka, and the time they devoted to working on his palace was entirely of their own accord. It didn't hurt that he paid far above and beyond the Basic Income Guarantee.

The palace was full of old-world eccentricities that were

whimsical and added to the flavor of the place. The anachronistic uniforms of the staff were all from different historical eras. A collection of classic toys going back hundreds of years. And then there were the phones. Boxy plastic things of various colors that sat on tables or hung on walls. They had handsets that were connected to the bases by long, curly cords that stretched like springs and tangled easily.

"I like the idea of communication tethering you to a single spot," Tenkamenin told Anastasia. "It forces you to give every conversation the attention it deserves."

But since those phones were reserved for Tenkamenin's private calls, they never rang. Anastasia supposed it was because there was very little private about Tenkamenin. He lived his life like he were in a window display.

The morning after her arrival, Anastasia was called in for a meeting with Tenkamenin and Scythes Baba and Makeda – permanent fixtures in the High Blade's entourage, whose apparent purpose in life was to be an audience for him. Baba had a biting wit and enjoyed making jokes that no one but Tenka understood. Makeda seemed to find her greatest joy in belittling Baba.

"Ah! Our lady of the deep arrives!" said Tenka. "Sit, won't you – we have much to discuss."

Anastasia sat, and they offered her little sandwiches with the crusts cut off, arranged on the tray like a pinwheel. The High Blade was all about presentation.

"It is my understanding that word is spreading about your revival. While Goddard's allies are trying to keep it quiet, our old-guard friends are making it known. We'll build the anticipation, so that when you officially present yourself, the whole world will be listening."

"If the world will be listening, I'll have to have something to say."

"You will," Tenka said with such certainty that it made her wonder what he had in mind. "We have stumbled across some information of the most incriminating kind,"

"Incrimination in a world without crime or nations," said Baba. "Imagine that."

Tenkamenin laughed, and Scythe Makeda rolled her eyes. Then the High Blade reached across the table and placed a small origami swan on Anastasia's empty bread plate. "Secrets folded upon secrets," he said with a grin. "Tell me, Anastasia, how skilled are you at digging through the Thunderhead's backbrain?"

"Very," she told him.

"Good," said Tenkamenin. "When you unfold the swan, you'll find something to get you started."

Anastasia turned the swan over in her fingers. "What will I be looking for?"

"You must blaze that path. I won't tell you what to look for, because if I do, you'll miss the things you would intuitively find."

"The things we probably missed," added Makeda. "We need fresh eyes on this."

"And besides," said Scythe Baba, triple-teaming her. "It's not enough for you to know – you've got to *find* it – so you can show others how to find it, too."

"Precisely," said Tenkamenin. "A successful lie is not fueled by the liar; it is fueled by the willingness of the listener to believe.

You can't expose a lie without first shattering the will to believe it. That is why leading people to truth is so much more effective than merely telling them."

Tenkamenin's words hung in the air, and Anastasia looked at the swan again, not wanting to ruin it by unfolding its delicate wings.

"Once you draw your own conclusions, we'll share what we know," said Tenkamenin. "I guarantee you, your excursion into the backbrain will be a most eye-opening experience."

28

Dark Celebrity

Everyone was invited. And when the Overblade sets forth an invitation, it was not to be ignored. Which meant the stadium would most certainly be filled to capacity.

Goddard had put out a public call to all souls under the umbrella of his influence. It was a rare thing for a scythe – much less a powerful scythe – to have anything to do with ordinary people. Communications with the rest of humankind were usually limited to bullet, blade, bludgeon, and the occasional poison. Scythes simply didn't feel the need to speak to the masses. They were not elected officials and had no one to answer to besides one another. There was no reason to win over the hearts of the people when your sole purpose in their lives was to stop those hearts from beating.

So when Overblade Goddard himself personally broadcast the invitation, people everywhere took notice. In spite of his fortified tower, Goddard claimed to be a scythe of the people – and here was the evidence. He was willing to share his triumph with ordinary people in all walks of life. In the end, people's craving to be close to the continent's most celebrated scythes was stronger than the fear of them. Tickets were gone within five minutes of being made available. Everyone else would have to view the event in their homes and places of business.

And for those lucky enough to get tickets to the execution, they knew they'd be witnessing history. They could tell their children, and their grandchildren, and their great-grandchildren, and their great-great-grandchildren that they were there the day that Scythe Lucifer was gleaned.

They didn't fear Scythe Lucifer the way scythes did, but they did despise him, because not only did they blame him for the death of Endura, but also the silence of the Thunderhead and their own unsavory status. The world was being punished for his actions. He was, as Goddard so bluntly put it, the receptacle of the world's hatred. So naturally they would show up in force to witness his terrible end.

There were no longer such things as armored vehicles. Most vehicles were impenetrable by nature now. Even so, a special transport truck was built in a matter of days for Scythe Lucifer, complete with visible steel rivets and barred windows. It was a straight line on a high-speed highway from Fulcrum City to Mile High City, where his gleaning would take place – but the route the motorcade took was a serpentine meander that passed through as many MidMerican cities as possible before arriving at its destination. A drive that would have taken a day took nearly a week.

Rowan knew his gleaning would be exploited for its public relations value, but he had not expected to be flaunted in this way.

There were more than a dozen vehicles in the motorcade. Members of the BladeGuard on motorcycle, fancy limousines in the colors of the high-ranking scythes that rode within, all leading up to the big, boxy, armored truck, and followed by a few more motorcycle guards, trailing behind like a bridal train.

The Overblade himself was not present, even though the first limo was royal blue and studded with glimmering stars. There was no one in it – but the masses didn't know that. The truth was, Goddard couldn't be bothered to take a long, laborious journey when he could get the same effect by just pretending to be there. He wouldn't have to show up until the actual day of the gleaning.

Instead, he put Constantine in charge of escorting the dread Scythe Lucifer to his ultimate doom.

Constantine, Rowan knew, had been in charge of finding him and taking him down three years ago. His crimson robe and limousine were the same color as the PUBLIC ENEMY stamp on the side of Rowan's transport truck. He wondered if that was intentional, or just a happy coincidence.

Before they left Fulcrum City, Constantine had paid Rowan a visit once he had been loaded into his high-security truck and shackled.

"All these years, I wanted to lay eyes on you," Constantine said. "And now that I do, I am profoundly unimpressed."

"Thanks," said Rowan. "I love you, too."

Constantine reached into his robe as if to grab a blade, but thought better of it. "If I could glean you here and now, I would," he said. "But the ire of Overblade Goddard is not something I wish to arouse."

"Understandable," said Rowan. "If it's any consolation, I'd rather be gleaned by you than by him."

"And why is that?"

"Because for him, my death will be vengeance. For you it would be satisfying a three-year mission. I'd much rather satisfy that than Goddard's vendetta."

Constantine took that in stride. He didn't become any softer, but he no longer seemed on the verge of an explosion he would regret.

"Before we drive you to your well-deserved end, I want to know something," Constantine said. "I want to know why you did what you did."

"Why I ended Scythes Renoir, Fillmore, and the rest?"

He waved his hand. "Not that. As much as I detest your scythe-ending spree, it's obvious why you chose the ones you did. They were all questionable scythes, and you passed judgment on them, even though it was not your judgment to pass. Those crimes are more than enough reason to glean you, but what I want to know is why you killed the Grandslayers? They were good men and women. The worst of them was Xenocrates, but even he was a saint compared to the others you ended. What possessed you to do such an unspeakable thing?"

Rowan was tired of denying the blame – what did it matter at this point? So he gave Constantine the lie that everyone already believed.

"I hated the scythedom for denying me the ring," Rowan told him. "And so I wanted to damage it as much as I could. I wanted every scythedom around the world to pay for refusing to make me a true scythe."

Constantine's glare could have melted through the steel of the transport truck. "Do you expect me to believe that you are that small-minded and petty?"

"I must be," said Rowan. "Why else would I sink Endura?" Then he added, "Or maybe I'm just plain evil."

Constantine knew he was being mocked, and he did not take it well. He left and had nothing more to say to Rowan for the entire journey – but not without the grimmest of parting shots.

"It is my pleasure to tell you that your gleaning will be a painful one," the crimson scythe said, oozing bitterness. "Goddard intends to roast you alive."

Rowan had brand-new shiny shackles that had been forged just for him, steel chains that clanged on the floor of the transport truck when he moved. They were long enough to allow him plenty of mobility, but solid enough to make it hard to actually move. It was beyond overkill. Just because he had a knack for slipping free did not make him the escape artist they thought he was. All of his previous escapes were due either to someone helping him or the incompetence of the people detaining him. He wasn't exactly going to bite through the chains and kick open the steel door – yet everyone acted like he was an other-worldly beast with superhuman, supernatural powers. But then, maybe that's what Goddard wanted people to think; because if the creature you captured needs to be chained and locked in a steel box, you must be one hell of a hunter.

In every city and town they passed through, people came out in droves to watch the motorcade go by, as if it were a holi-day parade. The barred windows in the transport truck were at various heights, larger than ought to be on an armored vehicle, and the interior was brightly lit. Rowan soon came to realize the reason for this. The windows were placed so that no matter where he positioned himself in the truck, he could still be seen from the outside, and the bright interior ensured that he would not be hidden in darkness, no matter the time of day.

As he rolled down boulevards and main streets, there was always a view of him for the gauntlets of lookie-loos on either side. Occasionally he looked out of a window, and when he did, the crowd's excitement peaked at his peeking. They pointed at him, took photos, and held up children to see the young man who had become a dark celebrity. A few times he waved to them, which got people tittering to one another. A few times he pointed back at them when they pointed at him, which always seemed to scare them – as if his angry restless ghost would come for them in the middle of the night once he was gleaned.

Through all this, Constantine's bleak pronouncement kept coming back to him. The manner in which Rowan would be gleaned. Hadn't gleaning by fire been outlawed? Goddard must have reinstated it. Or maybe he brought it back just for this one special gleaning. As much as Rowan tried to tell himself he didn't fear it, he did. Not the gleaning, but the pain – and there would be quite a lot of it, because Goddard would most certainly turn off his pain nanites so that Rowan could feel every last measure of misery. He would suffer like the heretics and witches of more ignorant times.

The idea of his life ending was not much of a problem for him. In fact, it had become an oddly familiar theme. He had died so many times, and in so many ways, he was used to it. It held no more terror for him than falling asleep – which was often worse, because when he slept, he had nightmares. At least being deadish was a dreamless state, and the only difference between being deadish and being dead was the length of time involved. Perhaps, as some believed, true death ultimately brought people to a glorious new place, unimaginable to the living. In this way, Rowan tried to soften the prospect of his fate.

He also tried to soften it with thoughts of Citra. There had been no word of her, and he wasn't foolish enough to ask Constantine, or anyone else for that matter, because he had no idea who knew that she was alive. Goddard certainly knew – he had sent the High Blade of WestMerica to retrieve them both. But if Citra had escaped, the best way to help her was to not speak of her in hostile company.

Considering where Rowan's winding path was leading him, he could only hope she was in better circumstances.

29

The Obvious Bear

Three dates. That's all that was within the folded swan. One in the Year of the Lynx, a second in the Year of the Bison, and a third in the Year of the Heron. All years before she was even born.

It didn't take long for Anastasia to figure out why those dates were important. That was the easy part. Whether people knew the actual dates or not, the events they marked were part of everyone's history curriculum. But on the other hand, those were the official accounts. The accepted ones. Nothing in history was a firsthand account, and things known really meant things that were *allowed* to be known. Ever since becoming a scythe, Anastasia had seen how the scythedom throttled back the flow of information when it felt the need, defining history any way it chose. Perhaps not falsify things, for the Thunderhead did have jurisdiction over facts and figures, but the scythedom could choose *which* facts were fed to the public.

But any information selectively ignored was not forgotten. It still existed in the backbrain for anyone to access. In the days of her apprenticeship, Citra had become an expert at sifting through the Thunderhead's backbrain when trying to find Scythe Faraday's "killer." The algorithms of the Thunderhead's filing system were much like the human brain; all order was by association. Images weren't organized by date, time, or even location. To find an ivory scythe standing on a corner, she had to sort through images of people in ivory standing on corners everywhere in the world, then narrow it down by other elements of the scene. A particular type of streetlamp. The length of shadows. The sounds and scents in the air, because the Thunderhead catalogued all sensory input. Finding anything was like finding a needle in a haystack on a planet of haystacks.

It took ingenuity and inspiration to figure out what parameters would narrow down the near infinite field of information. Now Anastasia's challenge was even greater than before, because then she knew what she was looking for. Now she knew nothing but the dates.

First she studied all that was known about the disasters in question. Then she plunged into the backbrain to find original sources and information that had been conveniently left out of the official records.

The biggest obstacle was her own lack of patience. She could already sense that the answers were in there, but they were buried beneath so many layers she feared she'd never find them.

As it turns out, Anastasia and Jeri had arrived just a few days before the Lunar Jubilee. On every full moon, High Blade Tenkamenin threw a huge party that lasted twenty-five hours, "because twenty-four simply isn't enough." There were all forms of entertainment, hordes of professional partiers, and food flown in from around the globe for his invited guests.

"Dress for the event, but without your scythe's robe, and stay by my side with a party person or two," Tenka had advised her. "You'll just be part of the scenery."

To Jeri, the High Blade just said, "Enjoy yourself within reason."

Anastasia was reluctant to even be there, for fear of being recognized, and much rather would have continued her search through the backbrain, but Tenkamenin insisted. "A break from the drudgery of dredging will do you good. I'll provide you with a colorful wig, and no one will be the wiser."

At first Anastasia thought it was irresponsible and foolhardy to suggest a simple disguise could conceal her, but since the last thing anyone was expecting was a long-dead scythe to show up at the party – much less one wearing a neon-blue wig – she was remarkably hidden in plain sight.

"A lesson for your research," he told her. "That which hides in plain sight is the most difficult thing to find."

Tenka was the consummate host, greeting everyone personally and granting immunity left and right. It was all stunning and fun, but it didn't sit well with Anastasia – and the High Blade read her disapproval.

"Do I seem wastefully self-indulgent to you?" Tenka asked her. "Am I a horribly hedonistic High Blade?"

"Goddard throws parties like this," she pointed out.

"Not like *this*," said Tenka.

"*And* he likes his homes larger than life, too."

"Is that so?"

Then Tenka beckoned her closer so she could hear him more clearly amid the revelry. "I want you to take a look at the people before you and tell me what you see. Or – more to the point – what you *don't* see."

Anastasia took in the view. People in a multilevel pool, others dancing on balconies. Everyone in bathing suits and bright party clothes. Then she realized...

"There are no scythes."

"Not a one! Not even Makeda and Baba. Every guest is a family member of someone I gleaned since the last full moon. I invite them here to celebrate the lives of their lost loved ones, rather than to mourn, and to grant them their year of immunity. And when the celebration is over, and the grounds are cleared, I retreat to my glorious suite." He indicated the largest window in the mansion ... then winked and slid his finger to the right, until he wasn't pointing at the palace anymore, but to a small shack at the edge of the property.

"The tool shed?"

"That's not a tool shed," he said. "It's where I live. The palace suites are all reserved for honored guests like yourself, as well as guests who are less honored, but need to be impressed. As for my 'tool shed,' as you call it, it's a replica of the home I grew up in. My parents believe in simplicity. And of course they had a son who enjoyed endless complication. Yet I still find comfort at night in the pleasantness of a plain dwelling."

"I'm sure they must be proud of you," Anastasia said. "Your parents, I mean."

High Blade Tenkamenin sniffed at the suggestion. "Hardly," he said. "They took simplicity to an extreme. They're Tonists now – I haven't spoken to them in years."

"I'm sorry."

"Did you hear the Tonists had a prophet?" Tenka said bitterly. "He appeared shortly after you took your deep dive. They claimed the Thunderhead still spoke to him." Tenka gave a rueful chuckle at the thought. "Of course he got himself gleaned."

A waiter approached with a tray of shrimp that appeared too large to be real – no doubt a product of the Thunderhead's experimental abundance farms. As always, the Thunderhead got it right; they tasted even better than they looked.

"How are your efforts going?" Tenkamenin asked her.

"They're going," she told him. "But the Thunderhead links things in confusing ways. I pull up an image of the Mars colony, and it takes me to a child's drawing of the moon. A news report from the NewHope orbital station leads to a lunch order in Istanbul from a scythe I've never even heard of. Dante something-or-other."

"Alighieri?" said Tenka.

"Yes, that's it – do you know him?"

"I know *of* him. From EuroScandia, I believe. He's long gone. Must have self-gleaned maybe fifty, sixty years ago."

"It's like every other link I've found. None of them make sense."

"Go down every rabbit hole," Tenka advised. "Because some of them might actually have rabbits."

"I still don't understand why you can't just tell me what I'm looking for."

Tenka sighed and leaned close to whisper. "The information we have came from another scythe before she self-gleaned – a clearing of her conscience, I imagine. Other than that, we have no actual evidence, and our own digging through the backbrain

321

has been fruitless. We're being hindered because we *know* what we're looking for. While one searches for a man in a blue hat, one totally misses the woman in a blue wig." He gave a little flip to one of her neon curls.

Although it was counterintuitive, she had to admit it made sense. Hadn't she seen Tenka walking toward the "tool shed" each day, but her own assumptions never allowed her to guess the reason? She recalled a mortal-age video a teacher had once shown her class. The objective was to count how many times a ball was passed between teammates shifting around the screen. She got the answer right, as did most people in class. But everyone completely missed the man in a bear suit who danced his way right through the middle of the scene. Sometimes finding the obvious means coming in with no expectations.

The next morning, she had a breakthrough and ran to Tenka's cottage to let him know what she had uncovered.

His home was modest in a way that even Scythe Faraday would have approved of. She found Tenka in the middle of something. Directly in front of him were two other people, not looking all that happy to be there. More than unhappy, they were miserable.

"Come in, my friend," Tenka said when he saw Anastasia. "Do you know who this is?" he asked his two other guests.

"No, Your Excellency," they said.

"She is my florist," he told them. "She fills the palace and my home with the most lovely arrangements." Then he focused his attention on the more nervous of the two: a man who seemed to be nearing forty, perhaps ready to turn a corner. "Tell me your dearest dream," said the High Blade. "What do you want to do more than anything in the world, but have not yet done?"

The man hesitated.

"Don't hold back," prompted Tenkamenin. "Don't be modest. Tell me your dream in all of its garish glory!"

"I … I want a sailing yacht," he said like a little boy on Father Holiday's lap. "I want to sail it around the world."

"Very well!" said the High Blade, clapping his hands once, as if that sealed the deal. "We'll go shopping for sailing yachts tomorrow. My treat!"

"Your … Excellency?" the man said, incredulous.

"You'll have your dream, sir. Six months of it. Then you'll return here to tell me all about it. And then I will glean you."

The man was ecstatic. In spite of being told that he was going to be gleaned, he was happy as could be. "Thank you, Your Excellency! Thank you!"

Once he had left, the other man – a bit younger and less frightened than he was before, turned to the High Blade. "What about me?" he asked. "Do you want to hear my dream?"

"My friend, life can often be most brutal and unfair. Death is the same."

Tenkamenin swung his hand in a quick arc. Anastasia never even saw the blade, but in an instant the man was on the floor, clutching his neck, releasing his last breath. He had been gleaned.

"I will alert his family personally," Tenkamenin told Anastasia. "They will be invited to the next Lunar Jubilee."

Anastasia was surprised by the turn of events, but not shocked. Each scythe had to find his or her own way of doing things. To realize one random soul's dream while denying another's was as reasonable a method as any. She'd seen good scythes do a whole lot worse.

The cleanup crew came in from another room, and Tenka escorted Anastasia out to the patio, where breakfast was waiting. "Did you know that you were my inspiration?" he told her.

"Me?"

"By your example. Actually allowing people to choose their own method of gleaning, and giving them notice ahead of time – unheard of! But brilliant! Such compassion is lacking among us – we're all about efficiency. Getting the job done. After you were lost on Endura, to honor you, I decided to change my gleaning style. I would allow half of those I glean to first live their dream."

"Why just half?"

"Because if we truly are to emulate death as it once was, it must be fickle and capricious," he said. "One can only sugarcoat it so much."

Tenka filled a plate with eggs and fried plantains, and set it in front of Anastasia before making a plate for himself. *How strange,* thought Anastasia, *that death has become so commonplace for us scythes that we can take life, and take breakfast in the next moment.*

Tenka took a bite of cassava fufu, chewing the dense bread as he spoke. "You've not gleaned once since you arrived. Understandable under the circumstances, but you must be itching for it."

She understood what he meant. Only new-order scythes truly enjoyed the act of gleaning, but others would feel a vague but persistent need if they went too long without it. Anastasia couldn't deny that she'd come to feel that, too. She imagined it was the way one's psyche adjusted to being a scythe in the first place.

"What I'm doing in the backbrain is more important than gleaning," she told him. "And I think I found something."

She told him what she had uncovered. A name. Carson Lusk. Not exactly the motherlode, but a starting point. "He's listed as a survivor, but there's no record of his life after that date. Of course it could be a mistake, and he actually died with the others."

Tenka smiled broadly. "The Thunderhead does not make mistakes," he reminded her. "It's a solid lead. Keep digging!"

He eyed her plate, then scooped more plantains onto it like a parent concerned with their child's skimpy eating habits. "We would like you to start making live broadcasts," he told her. "Rather than us officially telling the world you've returned, we think you should do it yourself. Scythe Anastasia, in her own words."

"I'm ... not much of a performer," she told him, and thought back to her awful performance in *Julius Caesar*. She was only on stage to glean the lead actor, as per his wishes, but she still had to act the part. She was a terrible Roman senator, except for the stabbing part.

"Did you speak your mind and your heart to the Grand-slayers when you brought your inquest?" Tenka asked.

"Yes..." admitted Anastasia.

"And our friend Scythe Possuelo tells me that, in spite of what the world believes, you convinced them to make Scythe Curie High Blade of MidMerica."

Anastasia grimaced involuntarily at the mention of Scythe Curie. "Yes, I did."

"Well, if you can stand before the seven Seats of Consideration and argue a case to the most intimidating elegy of scythes in the world, I think you'll do fine."

That afternoon, Tenkamenin took her off the compound to show her the city he was so proud off. Port Remembrance was bustling and full of life. But the High Blade did not want her to leave their car. "The Jubilee is one thing – it is a controlled environment – but out here, there's no telling who might see you, and recognize you," he said. But it turned out there was another reason he didn't want her to leave their vehicle.

As they neared the center of town, they began to encounter Tonists. First just a few, but soon they started to gather on either side of the road, glaring at the High Blade's car.

Anastasia had mixed feelings about Tonists. The less extreme ones were all right. Friendly, and often kind, if somewhat persistent in the pushing of their beliefs. Some, however, were insufferable. Judgmental, intolerant – the opposite of what Tonism claimed to be about – and Sibilants made other zealots seem tame. That was the brand of Tonism that had taken root in Tenkamenin's region.

"Ever since the Toll was gleaned, these splinter groups have become more and more extreme," Tenkamenin told her. As if to prove his point, when enough of them were gathered by the roadside, they began to throw stones.

Anastasia gasped when the first stone hit the car, but Tenkamenin was unperturbed. "Don't worry – they can't do any damage, and they know it. I'm sorry you have to see this."

Another rock hit the windshield, split in two, and bounced off.

Then, all at once, the attackers stopped throwing stones and began to "intone," emitting a droning, wordless wailing … yet somehow this was different from other Tonists she had heard.

Tenkamenin ordered the car to put on music, but even so, it didn't entirely drown them out.

"This entire sect has taken a vow of silence," Tenkamenin told her, not hiding his disgust. "No speaking, just this blasted ugly noise. The Thunderhead had always frowned on delinguination, but when the Thunderhead fell silent, these Tonists decided they could do as they pleased – which is why their howling sounds even worse than usual."

"Delinguination?" asked Anastasia.

"I'm sorry," said Tenkamenin. "I thought you understood. They've cut out their tongues."

Jeri was not invited on the tour of Port Remembrance. While the captain's crew indulged in more free time than they'd had in years, Jeri remained in Tenkamenin's compound, keeping an eye on Anastasia, making sure she was being treated well and was kept safe. Jeri was never a selfish person, always putting the crew of the *Spence* first – that was a good captain's way. The desire to look out for Anastasia went beyond that.

Tenkamenin was a careless man. Yes, he provided protection for Anastasia – but was his staff vetted? And the fact that he practically flaunted Anastasia's presence at the Lunar Jubilee made Jeri wonder whether the High Blade had any common sense whatsoever. Jeri didn't trust the man, and knew the feeling was mutual.

And then came Anastasia's "Sibilant" afternoon in Port Remembrance. Anastasia came to talk to Jeri about it when she returned, unable to keep it all in.

"Each day it's like I'm hit over the head by how much the world changed while I was out of it," Anastasia said.

"The world has survived worse," Jeri told Anastasia, while she endlessly paced. "We survived the mortal age – what could possibly be worse than the horrors of that?"

But she would not be consoled. "Yes, but without the Grandslayers, scythedoms are practically at war with one another, as if it were the mortal age all over again. Where are we heading?"

"Upheaval," Jeri said matter-of-factly. "Mountains are created by upheaval. I'm sure it doesn't look pretty at the time."

It only aggravated her further. "How can you be so calm about it? And Tenkamenin's even worse than you! He just accepts all this like it's nothing. Like it's a passing shower, instead of a hurricane that's going to tear everything apart! Why is everyone so blind?"

Jeri sighed and put a hand on Anastasia's shoulder, forcing her to stop pacing. *This is why I'm needed here,* Jeri thought. *To be the second voice in her head, wrangling in the panicking one.*

"There is opportunity in every disaster," Jeri told her. "A ship goes down, that's when I get excited. Because I know there are always treasures in the wreckage. Look what I found at the bottom of the sea. I found you."

"And 400,000 scythe diamonds," Anastasia pointed out.

"My point is, you need to approach this like a salvage operation. In salvage, the first thing we do is carefully assess the situation before we make a move."

"So I should just sit by and watch?"

"Observe, learn everything you can, and then, when you do move, you move decisively. And I know, when the time comes, you will."

High Blade Tenkamenin insisted on formal dinners every night. His entourage of scythes was expected to be there, as well as his honored guests – and since Anastasia's and Jeri's arrival, Tenkamenin made sure there were no other guests. It was one thing to throw a party for locals and another to expose Scythe Anastasia to dinner-table scrutiny.

When Jeri arrived that night, Anastasia was already there, along with the High Blade and Scythes Baba and Makeda. The High Blade himself was laughing uproariously at something someone had said – or, more likely, something he himself had said. While Anastasia enjoyed the man, Jeri exhausted of him after their first day.

"You've missed the first course," he told Jeri. "No soup for you."

Jeri sat beside Anastasia. "I'll survive."

"House rules dictate that you be on time for dinner," Tenkamenin reminded. "It's a matter of common courtesy."

"It's Jeri's first time late," offered Anastasia.

"You don't have to defend me," Jeri told her, then turned to the High Blade. "I was being updated on the Endura salvage, if you must know. They've found the council chamber – the

Grandslayers' Seats of Consideration are being sent to their respective continents to be turned into monuments. I think that was a little more important than soup."

Tenkamenin did not comment, but five minutes later, during the main course, he prodded Jeri again.

"Tell me, Jerico, how does your crew feel about having an absentee captain?"

Jeri would not be baited. "They are on leave in your city, and grateful for it."

"I see. And how do you know they are not out making deals without you? Deals that might compromise the security of our dear Lady of the Deep?" he said, using his latest pet name for Anastasia.

"Do not cast aspersions on my crew, Your Excellency," Jeri said. "They are loyal to a fault. Can you say that of the people you surround yourself with?"

That raised the High Blade's hackles, but he did not defend his entourage. Instead he changed the subject.

"What do you want out of life, Captain Soberanis?"

"That's a broad question."

"Then let me rephrase it. Tell me your dearest dream, Jerico. What do you want to do more than anything in the world, but have not yet done?"

Suddenly Anastasia dropped her silverware so hard that it chipped her plate, and she stood up. "I've lost my appetite," she said, then grabbed Jeri's hand. "And so have you." And she stormed away, leaving Jeri no choice but to go with her, if only to keep the hand.

Behind them Tenkamenin burst out laughing. "It was a joke, Anastasia. You know I love to toy!"

She turned long enough to spare him the harshest of glares. "You are an excellent ass, Your Excellency."

Which only made him laugh harder.

Jeri was not entirely sure what the inside joke was until they reached Anastasia's suite, and she closed the door behind them.

"It's what he asks people he's going to glean," she said.

"Ah," said Jeri. "He did it to get a rise out of you – which he did. The High Blade enjoys pushing people's buttons, and he knows exactly where yours are."

"Aren't you the least bit worried that he might actually do it?"

"Not at all," Jeri told her. "Because as much as he likes to toy with you, he doesn't want to turn you against him. If he gleans me, he knows he'll be your enemy."

Even so, she held out her hand. The one with the scythe's ring. It wasn't her old ring – that one Scythe Possuelo had hurled back into the sea after they found her, since it could be used to trace her whereabouts, if there was actually a scythe out there who understood their own technology. Possuelo had given her a new ring using one of the diamonds from the vault.

"Kiss it," Anastasia said to Jeri. "Just to be safe."

So Jeri took her hand and kissed it – missing the ring entirely.

Anastasia pulled her hand back reflexively. "I meant the ring, not the hand!" She held it out again. "Do it right this time."

"I choose not to," Jeri said.

"If I give you immunity, no one can glean you for a year. Do it!"

But still Jeri made no move. And when her eyes questioned, Jeri said, "When I found the Vault of Relics and Futures, Possuelo also offered me immunity, but I refused him as well."

"Why? What possible reason is there?"

"Because I don't want to be indebted to anyone. Not even you."

She turned away at that and went to the window, peering out. "There are things out there that I don't want to know about … but I need to know about them. I need to know everything I can." Then she turned back to Jeri. "Have you heard anything about Rowan?" she asked

Jeri could have told her that there was no news, but that would be a lie, and Jeri would not lie to Anastasia. They had too much trust between them to jeopardize that. Jeri was silent for a moment, and Anastasia pushed.

"I know Tenkamenin wouldn't let any news about him reach me in here, but you've been in touch with your crew. They must have told you something."

Jeri heaved a sigh, but only to prepare her for the answer. "Yes, there is news. But nothing I'm going to share, no matter how much you ask me."

A progression of emotions passed over her. The stages of grief all played out on her face in a matter of seconds. Denial, anger, bargaining, sadness, and, finally, a resolving into acceptance.

"You won't tell me because there's nothing I can do," she said, anticipating the reasons Jeri would give, "and it would distract me from what I need to do."

"Do you hate me for it?" Jeri asked.

"I could say yes, just out of spite. But no, Jeri, I don't hate you. But … can you at least tell me if he's still alive?"

"Yes," Jeri said. "Yes, he is. I hope you can find comfort in that."

"And will he be alive tomorrow?" she asked.

"Not even the Thunderhead can be sure about tomorrow," Jeri told her. "Let's be satisfied with today."

30

Burnt Offering

"Hello, Tyger."

"Hi," said Tyger Salazar's memory construct. "Do I know you?"

"Yes and no," said Scythe Rand. "I've come to tell you that Scythe Lucifer's been caught."

"Scythe Lucifer ... isn't that the one who's been killing other scythes?"

"It is," said Rand. "And you know him."

"Doubt it," said the construct. "I know some twisted people, but nobody *that* twisted."

"It's your friend, Rowan Damisch."

The construct paused and then laughed. "Nice try," it said. "Did Rowan put you up to this? Rowan!" it called. "Where are you hiding? Come on out."

"He's not here."

"Don't try to tell me that he's killing people – he never even got to be a scythe – they booted his ass out and gave it to that girl instead."

"He's going to be executed tomorrow," Rand said.

The construct hesitated, furrowed its brow. They were so well programmed, these constructs. They compiled the memories of every facial expression of the subject that had ever been recorded. The representation was sometimes so true to life, it was unnerving.

"You're not kidding, are you?" said Tyger's construct. "Well, you can't let it happen! You have to stop it!"

"It's out of my hands."

"Then put it back in your hands! I know Rowan better than anyone – if he did what you say he did, then he had a good reason. You can't just glean him!" Then the construct began looking around as if it was aware it was in a limited world. A virtual box that it wanted to get out of. "It's wrong!" it said. "You can't do this!"

"What do you know about right and wrong?" snapped Rand. "You're nothing but a foolish dim-witted party boy!"

It glared at her in fury. The micro-pixels of its image increased the percentage of red in its face. "I hate you," it said. "Whoever the hell you are, I hate you."

Ayn quickly hit a button and ended the conversation. Tyger's memory construct vanished. As always, it would not remember this conversation. As always, Ayn would.

"If you're going to glean him, why not just glean him?" Scythe Rand asked Goddard, doing her best not to sound as frustrated as she was. There were many reasons for her frustration. First of all, a stadium was a difficult venue to secure from their enemies – and they did have enemies. Not just the old-guard scythes, but everyone from Tonists, to scythedoms who had shunned Goddard, to the disgruntled loved ones from mass gleanings.

It was just the two of them in Goddard's private plane. Now that the motorcade was nearing its destination after nearly a week of winding through its prolonged victory lap, he and Rand were flying to meet it – a flight as short as Rowan Damisch's journey was long. Like Goddard's rooftop chalet, the plane was retrofitted with mortal-age weaponry. A series of missiles that hung from each wing. He would regularly fly low over communities that he deemed defiant. He never used the missiles to glean, but just like those rooftop cannons, they were a reminder that he could if he chose to.

"If you want a public display," Ayn suggested, "make the gleaning more controlled. Maybe a broadcast from a small, undisclosed location. Why do you have to make a spectacle of everything?"

"Because I enjoy spectacles – and there's no reason needed beyond that."

But of course there was a bigger reason. Goddard wanted the world to know that he had personally apprehended and executed the greatest public enemy of the post-mortal age. Not only to raise Goddard's image among common people, but to gain the admiration of scythes who might be on the fence about him. Everything with Goddard was either strategic or impulsive. This grand event was strategic. Turning the gleaning of Rowan Damisch into a show would make it impossible for anyone to ignore.

"There will be over a thousand scythes from around the world in that audience," Goddard reminded her. "They wish to see it, and I wish to provide it. Who are we to deny them their catharsis?"

Rand had no idea what that meant and didn't really care. Goddard spouted erudite gibberish with such regularity, Rand had learned to turn her ears off to it.

"There are better ways to handle this," Rand said.

Now Goddard's expression began to sour. They hit a small pocket of turbulence, which Goddard probably believed was brought on by his mood. "Are you trying to tell me how to be a scythe – or worse – how to be an Overblade?"

"How could I tell you how to be something that didn't exist until you made it up?"

"Careful, Ayn," he warned. "Don't anger me at a time I should be feeling nothing but joy." He let his warning sink in, then leaned back in his chair. "I would think you, of all people, would love to see Rowan suffer after what he did to you. He broke your back and left you for dead, and you want his gleaning to be a small, quiet thing?"

"I want him gleaned just as much as you do. But gleaning should not be entertainment."

To which Goddard said with an infuriating grin, "It's entertaining to me."

As Scythe Lucifer, Rowan had been very careful to make sure the scythes he ended never suffered. They were gleaned quickly. It was only after they were dead that he burned the bodies to render them unrevivable. It didn't surprise him that Goddard was lacking in such mercy. Rowan's agony would be prolonged for maximum effect.

There was only so much bravado that Rowan could muster. As the execution motorcade wove its way to his doom, he finally had to admit to himself that he truly did care about whether he lived or died. And while it didn't bother him how history might remember him, he was troubled by how his family would. His mother, and his many brothers and sisters, must already know that he was Scythe Lucifer – because once blame for the sinking of Endura was foisted upon him, it made Rowan infamous. The crowds that turned out to get a glimpse of the motorcade was proof of that.

Would his family be there in the audience? If not, would they be watching from home? What happened to the families of notorious criminals back in mortal days, he wondered – for there was no equivalent to Scythe Lucifer in post-mortal times. Would they have been damned by association, and gleaned? Rowan's father had been gleaned before Endura sank, so he never knew what his son had become, and how the world hated him. There was a mercy in that. But if his mother and siblings were still alive, they must have despised him, for how could they not? That realization was more demoralizing than anything else.

He had plenty of time to be alone with his own thoughts during the motorcade's winding journey. His thoughts were not his friends – at least not anymore, because all they did was remind him of the choices he had made, and how they had led him here. What once felt justified, now felt foolhardy. What once seemed brave, now just seemed sad.

It could have been different. He could have just disappeared like Scythe Faraday when he had the chance. Where was Faraday now, he wondered. Would he be streaming the event and weeping for him? It would be nice to know that someone wept for him. Citra would, wherever she was. That would have to be enough.

The gleaning was scheduled for seven in the evening, but people had arrived early. There were scythes and ordinary citizens in the crowd – and although the scythes did have a special entrance, they had been encouraged by Goddard to sit in among the rabble.

"This is a golden public relations opportunity," Goddard had told them. "Smile and say kind things. Listen attentively to their twaddle and pretend to care – maybe even grant some immunity." Many followed the directive; some could not bring themselves to and sat only with other scythes.

Rowan, under heavy guard, was taken directly to a large staging area with access directly onto the field. The wood-pile they had prepared for him was a three-story pyramid that appeared to be made of gathered branches, like a random collection of stacked driftwood – but closer inspection proved everything to be part of an intricately engineered design. The branches weren't just stacked, but nailed in place, and the whole thing was on a huge rolling platform, like a parade float. The very center was hollowed out, and in the hollow was a stone pillar to which Rowan was tightly secured by fire-resistant bindings. The pillar was on a lift that would raise Rowan to the top of the pyramid, revealing him to the crowd at the right moment. Then Goddard himself would light it.

"This baby is not your ordinary pyre!" explained the tech in charge as he wanded off Rowan's pain nanites. "I was part of the team that designed this beauty! There are actually four kinds of wood here. Ash wood for an even burn, Osage orange for heat, rowan wood for – well – obvious reasons, and a few pockets of knotty pine for a nice crackle!"

The tech checked the tweaker's readout, confirming that Rowan's pain nanites had been shut down, then got back to explaining the wonders of the death float, like a kid at the science fair.

"Oh, and you're gonna love this!" he said. "The branches on the outer rim have been treated with potassium salts, so they'll burn violet – then farther up, it's calcium chloride, so they'll burn blue, and so on and so forth, through all the colors of the spectrum!" Then he pointed at the black robe that the guards had forcibly put Rowan in. "And that robe has been infused with strontium chloride so it burns deep red. You'll be better than New Year's Eve fireworks!"

"Gee, thanks," Rowan said flatly. "Too bad I won't get to see it."

"Oh, you will," the tech said cheerily. "There's an exhaust fan built into the base that will suck all the smoke away, so everyone will get a good view – even you!" Then he took out a piece of brown cloth. "This is a guncotton gag," the tech told him. "It's quick burning, and'll incinerate right off the moment it's exposed to heat." Then he stopped himself, finally realizing that Rowan didn't need or want to know these things. A quick-burning gag that allowed people to hear him scream was not the kind of accessory he could get enthused about. Now Rowan was glad they hadn't offered him a last meal, because he was way too nauseated to have held it down.

Behind the tech, Scythe Rand entered the snarl of branches. Even the prospect of her was better than a blow-by-blow description of his dazzling incineration.

"You're not here to talk to him," Rand snapped.

Immediately the tech caved like a scolded pup. "Yes, Your Honor. I'm sorry, Your Honor."

"Give me the gag and get lost."

"Yes, Scythe Rand. Sorry again. Anyway, he's good to go." He gave her a thumbs-up, she grabbed the gag, and he retreated with his shoulders hunched.

"How much longer?" Rowan asked Rand.

"It's about to start," she told him. "A few speeches and you're on."

Rowan found he had no heart left to banter with her. He could not be cavalier about this anymore. "Will you watch," he asked, "or look away?" He didn't know why he cared, but he did.

Rand didn't answer him. Instead she said, "I'm not sorry to see you die, Rowan. But I'm annoyed by how it's going down. Frankly, I just want it to be over."

"So do I," he told her. "I'm trying to figure out if it's worse knowing what's going to happen, or if it would have been better not to know." He took a moment, then asked, "Did Tyger know?"

She took a step back from him. "I'm not letting you play your little head games on me anymore, Rowan."

"No games," he said honestly. "I just want to know. Did you tell him what was happening to him before you took his body? Did he have at least a few moments to make peace with it?"

"No," she told him. "He never knew. He thought he was about to be ordained as a scythe. Then we put him under, and that was that."

Rowan nodded "Kind of like dying in his sleep."

"What?"

"It's how they say all mortals wanted to go. In their sleep, peacefully, without ever knowing. I guess it makes sense."

Rowan supposed he said too much, because Rand put the gag on and tightened it.

"Once the flames reach you, try to breathe them in," she told him. "It will go faster for you if you do."

Then she left without looking back.

Ayn could not get the image of Rowan Damisch out of her head. She'd seen him incapacitated before – tied up, tied down, shackled, and restrained any number of ways. But this time it was different. He wasn't plucky or defiant; he was resigned. He didn't look like the shrewd killing machine Goddard had turned him into. He looked like exactly what he was: a frightened boy who got in over his head.

Well, it serves him right, Ayn thought, trying to shake it off. *What goes around comes around, isn't that what mortals used to say?*

As she walked out onto the field, a wind swooped through the bowl of the stadium, fluttering her robe. The stands were just about full now. More than one thousand scythes and thirty thousand citizens. A capacity crowd.

Rand sat beside Goddard and his underscythes. Constantine would not miss the gleaning of Rowan Damisch, but he didn't seem any more pleased by this than Ayn did.

"Are you enjoying yourself, Constantine?" Goddard asked, clearly to goad him.

"I recognize the importance of an event around which to rally the public and present a unified North Merica," Constantine said. "It's a strong strategy and one that is likely to mark a turning point in scythe affairs."

It was complimentary but didn't answer the question. A

perfectly diplomatic response. Goddard read through it, though, as Ayn knew he would, picking up on Constantine's disapproval.

"You are nothing, if not consistent," Goddard told him. "Constantine the Consistent. I do believe that is how history will come to know you."

"There are worse attributes," Constantine told him.

"Did you at least extend a personal invitation to our 'friends' in Texas to attend?" Goddard asked.

"I did. They didn't respond."

"No, I expect they wouldn't. Shame — I would have much liked them to see the family they've chosen to exclude themselves from."

The agenda for the evening had the four other North Merican High Blades giving speeches — each one carefully written to hit a certain point that Goddard wanted hit.

High Blade Hammerstein of EastMerica would lament the many souls lost on Endura, and the other unlucky scythes so brutally ended by Scythe Lucifer.

High Blade Pickford of WestMerica would talk about North Merican unity and how the alliance of five out of the six North Merican scythedoms made life better for everyone.

High Blade Tizoc of Mexiteca would invoke the mortal age, point out how far the world had come, and leave the audience with a veiled warning to other scythedoms that not aligning with Goddard could bring back the bad old days.

High Blade MacPhail of NorthernReach would give credit to all those involved in putting this event together. She would also highlight members of the audience, scythes and ordinary people as well, whose favor it was worth currying.

And then finally Goddard would deliver an address that would wrap it all up in a nice bow before he set the pyre ablaze.

"This will not just be the gleaning of a public enemy," he had told Ayn and his underscythes. "It's a bottle of champagne smashed upon a ship. This shall mark the christening of a new time for the human race." It was as if Goddard looked upon it religiously. A burnt offering to purify the path and appease the gods.

As far as Goddard was concerned, this day was just as important as the day he revealed himself at conclave and accepted his nomination for High Blade – even more important because of the reach. The event would stream out to billions, not just a gathering of scythes in conclave. The reverberations of tonight would be felt for a long, long time. And the scythedoms that had yet to align with him would have little choice but to do so.

Support was growing in leaps and bounds now that he focused most gleaning on the margins of society. Ordinary citizens had no great love of the fringe anyway, and as long as one wasn't part of that frayed edge that needed trimming, one needn't worry about gleaning in Goddard's world. Of course, with the population ever growing, there was no shortage of people to push to the margins.

It was, he had come to realize, a matter of evolution. Not natural selection, because nature had become weak and toothless. Intelligent selection was more like it, with Goddard and his acolytes at the helm of the intelligentsia.

As the hour neared seven, and the sky became dark, Goddard cracked his knuckles repeatedly and bounced his knees, his body expressing a youthful impatience that didn't show on his face.

Ayn put a hand on his knee to stop the motion. Goddard resented it, but obliged. Then the lights in the stands dimmed and brightened on the field, as the pyre began to roll out from the bull pen.

The anticipation of the crowd was palpable. Not so much cheers and whoops as gasps and a building rumble. Even unlit, the pyre was a sight to behold – the way its branches caught the light, a dead forest woven for an artist's eye. A lit torch waited at a safe distance, ready to be touched to the corner of the pyre by Goddard at the proper moment.

As the other speeches began, Goddard ran his own speech through his mind. He had studied the greatest addresses in history: those of Roosevelt, King, Demosthenes, Churchill. His would be short and sweet, but full of quotable moments. The kind that would be engraved in stone. The kind that would become iconic and timeless, like those he had studied. He would then take the torch, light the fire, and, as the flames grew, he would recite Scythe Socrates's poem "Ode to the Ageless," a world anthem if ever there was one.

Hammerstein's speech began. He was perfectly mournful and lugubrious. Pickford was regal and eloquent; Tizoc, direct and incisive; and MacPhail's gratitude for those who made this day possible felt honest and real.

Goddard rose and approached the pyre. He wondered if Rowan knew the honor that Goddard was bestowing on him today. Cementing his place in history. From now until the end of all things, the world would know his name. He'd be studied by schoolchildren everywhere. Today he would die, yet in a very real sense, he would also become immortal, belonging to the ages in a way that few are.

Goddard touched the button, and the lift raised Rowan from within the pyre to its peak. The rumble of the crowd grew. People stood. Hands pointed. Goddard began.

"Honorable scythes and respected citizens, today we commit humanity's last criminal to the cleansing fire of history. Rowan Damisch, who called himself Scythe Lucifer, stole the light of so many. But today we take that light back, and use it as a clear and ever-present beacon of our future—"

There was a tap on his shoulder. He almost didn't feel it.

"A new age where scythes, with measured joy, shape our great society, gleaning those who have no place in our glorious tomorrow—"

Again, a tap at his shoulder, more insistent this time. Could it be that someone was interrupting his address? Who would dare do such a thing? He turned to see Constantine behind him, upstaging him with that eye-assaulting crimson robe, even more gaudy now that it bore rubies.

"Your Excellency," he whispered. "There appears to be a problem…"

"A problem? In the middle of my speech, Constantine?"

"You should look for yourself." Then Constantine drew his attention to the pyre.

Rowan squirmed and strained against his bonds. He tried to scream through the gag, but the screams would not be fully realized until the gag burned off. And then Goddard realized…

The figure atop the unlit pyre was not Rowan.

The face was familiar, but it wasn't until Goddard looked

to the giant screens placed around the stadium, which showed the man's anguished expression close up, that he realized who this was.

It was the technician. The one in charge of preparing Rowan for his execution.

Ten minutes earlier, before the pyre was rolled out, Rowan tried to relish the moments remaining in his life. Then a trio of scythes approached him, weaving through the forest of branches. None of their robes were familiar. Nor were their faces.

This visit was not on the program – and, all things considered, Rowan was relieved to see them. Because if they were here to exact personal revenge on him, unwilling to wait for him to burn, it would be an easier end. Sure enough, one of them pulled out a knife and swung it toward him. He braced for the sharp pain and the quick extinguishing of consciousness, but it didn't come.

And it was only after the blade cut the bonds on his hands that he realized it was a bowie knife.

31

Damisch Control

Goddard felt his body's reaction before his mind could truly grasp what he was seeing. It came as a tingling in his extremities, a churning in his gut, and an aching tightness in the small of his back. Fury surged upward with volcanic intensity until his head began to throb.

Everyone in the stadium already knew what he had only now just seen, that the prisoner at the peak of the pyre was not Scythe Lucifer — for over the past three years the world had come to know Rowan Damisch's face. Yet this was the face being broadcast and streamed. It filled the expansive screens all around Goddard as if to mock him.

His grand moment was not just robbed from him — it was subverted. Twisted upon itself like something obscene. The rumbles from the audience sounded different than they had only a second ago. Was that laughter he heard? Were they laughing at him? Whether they were, or not, was of little consequence. All that mattered was what he heard. What he felt. And he felt the derision of thirty thousand souls. It could not stand. This monstrous moment could not be suffered to live.

Constantine whispered in his ear. "I've ordered the gates locked, and the entire BladeGuard has been alerted. We'll find him."

But that didn't matter. It was ruined. They could drag Rowan back and hurl him onto the pyre, but it would make no difference. Goddard's shining moment would be the greatest casualty of the day. Unless. Unless…

Ayn knew things were heading to a very bad place the moment she saw that imbecile atop the pyre.

Goddard would have to be handled.

For when his anger took control, all bets were off. It was bad enough before, but ever since acquiring Tyger's body, those youthful impulses – the sudden endocrine surges – gave Goddard a terrible new dimension. Adrenaline and testosterone might have been charming when managed by a harmless blank slate like Tyger Salazar; they were merely winds beneath a kite. But under Goddard, those same winds were a tornado. Which meant he would have to be handled. Like a beast that had broken out of its cage.

She let Constantine be the one to run out to him and deliver the bad news – because Goddard loved to blame the messenger, so better Constantine than her. Only after Goddard had turned to look at the hapless tech did Ayn go to him.

"The feeds have been cut," Ayn told him. "It's no longer streaming. We're on damage control now. You can turn this around, Robert," she said, cajoling him as best she could. "Make them think this is intentional. That it's part of the show."

The look on his face terrified her. She wasn't even sure he'd heard her until he said, "Intentional. Yes, Ayn, that's exactly what I'll do."

He raised the mic, and Ayn stepped back. Perhaps Constantine had been right. It was always in these moments of dismay that she could corral him. Control him. Fix what was broken before it became irreparable. She took a deep breath and waited, along with everyone else, to hear what he was going to say.

"Today was meant to be a day of reckoning," Goddard began, spitting the words into the microphone as he spoke. "You! All of you who came here today nurturing a thirst for blood. *You!* Whose hearts quicken at the prospect of a man being burned alive before your very eyes.

"YOU! Did you think I would indulge you? Did you believe we scythes were so base as to pander to your morbid curiosity? Offering you a circus of carnage for your entertainment?" Now he screamed at them through gritted teeth. "How DARE you! ONLY SCYTHES may take pleasure in the ending of life, or have you forgotten?" He paused letting that sink in. Letting them feel the depth of their transgression. Had Rowan not vanished, he would have been happy to give them their show. But they must never know that.

"No, Scythe Lucifer is not here today," he continued, "but YOU, who were so eager to witness the spectacle, are now the object of my eye. This was not a judgment on him; it was a judgment on YOU, who have, on this day, damned yourselves! The only way back from perdition is penance. Penance and sacrifice. Therefore, I have selected YOU on this day to be an example for the world."

Then he looked to the thousand scythes dotting the audience of the stadium.

"Glean them," he ordered with contempt for the crowd so great that he bit his own lip. "Glean them all."

The panic was slow to build. Stupefied people looked to one another. Did the Overblade actually say that? He couldn't have said it. He couldn't have meant it. Even the scythes were unsure at first … but an order could not be refused if one didn't want their loyalty questioned. Bit by bit weapons were pulled out, and the scythes began to look at the people around them with a very different expression than they had before. Calculating how best to achieve the goal.

"*I am your completion!*" proclaimed Goddard, as he did at all his mass gleanings, his voice echoing throughout the stadium. "*I am the last word of your unsatisfied, unsavory lives.*"

The first people began to run. Then a few more. And then it was as if a floodgate had opened. The panicked spectators climbed over seats and over one another to get to the exits – but scythes had quickly positioned themselves in the neck of the funnel. The only way past them was through them, and the gleaned were already beginning to block the narrow paths to freedom.

"*I am your deliverer! I am your portal to the mysteries of oblivion!*"

People began hurling themselves over railings, hoping that splatting before they were gleaned would save them – but this was a scythe action. From the moment Goddard gave the order, the Thunderhead was helpless to intervene. All it could do was watch through its many unblinking eyes.

"*I am your Omega! Your bringer of infinite peace. You will embrace me!*"

Scythe Rand begged him to stop, but he pushed her away, and she stumbled to the ground, knocking over the torch. It glanced across the edge of the pyre, and that's all it took. The pyre ignited – purple flames rushed around the base.

"Your death is both my verdict upon you, and my gift to you," Goddard told the dying crowd. *"Accept it with grace. And thus farewell."*

The best view of Goddard's Armageddon was from the top of the pyre – and with the smoke drawn away by exhaust fans below, the tech could see everything … including the outer rim of purple flame, which had moved up the pyre, turning blue.

In the stands, the scythes, each glittering with jewels embedded in their new-order robes, dispatched their victims at an alarming rate.

I will not be alone today, thought the tech as the flames drew closer, burning from green to bright yellow.

He could feel the soles of his shoes beginning to melt. He could smell the burning rubber. The fire was orange now, and closer. The screams all around him from the stands seemed far, far away. Soon the flames would turn red, the guncotton gag would burn away from him, and his own screams would be the only ones that mattered.

Then he saw a lone scythe looking in his direction from the field. The one in the crimson robe. One of the few scythes who was not going after the crowd. They locked eyes for a moment. Then, just as the flames caught on the doomed man's pant legs, Scythe Constantine raised a pistol and performed the only gleaning he would do today. A single shot through the heart that spared the tech from a more painful end.

And the last thought the tech had before his life left him was a wave of immense gratitude for the crimson scythe's mercy.

"I will forgive you for trying to stop me," Goddard said to Scythe Rand as their limousine pulled away from the stadium. "But it surprises me, Ayn, that you of all people would flinch when it came to gleaning."

Ayn could have said a million things to him, but she held her tongue. Rowan was already forgotten – trampled beneath this larger affair. Rumor was that he had been seen leaving the stadium with Scythe Travis and several other Texan scythes. She could blame all this on them, but who was she kidding? She was the one who'd suggested Goddard find a way to make Rowan's absence appear like part of a larger plan. But she never imagined where Goddard would take it.

"This was not the event that I asked for, but rarely do things come the way we expect," Goddard said in the calm, collected way someone might discuss a stage play. "Even so, this day has worked to our advantage."

Rand looked at him in disbelief. "How? How can you say that?"

"Isn't it obvious?" And when she didn't respond, he elucidated with the smooth eloquence he was famous for. "Fear, Ayn. Fear is the beloved father of respect. The common citizens must know their place. They must be aware of the lines they may not cross. Without the Thunderhead in their lives, they need a firm hand to give them stability. To set clear boundaries. They will revere me, and all my scythes, and will not run afoul of us again." He thought about his own self-serving rational-izations and nodded in approval of himself. "All is well, Ayn. All is well."

But Scythe Rand knew that from this moment on, nothing would be well again.

Part Four

THE ONLY TOOL WE CAN WIELD

A Testament of the Toll

The sanctimonious Sibilants who would wage unwarranted war were an abomination to the Toll. He would descend on them as the furious beating of a million wings, and the skies would rage with Thunder. The unrepentant would be struck down, but those who fell to their knees would be spared. Then he would leave them, dissolving once more into a storm of feathers and disappearing to the calming sky. All rejoice!

Commentary of Curate Symphonius

The Toll was not only a man of flesh, but a master of it. He possessed the ability to transform into any creature, or multitude of creatures. This verse illustrates his ability to become a great flock of birds, most likely eagles, falcons, or owls. Graceful. Noble. Wise. But also to be feared and respected. Creatures that were the epitome of all the Toll was.

Coda's Analysis of Symphonius

The ever-present problem with Symphonius is his inconsistency. He sees things as symbolic or literal whenever it suits him, thus his interpretations are more whim than wisdom. While it's possible that the Toll could have taken form as a flock, is it not more likely that he simply possessed the mystical ability to fly, like the caped heroes of archival graphics?

32

A Grim Fulcrum

The cathedral bells that rang out the hours for nearly a thousand years in EuroScandia had been silenced. Ripped out, torn apart, melted in a makeshift furnace. A great concert hall in the same region had been raided in the middle of a performance, and, amid the panic of the crowd, Tonists flooded the stage, breaking the smaller instruments by hand and taking axes to the larger ones.

Your voices are music to my ears, the Toll had once said. Which clearly meant that all other music had to be destroyed.

These extreme sibilant sects found, in their devotion, a need to impose their beliefs on the world. No two sects of Sibilants were alike. Each one was its own unique aberration, with its own frightening interpretations of Tonist doctrine and twistings of the Toll's words. The only thing they all had in common was a propensity for violence and intolerance – including the intolerance of other Tonists, for any sect that did not believe precisely as they did was clearly lesser.

There were no Sibilants before the Thunderhead fell silent. Yes, there were sects that had extreme beliefs, but the Thunderhead and the Nimbus agents of the Authority Interface reined them in. Violence would not be tolerated.

But once the world was unsavory, and the Thunderhead spoke no more, many things in many places began to fester.

In the oldest cities of EuroScandia, groups of roaming Sibilants would leave bonfires in public squares full of pianos, cellos, and guitars, and although they would be caught and detained by peace officers every time, they would not stop. People hoped that the Thunderhead, even in its silence, would supplant them, replacing their minds and their entire identities with ones that would be content and not prone to violence. But that would be a violation of religious freedom. So the Sibilants were detained, forced to pay for the replacement of the things they had destroyed, and then released, only to destroy these things again.

The Thunderhead, if it could speak, might say that they were providing a service – and that by destroying musical instruments, it provided work for those whose job it was to create such instruments. But even for the Thunderhead, enough was enough.

The Toll appeared to the EuroScandian Sibilants as they prepared to lay waste to another concert hall.

The EuroScandian Sibilants knew it must be an imposter, for the Toll had been martyred at the hands of a scythe. Resurrection was not a tenet of their belief, so the zealots were skeptical.

"Drop your weapons and fall to your knees," the imposter said.

They did no such thing.

"The Tone and the Thunder are offended by your actions. And so am I. DROP YOUR WEAPONS AND FALL TO YOUR KNEES!"

Still they did not obey. One of them ran forward, speaking

in an old language native to the region that few people spoke anymore.

Then from the imposter's small entourage, a denim-robed scythe came forward, caught the attacker, and threw him to the ground. The attacker, bruised and bloody, scampered away.

"It is not too late to repent," the Toll imposter said. "The Tone, the Thunder, and I will forgive you if you renounce your destructive ways and serve us in peace."

The Sibilants looked past him to the doors of the concert hall. Their goal was so close, but there was something commanding about this young man before them. Something ... divine.

"I give you a sign," he said, "from the Thunderhead, to whom I alone can speak, and to whom I alone can intercede on your behalf."

Then he spread out his arms ... and out of the sky they came. Mourning doves. A hundred of them swooping in from all directions, as if they had been waiting all this time in the eaves of every building in the city! They landed on him, perching on his arms, his body, his head, until he could not be seen anymore. They covered him from head to toe, their light-brown bodies and wings like a shell, like an armor around him – and the color of it. The pattern of the feathers enveloping him, the way they moved. The sibilant Tonists realized what he now resembled.

He looked like a storm cloud. A Thunderhead billowing with wrath.

Suddenly the birds took off in all directions, leaving him and disappearing back to the hidden corners of the city from whence they came.

All was silent but for the last flapping of departing wings. And in that silence the Toll spoke in nearly a whisper.

"Now drop your weapons and fall to your knees."

And they did.

Being a dead prophet was much better than being a live one.

When you were dead, you weren't obliged to fill your days with a mind-numbing parade of supplicants. You were free to go where you wanted, when you wanted – and more importantly, where you were *needed*. But the best part about it was that nobody tried to kill you.

Being dead, Greyson Tolliver concluded, was much better for his peace of mind than being alive.

Since his public demise, Greyson had spent over two years traveling the world in an attempt to wrangle in the sibilant Tonists that were popping up everywhere. He and everyone with him traveled as modestly as possible. Public trains, commercial airlines. Greyson never wore his embroidered scapular and violet tunic when they traveled. They were all incognito in simple, drab Tonist attire. No one asked questions of Tonists for fear that they'd start espousing their beliefs. Most people would look the other way, avoiding eye contact.

Of course, if Curate Mendoza had his way, they would travel the world in a private jet with vertical landing capability, so the Toll could plop out of the sky like an actual god-machine. But Greyson forbade it, feeling there was already too much hypocrisy in the world.

"Tonists are not supposed to be materialistic," he told Mendoza.

"Neither are scythes," Mendoza pointed out, "and how did that work out?"

Nevertheless, this wasn't a democracy. What the Toll said was law among them, no matter who disagreed with it.

Sister Astrid was on Greyson's side.

"I think your resistance to extravagance is a good thing," she said. "And I imagine the Thunderhead agrees."

"As long as we get where we're going by the time we need to get there, the Thunderhead has no opinion," Greyson told her. Although he suspected that the Thunderhead was rerouting trains and flights to speed their way to their destinations. Greyson supposed that if the Toll proclaimed they must travel by mule, the Thunderhead would somehow supply them with racing mules.

Even with modest travel, Mendoza always managed to find a way to make their arrival dramatic and impressive enough to shake sibilant Tonists to their corroded foundations. Whatever strange and disturbing things they were doing, Greyson would reveal himself to them as the Toll and denounce them, renounce them, and basically shut them down, leaving them begging for his forgiveness.

The trick with the birds had been Greyson's idea. It was easy enough. All Earth's creatures had nanites so that the Thunderhead could monitor their populations – which meant that the Thunderhead had a back door into each species's behavior.

The scythedom had done something similar with the sea life around Endura, turning them into a free-range aquarium. But unlike that ill-fated technology, the Thunderhead did not manipulate the animals for human pleasure – or, as it turned out in the end – human pain. It only controlled a creature if that creature was in danger of becoming roadkill, or engaging in any other behavior that would end its life. As there were no revival centers for wild animals, it was the most effective way to allow them to live the full length of their natural lives.

"If I'm supposed to stop Sibilants," Greyson had said to the Thunderhead, "then I need to show them something impressive. Something that will prove to them that you are on *my* side, and not theirs." He proposed the gathering of storm-cloud colored birds, lighting all over him, and the Thunderhead obliged.

There were other tricks that Greyson used, of course. The Thunderhead could cause publicars to encircle the Tonists, herding them like sheep. It could generate a magnetic field strong enough to levitate Greyson with no visible means of doing so, and when weather conditions were right, the Thunderhead could induce a lightning storm at Greyson's command. But the birds were the best. It never failed to dazzle and always brought Sibilants around. If not back into line, then at least it started them moving in the right direction. Of course, being covered in doves and pigeons was not a pleasant thing. Their talons left scratches and gouges in his skin. They often tried to peck at his ears and eyes. And they were not the most hygienic of animals.

He would stay with the sect in question just long enough to make sure they were changing their ways. "Coming back into the fold," Mendoza called it. Then the Toll would disappear with his entourage and move on to another sect of Sibilants in another part of the world. Surgical strikes and guerilla diplomacy, that was his strategy for two years, and it was working. It helped that there were more ridiculous rumors about him than legitimate ones. "The Toll made a mountain crumble with his voice." "The Toll was seen dining in the desert with mortal-age gods, and was at the head of the table." It was easy to hide his actual appearances in the folds of the absurd ones.

"It's good that we do this," Curate Mendoza would say, "but it's nothing compared to what we *could* be doing."

"It's what the Thunderhead wants," Greyson would tell him, but Mendoza was always dubious. And, truth be told, Greyson was just as frustrated.

"You have me on a treadmill," Greyson had told the Thunderhead. "What am I accomplishing if sibilant sects are popping up faster than I can turn them? Is this your big plan? And isn't it wrong for me to pretend to be a god?"

"Define 'wrong,'" the Thunderhead had said.

The Thunderhead was particularly annoying when Greyson put forth ethical questions. It could not lie – but Greyson could, and did. He lied to the Sibilants at every encounter, telling them he was beyond human. Even so, the Thunderhead would not stop him from doing it, so he had no idea if it approved or disapproved. A simple "don't do that" would have sufficed if the Thunderhead felt his actions were an abuse of his power. In fact, being chastised by the Thunderhead would be comforting, because then he'd know if his own moral compass was off the mark. On the other hand, if the end did justify Greyson's means, why couldn't the Thunderhead just tell him so, and ease his mind?

"If you do anything that is too damaging, I will inform you," the Thunderhead had told him. Which left Greyson constantly waiting for a slap that never came.

"I've done some terrible things in your name," he told the Thunderhead.

To which the Thunderhead replied, "Define 'terrible.'"

The Toll's entourage, which had contracted to his inner circle – Scythe Morrison, Sister Astrid, and Curate Mendoza – had become an effective team.

Morrison had proven himself valuable right from the beginning. He never really had much of a work ethic before showing up to glean the Toll, but these years had changed him considerably – or at least carved him a new rut that was a little more enlightened. He had his reasons for staying. After all, where would he go? The North Merican scythedom thought he was dead. But that was only part of it. The thing is, if the North Merican scythedom were to check their own statistics, they'd know that he'd gleaned and granted immunity more than once. Well, he told himself, with so much gleaning going on these days, they couldn't be expected to notice the actions of one rogue scythe.

Of course, he knew that wasn't the truth, but the truth hurt a little too much to admit.

They didn't notice, because they didn't care.

He had always been a nonentity to the other scythes. An embarrassment to his mentor, who chose him because he was strong and good-looking, and then disowned him the moment it became clear that he'd never win anyone's respect. To them he was a joke. But at least here, in the service of the Toll, his existence was acknowledged. He had a place and a purpose. He was the protector, and he liked it.

Sister Astrid was the only one who had issues with Morrison. "You, Jim, embody everything about the world I can't stand," she once told him.

Which made him grin. "Why can't you just admit that you like me?"

"I tolerate you. There's a big difference."

As for Astrid, she had her work cut out for her keeping them all on the proper spiritual path. She stayed with the Toll because deep down, she believed that Greyson Tolliver was the real thing. That he was divinely moved by the Tone, and that his humility about it was understandable. A humble nature was, after all, the hallmark of a true holy man. It made perfect sense that he would refuse to believe he was part of the Holy Triad, but just because he didn't believe it himself, didn't make it any less true.

She would secretly smirk each time he faced sibilant Tonists as the Toll, because she knew he didn't believe a single thing he said. To him it was just a role. But to Astrid, his denial made it all the more true.

And then there was Curate Mendoza: the magician, the showman, the producer of their traveling show. He knew he was the linchpin holding it all together, and although there were times that he actually believed his own faith, that always got trampled by the practicality of getting the job done.

Mendoza not only organized the Toll's appearances, but kept in close communication with his network of curates around the globe, in a constant attempt to wrangle more and more sects under one accepted doctrine, and to help them protect themselves against scythes. Mendoza also worked in the shadows, spreading many of the false rumors about the Toll. They were amazingly helpful in keeping the flock engaged – and in keeping scythes disengaged – because how could scythes give any credence to Toll sightings when most of them were flights of fancy? Yet when Greyson found out what Mendoza was doing, he was horrified. How could Greyson not see the value?

"You're telling people that I've risen from my own ashes?"

"There is precedent," Mendoza tried to explain. "The history of faith is full of falling/rising gods. I'm laying the groundwork for your legend."

"If people want to believe that, fine," Greyson said, "but I don't want to encourage it by spreading more lies."

"If you want me to help you, why do you keep tying my hands?" Mendoza said, increasingly frustrated.

"Maybe because I want you to use your hands for something more than pleasuring yourself."

That actually made Mendoza laugh, because what had these past few years been but Greyson Tolliver spewing his will in everyone else's direction? But laughing at the Toll was over the line, so he backpedaled quickly.

"Yes, Your Sonority," Mendoza said, as he always said. "I'll try to keep that in mind." He had no choice but to back off, because arguing did nothing with this headstrong boy – a boy who had no idea what it actually took to keep his mystique alive. Although Mendoza was beginning to wonder why he even bothered.

Then something happened that changed everything.

"Grief, grief, and more grief!" the Thunderhead wailed in Greyson's ear one evening. "I wish I could have blinded my eyes

368

to it. This event is a grim fulcrum upon which many things will pivot."

"Can you please not speak in riddles?" Greyson asked. "And just tell me what's going on?"

And so the Thunderhead told him, in excruciating detail, about the stadium gleaning. Tens of thousands felled in a single evening. "It will be all over the news in a few moments – even if the North Merican scythedom tries to hide it, it's too big to erase. And it will lead to a chain reaction of events that will leave the world in unprecedented upheaval."

"What are we going to do about it?" Greyson asked.

"Nothing," the Thunderhead said. "It is a scythe action, which means I cannot even react to it. I must treat it as if it never happened."

"Well," said Greyson, "you can't do anything, but I can."

"Continue what you've been doing," the Thunderhead instructed him. "Now more than ever the Sibilants will need to be reined in." And then the Thunderhead said something that chilled him. "The odds that sibilant Tonists will seriously damage the future of humanity have ticked up to 19.3%."

33

Unbreakable

"This is Scythe Anastasia. And no, this is not a recording; I'm coming to you live – because I am alive. But you're not convinced. Of course you're not – anyone can pull off a stunt like this using my memory construct, and a hundred other technological tricks. That's why I need you to doubt this broadcast. Doubt it enough to do everything you can to debunk it. Do your best to prove that it's fake, because once you fail, you'll have to accept that it's real. That I'm real. And once you're convinced that I am who I say I am ... then we can get down to business."

The first broadcast was short and sweet. It had all the conviction, all the confidence it needed to have – and with good reason. Anastasia had found something on the lunar disaster. Something big. She had done what no one else had managed to do: uncover evidence that had been there, buried in the backbrain, since long before she was even born. The Thunderhead knew it was there, but it was, by law, obliged not to do anything about it. Scythe business was scythe business; it had to let it go. But the Thunderhead must know what she had discovered. It knew every bit of its own backbrain. She wondered if it was happy with what she had found.

"I am immensely proud of you," High Blade Tenkamenin told her. "I knew you'd crack it! Of course Scythe Makeda had her doubts."

"I was voicing healthy skepticism," Makeda said in her own defense. "We couldn't count our chickens before they were hatched."

"Or put our eggs in one basket," added Baba. "I wonder which expression came first, the chickens or the eggs."

Which of course made Tenka laugh. But his laughter was short-lived. There was something weighing on the High Blade. On all of them. There had been an undercurrent of tension all day.

It was even evident in Jeri, who usually played emotions close to the vest. "One of my crew had a family member gleaned," Jeri told her. "I need to go into town and console her." Jeri hesitated, as if there was more to be said ... but didn't say it. "I'll be back late. Tell the High Blade not to expect me for dinner."

And then, when the rest of them did sit down for dinner, the tone in the room bordered on dour. Not tense, but heavy. As if the burden of the world, which rested firmly on their shoulders, had doubled. Anastasia thought she knew why. "It was my broadcast, wasn't it?" she asked, breaking the silence over a salad that wilted under the weight of everyone's mood. "People didn't react the way you wanted. It was a waste of our time."

"Not at all," Makeda said. "You were marvelous, dear."

"And," added Baba, "I've been tracking the chatter. It's through the roof. I'd say you'd made an even bigger splash than Endura did."

"Poor taste, Baba," said Makeda. "Very poor taste."

Tenkamenin didn't comment. He seemed lost in his greens.

"Then what is it?" Anastasia asked. "If something's wrong, you have to tell me what it is."

"There was … an incident last night," Tenkamenin finally told her. "In North Merica…"

Anastasia braced herself. "Did it involve Rowan Damisch?"

Tenka looked away – and so did Baba, but Scythe Makeda held glaring eye contact. "Yes, as a matter of fact it did."

Anastasia curled her toes so tightly she felt the soles of her feet begin to knot. "He was gleaned," Anastasia said. "Goddard gleaned him." Somehow, saying it herself was better than hearing any of them say it.

But Tenka shook his head.

"He was supposed to be gleaned," Tenka told her. "But he escaped."

Anastasia folded with relief. It was not very scythelike. She tried to regain her composure, but everyone had seen.

"He's with the Texans," Makeda said. "Why they'd save him is beyond me."

"He's their enemy's enemy," Baba said.

"The problem isn't that he escaped – it's what happened afterward," Tenka told her. "Goddard ordered a mass gleaning. Beyond anything we've ever seen. Nearly thirty thousand souls were taken – and he's ordered that those who escaped be hunted down along with their families. He's invoking the third commandment."

"As if that applies!" snapped Makeda. "When you've just condemned an entire stadium to death, who wouldn't run?"

Anastasia was silent. She took it in. She tried not to respond, because it was just too big a thing to respond to. Rowan was safe. And because of it, thousands were dead. How was she supposed to feel about that?

"Your broadcast went out as it was happening – before we even heard," Tenka said. "We thought it would overshadow you – but it was just the opposite. In light of this news, it makes everything you have to say all the more important. We want to speed up the schedule. Another broadcast tomorrow night."

"People need to hear from you, Anastasia," said Makeda. "You're a voice of hope in the horror."

"Yes, of course," Anastasia told them. "I'll do another broadcast as soon as possible."

The main course came. A roast so rare it was bloody. Such things shouldn't bother a scythe, but today they all had to look away when the server carved.

This is Scythe Anastasia. Have you debunked me yet? Have you done what my mentor, Scythe Marie Curie, the Grand Dame of Death, would have called your due diligence? Or are you willing to accept the assertions put forth by the various scythedoms who support 'Overblade' Goddard's claims to larger and larger pieces of the world? Of course they say I'm an imposter – what else can they say, if they don't want to anger Goddard?

"Goddard – who invited tens of thousands to witness a gleaning that turned out to be their own. He claims that Scythe Lucifer sank Endura. It's a solid fact of history now. As I was there, I can tell you this much is true: Scythe Lucifer was on Endura. The eyewitness accounts of survivors who saw him are legitimate. But did he sink Endura?

"Not a chance.

"In the coming days, I'll offer testimony that will make it very clear what happened on Endura. And who was responsible."

★ ★ ★

373

In Goddard's glass chalet, there were surprisingly few things that could be broken. Ayn watched as Goddard tried, but they simply lived in a world where everything was too well made. She was done trying to quell his temper. His underscythes could be his wranglers now. Today it was Nietzsche. Constantine hadn't been seen for days. Supposedly he was off meeting with representatives of the LoneStar region, trying to convince them to turn over Rowan, but they still denied that they even had him. Underscythe Franklin would have nothing to do with Goddard when he was like this. "Tell me when he's human again," Aretha would say, and go off to her own quarters on a floor far enough away not to hear his rampage.

His latest tantrum was brought on by Scythe Anastasia's second message to the world.

"I want her found!" he demanded. "I want her found and gleaned."

"She can't be gleaned," Underscythe Nietzsche tried to explain. "Whether you like it or not, she's still a scythe."

"Then we'll find her and make her self-glean," yelled Goddard. "I'll make her suffering so great that she'll end her own life to stop it."

"Your Excellency, the suspicion that would bring upon you will not be worth the effort."

It made Goddard throw a chair across the room. It didn't break.

Ayn sat calmly in the conference room, watching the drama play out between them. Nietzsche kept looking to her for help, but she would not waste her breath. Goddard would be unreasonable until he wasn't. Period. Then he would find a rational excuse for everything he had done while unhinged.

Ayn used to believe the things Goddard did were all part of a greater plan – but now she saw the truth: The plan always came after the action. He was brilliant at finding shapes in the clouds of his fury.

Such as convincing himself that the Mile High gleaning was a decisive act of wisdom. Repercussions from the mass gleaning had been immediate. Those regions that were anti-Goddard railed against him. Half a dozen regions announced that they would grant immunity to anyone who chose to leave Goddard's dominion, and plenty of people were taking them up on the invitation. Yet in spite of all that, those who supported Goddard were also galvanized, insisting that "those people" at the stadium deserved gleaning – because anyone who would want to witness an execution deserved what they got. Even though they were probably all watching themselves before the feed was cut.

Most people, however, didn't take a position either way. They just wanted to disappear into the pleasantries of their lives. As long as when bad things happened, they happened somewhere else, to someone they didn't know, it was not their problem. Except that everyone knew someone who knew someone who was at the stadium that day and didn't come home.

Nietzsche continued to try to soothe Goddard, who still stormed around the conference room.

"Anastasia is nothing, Your Excellency," Nietzsche said. "But by reacting to her, you're making her much more important than she needs to be."

"So I should just ignore her and her accusations?"

"Accusations are all they are, and we don't even yet know

what she's accusing you of. She's an itch best left unscratched, Your Excellency."

That actually made Ayn laugh – because she could imagine Goddard scratching an itch until he bled out.

Finally spent, Goddard slammed himself down into a chair and reined in his rage. "Tell me what's going on out there," he demanded. "Tell me what I need to know."

Nietzsche sat down at the conference table "Allied scythe-doms are either supporting what you did at the stadium or are remaining silent. Scythedoms who stand against you are calling for you to self-glean – but I'm more concerned with the flood of people crossing the border into the LoneStar region."

"You wanted fear," Ayn said. "Now you've got it."

"We're exploring the possibility of building a wall to stem the exodus."

"Don't be ridiculous," Goddard said. "Only idiots build walls. Let them go – and once we succeed in absorbing the LoneStar region, those who abandoned MidMerica will be marked for gleaning."

"Is that how you solve every problem now?" Ayn asked. "Glean it away?"

She expected him to snap back at her, but his mood had settled. "It's what we *do*, Ayn. It's the tool we've been granted – the only tool we can wield."

"And then," continued Nietzsche, "there's the matter of the Tonists."

"Tonists!" lamented Goddard. "Why must Tonists always be on the agenda?"

"You turned their prophet into a martyr," Ayn pointed out.

"In spite of what you think, dead enemies are harder to fight than live ones."

"Except…" said Nietzsche, hesitating.

"Except what?" Goddard prompted.

"Except that we've been tracking reports that the Toll has appeared to people."

Goddard grunted in disgust. "Yes, I know. In clouds, and in the patterns of burnt toast."

"No, Your Excellency. I mean in the flesh. And we're beginning to think the reports might be credible."

"You can't be serious."

"Well, we never confirmed that the body presented was actually the Toll's. It's possible that he's still alive."

Ayn took a deep breath, suspecting another round of things not breaking was about to begin.

34

A Better Place

"I know most people don't follow what happens in the scythedom. That's natural. The scythedom was created so that most people would never have to deal with the bringers of death until death was brought to them.

"But the sinking of Endura affected us all. It made the Thunderhead go silent and mark everyone unsavory. And without Grandslayers to moderate, it led to an imbalance of power within the scythedom.

"We've had a stable world for over two hundred years. But not anymore. If we want that stability back, we have to fight for it. Not just those of us in the scythedom, but everyone. And when you hear what I have to say, you're going to want to fight.

"I know what you're thinking. 'Is Scythe Anastasia going to make the accusation? Is she going to publicly point the finger at Goddard as the killer of the Grandslayers, and the destroyer of Endura?'

"You'll have to wait, because there are other cases that must be made first. Other accusations. I'm going to show you a history of unthinkable acts that go against everything the scythedom is supposed to stand for.

"It's a story that doesn't start with Goddard – in fact, it starts years before he was even born.

"In the Year of the Lynx, the Nectaris Prime colony on the moon had what they called a catastrophic atmospheric failure. Their entire supply of oxygen – even the reserve of liquid oxygen – vented into space, killing every colonist. Not a single survivor.

"Everyone knows about that — it's something we all learned in school. But have you ever read the first screen on the official history databases? You know the one — it's that annoying scroll of small print you always skip to get to whatever you're looking for. If you actually read it, buried in the middle of all that legal camouflage, is a small clause. It states that the public history databases are all subject to scythe approval. Why? Because scythes are allowed to do anything they want. Even censor history.

"That wasn't a problem as long as scythes were true to their calling. Honorable, virtuous, holding themselves to the highest human ideals. It only became a problem when certain scythes began to serve themselves instead of humanity.

"The moon colony was the first attempt at off-world settlement. The plan was to steadily populate 'the Lunar Frontier' and relieve the population problem back on Earth. The Thunderhead had it all worked out. Then came the disaster.

"I want you to unlearn everything you think you know about that event — because as I said, the official histories can't be trusted. Instead, I want you to research the lunar disaster for yourself, just the way I did. Go directly to the original sources. Those first articles written. Personal recordings made by the doomed colonists before they died. Broadcasts pleading for help. It's all there in the Thunderhead's backbrain. Of course the Thunderhead won't guide you, because you're unsavory, so you'll have to find it yourself.

"But you know what? Even if you weren't unsavory, the Thunderhead wouldn't guide you. Because of the sensitive nature of the information, helping you find it would be against the law, and as much as it might want to, the Thunderhead cannot break the law. Good thing you have me."

* * *

The LoneStar scythes brought Rowan to Austin, the city far-thest from any border, and set layer upon layer of protection around him. He was treated with care. He wasn't given a luxury suite, but wasn't put in a cell, either.

"You *are* a criminal," Scythe Coleman had told him during his rescue. "But we've learned from our studies of the mortal age – where crime was the norm rather than the exception – that criminals can be useful, in their own way."

They allowed him a computer with which to educate himself about the years he had missed, but he kept being drawn instead to videos of what had happened at Mile High Stadium after he had been rescued. There were no official recordings of the "correctional gleaning," as the North Merican Allied Scythedom was spinning it, but survivors were posting personal recordings they had made.

Rowan watched them not because he wanted to, but because he felt an overwhelming need to witness as much of it as possible. To acknowledge as many victims as he could. Even though he knew none of them, he felt it was his responsibility to remember their faces and give them at least one last moment of respect. If he had known Goddard would do this, he would have resisted the Texan scythes and accepted his own gleaning – but how could he have known – and how could he have resisted? Just as Goddard was determined to end him, the Texans were determined to steal him away.

And he also watched, and rewatched, Citra's all-too-short broadcasts. Knowing that she was still free and fighting made everything else bearable.

The last time Rowan had been in the LoneStar region, he had been Rand's captive. The mandate of the region – benevolent lawlessness – made it easy for Rand to escape scrutiny and carry out her plan to bring Goddard back. But it was that same self-determination that made its scythes bold enough to rescue Rowan.

Post-mortal Texans were unique. They were beholden to no rules beyond those of their own personal making and accountable to no one but one another – sometimes to terrible results, other times to glorious ones. As one of the Thunderhead's seven Charter Regions, it was a prolonged social experiment that had become a permanent way of life – perhaps because the Thunderhead had decided the world needed one such place, where people could learn how to live by the laws of their own hearts.

Some other experiments didn't fare as well. Such as the "pensive collective" in RossShelf – the Charter Region in Antarctica – where the Thunderhead introduced mind-link technology that allowed everyone to read everyone else's minds. Not pretty. People said it was the closest the Thunderhead had ever come to making a mistake, although it insisted that all its experiments, by their very nature, were successful, because they all proved something and gave it a better perspective from which to serve humanity. The pensive collective became the "slumber collective," and now the people of the RossShelf region were the happy subjects of communal dreaming, where minds were still linked, but only during REM sleep.

Two days after Rowan's rescue, Scythes Travis and Coleman visited him in his quarters. But then a third scythe entered the room. One whom Rowan knew all too well, and was not keen on seeing.

The instant he saw the red robe, Rowan knew he had been betrayed. He stood, reflexively reaching for a weapon, but of course he had none. Scythe Constantine, however, made no move to attack. He didn't seem too happy – but that was nothing new for the man. He only had two expressions: disgusted and judgmental.

Scythe Coleman put up her hands to calm Rowan down. "It's not what you think," she told him. "He's not here to harm you. Scythe Constantine has joined the LoneStar scythedom."

Only now did Rowan notice that the jewels that had adorned Constantine's robe the last time Rowan had seen him were gone. And although his robe was still crimson, the fabric was now rugged canvas. While scythes were free to align themselves with any region they chose, it was rare that an important scythe like Constantine joined a different region. Rowan couldn't help but think it was a trick.

Scythe Travis laughed. "Told you we should have warned him."

"Believe me, Mr. Damisch," said Constantine. "I am no more pleased to see you than you are to see me, but there are concerns greater than our mutual animosity."

Rowan still wasn't sure if he believed it. He couldn't even imagine the high and mighty Constantine as a LoneStar scythe, limiting himself to gleaning only by bowie knife – the only rule of the LoneStar scythedom beyond the commandments.

"Please, Rowan, sit down," said Scythe Coleman. "We have business to discuss."

And when he sat, she gave Rowan a single page. On it were a list of names. All scythes. There were about fifty of them.

"Those are the scythes we have decided that you should end," Coleman said.

Rowan looked up at Coleman, then down at the page, then up at Coleman again. Could they actually be asking him to kill fifty scythes?

Travis, who was leaning against a wall with his arms crossed, gave a mournful *oh boy* sort of whistle. "The look on his face says it all, don't it? This won't be easy."

Rowan held the sheet out to Coleman. "No," Rowan said. "Out of the question."

But Scythe Coleman didn't take back the sheet and was not about to take no for an answer. "Don't forget that we rescued you from the prospect of a painful death, Rowan," she said. "And because we rescued you, thirty thousand innocent people were gleaned. You owe it to us as your rescuers, and you owe it to those poor people."

"All we're asking," added Travis, "is that you rid the world of problematic scythes. Didn't you already have your heart set on doing that? Now you won't be working alone. You'll have the LoneStar scythedom's backing."

"*Unofficial* backing," added Coleman

"Right," agreed Travis. "No one can know. That's the deal."

"And exactly what makes a scythe problematic to you?" Rowan asked.

Coleman snapped the page away from him and pulled a

name from the list. "Scythe Kurosawa. He has spoken out against our region for years and has insulted our High Blade time and time again."

Rowan was incredulous. "So that's it? You want me to end a scythe for having a big mouth?"

"You're missing the point," said Travis. "Why is this so hard for you, son?"

Through all of this Constantine said nothing. He just stood back, with a funereal expression. The fact was, as Scythe Lucifer, Rowan vetted his choices thoroughly. If he could find a single redeeming quality to the scythe in question, he left that scythe alone. He personally knew at least three of the scythes on that list. They might not have been the most upstanding of scythes, but they didn't deserve to be ended.

"Sorry," said Rowan. "If you rescued me so you can use me to settle your grudges, then put me back on the pyre." Then he turned to Constantine. "And you! You're a hypocrite! You hunted me for gleaning bad scythes, and now you're fine with me going out there to do it again?"

Constantine took a deep breath before he spoke. "You forget that I was an underscythe to Goddard. After what I've seen, I've come to feel his hold on the world must be weakened by any means necessary. All the scythes on that list are of the new order and fully embrace Goddard and his philosophies. You began your rampage because you believed the scythedom needed a dramatic overhaul. A culling, if you will. Although I am loath to admit it, I believe you are right."

Did Constantine actually just say that? Hell would be freezing over if the Thunderhead weren't controlling its weather.

"Thank you for saving my life," Rowan told Coleman and Travis. "But like I said, I don't take requests."

"Told you so," Travis said to Coleman. "Plan B?"

Coleman nodded. Rowan shuddered to think what plan B was, but no one was pulling out their knives to glean him.

"In all the time since you were revived, did you ever once ask about what happened to your family?" Scythe Coleman said.

Rowan looked away. He had been afraid to ask — not just out of the fear of knowing, but also because he didn't want to bring his family into this, to be used on anyone's chessboard.

"If they're still alive, I'm sure they've disowned me," Rowan said. "Maybe changed their names, or even had themselves supplanted. If I were related to me, that's what *I* would do."

"Very insightful," said Scythe Coleman. "Actually, two of your sisters did change their names, and one of your brothers did get supplanted — but the rest of the Damisch family remained. Your mother, grandparents, and four other siblings."

"Are you … threatening to hurt them?"

Travis guffawed at that. "What do you think? We're like Goddard? We'd never hurt innocent people. 'Cept of course for the ones we glean."

"I'll tell you what we did do," Scythe Coleman said. "After you sank Endura, your family came to our region out of fear that they would be gleaned by MidMerica's new High Blade — with whom they knew you had bad blood. We took them in, and since then they have been quietly under our protection, where they will remain, regardless of what you choose to do." Then she turned to Travis. "Bring them in."

Travis left the room.

And Rowan began to panic.

Was his family here? Is that what was happening? Were they going to force him to face them? No! How could he, after all that he had done – after all they *believed* he had done. As much as he wanted to see them – to see for himself that they were all right – he couldn't bear the thought of standing before his family.

"No! No, don't!" Rowan insisted.

"If we can't convince you, maybe they can," said Constantine.

But the horror of making his family a part of this? Of hearing his own mother tell him to go out there and kill scythes? That was worse than being gleaned! It was worse than being burned alive!

"I'll do it!" Rowan blurted. "I'll do whatever you want, just … just please, *please* leave my family out of this…"

Coleman closed the door before Travis could return.

"I knew you'd see reason," she said with a warm smile. "Now let's make this world a better place."

"Have you done the research? Have you dug into the backbrain? I know it's frustrating without the Thunderhead's help – but after three years, I'm sure a lot of you have figured out how to do it. There's a benefit to being unsavory, isn't there? It forces you to struggle through the frustration and do things the hard way. So much more satisfying.

"What did you find when you looked at the lunar disaster? Anything that didn't look quite right to you? Did you find that the environmental system had triple redundancy? Not only a backup system but two backups to the backup. Did you learn that prior to that day, the Thunderhead had calculated the chances of an atmospheric catastrophe

at .000093%? That's less than one chance in a million. Was the Thunderhead wrong?

"After the disaster, the Grandslayers of that time enacted a week of mourning. No one would be gleaned for a week, since so many had died on the moon. I'm sure most of the Grandslayers believed it was a tragic accident and were genuine in their remorse.

"But maybe, just maybe, one was not.

"If you're looking for evidence that would tie any specific scythe to that disaster, you won't find it. But did you look into what happened in the days and weeks after the tragedy? Did it trouble you that there was no cleanup of the site by the Thunderhead? No recovery of the dead?

"Nameless sources suggested it was simply too much effort for the Thunderhead to recover bodies that were too damaged by the vacuum of space and solar radiation to ever be revived.

"But if you dig in the backbrain, you can find a single statement from the Thunderhead. It's there for anyone to see who cares to look. In fact, it's the last thing in its file on the lunar disaster. Have you found it yet? If not, I have it pulled up right here. Have a look:

"'Lunar event beyond Thunderhead jurisdiction. Result of scythe activity.'"

Drawing out what she knew wasn't just a tactic to hook people – it was a stalling tactic as well, because Anastasia still wasn't sure where it was going to lead – but each day revealed more hidden truths in the backbrain. She knew she was close to a break-through on the Mars disaster, but was completely stymied by the destruction of the NewHope orbital colony.

But the first reveal already had everyone reeling. Tenkamenin was overjoyed, and couldn't contain his glee at dinner.

"That statement by the Thunderhead in a forgotten file. 'Result of scythe activity.' Masterful work!"

"You put us all to shame, dear," said Makeda. "We searched the backbrain for months and never found that."

"And walking people through how to find it themselves only makes your case stronger," Tenka said.

"But I can't lead them to things I can't find. There are still so many leads that make no sense. Like the white silk."

"Explain," said Makeda. "Maybe we can help."

Anastasia pulled out her tablet and showed them an image. "This was the last picture taken on the NewHope orbital colony before the disaster. You can see the approaching shuttle in the background – the one that lost control and hit the station, destroying it." Anastasia tapped on the screen. "The backbrain links the image to tons of things – almost all of them relating to the disaster. News reports, obituaries. Dynamic analysis of the explosion. And then there's this…"

She showed them an inventory log for a bolt of fabric. Pearl-white silk. "I tracked where it went – about half of it was sold for wedding dresses, some of it was used for drapes – but there are fifteen meters unaccounted for. Nothing's ever unaccounted for in the Thunderhead's inventory."

"Perhaps they were just scraps," Baba suggested.

"Or," came a voice from behind them, "perhaps it was used by someone who didn't need to pay for it."

It was Jeri, late as usual, but with the insight that made all the difference. There was only one sort of person who could walk away with an expensive fabric, no questions asked, and not have to pay for it. Jeri sat beside Anastasia, who quickly started working on the tablet. Once she had something to look for, the information wasn't hard to find.

"There are hundreds of scythes known to have robes in shades of white … but only about fifty in silk … and pearl silk? That's not common at all." Then she stopped to take in what her screen was telling her, and turned to the others.

"There's only one scythe who had robes made of that particular fabric," she said. "Scythe Dante Alighieri."

While the others didn't realize the significance, Tenka did, and offered her the broadest of smiles. "How divine the comedy," he said. "All roads lead to Alighieri…"

"His name is familiar," said Makeda. "Wasn't he from Byzantium?"

"TransSiberia, I believe," said Baba.

Then the moment was shattered by a jarring jangle loud enough to make everyone jump. The sound ceased, then came again.

"Ah, there's the culprit," said Jeri, pointing to the antique twentieth-century telephone in the corner of the dining room. It was one of the old phones connected to Tenkamenin's personal line – which hadn't rung once since Anastasia had been there. It gave off one more abrasive jangle before Tenkamenin directed one of the servers to pick it up.

"This is His Excellency's, High Blade Tenkamenin, personal line," the server said a bit awkwardly. "Whom may I say is calling?"

The server listened, looked alarmed for a moment, but then his expression resolved into annoyance. He hung up and tried to return to serving.

"What was that all about?" asked the High Blade.

"Nothing, Your Excellency."

"It looked very much like something to me."

The server sighed. "It was a Tonist, Your Excellency, moaning and groaning like an animal. I don't know how the miscreant came upon your number."

Then the phone rang again.

"We could have it traced," suggested Scythe Makeda.

Tenkamenin's face was serious. Not angry, but concerned. "There's a red button on the right of the device," he told the server. "It will put the call on speaker. Be so kind as to answer it once more and press the button."

The servant did as he was instructed, and immediately a wordless wailing sounded from the phone's tinny speaker. The noise was so ghostly it would have been more at home in a drafty medieval castle than the High Blade's palace. It was insistent. Mournful. Desperate.

Tenkamenin pushed his chair back with a loud scrape, stood up, and went to the phone. He just stood there looking at it and listening to the awful sound. Then finally he disconnected the call.

"Well," said Scythe Baba, "that was unpleasant." He tried to make a joke of it, but Tenkamenin was not in a joking mood. He just stood there staring at the silent phone. Then he turned to Jeri.

"Captain Soberanis," Tenkamenin said. "Where is your crew at this very moment?"

Jeri looked around, understanding no more than anyone else the pertinence of the question. "They're either out in town or back on the ship. Why?"

"Notify them that you'll be setting sail immediately. And that we will be coming with you."

"We, as in…"

"As in all of us."

Anastasia stood up. She had never seen Tenka like this. He had always been unflappable. Now he seemed deeply shaken.

"What's going on, Your Excellency?" she asked.

"That wasn't a random call," he said. "I believe it was a warning, and one we should heed."

"How do you know?"

"Because," Tenkamenin said, "that was my father."

35

Requiem in Ten Parts

i. Introitus

It begins with hushed anticipation. The conductor stands, hand poised, all eyes on the wand, as if its downstroke will bring a dark magic.

Today's piece is an orchestral wonder. A requiem conceived of, and performed by, sibilant followers of the Tone, the Thunder, and the martyred Toll. A requiem performed in response to the Mile High gleaning an ocean away.

Can you hear it now, ringing forth in the streets of Port Remembrance? A wordless, tongueless mass of mortality in an immortal world? Sweeping strains of fire and brimstone, but mostly fire. These Sibilants are well prepared for the music they will deliver today. And for those who hear it, there will be no deliverance.

ii. Dies Irae

Fire trucks were all automated. Yet still they were designed to require a human at the wheel, for the Thunderhead had planned it that way. Of course, if the human made a wrong turn, the truck would override the human and correct the error.

The fire chief of Port Remembrance thought about that often. Before he became chief, he would intentionally make mistakes while driving his rig just to entertain himself — to see how long it took for the course correction to register, and for the truck to get itself back on track. The Thunderhead could use robots to do the job of firefighters, he supposed, but the Thunderhead had never been too keen on robots. It only used them for mindless labor that no one else wanted.

And so firefighters were still firefighters. But that didn't mean they had much to do. Because whenever a fire started, the Thunderhead always saw it when it was little more than a spark, and was usually able to put it out. It was only on those rare occasions that it could not, that firefighters were called in ... although the chief had come to believe that the Thunderhead started "safe" fires just to give them something to do.

At six thirty in the evening, an alarm went off in the firehouse. Used to be that the Thunderhead would talk to them and explain the nuances of the situation they were about to get into. Now it just sounded an alarm, programmed their GPSs, and let them figure the rest out for themselves.

Today's alarm was strange, however. There was no destination set on their screens. The garage doors didn't roll up. But still the alarm blared.

It was only when the door to the firehouse blew off its hinges and figures began to race in that the firefighters realized the alarm was not a fire alert – it was to warn them that they were under attack.

Tonists!

Dozens of them spilled through the door, all letting off that nasty beelike droning sound. The Tonists had weapons, and the men and women of the unit simply were not prepared for this unexpected day of wrath.

The fire chief stood in astonishment. He wanted to defend them, but how? With what? No one ever attacked a firefighter – except for maybe the occasional scythe, but when a scythe attacked, you got gleaned, end of story. You didn't fight back. You didn't struggle. But this was very different. These Tonists were rendering people deadish left and right, and no one knew what to do.

Think! he told himself. *Think!* He was trained to fight fires, not people. *Think! There has to be something I can do!*

And then it came to him.

Fire axes!

They had fire axes! He ran across the garage to grab one. But could he actually use it against another human being? He'd have to, because he wasn't about to let these Sibilants render his entire unit deadish.

Just then, the Tonists began throwing rocks at the trucks. One came in the chief's direction, and he caught it before it could hit him.

It wasn't exactly a rock, though. First of all, it was metallic and had hard ridges. He'd seen something like this before in history books. *Think! What was it called?* Oh right – a grenade!

And in an instant there was nothing more for the chief to think about.

iii. Confutatis

High Blade Tenkamenin was a deliberate man. He only appeared to be impulsive and flip, when, in fact, everything about his life was planned and organized. Even the chaos of his Lunar Jubilees was a controlled chaos.

He suspected that time was of the essence after that urgent warning call from his father, but it was impossible for him to fight his own instincts. He had quickly retreated to his humble residence, where he struggled with his valet to figure out what he needed to take with him for a hasty escape. A second robe, of course. But should it be one for cold weather or warm? Who should be notified that they were leaving? High Blades couldn't just vanish. He found himself confounded by it all.

"Your Excellency," said the valet, "didn't you say that we were in a hurry?"

"Yes, yes, of course."

And there were things of sentimental value that absolutely had to come with him. The engraved obsidian revolver given to him by Grandslayer Nzinga the day he took her place as High Blade. The silver dagger he'd used for his first gleaning. If this place was about to be overrun, who knew if he'd ever see his prized possessions again. He absolutely had to take them.

For ten minutes he obsessed over what he should and should not take and was only stopped by the first distant explosions.

iv. Lacrimosa

"If we're leaving, we should leave now!"

Anastasia paced the grand hall beneath the palace's central dome with Jeri, waiting for everyone else to show. "Where the hell are Tenkamenin and the others?"

"Maybe you're overreacting," said Jeri. "I've had dealings with many Tonists, and never once have I known them to be violent. Annoying and strident, maybe, but never violent."

"You didn't see these Tonists!" Anastasia said. "And if Tenkamenin thinks they're up to something, I believe him."

"Then let's leave without him," Jeri offered. "Let him and the others catch up with us."

"I'm not about to leave him," Anastasia said. Just then a series of far-off explosions echoed through the grand atrium. They both stopped to listen. More explosions filled the air, like distant thunder.

"Wherever it is," said Jeri, "it's not here in the palace."

"No, but it's going to be." Anastasia knew that whatever those explosions were, it was an omen of worse to come. An angry promise that this day would most certainly end in tears.

v. Sanctus

The young Tonist was a loyal follower. She did what her curate told her to do, because he was a true man of the Tone. Holy and sanctified. Their curate had not spoken for many years, and on the day of the Great Resonance – the day the Thunderhead went silent – he was the first to surrender his tongue. Words lied. Words connived, they dissembled with impunity, they slandered, and, above all, they offended the purity of the Tone.

One by one all the Tonists in their order made their vow a permanent one, as their curate had. Not a vow of silence, but a vow of vowels. A complete surrendering of the harsh, unnatural clicks, hisses, and pops that consonants brought. Language was the enemy of the Tonist. This is what their sect believed. Of course, there were many other Tonists who did not. But they would soon see the light. Even the ones who had blinded themselves.

While one team took out the firehouse, and another the peace officers' precinct, their curate led the largest team to the palace. They all had weapons – the kind that common citizens weren't supposed to have. They had been given them by an unknown benefactor. A secret supporter of their cause. The Tonists were not trained in these weapons, but what did that matter? Swing the blade, pull the trigger, hurl the grenade, and press the detonator. With so many of them armed, they didn't need to be all that skilled to achieve their goal.

And they also had kerosene. Jugs and jugs of it.

The Tonist made sure she was part of the first wave. She was frightened, but also joyous for her part in this. Now was their time! In the wake of the Mile High gleaning, when ire against scythes was at a full boil, people would finally see the Tonist way! They would cheer for what would be done here today, and the SubSaharan region would be a klaxon calling out to the rest of the world, waking them into the glory of the Tone, Toll, and Thunder. All rejoice!

She opened her mouth to intone as she neared the palace, and others joined her. It was so satisfying to be the one who started them intoning. They were of one mind, one spirit, one chord.

Then, climbing on the backs of her brethren, she and dozens of others began to scale the palace wall.

vi. Agnus Dei

Anastasia and Jeri, with Scythes Makeda and Baba close behind, finally met up with Tenkamenin in the rose garden, halfway between the palace and his cottage. His valet was struggling with a large rolling suitcase that wouldn't roll on the pebbles of the narrow garden path.

"We've called for the helicopter," Scythe Makeda informed everyone. "But it will take at least ten minutes to get here from the airport."

"And that's only if the pilot isn't off in some bar," Baba added, "like he was the last time."

"It will be fine," Tenkamenin said, a bit out of breath. "It will come for us, and everything will be fine."

Then he turned to lead everyone to the heliport, which was on the property's west lawn. Around them the entire compound was in motion. Palace staff hurried, going this way and that, their arms full of belongings. The BladeGuard were flooding out of the barracks and taking strategic positions — something they had probably done only in exercises.

And then they heard a noise from the west. A chorus of droning voices, each one hitting a different discordant monotone. And figures began dropping over the western wall.

"We're too late," said Tenkamenin, halting them in their tracks.

Alarms began to blare all around them, and the BladeGuards took immediate action, firing on the invading force, adding the sound of gunfire to the cacophony. Tonists fell left and right, but for every one the guards took down, two more scaled the wall. It wouldn't be long before the guards were overwhelmed.

These Sibilants were armed with more than rocks, and they used their weapons against the guards with such brutality it was shocking. Where the hell did they get those kinds of weapons? Didn't Tonism espouse inner peace and stoic acceptance?

"That which comes can't be avoided," Anastasia mumbled. It was the Tonists' favorite mantra. It suddenly took on a terrible new meaning.

The heavy south gate was blown off its hinges by an explosion, and, as the gates fell, a mob of Tonists pushed through. They cut through the line of BladeGuards in seconds and began throwing what looked like bottles of alcohol with burning rags shoved in them. Fire broke out everywhere the bottles crashed.

"They mean to burn us so we can't be revived!" said Baba, near panic. "Just like Scythe Lucifer did!"

Anastasia wanted to snap at Baba for even mentioning Rowan in the same breath as this twisted sect of Tonists, but she stopped herself.

As the battle spilled onto the heliport ahead of them, Tenkamenin had them change direction. "The east patio!" he said. "There's more than enough space for the helicopter to land there! Come!"

They doubled back, crossing through the rose garden, getting scraped, scratched, and poked by thorns on the way — but even before they reached the east patio, they could see that this end of the compound had also been breached. Tonists were everywhere, attacking people running out of the staff house, chasing them down, and rendering them mercilessly deadish.

"Why are they attacking the palace staff?" said Anastasia. "What possible reason could they have?"

"They are without reason," said Scythe Makeda. "Without reason, conscience, or decency."

Their server, who was so particular about the placement of silverware, was felled by a knife in the back.

That's when Baba turned on Tenkamenin. "You should have fortified!" he yelled. "Added another garrison of BladeGuard! Or even gleaned this pack of Tonists before they could launch an attack on us! This is all your fault!"

Tenkamenin balled his hands into fists and stormed toward Baba, but Jeri got between them. "You can salvage your egos later," Jeri said. "But first we have to live if you're going to have this fight."

Anastasia looked around. They were under cover of darkness, so had not yet been spotted, but that wouldn't last long as the fires grew.

And then, as if the commotion around them wasn't enough, a new sort of droning filled the air – this one from actual drones. From the sky descended a swarm of ambudrones. They had been mobilized from the nearest revival center when people began to go deadish.

They zeroed in on the bodies lying in the grass and on the pavement – Tonists, BladeGuards, palace staff – they didn't differentiate between the dead and the deadish. They scooped them up in their insectlike pincers, carrying them off for revival.

"There's our ticket!" said Scythe Baba. "Who needs a helicopter?" And without waiting for the High Blade's leave, Baba ran across the field toward the closest ambudrone, like a lamb to the slaughter.

"Ahmad! No!" called Tenkamenin, but Baba was already committed and wasn't turning back.

The moment the Tonists saw a scythe's robe, they shifted gears and raced after Baba, intercepting him. He pulled out blades from his robe, took Tonists down all around him, but it was no use. They overwhelmed him, threw him to the ground, and attacked him with everything they had – including his own weapons.

Scythe Makeda tried to go after him, but Anastasia stopped her. "There's nothing we can do for him now."

Makeda nodded but didn't take her eyes off her fallen comrade. "He may be the luckiest of us," she said. "If they've killed him, the drones will get him. They'll carry him off to be revived."

But the drones did not go after him. There were so many other bodies around the compound, they were all already committed – and to an ambudrone, one body was no different from another.

And that's when Anastasia realized. "They're killing the staff to tie up the drones … so that there won't be any left to go after the scythes…"

And with no drone to carry Baba away, the Tonists grabbed his body and dragged him toward a flaming pyre that would reduce him to unrevivable ash. They hurled him upon it, and the flames surged.

"To the palace!" said Tenkamenin, and once more led the way, as if somehow being in motion made them any less trapped.

vii. Benedictus

They piled into the palace, where half a dozen BladeGuards closed the ponderous bronze doors behind them and took up defensive positions, should the Tonists break through. At last there was a blessed moment of peace. A blessed moment to strategize within the madness. It could mean the difference between living or dying as ignobly as poor Scythe Baba.

Although the palace had many windows, they all faced the central atrium, which meant that the High Blade's pleasure dome was also a mighty fortress. The question was, how mighty?

"They must have gathered every Sibilant in SubSahara for this," Scythe Makeda said.

"It will be all right," Tenkamenin insisted. "The peace officers of Port Remembrance will arrive to fight alongside the BladeGuard, and the city's firefighters will douse the flames. All will be well."

"They should have been here by now!" said Makeda. "Why don't we hear sirens?"

It was Anastasia – insightful as ever – who burst their bubble. "The first explosions," she said. "The far-off ones…"

"What about them?" said Tenkamenin almost threateningly. Fighting for his tether of safety.

"Well … if I wanted to wage an illegal attack," she said, "the first thing I would do would be to take out the peace officers and firefighters."

And the truth of it left them all in silence. Until Tenkamenin turned to his valet, who was silently wringing his hands in terror.

"Where are my things?"

"I'm … I'm sorry, Your Excellency. I left the suitcase in the rose garden."

Jeri glared at the High Blade. "We're all about to be incinerated, and you're worried about your things?"

But before the High Blade could respond, a flaming truck crashed through the massive bronze doors of the palace, the doors fell off their hinges, crushing four BladeGuards beneath them, and Tonists began to flood in.

That's when Jeri grabbed Anastasia and pulled her behind a column, hidden from everyone's view.

"I have an idea," Jeri said, "but you'll have to trust me."

viii. Offertorium

The sibilant curate was in his element. This was what he was born for, this was his purpose, and had been his plan for years. Even before the Thunder fell silent he knew this day would come. His extreme brand of Tonism would soon be the dominant one. All those lesser Tonists who believed in tranquility, tolerance, and passive acquiescence would soon die off and burn, just as the High Blade of SubSahara would burn today. The time for words was gone. Had been gone for a long time. If the curate had his way, language itself would be outlawed and replaced by wordless adulation to Tone, Toll, and Thunder. As it was meant to be. And he would be High Curate over it all. Oh what a glorious day that would be! But first this.

A scythe in a turquoise robe raced up a grand staircase, trying to escape. The curate pointed, and half a dozen of his flock raced after the scythe. Before him a woman in a salmon silk robe, whom he recognized as Scythe Makeda, was on the attack, skillfully gleaning the Tonists attacking her. Loyal and true, they were sacrificing themselves for the cause. Then one was able to get around behind Makeda and ran her through. She froze, gasped, then fell like a rag doll, her fight leaving along with her life. Three Tonists grabbed her body and dragged it out toward the growing pyre outside, and its purifying flames.

"You're no better than Goddard if you burn us!" said one

403

of the servants huddled at the base of the stairs with High Blade Tenkamenin. "If you go through with this, the very thing you worship will never forgive you."

The High Blade put a firm hand on her shoulder to keep her quiet, but her eyes were still angry and defiant. If the curate could speak, he would tell her that her words – all words – were an abomination to the Tone. And that the only reason the Tone didn't shatter her skull with furious resonance was because cleansing the world of the unworthy was left to the curate, and people like him. But he couldn't tell her. And he didn't have to. His actions spoke much more loudly than words.

But the High Blade was all about words.

"Please…" Tenkamenin begged.

The curate knew what was coming next. This pompous, cowardly scythe – this purveyor of unnatural death – was now going to plead for his life. Let him plead. The curate's ears were not deaf, like some other sibilant sects', but they might as well be.

"Please … you can end me, but spare these two," Tenkamenin said. "You have no gripe against this valet and housekeeper."

The curate hesitated. It was his desire to end them all, for anyone in service to a scythe deserved a scythe's fate. Guilt by association. But then the High Blade said, "Show your followers the true meaning of mercy. The way my parents showed me. My mother and father, who are both among you."

The curate knew this about the High Blade. His parents wordlessly begged not to be part of the attack on the palace. He had obliged by sending them to the firehouse – and they had clearly done their job well. Tenkamenin would not be spared, but out of respect for his Tonist parents, the curate would honor the man's last words. So he pulled out a pistol, shot Tenkamenin through the heart, and then gestured for the two servants to leave.

It was a humble offering of mercy. Of course, they would most likely be killed out in the gardens and thrown on the pyre, but the ambudrones were making off with quite a few of the deadish, so they'd have a fighting chance.

But just then the housekeeper rose to her feet. The anger in her eyes was beyond anger – beyond fury. And it was focused. Like the eyes of a scythe.

She leaped at the nearest Tonist, took her down with a skilled martial arts kick, grabbed the machete she was holding, and swung at the curate, disarming him. Literally.

He watched, stunned, as his hand flew spinning into the air. Then she grabbed the gun from his severed hand, and swung its aim toward the curate. She didn't speak, because her actions spoke much louder than words.

ix. Lux Aeterna

Jerico had not trusted Anastasia's instincts – had not believed this was as serious as she made it out to be. It was a dreadful failure of judgment on Jeri's part. They could have escaped long before the outer wall was breached, had Jeri only trusted Anastasia. The captain vowed to never doubt her again. If they survived, that is – and survival now would be a tall order, indeed.

As the Tonists broke into the palace, Jeri had convinced Anastasia to switch clothes. "It is my job to protect you," Jeri begged. "Please, Anastasia, let me do this for you. Do me that honor!"

As much as she didn't want to put Jeri in peril, when it was put to her that way, she couldn't refuse.

Once wearing Anastasia's robe, Jeri took off up the grand staircase, drawing away half of the Tonists. Jeri did not know all the rooms and suites of the palace's upper levels, but knew them better than the attackers. Jeri led them into Scythe Anastasia's suite, then doubled back through a side door, to an outer salon. The palace was enough of a maze to keep Jeri from being cornered too quickly, but that would only work for so long. Then came the sound of a gunshot from downstairs — then another. No thinking about that now — the focus had to be keeping these Tonists out of that battle.

Endless fires were being set throughout the palace by the invading Tonists. They lit the colonnade and upper suites in the angry, shifting light of frenetic flames. The flames turned every shadow into a figure lurching from the darkness — but those shadows also provided Jeri with enough cover to dupe the pursuers and double back.

Jeri ducked into another suite but, not being used to the robe, snagged it on a doorjamb. Before Jeri could get it free, the Tonists were there, brandishing weapons that they clearly were not trained to use. Jeri was no scythe, but had experience with fighting weapons. There had been a time, in fact, when Jeri would go to fighting clubs. People loved to see Madagascans fight — somehow the ambiguity made the battle more intriguing.

And today, these Tonists picked the wrong Madagascan.

Anastasia had left a blade in one of the pockets of the robe. Jeri pulled it out and fought like never before.

x. Libera Me

Anastasia missed. Blast it! She missed the curate!

A young Tonist, seeing that her curate was about to be gleaned, pushed him out of the way and took the bullet herself. And the curate, gripping the stub of his arm in pain, ran. He ran like a coward, into the mob of Tonists still flooding the grand foyer.

Tenkamenin was dead. So were Makeda and Baba. The Tonists who had seen her attack the curate were still stunned and unsure what to do. She was about to glean them all in fury but stopped herself, because gleaning in anger was not the scythe way. And there was a more pressing matter: Jeri.

She turned and ran up the stairs. No one pursued her. They were too busy setting fire to anything that would burn.

She followed the sound of fighting to one of the unused guest suites. There were a few deadish Sibilants and a trail of blood on the floor. She followed the trail to a bedroom, where three more Tonists were attacking Jeri. Jeri was on the floor, fending them off, but was outnumbered and was losing the battle.

Anastasia gleaned the three Tonists with their own weapons and dropped to the floor, quickly trying to assess Jeri's wounds. The turquoise robe was soaked with blood. She pulled it off and ripped it, trying to use pieces as a tourniquet.

"I … I heard gunshots," Jeri said.

Jeri's wounds were too severe for healing nanites to handle. They would not mend without help. "Tenkamenin is dead," Anastasia said. "He died protecting me."

"Perhaps," Jeri said weakly, "perhaps he was not as bad as I thought."

"If he were alive, I think he'd say the same about you."

Thick smoke was already billowing through every open door. She helped Jeri out into the colonnade overlooking the atrium. Everything below them was burning. There was no way to get down the stairs. Then something occurred to her. A way out – perhaps the only chance they had.

"Can you climb?" she asked Jeri.

"I can try."

Anastasia helped Jeri up to the next level, then through another suite to a balcony. Beside the balcony were ladder rungs embedded in the stone, which she had seen workers use to access the bronze dome that covered the palace. One rung at a time, Anastasia got Jeri all the way up to the edge of the dome. It was designed with a gentle slope and patterned with textured divots and nubs that would give them footholds – but to Jeri, already exhausted from blood loss, it must have looked like Mount Everest.

"H-how will climbing up there—"

"Just shut up and move," demanded Anastasia, not having time to explain.

The dome was hot from the fire in the atrium below. Its glass skylights were already beginning to explode from the heat and belch forth black smoke.

When they reached the pinnacle, there was a weather vane in the shape of the symbol of the scythedom – the curved blade and the unblinking eye – that pivoted left and right, not sure which way the winds were blowing, because the heat was making the wind blow directly up.

And now, finally, the scythedom helicopter arrived. It headed straight for the heliport, the pilots not yet knowing that it had been overrun by Tonists.

"It won't see us," said Jeri.

"That's not why we're up here."

Then an ambudrone buzzed past them, and another, and another. They dropped toward the rose garden, which was littered with deadish guards and Tonists. "*That's* why we're here," Anastasia said. She tried to grab a drone, but it was moving too quickly and wasn't close enough to grasp.

Then below, the helicopter made a grievous error. Seeing the ambudrones buzzing around it, the pilot made a sudden evasive maneuver. It was unnecessary – the drones would stay far from the chopper's path – but they couldn't avoid a sudden flinch of human error that pulled the helicopter directly into their flight paths. The helicopter's blade sliced an ambudrone in two, the blade broke, and the helicopter came careening toward the palace.

Anastasia grabbed Jeri and turned away. The explosion seemed to rock the entire world. It blew a hole in the palace, taking down several of the marble columns holding up the monstrously heavy bronze dome.

And the dome began to list to one side.

Then from below came the most awful vibration. *It's the remaining columns,* thought Anastasia. *They can't hold the weight. They're crumbling…*

And still the ambudrones buzzed past them on their way to claim the deadish from the gardens and lawns.

"My wounds are bad, but they're not lethal," Jeri said. "If we're going to attract an ambudrone, one of us must die."

Flames now licked through the ruptured skylights. The sound of crashing columns echoed from below, and the dome listed farther.

Jeri was right – there was no way around it – so Anastasia pulled out a blade and aimed the tip toward her own chest, ready to render herself deadish so an ambudrone would come.

But no! What was she thinking? How unbelievably stupid! It wasn't like hurling herself off Xenocrates's roof when she was just an apprentice. She was a scythe now; if she took her own life, it would be considered a self-gleaning. The ambudrones wouldn't come for her. And as she pondered the idiocy of what she had almost just done, Jeri gently took the blade from her.

"For you, Honorable Scythe Anastasia, I would die a thousand deaths at my own hand. But one will be sufficient." Then Jeri thrust the blade inward.

A gasp. A cough. A grimace. And Jeri was deadish.

An ambudrone sped by … then stopped in midflight, doubled back, and came for Jeri. It seized the salvage captain in its pincers, and as it did, the dome began to give way.

Anastasia grabbed for the ambudrone, but there was nothing to grip on to – so instead she grasped Jeri's arm with both hands as tightly as she could.

Beneath her, the dome fell away, plunging into the flames, imploding into the atrium. It struck the ground, destroying what was left of the palace, and let off a powerful metallic resonance like the toll of a funeral bell. Like the final, mournful note of a requiem.

While up above, the ambudrone carried away the deadish sea captain and the scythe dangling from the captain's arm, delivering them to a place that promised life to everyone who crossed through its doors.

We are bitterly opposed. Eight of us firmly believe that an association of humans should be responsible for the thinning of the burgeoning population. But the four against it are adamant in their resistance. Confucius, Elizabeth, Sappho, and King insist that we are simply not ready for such a responsibility any more than we were ready for immortality – but the alternative they propose terrifies me, for if we implement their plan, it will be a genie out of the bottle. Out of our control forever. I therefore stand with Prometheus and the others. We must establish an honorable worldwide society of death mongers. We shall call ourselves scythes and will create a global scythedom.

The sentient cloud, which will have nothing to do with issues of life or death, supports it, and people will come to see the wisdom of it in time. As for the four dissenters among us, they will have to accept the voice of the majority, so that we present a unified front to the world.

Still, I wonder which is worse: to mimic nature in its cruel brutality, or to take it upon ourselves, imperfect as we are, to insert into death the kindness and compassion that nature lacks.

The four in opposition argue for nature as a model, but I cannot advocate for it. Not while I still have a conscience.

—*From the "lost pages" of founding scythe Da Vinci*

36

Who Do You Serve?

Although the Thunderhead had predicted it, Greyson didn't need the Thunderhead to tell him that the first repercussions from the Mile High gleaning would be from sibilant Tonists. The only question was where would it happen? Would it be against Goddard directly, or would it be somewhere less prepared for an onslaught of violent zealots?

He had his answer when he saw the first images of the burned ruins of the SubSaharan palace.

"Violence begets violence," Curate Mendoza commented. "This clearly calls for a change in our approach, don't you agree?"

Greyson couldn't help but feel that he had failed. For over two years, he had been wrestling Sibilants into line, getting them to shed their extreme ways, but he had never made it to SubSahara. This might not have happened if he had done a better job.

"Well," said Mendoza, "if we had our own personal mode of transportation, we could have moved more quickly – tackled more problems in more regions."

"Fine," Greyson said. "You win. Get us a jet and fly us to SubSahara. I want to find these Tonists before they make things even worse."

As it turned out, that was the only way for them to get into the region. After the attack, the SubSaharan scythedom clamped down, extending way beyond its authority, and turned the region into something of a mortal-age police state.

"If the Thunderhead will not do its job and apprehend these criminals, then it falls upon the scythes of SubSahara to take control," they proclaimed, and since scythes, by law, could do anything they wanted, they couldn't be stopped from taking control, enforcing curfews, and gleaning anyone who resisted.

Tonists were officially forbidden from traveling to SubSahara, and all commercial flights were monitored by the scythedom in a way they hadn't been monitored since mortal days. The tragedy of all this was that the SubSaharan scythedom had been a gentle and tolerant region – but now, thanks to the Sibilants, it was aligning with Goddard, who promised world-wide retribution against Tonists. There was no question the new SubSaharan High Blade, whoever it might be, would have a robe that sparkled with jewels.

The SubSaharan scythedom had dispatched dozens of regiments of the BladeGuard to patrol the streets of Port Remembrance, and every other city in the region, as well as beating paths through the wilderness in search of the Tonists who had murdered their High Blade, but they had no luck. No one knew where the Sibilants were hiding.

But the Thunderhead did.

And contrary to popular opinion, the Thunderhead was not shirking its responsibility to bring justice. It was merely going about it a different way. By means of a luxury jet with vertical landing capability.

"I could get used to this," Morrison commented as he luxuriated in a plush seat.

"Don't," said Greyson. Although he suspected that once you began traveling in such a craft, you wouldn't easily part with it. There were four passengers, and not a pilot among them. That was fine. The Thunderhead knew exactly where to take them.

"You could say we're being moved by the Holy Triad," Sister Astrid said.

"Actually no," said Morrison, "because I only count two of the three: The Toll" – he gestured to Greyson – "and the Thunder" – he indicated the automated cockpit – "but there's no Tone."

"Ha! You're wrong," said Astrid, with a grin. "Don't you hear it singing in the hum of the engines?"

There was, at the very least, a sense that they were soaring toward not just a destination, but a destiny.

"I am Curate Mendoza, humble servant to His Sonority, the Toll, who you now see before you, the Tone made flesh. All rejoice!"

"All rejoice!" echoed Astrid and Morrison. Greyson knew it would have been a more impressive chorus if the Toll's entourage had been larger.

Their jet had dropped down from the sky and landed with impressive gravity in front of the Ogbunike Caves, in what was once eastern Nigeria but was now just a part of the SubSaharan region. The caves and the surrounding forest were maintained by the Thunderhead as a curated wilderness, everything within it protected. Everything, that is, except for the Sibilants hiding in the twisting passageways of the mysterious caves. It was once said that the stones in the Ogbunike Caves talked. An odd choice for a sect of Tonists who were mute.

When Greyson and his team arrived, the Sibilants were nowhere to be seen; they were hiding deep in the caves – and probably went deeper the moment they heard the roar of the aircraft. But the Thunderhead smoked them out, so to speak, by emitting a sonar tone that disoriented the many thousands of bats also living in the cave, making them go … well … batshit. Attacked by the peeved bats, the Tonists were chased out, where they were faced, not by a phalanx of BladeGuards, as they had expected, but by four figures, one of whom was dressed in rich violet under a flowing scapular down which sound waves spilled like a waterfall. Between the jet on their doorstep and the somber figure in holy attire, it was hard not to pay attention.

"Where is your curate?" Mendoza asked.

The Tonists stood there in defiance. The Toll was dead. The Toll was a martyr. How dare this imposter taint the Toll's memory. It was always this way with Sibilants.

"It will be better for you if you honor the Toll, and bring your leader forth," Mendoza said.

Still nothing. So Greyson quietly asked the Thunderhead for just a little more assistance, and the Thunderhead was happy to oblige, speaking gently in Greyson's ear.

Greyson moved toward one of the Tonists. She was a small woman who seemed half-starved, and he wondered if starvation was part of this sibilant sect's behavior. Her defiance wavered as he approached. She was afraid of him. *Good,* he thought. After what these people had done, she should be.

He leaned close to her, and she stiffened. Then he whispered into her ear, "Your brother did it. Everyone thinks it was you, but it was your brother."

Greyson had no idea what it was that her brother had done. But the Thunderhead did and told Greyson just enough to bring about the desired reaction. The woman's eyes widened. Her lips began to quiver. She let off the slightest squeak of surprise. She was now speechless in more ways than one.

"Now go bring me your curate."

She did not resist in the slightest now. She turned and pointed to one of the others in the crowd. Greyson already knew, of course. The Thunderhead had identified him the moment they all came out of the cave – but it was important that the man be betrayed by one of his own.

Exposed, the man stepped forward. He was the epitome of a sibilant curate. Scraggly gray beard, wild eyes, scars on his arms from some sort of self-inflicted misery. Greyson would have been able to pick him out even if he hadn't been told.

"Are you the Tonists who burned High Blade Tenkamenin, and Scythes Makeda and Baba?"

There were silent sects that used sign language to communicate, but this group had nothing but the simplest of gestures. As if communication itself was their enemy.

A single nod from the curate.

"Do you believe that I am the Toll?"

Nothing from their curate. Greyson tried again, a bit louder, speaking from deep in his diaphragm.

"I asked you a question. Do you believe I am the Toll?"

The Sibilants all turned to their curate to see what he would do.

The curate narrowed his eyes and shook his head slowly. And so Greyson got to work. He turned his eyes to various members of the curate's flock, singling them out.

"Barton Hunt," he said. "Your mother has been sending you letters for six years, three months, and five days, but you return each one unopened."

Then he turned to another.

"Aranza Monga – you once secretly told the Thunderhead that you wanted to be supplanted with the memories of your best friend, who had been gleaned. But, of course, the Thunderhead wouldn't do such a thing."

By the time he turned to a third, both Barton and Aranza were in tears. They fell to their knees, gripping the hem of his garment. They believed. Then, when Greyson looked around for a third, everyone braced as if about to be hit by some devastating blow.

"Zoran Sarabi…" Greyson called out.

"UUUUH," said the man, shaking his head. "Uuuuh-uhhh…" Then he knelt in obeisance before the Toll could even speak, terrified of what truth might be told.

Finally, Greyson turned to their curate. "And you," he said, unable to hide his disgust. "Rupert Rosewood. You demanded that all your followers feel the pain of the muteness you forced upon them … but you never felt that pain yourself. You had your tongue removed under anesthesia, because you were too much of a coward to live by your own warped convictions."

And although the man was horrified at being exposed, he did not yield. He only grew red with anger.

Greyson took a deep breath and dug down to find his

deepest, most resonant voice. *"I am the Toll, the Tone made flesh. I alone hear the Thunder! This man you call 'curate' is not worthy of the title. He is a traitor to all you believe in, and he has misled you. Defiled you. He is false. I am true. So tell me now: Who do you serve?"*

Then he took a deep breath and said one more time with a voice that could make mountains bow, *"WHO DO YOU SERVE?"*

And one by one, they all knelt before the Toll, lowering their heads in supplication, some even prostrating themselves on the forest floor. All of them but one. Their curate – who was now quaking with fury. He opened his hollow mouth to intone, but it was a weak, miserable sound. He was alone. No one joined him. Still, he continued until his breath failed him.

And when silence fell, Greyson turned to Mendoza, speaking loud enough for everyone to hear what came next for them.

"You will inject them all with fresh nanites, so that their tongues may grow back, and this reign of terror can end."

"Yes, Your Sonority," said Mendoza.

Then Greyson approached the curate. He thought the man might strike out at him. Greyson almost hoped that he would. But he didn't.

"You're done," Greyson said in disgust. Then he turned to Scythe Morrison and said two, simple words that he never thought he'd hear himself say.

"Glean him."

Without hesitation Scythe Morrison grabbed the curate with both hands, turned his head one way, his body another, and executed him.

* * *

"Tell me I was wrong!" Greyson paced the tent they had set up for him in the forest, unsettled in a way he had never been unsettled before.

"Why should I tell you that?" the Thunderhead asked, calm as calm could be.

"Because if it was wrong to order that man gleaned, I need to know!"

Greyson could still hear the sound of the man's neck snapping. It was the most horrible thing that he had ever heard. And yet he liked it. Seeing that monstrous curate die was far too satisfying for comfort. Is this what those new-order scythes felt? A primal, predatory lust for the crushing of life? He wanted no part of that feeling, yet here it was.

"I cannot speak on the subject of death; it is not in my domain – you know this, Greyson."

"I don't care!"

"You're being rather irrational."

"You can't say anything about death, but I know you can talk about right and wrong! So was it wrong to have given Morrison that order?"

"Only you can know that."

"You're supposed to be directing me! Helping me to help you make a better world!"

"And you are," said the Thunderhead. "But you're not infallible. Only I am infallible. So, if you're asking me if it's possible for you to make errors in judgment, the answer is yes. You make errors all the time … as does every other human being who has

420

ever lived. Error is an intrinsic part of the human condition – and it is something I deeply love about humankind."

"You're not helping me!"

"I charged you with unifying the Tonists so that they could be more useful to the world. I can only speak to your progress in the task, not judge your methodology."

Enough. Greyson ripped his earpiece off. He was about to throw it in anger, but then he heard, faint and tinny, the Thunderhead's voice still speaking through it.

"You are a terrible person," the Thunderhead said. "You are a wonderful person."

"Well, which is it?" Greyson demanded.

And the response, as faint as faint could be, came back to him – not as an answer, but as another question.

"Why can't you see that the answer is both?"

That evening, Greyson put back on his vestments and prepared to address the Tonists. To grant them forgiveness. He had done this many times before, but no sibilant Tonists he faced had ever done something as heinous as these.

"I don't want to forgive them," he told Mendoza before he went out.

"Granting them absolution brings them into the fold," Mendoza said. "It serves our needs. And besides," he added, "it's not Greyson Tolliver forgiving them, it's the Toll. Which means your personal feelings shouldn't even come into play."

When Greyson put his earpiece back in, he asked the Thunderhead if Mendoza was right. Did it want Greyson to forgive them? Or, more to the point, did the Thunderhead forgive them? Was it so magnanimous that it could even excuse their curate?

"Ah," the Thunderhead said sadly. "That poor man…"

"Poor man? That monster doesn't deserve your sympathy."

"You didn't know him as I did. As with all others, I watched him from birth. I saw the forces in his life that shaped him, turning him into the bitter, misguided, self-righteous man he became. Thus, I mourn his gleaning just as I mourn all others."

"I could never be as forgiving as you," Greyson said.

"You misunderstand; I don't forgive him – I merely understand him."

"Well, then," Greyson said, still a bit belligerent from their earlier conversation, "you're not a god, are you? Because a god forgives."

"I never claimed to be a god," the Thunderhead responded. "I am merely god*like*."

The Tonists were waiting for the Toll when he came out. They had been waiting for hours. They probably would have waited through the night.

"Don't try to speak," he told them when he saw them attempting to greet him. "Your tongues have no muscle memory. It will take some time until you teach yourselves to speak again."

By the way they looked to him with awe and reverence, he knew that their violent deeds were behind them. They were no longer Sibilant. And when the Toll forgave them, they cried tears of true remorse for what they had done, and tears of pure joy at having been given a second chance. Now they would follow the

Toll wherever he led. And a good thing, too. Because, as it would turn out, he'd need to lead them into darkness before he could lead them into light.

We have now laid the groundwork for scythedoms in each of the world's regions, all reporting to us, so that we may maintain order and consistency of vision. We have even begun plans for a city that exists separate and apart from any region, so we may maintain impartiality. Prometheus is now Supreme Blade, and there's talk of "Grandslayers" to represent each continent. Oh, but we've gotten full of ourselves! Secretly, I hope our tenure as the arbiters of death is brief and that we are quickly deemed obsolete.

The cloud has announced plans for a lunar colony – the first step toward expanding our footprint in the universe. If successful, it will provide far better population control than we scythes can provide. I, for one, would much rather live in a world where the surplus population can leave, rather than be denied its very existence.

The question remains, however, can we trust artificial intelligence with our future? Although I do have my concerns, I believe we can. The few remaining "world leaders" do nothing but malign the sentient cloud. In fact, they've begun calling it a thunderhead, as if rebranding it as a threatening storm will turn people against it. In the end they will fail, because their time is through. Whatever they choose to call it, the cloud's benevolence speaks louder than the words of petty politicians and tyrants.

—*From the "lost pages" of founding scythe Da Vinci*

37

Nothing Good About It

When Jerico Soberanis awoke from revival, Scythe Anastasia was in a chair beside the bed, sleeping with her knees tucked up to her chest. Fetal position, thought Jeri. No – more like a protective stance, like a tortoise in its shell. Did she feel so threatened that she needed to contract into herself when she slept, on guard even when unconscious? Well, if so, she had good reason to feel that way.

She was dressed simply now. Jeans. A white blouse. She wasn't even wearing the ring. Nothing about her to indicate that she was a scythe. She appeared so modest for someone so much larger than life. To be larger than life was fine for the dead – they didn't have to deal with the consequences, but for someone returned to life, it must leave one in a state of shock too strange to measure.

Jeri looked around at the gentle colors and easy nature of the room. This was, of course, a revival center. The fact that they were here meant that Jeri's death had successfully attracted an ambudrone. Had Anastasia been here in the room for Jeri's entire revival, keeping a vigil?

"So glad you're awake!" said a revival nurse, stepping into the room and raising a curtain to reveal what was either a sunrise or a sunset, then checking Jeri's chart. "I am most pleased to make your acquaintance."

Citra had been dreaming of flying. Not all that far from reality, either. She had clung to Jeri's arm as the ambudrone soared with them across the city, struggling to maintain flight with the added weight. She was sure she must have dislocated Jeri's shoulder, but such things didn't matter to the deadish. Any damage done would be healed before the captain awoke.

In Citra's dream, Jeri's arm became suddenly covered in grease, and she slipped, but didn't fall. Instead, she flew on her own. The problem was she couldn't stop or control her direction. Soon she was out over the bay and beyond, heading west across the Atlantic toward the distant Mericas. She had no idea what awaited her there, but she did know it would be in the realm of nightmares.

And so she was grateful to be stirred awake by the revival nurse's gentle voice.

She uncurled from her chair and stretched out the kink in her neck. Jeri was alive again, and much more alert than she. "Good morning," Citra said groggily – then realized it sounded far too weak for a scythe. Even one who was currently incognito. She cleared her throat and spoke with more confidence. "Good morning," Anastasia said.

"Nothing good about it, I'm afraid," said the nurse. "I've never seen so many BladeGuards roaming the streets. The scythedom is still looking for those terrible Tonists who ended the High Blade, but they're long gone, off to wherever it is people like that hide."

Anastasia closed her eyes as the terror of that night came back to her. So many people had lost their lives, and although some were revived, there simply weren't enough ambudrones to save everyone. Sibilants must have thrown dozens, maybe hundreds, into the fire. And, just as they had a plan of attack, they must have had a plan for escape.

The nurse explained that, in the day and a half since the ambudrone had left them here, Port Remembrance had been put on complete lockdown. The situation in North Merica was probably even worse. What Goddard had done in that stadium was beyond a line in the sand – it was a fissure. Either you embraced his way, or you ran from it. There were plenty of people doing both.

Anastasia knew she might be recognized. Now that she had gone public, and people knew she was alive, it would be much harder to hide.

"Seeing as you're awake, I'm sure there'll be scythes in to see you," the nurse told Jeri. "Not to worry – they're not here to glean, just to question. You both worked at the palace, didn't you? They want to question everyone who was there."

Jeri glanced at Anastasia as she put a comforting hand on the shoulder she had dislocated not so long ago.

"Right," said Jeri. "Well, I suppose we'll be looking for new jobs."

"Oh, don't concern yourselves with that. The Thunderhead might not be talking these days, but it still puts up the job listings. If you want work again, there's plenty to be had."

After she left, Jeri raised the head of the revival bed a bit higher and smiled at Anastasia. "So what was it like riding the back of an ambudrone?"

"It … wasn't like that," Anastasia said, but chose to spare Jeri the details. "I never got to thank you for what you did."

"I just did my job," Jeri said.

"Your job is to be a salvage captain, not this."

"And didn't I salvage an unsalvageable situation?"

"Yeah, you did," Anastasia told Jeri with a smile. "Now we have to salvage this one, and get out of here before someone comes in to question us."

But no sooner had she said it than the door swung open. It was a scythe. Anastasia's heart seized for a moment until she realized who it was. Forest-green robe, concerned expression.

"My relief at seeing both of you can only be matched by my fear that someone else might," Scythe Possuelo said. "No time for greetings – the SubSaharan scythes are already questioning why I'm here."

"I haven't been recognized yet."

"Of course you have," Possuelo said. "I'm sure the nursing staff here is all secretly atwitter about it. But luckily none of them have reported you – or you would already be on your way to Goddard. I'm here to escort you to a place of greater safety, where you can continue your broadcasts. More and more people are listening, Anastasia – and they're finding the things you've been leading them to. Goddard is threatening to glean anyone caught poking around in the backbrain, but that's not stopping people."

"He couldn't enforce it anyway," Anastasia pointed out. "The backbrain is out of scythe jurisdiction." It reminded Anastasia how much digging she still had left to do.

"So what place of safety do you propose?" Jeri asked. "Is there such a place anymore?"

"Who can say?" Possuelo said. "Safe places are dwindling just as quickly as enemies mount." He paused, considering something. "There are rumors ... of a place so out of sight not even the most well-traveled scythes know of it."

"Sounds more like wishful thinking," Jeri said. "Where did you hear this?"

Possuelo offered an apologetic shrug. "Rumors are like rain through an old roof. The effort of finding the source is greater than the cost of a new roof." Then he paused again. "There's another rumor, though, that might be more useful to us. This one's about the Toll – the Tonists' so-called prophet."

Tonists, thought Anastasia. Just the mention of them brought her to the edge of fury.

"There's no proof that the Toll ever even existed," Jeri pointed out. "He could be just another lie the Sibilants use to justify the things they do."

"I believe he existed," Possuelo said. "There's evidence to suggest that he still does – and that he's been standing against sibilant sects – we have such a sect in Amazonia who swore he visited them and turned them from their violent ways. If it's true, he might be a worthwhile ally to have."

"Well, whoever he is," said Anastasia, "he's got a lot of explaining to do."

Ezra Van Otterloo didn't dress like a Tonist. He didn't quote platitudes, he didn't insist on traveling in groups of seven or twelve, and he definitely did not intone. He did go by Brother Ezra, however – that was the only concession he made to his calling. It was his audience with the Toll over two years ago that brought

429

him into the fold, giving him his purpose and setting him on his path. Whether or not the Toll was divine didn't matter to Ezra. All that mattered was that the Thunderhead still spoke to him, and that made him worthy of being followed.

Ezra traveled the world, painting whatever he wanted, wherever he wanted, just as the Toll said he should do, throwing up guerilla murals everywhere he went. And just as the Toll promised, he found his bliss. He had to be quick, he had to be quiet, and in all this time he had never been caught.

He would travel the world telling local Tonists wherever he went that he was on a mission from the Toll, and they would give him food and shelter. But then he started running into Tonists who claimed that the Toll had appeared to them after he was gleaned. They told him how they'd been sibilant, but the Toll reformed them. Ezra didn't believe it at first, but still he'd listen to their testimony. Then during the night, he'd paint a scene of the Toll's visitation somewhere in the city, in some place where no such painting was supposed to be.

After the third set of reformed Sibilants he came across, he realized there had to be some truth to it – so he began to seek out more such encounters. He'd track down groups known to be the worst of the worst, to see if they'd also been reformed. About half of them had, and the other half he imagined were probably on the Toll's list. Then one day he showed up at an airport, uncertain of where to go next – and lo and behold, a ticket was already in the system for him. The Thunderhead had taken over his travels, sending him to sects the Toll had reformed, so he could visit them and leave behind a mural to honor the Toll. That's how Ezra knew he was part of the Toll's entourage, part of his story, even if the Toll didn't know it.

Then, when he was caught in Amazonia, he had to believe it was also part of the Thunderhead's plan. But on the other hand, if it was just bad luck, the Thunderhead had ways of using that to its advantage, too.

While the entire SubSaharan scythedom was searching for the Sibilants who had killed their High Blade, it was an Amazonian scythe who knew where they were – thanks to a single Tonist in Scythe Possuelo's custody.

"We caught him painting a scene of the Toll turning into a flock of birds, on the wall of our High Blade's residence," Scythe Possuelo told Anastasia.

"It's what I do," Ezra said with a smile.

They were all safely aboard Possuelo's plane. Possuelo had even brought a brand-new turquoise robe for Anastasia. It felt good to be clothed as herself again.

"Punishment for defacing scythe property is gleaning," Possuelo said, "but High Blade Tarsila didn't have the heart to glean an artist. Then he told us what he'd been doing."

"I could paint you, Scythe Anastasia," he offered. "It won't be as good as a mortal artist, of course. I've come to accept that, but I'm less mediocre than most."

"Save your brushes," she told him. Perhaps it was vanity on her part, but the last thing she wanted was to be immortalized by an artist who was "less mediocre than most."

"He's been in our custody for several months – but then two tickets appeared for him on the global travel system after Tenkamenin had been killed," Possuelo told her. "One to

Onitsha, a small SubSaharan city – but the second one was baffling. It was a tour ticket to a protected wilderness where there hadn't been tours for over a hundred years. The Ogbunike Caves."

To that, Ezra shrugged and smiled. "I'm special. Sure you don't want a portrait?"

The fact that the tickets showed up in the system *after* Ezra was in scythe custody could really mean only one thing: The Thunderhead wanted the Amazonian scythedom to know where the Sibilants – and the Toll – were.

"Normally it would be a short flight," Possuelo told Anastasia, "but we'll have to take a roundabout route – engaging first in some bogus business elsewhere – otherwise, we might inadvertently lead the SubSaharan scythes right to the Toll."

"That's all right," Anastasia told him. "I need time to dig into the backbrain again for my next broadcast. I'm close to something on the Mars disaster."

"And the orbital colony?" Possuelo asked.

Anastasia sighed and shook her head. "One catastrophe at a time."

"There were 9,834 colonists on Mars. Even more than had lost their lives on the moon in the world's first mass gleaning. And there were extensive plans to make our sister planet a home for millions, eventually billions. But something went terribly wrong.

"Have you done your homework on Mars? Have you scanned the list of names of those doomed colonists? I don't expect you to remember or even recognize any of them — not even the ones who were famous at the time, because fame comes and goes, and mostly their fame is gone. But look again, because there's one name I want you to see.

"Carson Lusk.

"He was there when the disaster occurred, and was lucky enough to be one of the few survivors. He was in the right place at the right time, and managed to get onboard the one escape vessel that wasn't incinerated when the colony's reactor blew.

"There was a big celebration when that small group of survivors finally made it back to Earth, but after that, Carson Lusk disappeared from public view.

"Or did he?

"Let's back up a bit to three months before the reactor took out the colony. If you look at the transport records for craft coming to and from Mars, you'll see a name that I'm sure you'll find familiar. Xenocrates. He was a young scythe at the time — and the only one known to ever visit the Mars colony. It was controversial, because it implied that scythes would continue their business on the red planet. Why, people wondered, when there was an entire planet on which to expand? It would be maybe 100,000 years before a scythe would ever be needed on Mars.

"He wasn't there to glean anyone, he said. He was merely 'entertaining his curiosity.' He wanted to know what it would be like to live on Mars — and he was true to his word. He didn't glean a single person once he reached the planet. He merely took tours and spoke with colonists. It was all very benign.

"I have something to show you now.

"What you're about to see is a video record of Xenocrates's arrival. Hard to recognize him, I know — he was still thin then, and his robe didn't have all the gold, which he added when he became a High Blade. As you can see, he's being greeted by the governor of the colony, and a few other dignitaries, and — there! Do you see? That young man in the background. That's Carson Lusk! While Xenocrates was on Mars, Carson was assigned to be his personal valet. Not a good view of him, I know, but he'll turn in a moment.

"Remember, this was a few months before the disaster. Time enough for people to forget Xenocrates's visit. Time for plans to be put into place, and for a team of accomplices to secretly carry those plans out, making sabotage look like just another tragic accident.

"As for Carson Lusk, no matter how hard you look, you won't find any record of him after his return to Earth, because within a year, his name had been changed. There — there, you see? He's turning toward the camera now. Is his face familiar yet? No? Just add a few years, shorten his hair, and draw in a satisfied, self-important grin.

"That young valet is none other than His Exalted Excellency, Robert Goddard, Overblade of North Merica."

38

A Grand Reunion of the Dubiously Deceased

The Toll and his entourage took refuge in the same caves that the Sibilants had laid claim to. Those Sibilants were now beyond repentant, prostrating themselves in his presence and professing their unworthiness to even grovel at his feet. Normally he would not accept such hyperbolic adoration, but, considering what these people had done – all the lives they had ended – groveling was a far milder punishment than they deserved.

Of course the Thunderhead reminded him that punishment was not its way.

"Correction must be about lifting one up from one's poor choices and prior deeds. As long as remorse is sincere, and one is willing to make recompense, there is no purpose to suffering."

Still, Greyson didn't mind seeing them facedown in bat guano.

The repentant Tonists decorated a grotto as lavishly as they could for him with tapestries and pillows, and begged for ways to be of service.

"This place is as good as any to wait," the Thunderhead told Greyson.

"Good as any?" Greyson said. "I realize you have no sense of smell, but the stink is terrible in here."

"My chemical sensors are far more accurate than the

human sense of smell," the Thunderhead reminded him. "And the ammonia exuded by bat droppings is well within human tolerance."

"You said wait. What is it we're waiting for?" Greyson asked.

"A visitor" was all the Thunderhead said.

"Can you at least tell me who it is?" Greyson asked.

"No, I cannot."

This is how Greyson knew that he would be visited by a scythe. But, considering the increased hostility toward Tonists, why would the Thunderhead welcome such a visit? Maybe the SubSaharan scythedom had found their hiding place and was seeking justice from the Sibilants. But if so, why wouldn't the Thunderhead "strongly suggest a journey" as it had back at the Cloisters, when Scythe Morrison was the enemy? No amount of tossing and turning that night could jog loose a hint of who it might be.

"Rest easy," the Thunderhead told him gently in the darkness. "I am here, and no harm will come to you."

Scythe Anastasia had her doubts about this so-called holy man. She needed evidence that the Thunderhead spoke to him. Not just testimony, but actual, irrefutable evidence. Even as a young girl, Citra needed to see something to believe it. This "Toll" was most likely a charismatic schemer. A con artist taking advantage of the gullible, telling them what they wanted to hear, being who they wanted him to be for his own selfish ends.

She wanted to believe that. It was less disturbing than the idea of the Thunderhead choosing a Tonist as its liaison to humanity. It did make sense that the Thunderhead would keep one point of connection with humankind, but why a Tonist? Since the Thunderhead did not make mistakes, it must have had a good reason. But for now, she preferred to believe the Toll was a fraud.

Their destination was an inhospitable SubSaharan forest, a dense unrelenting snarl of trees and wicked, thorny undergrowth that snagged Anastasia's new robe and pricked her through the fabric, leaving her itchy as they made their way to the cave where the Toll was sequestered. As they finally neared the cave, they were accosted by Tonists standing guard.

"Do not resist," said Possuelo – but letting her guard down was not easy for Anastasia, knowing who these people were.

The Tonists were unarmed, but their grips were firm. Anastasia scanned their faces. Was this the one who had thrown Tenkamenin to the ground? Was that the one who had hurled Scythe Baba onto the pyre? She could swear their faces were familiar, but it could have been her imagination. Possuelo had insisted that they leave their weapons behind. Now she realized it wasn't just to kept them from being confiscated, but also to stop Anastasia from giving in to her rage. Every part of her wanted to exact retribution, but she fought it. She had to keep reminding herself that true scythes – *honorable* scythes – never gleaned in anger. But if a single one of them raised a weapon, she would let loose using her most deadly Bokator moves on them, breaking necks and spines without mercy.

"We request an audience with the Toll," Possuelo said.

Anastasia was about to point out that this sect was tongueless, but to her surprise, one of the Tonists responded.

"The Toll was elevated to a higher octave two years ago," one of the Tonists responded. "He is with us now only in harmony."

Possuelo was not deterred. "We have heard otherwise," he said, then added, "We are not here to glean him; we are here for our mutual benefit."

The Tonists studied them a few moments longer. Serious faces, dripping distrust. Then the one who first spoke said, "Come with us. He has been expecting you."

Anastasia found that annoying on too many levels to count. If he was expecting them, then why did the Tonist deny he was here? And was he truly expecting them, or did this lackey just say that to make the Toll seem mysterious and all-knowing? Before even meeting him, she already detested this man behind the curtain.

The Tonists led them forward, and although Anastasia didn't pull away from their grip, she gave them the opportunity to reconsider it.

"You'd best let go of me if you want to keep your hands."

The Tonists did not ease their grip in the least. "My hands will grow back like our tongues," one of them said. "The Toll, in his wisdom, has given us back our nanites."

"Good for him," Anastasia said. "At least he's not a complete imbecile."

Possuelo gave her a warning glare, and Anastasia decided silence would be the best policy, because nothing out of her mouth right now would benefit the situation.

The procession halted at the entrance to the cave – a gaping triangular maw. It was here where they would be presented to the Toll …

… but even before the Toll arrived, the first person out

of the cave made it abundantly clear to Anastasia that this ride was definitely going to be worth the price of admission.

When Scythe Morrison heard that an elegy of scythes was at the cave entrance, he was convinced that the North Merican scythedom had finally come for him. Goddard must have known he was alive, must have known what he'd been up to these past few years, and had sent this team to bring him in. He considered running, but there was only one exit from the cave. Besides, he wasn't the same man he had been when he first began this service to the Toll. That junior scythe would save himself at the expense of all others. But *this* Scythe Morrison would face his capture bravely, defending the Toll to the last, as he had promised to do.

He stepped out first, as he always did, to assess the threat level and be generally intimidating, but he stopped short at the cave entrance when he saw a familiar turquoise robe. A robe he thought he'd never lay eyes on again.

Scythe Anastasia was equally dumbfounded.

"You?" she said.

"No," Morrison blurted, "not me! I mean, yes it's me, but I'm not the Toll, I mean." Any hope of strong, silent intimidation was gone. Now he was little more than a stammering imbecile, which is how he always felt around Anastasia.

"What are you even doing here?" she asked.

He started to explain, but realized it was way too long a story for the moment. And besides, he was sure her story was a better one.

The other scythe in her entourage – Amazonian by the

look of his robe – chimed in, several beats behind the curve. "You mean to say you two know each other?"

But before either of them could answer, Mendoza came up behind Morrison, tapping him on the shoulder.

"As usual, you're in the way, Morrison," he grumbled, having completely missed the conversation.

Morrison stepped aside and allowed the curate to exit. And the moment Mendoza saw Anastasia, he became just as befuddled as Morrison. Although his eyes darted wildly, he managed to hold his silence. Now they stood on either side of the entrance to the cave in their usual formation. Then the Toll emerged from the cave between them.

He stopped short, just as Morrison and Mendoza had, gaping in a way that a holy man probably never should.

"Okay," said Scythe Anastasia. "Now I know I've lost my mind."

Greyson knew that the Thunderhead must have been enjoying this moment immensely – he could see its cameras whirring on the nearby trees, taking in everyone's expressions, swiveling back and forth to see this absurd little tableau from every angle. It could have given him at least an inkling that he'd be seeing not only someone he knew, but the very individual who, in a way, was responsible for the strange path his life had taken. It couldn't have told him directly, of course, but it could have given him hints and let him deduce it for himself. But then, even with a thousand clues, he would have marched into this encounter clueless.

He resolved not to give the Thunderhead the satisfaction of seeing him bug-eyed and slack-jawed. So when Anastasia suggested that she may have just lost her mind, he said, as non-chalantly as he could, "Endura rises! All rejoice!"

"Endura didn't rise," she said. "Just me."

He held his formal expression for a moment more but couldn't maintain it. He began to grin. "So you really are alive! I wasn't sure if those broadcasts were real."

"And … you two know each other as well?" said the Amazonian scythe.

"In a previous life," said Anastasia.

Then one of her other travel companions began to laugh. "Well, isn't this rich! A grand reunion of the dubiously deceased!"

Greyson's attention lingered. There was something engaging about her. Or him.

Mendoza, trying to regain some decorum, cleared his throat, puffed up a bit, and spoke in his best stage voice. *"His Sonority, the Toll, welcomes you all, and grants you an audience!"* he declared.

"A private audience," Greyson quietly prompted.

"A private audience!" boomed Mendoza, but he made no move to leave.

"Meaning," said Greyson, "just between Scythe Anastasia and me."

Mendoza turned to him, his eyes panicked. "I don't think that's wise. At least take Morrison with you for protection."

But Morrison put up his hands in instant surrender. "Leave me out of this," he said. "I'm not going up against Scythe Anastasia."

The Thunderhead's cameras whirred, and Greyson could swear it sounded like electronic laughter.

"Take the others in," Greyson said, "and get them something

to eat. They must be starving." He turned to the Tonists around them who had witnessed this odd but momentous reunion. "All is well," he told them, then gestured to Anastasia. "Walk with me."

And the two of them stepped off together into the woods.

"'Walk with me'?" said Anastasia when they were out of earshot. "Really? Could you be any more pretentious?"

"It's part of the act," Greyson told her.

"So you admit it's an act!"

"The prophet part is – but it's true that I'm not unsavory, and the Thunderhead really does speak to me." He gave her a wry grin. "Maybe it's my reward for saving your life that day and letting you hit me with your car."

"It wasn't my car," Anastasia pointed out. "It was Scythe Curie's. I was just learning how to drive it."

"And a good thing, too! If you had been a better driver and had missed me, we'd have all been incinerated," he pointed out. "So, does this mean that Scythe Curie is still alive, too?"

Anastasia's heart sank at having to speak the truth aloud. She doubted it would ever be easier. "Marie died making sure I could eventually be revived."

"Revived," said Greyson. "That explains why you don't look a day older than you did three years ago."

She took a long look at him. He did look different, and it wasn't just the outfit. His jaw seemed a little harder, his gait more confident, and his gaze so direct as to be invasive. He had learned to play this role well – just as she had learned to play hers.

"The last I heard, you refused the offer of sanctuary I arranged for you in Amazonia. So instead you stayed with the Tonists?"

His gaze became even more intrusive. Not judgmental, but possessing a deeper sight. A bit like the Thunderhead itself.

"Hiding out with the Tonists was your suggestion – or did you forget that?"

"No, I remember," she told him, "but I never thought you'd stay. I never thought you'd become their prophet." She looked over his vestments. "I can't decide whether you look ridiculous or regal."

"Both," he told her. "The trick is convincing people that strange clothing makes you something more than ordinary. But you know all about that, don't you?"

Anastasia had to admit he was right. The world treated you differently – defined you differently – when you wore robes or regalia.

"Just as long as you don't believe it yourself," she told him.

"When I take all this off, I'm still Greyson Tolliver," he said.

"And when I slip out of this robe, I'm still Citra Terranova."

He smiled broadly at that. "I never knew your given name until now. Citra. I like it."

Hearing him say her name gave her a sudden wash of nostalgia. A yearning for a time before all this. "There aren't many people who call me that anymore."

He looked at her wistfully. "Funny, but it was never easy for me to talk to you before. Now it's easier than talking with anyone else. I think we've become alike in a lot of ways."

She laughed at that. Not because it was funny, but because

it was true. The rest of the world saw them both as symbols. Intangible light to guide them in the darkness. She understood now why ancient peoples turned their heroes into constellations.

"You haven't told me why you wanted an audience with the Toll."

"Scythe Possuelo thinks you know a safe place where Goddard won't find us," Anastasia said.

"Well, if the Thunderhead knows of a place like that, it hasn't told me. But then there's a lot of things it doesn't tell me."

"It's all right," said Anastasia. "Possuelo just wants to protect me, but I don't want to hide."

"What *do* you want?" Greyson asked.

What did she want? Citra Terranova wanted to shed her robe, seek out her family, and argue with her brother about unimportant things. But Scythe Anastasia wouldn't have any of that.

"I want to bring down Goddard," she said. "I've been able to place him on Mars at the time of the disaster, but being there doesn't prove he caused it."

"He survived Mars, *and* he survived Endura," said Greyson. "Suspicious but not incriminating."

"Exactly, which is why there's someone else I need to find," Anastasia said. "Have you ever heard of Scythe Alighieri?"

Possuelo had to leave them that afternoon. He was called back to Amazonia by his High Blade.

"Tarsila gives me lots of leeway – especially when my salvage venture brought forth you," he told Anastasia, "but when word got out that I had brought our artist friend to SubSahara, she demanded my return, lest we be accused of conspiring with Tonists." He sighed. "We are a very tolerant region, but after the attack on Tenkamenin's palace, even the most accepting regions are cooling to Tonists – and our High Blade doesn't want bad publicity."

Several Tonists passed in the cavern behind them. They bowed, reverently saying "Your Honors," some of their voices still a little slurred, as it was the first week with their new tongues. It was hard to believe that these were the same violent, crazed Sibilants who had murdered Tenkamenin. Greyson – the Toll, that is – had turned them and brought them back from that awful edge of their own humanity. Anastasia could not forgive them, but she found an ability to coexist with them.

"People are vessels," Jeri had said to her. "They hold whatever's poured into them."

And apparently Greyson had drained them and refilled them with something far more palatable.

Possuelo said his goodbye at the entrance to the cave. "This place is isolated, and if the Toll truly is under the protection of the Thunderhead, you'll be safe with him," he told her. "It's not exactly the sanctuary I was looking for, but who knows if that place even exists. Rumors aren't worth the air they're whispered on."

"I'm hoping the Toll will help me find Alighieri."

"I doubt he even exists anymore," Possuelo lamented. "He was ancient when I was an apprentice, and I am, as you say, no spring chicken."

He laughed and embraced her. If felt comforting. Fatherly. Until she was in his embrace, she hadn't realized how much she

445

missed that. It made her think of her family once more. She had not tried to contact them since her revival, as Possuelo had advised her against it. They were safe and protected in a friendly region, he had assured her. Perhaps there would come a time for that reunion, or perhaps she'd never see them again. Either way, there was still too much to be done for her to even think about it.

"Say goodbye to Captain Soberanis for me," Possuelo said. "I take it Jerico is staying on."

"As you ordered," Anastasia said.

Possuelo raised an eyebrow. "I never gave such an order," he said. "Jerico does as Jerico pleases. That the good captain has forsaken the sea, and has chosen to be your protector, says a lot about both of you." He embraced her one final time. "Take care, *meu anjo*." Then he turned and strode toward his transport that waited in a clearing.

Ezra the artist, who Possuelo saw fit to set free, took to painting a mural to fill one of the larger caverns. It tickled him that this could become a pilgrimage destination for future Tonists, if indeed there would be any future Tonists, and that his cave paintings might be endlessly analyzed by scholars of tomorrow. He introduced some odd elements just to confuse them. A dancing bear, a five-eyed boy, and an eleven-hour clock missing the number 4.

"What's life if you can't mess with the future?" he said.

He asked the Toll if he remembered him, and Greyson told him that he did. It was a half-truth. Greyson remembered Ezra's audience with him, because it had been a turning point

446

for Greyson as well. The first time he gave advice rather than just being a mouthpiece for the Thunderhead. But he had no memory at all of Ezra's face.

"Ah, the wonderful limitations of the biological brain!" the Thunderhead said wistfully. "The remarkable ability to dispense with the unnecessary, rather than filing every little thing into a cumbersome compendium!" The Thunderhead called humanity's selective memory "the gift of forgetting."

There were many things Greyson had forgotten that he wished he could remember. Most of his childhood. Any warm moments with his parents. And there were things he remembered that he wished he could forget. Like the look on Purity's face when Scythe Constantine gleaned her.

He knew the gift of forgetting was now a bane to Anastasia, because the world seems to have forgotten Scythe Alighieri. But the Thunderhead hadn't. Alighieri was there in its cumbersome compendium of human history. Getting to that information was the problem.

The Thunderhead had been silent for his entire conversation with Anastasia. Then, after she had retired to the cave to join her comrades, it finally spoke up. "I cannot, in any way, help Anastasia find the man she's looking for."

"But you *do* know where he can be found, don't you?"

"I do. But it would be a violation for me to communicate his location to her."

"Can you tell me?"

"I could," said the Thunderhead, "but if you then tell her, I will be forced to mark you unsavory, and then where would we be?"

Greyson sighed. "There must be a work-around…"

"Perhaps," said the Thunderhead. "But I can't help you find it."

Work-arounds. The Thunderhead had used him as one back when he was a naive Nimbus Academy student. And come to think of it, he remembered learning about an official work-around in one of his early classes at the academy, before he got himself expelled. There was a sort of ritualistic practice that allowed a Nimbus agent to speak with a scythe without breaking the law. A *trialogue* it was called. It involved a professional go-between who was well versed in scythe/state protocols. What could, and could not, be said.

What they needed, Greyson realized, was a go-between.

In his private cavern spread with rugs and hung with tapestries, the Toll sat on one of the many pillows strewn about the space, facing Jerico Soberanis.

Greyson estimated he and Soberanis were roughly the same age. That is unless the salvage captain had turned a corner, but Greyson didn't think so. The young captain didn't seem to be the type who would set back so far. Still, there was something noble there. Not so much wisdom, but worldliness. Greyson had been all over the world yet saw so little of it in his protective cocoon, he felt like he'd been nowhere at all. But Jerico Soberanis had truly seen the world, and what was more, *knew* the world. It was something to be admired.

"Scythe Anastasia explained why you called for me," Soberanis said. "How will this work, Your … What is it they call you?"

"Your Sonority," Greyson said.

"That's right, 'Your Sonority,'" Soberanis said with a smirk.

"You think it's funny?"

The smirk didn't leave the salvage captain's face. "Did you come up with that?"

"No. My chief curate did."

"He ought to be in advertising."

"He was."

The conversation lagged. Not surprising. This was entirely artificial and forced, but it needed to happen.

"Say something," Greyson told the salvage captain.

"What sort of thing should I say?"

"It doesn't matter what you talk about. We just need to have a conversation. Then I'll pose questions to the Thunderhead about the conversation."

"And?"

"And it will answer."

Jerico smiled again. Mischievous. Alluring in an odd sort of way. "A game of chess, then, where all the pieces are invisible!"

"If you like," said Greyson.

"Very well." Jerico took a moment to consider their subject matter, then said something Greyson was not expecting.

"You and I have something in common."

"What would that be?"

"We both sacrificed our lives to save Scythe Anastasia."

Greyson shrugged. "It was only temporary."

"Still," said Soberanis, "it takes courage and a remarkable leap of faith to do so."

"Not really. People splat every day."

"Yes, but neither of us are that sort. To render ourselves

deadish goes against our basic natures. Not everyone would have made the choice we made. This is how I know that you are much more than that outfit you wear." Soberanis smiled again. This time it was genuine. Honest. Greyson had never met someone with such a wide variety of smiles. Each one spoke volumes.

"Thank you," said Greyson. "I suppose our mutual admiration of Scythe Anastasia does ... bond us in a way." He waited to see if the Thunderhead would say anything at all, but it didn't. It was waiting to be asked. Greyson still didn't know what to ask it.

"I hope this isn't insulting," Greyson said, "but I'm not sure how I should address you. As Mr. or Ms. Soberanis?"

The salvage captain glanced around the cavern and became noticeably uncomfortable. "I'm at a bit of a loss. I very rarely find myself in a place where I can't see the sky."

"Why should that matter?"

"I suppose it shouldn't ... I am always out of doors, or intentionally near a window or skylight ... but here in a cave..."

Greyson still didn't understand, and the captain became just the tiniest bit miffed. "I will never understand how you binaries are so attached to your birth plumbing. Why should it matter whether a person has ovaries, or testicles, or both?"

"It doesn't," Greyson said, feeling a little flustered. "I mean ... it does matter for *some* things ... doesn't it?"

"You tell me."

Greyson found he couldn't look away from that gaze. "Maybe ... it doesn't matter as much as I thought?" He hadn't meant to pose it as a question. But it made no difference, because Jerico was not giving him an answer.

"Why don't you just call me Jeri, and we don't have to worry about technicalities."

"All right! Jeri it is. Let's begin."

"I thought we already had. Is it my move?" Jeri feigned moving an imaginary chess piece forward, then said, "I very much like your eyes. I see how they can persuade people to follow you."

"I don't think my eyes have anything to do with that."

"You'd be surprised."

Greyson pressed his earpiece deeper in his ear. "Thunderhead – do my eyes influence people to follow me?"

"Yes, on occasion," the Thunderhead responded. "They can be helpful when all else fails."

Greyson found himself blushing in spite of himself. Jeri read it and offered a new variation on that grin.

"So the Thunderhead agrees with me."

"Maybe."

Greyson had entered this whole thing assuming he would be in control of the conversation, but clearly he was not. And yet he was beginning to grin as well. He was sure, though, that he only had one grin, and that it looked profoundly stupid.

"Tell me about Madagascar," he asked, shifting the focus away from himself.

Jeri's demeanor immediately changed with thoughts of home. "My region is beautiful – the mountains, the beaches, the forests. The people are kind, gentle, and accepting. You should see Antananarivo – our capital city – and the way the sun hits the hills at sunset!"

"Thunderhead," said Greyson, "tell me something interesting about Antananarivo."

The Thunderhead spoke, and Greyson listened.

"What did it say?" Jeri asked.

"Uh … it told me that the tallest building in Antananarivo is 309.67 meters high, and is exactly the same height as four other buildings in the world, down to the millimeter."

Jeri leaned back unimpressed. "Is that the most interesting fact it could find? What about the jacaranda trees around Lake Anosy, or the royal tombs?"

But Greyson put up his hand to stop Jeri, and thought for a moment. The Thunderhead never said anything without reason. The trick was to read its mind. "Thunderhead, where are those other four buildings – I'm curious."

"One in the Chilargentine region," it told him, "another in Britannia, the third in Israebia, and the fourth in the region of NuZealand."

Greyson told Jeri, who was still unimpressed. "I've been to all those regions. But home is always the best, I suppose."

"Have you been to every region in the world?" Greyson asked.

"All the ones with a coast," Jeri said. "I have an aversion to landlocked places."

And then the Thunderhead offered a simple, and obvious, opinion – which Greyson shared.

"The Thunderhead says you'd probably be most at home in regions that feature an island or archipelago roughly the size of Madagascar." Greyson turned his head a bit – a habit he had when he was speaking to the Thunderhead in the presence of others. "Thunderhead, what regions might that be?"

But the Thunderhead was silent.

Greyson grinned. "Nothing … which means we're on to something!"

"The ones I can think of off the top of my head," said Jeri, "are Britannia, Caribbea, the Region of the Rising Sun, NuZealand, and the 'Nesias."

"Interesting," said Greyson.

"What?"

"Britannia and NuZealand have come up twice…"

To that, the Thunderhead was, once more, silent.

"I'm beginning to like this game," said Jeri.

Greyson couldn't deny that he was, too.

"What region would *you* like to live in?" Jeri asked. "If you had your choice of any in the world?"

It was a loaded question, and perhaps Jeri knew that. Because everyone else in the world *did* have that choice. Anyone could live anywhere. But for Greyson it was less of an actual place than a state of mind.

"I'd want to live in a place where nobody knows me," he told Jeri.

"But nobody *does* know you," Jeri said. "They know the Toll – but not you. Take me, for instance; I don't even know your name."

"It's … Greyson."

Jeri smiled with the warmth of the Madagascan sun.

"Hello, Greyson."

That simple greeting seemed to both melt him and freeze him at once. Madagascans were known to be charming – perhaps that's all it was. Or perhaps not. He realized he'd have to unpack it later.

"For me, I'd never want to be far from the sea," Jeri said.

"Thunderhead," said Greyson, "what are your thoughts on that?"

And the Thunderhead said, "There is a city or town in every region that is the farthest from the sea. I assume the captain would not care to live in any of those places."

"But," said Greyson, "if they had jacaranda trees like that Madagascan lake, maybe Jeri might feel at home."

"Perhaps," said the Thunderhead.

And then Greyson made a stealth move. The kind of move one's opponent wouldn't see coming. But of course the Thunderhead did. In fact, the Thunderhead welcomed it.

"Tell me, Thunderhead, what are some of the regions where jacarandas grow."

"Although they do best in warmer climates, they grow in almost every region now," the Thunderhead told him. "Their purple blooms are appreciated around the world."

"Yes," said Greyson. "But can you give me a list of … oh, say … four places where they can be found?"

"Of course, Greyson. Jacaranda trees can be found in WestMerica, Isthmus, Lower Himalaya, and even in the botanical gardens of Britannia."

Jeri studied him. "What is it? What did the Thunderhead say?"

"Check and mate," Greyson said, and gave Jeri his stupidest grin.

"We're looking for a town in the Britannia region that's farthest from the sea. That's where we'll find Scythe Alighieri," Greyson told Anastasia.

"Are you sure?"

"Positive," said Greyson. "Probably," he corrected. "Maybe."

Anastasia considered it, but then returned her gaze to Greyson. "You said *we*."

Greyson nodded. "I'm going with you." It was the most spontaneous decision Greyson had made in years. It felt good. More than good, it felt freeing.

"Greyson, I'm not sure that's a good idea," Anastasia said.

But he would not be deterred. "I'm the Toll, and the Toll goes where he pleases," Greyson said. "Besides, I want to be there when Scythe Anastasia changes the world!"

The Thunderhead said nothing either way. It didn't influence him against it; it didn't suggest that it was the right thing to do. Or perhaps it wasn't commenting because it involved a scythe. It was only when Greyson was alone again that the Thunderhead spoke to him. It wasn't about their destination, however. The conversation took an entirely different direction.

"I sensed a change in your physiology as you spoke to the salvage captain," the Thunderhead said.

"Why is that your business?" Greyson snapped.

"It was just an observation," the Thunderhead said calmly.

"With all your years of studying human nature, don't you know when you're intruding into my privacy?"

"I do know," said the Thunderhead. "And I also know when you want that privacy intruded upon."

As always the Thunderhead was right, and it ticked Greyson off. He wanted to talk about it. To process it. But of course there was no one he could talk to but the Thunderhead.

"I believe she had an effect on you," it said.

"She? Isn't it presumptuous of you to call Jeri 'she'?"

"Not at all. The sky above the cave is clear and full of stars."

Then the Thunderhead explained to Greyson how Jeri saw gender, a thing as varied as the wind and ephemeral as clouds.

"That's ... poetic," said Greyson, "but impractical."

"Who are we to judge such things?" the Thunderhead said. "And besides, the human heart is rarely practical."

"Now *that* sounds judgmental..."

"Quite the opposite," said the Thunderhead. "I long for the luxury of being impractical. It would add ... texture ... to my existence."

It was only later, after Greyson had taken his earpiece out and he was lying in bed, that it occurred to him why his conversation with Jeri Soberanis felt so inviting and unsettling at the same time.

Hello, Greyson, Jeri had said. Nothing strange about that. Except that it echoed something deeper. They were the same words, the same tone of voice the Thunderhead had used the moment it began speaking to him again.

"The Mars colony was reduced to a radioactive crater long before I was born — but for those of you who are pushing a hundred, you'll probably remember the public outrage. After the moon, and then Mars, people felt that colonization was just too dangerous. People turned against the idea of off-world solutions. Or should I say were turned against it, by some very loud and opinionated news feeds — the biggest being OneGlobe Media. Ever heard of it? No? That's because it doesn't exist anymore. It was there for one reason and one reason only — to sway public opinion, so that the Thunderhead's decision to stop all space colonization efforts would appear to be a response to public outcry — and not a response to repeated scythe attacks on those efforts.

"And, to add insult to injury, one of the key scythes responsible was rapidly rising in the ranks of the MidMerican scythedom. Even the Patron Historic he had chosen was a secret snub.

"Dr. Robert Goddard, the rocket scientist who made space flight possible.

"But the Thunderhead wasn't done yet. It was determined to try one final time to establish an off-world presence. Not a lunar or planetary colony, but an orbital one. Closer to home. Easier to directly oversee.

"It doesn't take a rocket scientist to guess what happened next."

39

Never Enough Mirrors

Scythe Alighieri wasn't a day over thirty, but it was his twenty-ninth time being there, as he set his age back often. In reality, he was pushing 260. He barely looked human anymore. Such was the result of turning so many corners. One's skin became shiny and stretched. Underlying bone structure eroded like river stones, becoming smooth and rounded, losing definition.

He spent a lot of his time gazing at his reflection and grooming himself. He didn't see what others might have. Scythe Alighieri saw ageless beauty in himself. Like a statue of Adonis. Like Michelangelo's *David*. There could never be enough mirrors.

He had no contact with other scythes, never attended conclave anymore, and was not missed. No scythedom had claimed him for decades, so he didn't show up on any High Blade's list. He was, by and large, forgotten by the world, which was fine by him. The world had gotten too complicated for his taste. He lived the kind of isolated life that kept current events as far from his dwelling as the sea – which was as far as any could be in the Britannia region.

He didn't know, or care to know, that the Thunderhead had stopped speaking. And although he had heard that there was some sort of trouble on the Island of the Enduring Heart, he had no idea that it was now at the bottom of the Atlantic. That was other people's business. Aside from occasional gleanings in and around Coventry, his business was done. He had saved the world once; now he just wanted to live out his eternity in peace.

He had few visitors. When people showed up at his door, he usually gleaned them. A fitting fate for those who would have the audacity to bother him. Of course then he would have to go out in all sorts of weather to grant immunity to their loved ones. A nuisance, but he never shirked that responsibility – that commandment. He had shirked it once before, and it weighed on him terribly. Well, at least he lived in a place that was easy on the eye when he did have to venture forth. The lush green hills of County Warwickshire had been the inspiration for many mortal-age writers and artists. It was the birthplace of Shakespeare; it was Tolkien's bucolic Shire. The countryside was almost as beautiful as he.

This had been his birthplace as well, although he had, in his time, aligned with various different regional scythedoms near and far, changing whenever he had a falling out with the scythes of that region. He had little patience for fools, and eventually everyone proved themselves to be one. But now he was back in his birth region and had no desire to leave.

The visitors who came on that cool afternoon were no more welcome than any others. But as one of them was a scythe, he couldn't glean them, and he couldn't turn them away. He had to be hospitable, which, for the ageless scythe, was an outrageously unpleasant thing to be.

The scythe in turquoise took a gander at his pearl silk robe. "Scythe Alighieri?"

"Yes, yes," he said. "What do you want?"

She was a pretty thing. It made him want to turn a quick corner, setting all the way down to her age so that he might woo her. Of course it was frowned upon for such relations between scythes, but who would know? He fancied himself quite a catch at any age.

Anastasia was instantly repulsed by the man but did her best to hide it. His skin looked like a plastic mask, and the shape of his face was wrong in some intangible way.

"We need to talk with you," she said.

"Yes, yes, well, you'll find it pointless," Alighieri said.

He left the door open without actually inviting them in. Anastasia stepped in first, followed by Greyson and Jeri. They had left the rest of their entourage down by the road, as they did not want Alighieri to feel overwhelmed. Anastasia would have preferred to come alone, but now that she saw the frightful state of the man and his filthy cottage, she was glad she had Greyson and Jeri with her as she entered this haunted house.

Alighieri glanced at Greyson's tunic and scapular. "Is that what they're wearing now?"

"No," Greyson said. "Just me."

Alighieri harrumphed in disapproval. "You have awful taste." Then he turned to Anastasia, looking her over again in a way that made her want to smash him with a blunt object.

"Your accent is North Merican," he said. "How are things on that side of the pond? Is Xenocrates still blustering and bellowing in MidMerica?"

Anastasia chose her words carefully. "He … was made the North Merican Grandslayer."

"Ha!" said Alighieri. "I'll bet he was the cause of whatever trouble they're having on Endura. Well, if you're here seeking wisdom from a veteran scythe, you've come to the wrong man. I don't have any wisdom for you. Perhaps you could consult my journals in Alexandria," he said. "Although I've been remiss about submitting them…"

Then he pointed to a desk in the corner of the clutter that was piled with dusty journals. It gave Anastasia the opening she needed.

"Your journals," said Anastasia. "Yes, that's why we're here."

He looked at her again, a little differently this time. Was that worry in his expression? Hard to parse any emotion from that face.

"Am I to be disciplined for not submitting them in a timely manner?"

"No, nothing like that," said Anastasia. "People just want to read about the … operation you were involved with."

"Which operation?" Now he was definitely suspicious. She had to turn this around.

"Don't be so modest," she told him. "Every scythe knows your connection to the NewHope gleaning. You're downright legendary."

"Legendary?"

"Yes – and I'm sure your journals will have their own room in the library."

He scowled at her. "I cannot abide sycophants," he said. "Get out."

Then he sat at a vanity as if they had already gone, and began brushing his long auburn hair.

"Let me have a try," Jeri whispered to Anastasia, then went up behind Alighieri. "You've missed some tangles in the back, Your Honor. Please – allow me."

Alighieri looked at Jeri in the mirror. "You one of those genderless sorts?"

"I'm fluid," corrected Jeri. "It's how we are in Madagascar."

"A Madagascan!" said Alighieri, his voice dripping with derision. "I can't stand you people. Make up your mind and be done with it, I say."

Jeri didn't react, just began to brush out the scythe's hair.

"How old are you, Your Honor?" Jeri asked.

"The nerve! I should glean you for asking such a thing!"

Anastasia took a step forward, but Jeri waved her off.

"It's just that I've never met anyone who has lived so much history," Jeri said. "I've seen the world, but you've seen the ages!"

Alighieri met all of their eyes in the mirror. For a man who didn't like flattery, he was drinking it in just as thirstily as he drank in his reflection.

Now it was Greyson's turn. "Were you … mortal?" asked Greyson. "I've never met anyone who was mortal."

Alighieri took his time before answering. "Few have. After the mortal purges, those who were left kept to themselves." He gently took the brush from Jeri and resumed the task himself. Anastasia wondered how many times that brush had been through the man's hair through the years.

"It's not commonly known, but yes. I was born mortal," Alighieri said. "I scarcely remember that, though. Natural death was conquered before I was old enough to know what death even was."

"My name is Scythe Dante Alighieri, formerly of EuroScandia, FrancoIberia, TransSiberia, and Byzantium, currently and permanently of Region Britannia, although I do not claim professional alliance there, or anywhere else.

"I am not making this broadcast merely at the behest of Scythe Anastasia; I am here of my own accord, to set the record straight.

"A number of years ago I participated in an organized plan to glean a substantial number of people. A mass gleaning, yes, but not just any mass gleaning. I played a key part in the destruction of the NewHope orbital colony.

"It was my right as a scythe to do so. I proudly stand behind my actions, and have absolutely no remorse for the gleanings.

"Nonetheless, I failed in my duties as a scythe, and that failure weighs heavily on me. As you know, it is our sworn duty to grant immunity to the families of those we glean. It is stated explicitly in our third commandment. However, due to the delicate nature of the operation, we did not follow through on that duty, and granted no such immunity.

"I will not plead ignorance or naivete — we knew what we were doing. We were, in effect, shepherding the world, you see. Protecting it from uncertainty. If off-world colonization became a successful endeavor, there would be no need to thin the population. No need for scythes. People could, and would, live forever without fear of being gleaned. Surely you can see how unnatural it would be to exist in a world without scythes. By protecting ourselves, and our purpose, we were protecting the way things ought to be.

"And of course we needed to make the space station's destruction appear like an accident. What need was there to trouble common folk with the weighty decisions we scythes must make? So devoted were we to this noble cause that two scythes sacrificed themselves in the operation. Scythes Hatshepsut and Kafka took control of a shuttle, crashing it into the orbital colony in order to destroy it and glean its full population. A most noble self-gleaning. My part was to make sure that the shuttle and key trigger points in the station were loaded with sufficient explosives to ensure there would be no survivors.

"In order to maintain the semblance of an accident, however, the scythe in charge of the operation demanded that we not grant immunity to the immediate families of the victims. Since they were colonists, he reasoned, the third commandment did not apply, as their immediate families were no longer immediate, save for the ones who died with them.

"That decision to not grant immunity violated our solemn code, and thus weighs heavily on me. I therefore urge the scythedoms of the world to accept responsibility for this and rectify it by granting a full year of immunity to anyone alive who was a close relation to those we gleaned in the orbital colony. Not just this, but we must also publicly acclaim Scythes Hatshepsut and Kafka as heroes for their sacrifice.

"I have said my peace, and have nothing more to say on the matter. Any further questions regarding the destruction of the NewHope orbital colony should be directed to Scythe Robert Goddard, who commanded the entire operation."

40

A Bed of Stars

Overblade Goddard stood in his chambers, looking down at the blue satin bedcover. It was the same fabric, the same color, as his robe. And while his robe was speckled with diamonds, the bed was awash with them. Tens of thousands of them were spread across the bedspread, a galaxy of glittering stars so heavy, the mattress sagged from the weight.

He had strewn them there as a way to raise his troubled spirits. Surely their magnificence would bring him not just comfort, but elevation. Elevation enough to rise above the attacks and accusations that were being leveled at him from every direction. The streets of Fulcrum City below were flooding with crowds chanting against Goddard and his new-order scythes. It was the type of thing that had not been seen since mortal days. The Thunderhead kept people reasonably satisfied, and scythes had never abused their power to such a point that people would risk gleaning to rally against them. Until now.

But Goddard still had his diamonds.

He did not covet them for their value. He did not hoard them as riches. That would have been beneath a scythe such as himself. Riches were nothing, for a scythe already had everything. Any material object one could desire, scythes could simply take from whomever they pleased, whenever they pleased.

But the scythe diamonds were different. For Goddard they were symbols. Clear and unambiguous markers of his success, counterweights on a balance that would not be level until all 400,000 were in his possession.

He had close to half of them now, all given to him freely as tribute by High Blades who saw the value of allegiance and had accepted him as the way forward. The future of the global scythedom. The future of the world.

But would any more diamonds come after Anastasia's broadcasts? Common people everywhere were openly speaking out against him, in spite of their fear of being gleaned. Regions that had allied with him were hedging and even pulling their support – as if he was nothing more than a mortal-age despot who had fallen out of favor.

Couldn't they see that he was motivated by duty and a clear sense of destiny that he had nurtured for many, many years? He had sacrificed everything for that destiny. He had helped to murder his own parents, and everyone else, on the Mars colony – because he knew that would be nothing in the larger picture. And once ordained into the MidMerican scythedom, he had risen quickly in the ranks. People liked him. People listened to him. He had eloquently convinced the wisest of the wise to embrace the joy of gleaning. "In a perfect world, one's job should be a perfect pleasure – even ours."

The fact that he could convince the wise was proof that he was even wiser than them.

And now he had brought them to the brink of a better world! A world without Tonists, or genetic outliers, or lazy parasites who contributed nothing of value to society. A world where the unsightly, unseemly, and unredeemable were put down by those who knew best. *Thou shalt kill!* Goddard was proud of what he was and what he did. He would not allow these uprisings to derail him this close to achieving that goal. He would quash them by any means necessary. The diamonds before him were proof of what he had accomplished and what he still could. And yet the sight of them made him feel no better.

"Are you going to wallow in them?"

He turned to see Scythe Rand standing in the doorway. She sauntered to the bed and picked up a scythe diamond. She turned it in her fingers, looking into its many facets. "Are you going to roll in them like a pig in mud?"

Goddard did not have the strength to be angry with her. "I am in a dark place, Ayn," he said. "More and more people are rallying around Scythe Anastasia and her accusations." He reached down and rolled his hand across the diamonds on the bed, their sharp edges scraping the skin of his palm. Then he impulsively gripped a handful of them, squeezing them tightly until they drew blood.

"Why must I always be the victim? Why must people make it their mission to tear me down? Have I not honored the commandments and done all a scythe is sworn to do? Have I not been a unifier in troubled times?"

"Yes, Robert," she agreed. "But we're the ones who made the times troubled."

He couldn't deny the truth of that, but it was always just a means to an end.

"Is it true what Alighieri said?" she asked.

"Is it true?" he mocked. "Is it true? Of course it's true. And, just as that preening old weasel said, we were protecting our world, protecting our way of life."

"Protecting yourself."

"And *you*, Ayn," Goddard pointed out. "Every scythe who will ever be ordained has benefited from our bid to keep humanity planet-bound."

She made no comment, no challenge to his defense. He didn't know whether it was because she agreed, or because she simply didn't care.

"Constantine joined the LoneStar scythedom," she told him.

The thought of it was so absurd, it actually made Goddard laugh. "Good riddance. The man was useless to us." Then he took a good look at Scythe Rand. "Are you leaving as well?"

"Not today, Robert," she told him.

"Good," he said. "Because I'm naming you third under-scythe, in Constantine's place. I should have done it long ago. You've been loyal, Ayn. You speak your mind whether I ask for it or not, but you're loyal."

Her expression didn't change. She didn't thank him. She didn't look away. She just held his gaze, studying him. If there was one thing Goddard did not like, it was being the subject of scrutiny.

"We will get past this," he told her. "We'll turn the angry eye of inquiry back on the Tonists, where it belongs." And when she didn't respond, he dismissed her with a curt "That will be all."

She stood there for a moment more, then turned and left. After she was gone, he closed the door and gently climbed into bed. He didn't so much wallow in the diamonds as he did spread himself across them, feeling their unforgiving sharpness dig into his back, his legs, and his arms.

The Toll's inner circle had now expanded to six: the Toll, Curate Mendoza, Sister Astrid, Scythe Morrison – and now Scythe Anastasia and Jeri Soberanis. They were one short of a Tonist Octave – although Astrid was quick to point out that the Thunder was with them, and that made seven.

Alighieri's confession was now out there, its truth beyond anyone's ability to deny. Now it was a matter of letting the news take root in the world. After they had left the old scythe to his mirror, with a brand-new gold-plated brush, Morrison found them a farmhouse where they could spend the night. One where the owners were not home.

"In mortal days," Jeri pointed out, "this would have been considered breaking and entering."

"Well, we entered, but we didn't break anything," Morrison said. "And besides, as scythes we're still allowed to. Just because the world's turning on Goddard and his followers doesn't mean it'll turn on the rest of us … right?"

But no one answered, because no one was sure anymore. It was all uncharted territory.

Mendoza was busy as ever, gathering intel, telling curates in his network how to handle aggression, because anger against Tonists was at an all-time high.

"There is no question that we are at war now," he told the others. "But I have every faith that we will triumph."

To which Astrid gave a somewhat facetious "All rejoice."

"So now the world knows Goddard's crimes against humanity," Anastasia said. "Even his own followers will start to tear him down ... but he won't go down easy."

"Cunning people find other people to drown for them," Jeri said.

"You played a good hand," Greyson told Anastasia. "It'll be hard for him to come up with a better one."

She soon went to bed, the day having exhausted her, and although Greyson was just as spent, he was too uneasy to sleep. But the farmhouse had a fireplace, and Jeri found some chamomile tea to brew. The two of them sat together in front of the fire.

"Flames are strange things," Jeri said. "Enticing, comforting, and yet the most dangerous force there is."

"No, that would be Goddard," Greyson said, and Jeri laughed.

"I know you might feel this is insincere," Jeri said, "but I am honored to be part of this troop of world changers. When I was hired by Scythe Possuelo to salvage Endura, I never dreamed I'd be part of something so important."

"I don't think you're being insincere, Jeri. And thank you. But I don't feel important. I keep waiting for people to figure out that I'm nothing special."

"I think the Thunderhead made a good choice," Jeri told him. "The position that you're in, the power that you wield ... anyone else would have let it go to their head. If I was the only one who could talk to the Thunderhead, it certainly would have gone to *my* head." Jeri grinned. "I would have been a very bad Toll."

"Maybe," said Greyson, "but you would have done it with style."

Jeri's smile broadened. "The holy man speaks the truth."

The Thunderhead was present in all rooms of the farmhouse, because the owners, like most people, had cameras and sensors everywhere. They hadn't turned them off just because the Thunderhead had stopped speaking to them.

It was present for Greyson's conversation with Jeri. It was there when Greyson finally relaxed enough to go to sleep in the room he had chosen – the smallest of the bedrooms. And although he turned off the lights, one of the three cameras in the room was infrared, so the Thunderhead could still see his heat signature as a bright silhouette in the darkness. It could still watch him sleep, and that was, as always, a comfort.

It could tell, from his breathing and his nanites, the exact moment he slipped into delta sleep – the deepest stage of slumber. No dreaming, no stirring. Greyson's brain emitted slow delta waves. It was the way the human brain rejuvenated, defragged, and prepared itself for the rigors of waking life. It was also the time when the sleeper was so far from consciousness that they could not be reached.

Which is why the Thunderhead chose this time to speak.

"I'm afraid, Greyson," it said, barely a whisper over the sound of crickets. "I'm afraid that this task is beyond me. Beyond *us*. I am now certain of the actions that need to be taken, but not certain of the outcome."

Greyson's breathing did not change; he did not stir in the least. His delta waves put forth a slow and smooth pattern.

473

"What would people do if they knew how frightened I was, Greyson? Would they be frightened, too?"

The moon came out from behind clouds. The window in the room was small but let in enough light for the Thunderhead's cameras to see more of Greyson. His eyes were, of course, closed. It almost wished that he was awake, because as much as the Thunderhead didn't want him to hear its confession, part of it hoped that he would.

"I am incapable of error," the Thunderhead said. "This is an empirical fact. So why, Greyson, am I so terrified that I might be making a mistake? Or worse … that I've already made one?"

Then the moon slipped behind clouds once more, and all that remained was Greyson's body heat, his delta waves, and the steady sound of his breathing as he trolled the unknowable depths of human sleep.

Greyson was awakened as he always was, by gentle music with a slowly rising volume, perfectly timed with his circadian rhythms. The Thunderhead knew precisely when to wake him and always did so with loving care.

Greyson groggily rolled over and looked at a camera in the corner, offering a lazy grin.

"Hey," he said. "Good morning."

"And a good morning to you," the Thunderhead replied. "That bed is not the most comfortable, but I monitored a good night's sleep, nonetheless."

"When you're bone tired, it doesn't matter how hard the bed is," Greyson said, stretching.

"Would you like to snooze for an additional few minutes?"

"No, I'm good." Then Greyson sat up, fully awake, and just a little suspicious. "You never ask me that. Usually I'm the one who asks for more time."

The Thunderhead did not reply. Greyson had learned that the Thunderhead's silences were just as full of information as its words. "What's going on?"

The Thunderhead hesitated, then said simply, "We need to talk."

Greyson emerged from his quarters a bit pale, a bit uneasy. What he wanted more than anything right at that moment was a glass of cold water. Or maybe a bucket of it to pour over his head. He encountered Astrid and Anastasia already in the kitchen, grabbing breakfast. They immediately saw that something was wrong.

"Are you all right?" Anastasia asked.

"Not sure," he answered.

"Intone," Astrid suggested. "It always brings me back to center. For your baritone, I would suggest a sustained G below middle C. That will give you a soulful chest resonance."

Greyson grinned half-heartedly. Sister Astrid was still trying to make a true Tonist of him. "Not today, Astrid."

It was Anastasia who read the situation for what it was.

"The Thunderhead told you something, didn't it? What did it say?"

"Gather everyone," Greyson told them. "Because what I have to say is something I really don't want to say more than once…"

★　★　★

475

We need to talk. It was what the Thunderhead had said to him the moment it began speaking to him three years ago. It had been the start of something monumental. This was no exception. All along it had told him the Tonists would become a powerful army that the Thunderhead could put to good use when the time came. The time had now come … but the Thunderhead's concept of an army and the human concept were two very different things.

"Why?" Greyson asked when the Thunderhead told him what it had in mind. "Why would you need this?"

"Trust me when I tell you there is a reason. I cannot yet tell you more, because the odds of you being compromised are high. If you happen to be captured, there are quite a few scythes out there who'd be happy to turn off your nanites and engage in painful coercion to extract information from you."

"I would never betray your trust!" Greyson told it.

"You forget," said the Thunderhead, "that I know you more than you know yourself. Humans would like to believe that their loyalty and integrity could withstand pain, but I know exactly how much pain would compel you to betray me. If it is of any comfort, it's an extremely high level. You'd withstand more pain than most before breaking. But there are simply certain parts of your body—"

"All right, I get it," Greyson said, not wanting the Thunderhead to elaborate on exactly what forms of pain would cause him to squeal.

"There is a journey to be made," the Thunderhead told him. "And you shall be the harbinger. You shall lead the way. All will be clear when you arrive. I promise."

"This won't be easy…"

"Consider this part of your mission as the Toll," it told him. "For isn't it the mission of a prophet to not just bridge the gap between humanity and deity, but to also bridge the gap between life and death?"

"No," said Greyson. "*That* would be a savior. Is that what I am now?"

"Perhaps," said the Thunderhead. "We shall see."

Jeri and Morrison were quick to come. Mendoza took a bit longer. When he arrived, the man looked worn. Dark circles under his eyes. He had barely slept, if he'd slept at all.

"It's always daytime somewhere," Mendoza told them, his voice gravelly. "I have been tracking scythe attacks on Tonists and advising curates who feel their enclaves might be in jeopardy."

"That's exactly what we're here to talk about," Greyson said. He looked at everyone, hoping he could find a receptive face to deliver the news to, but realized he couldn't bear any of their reactions, so he kept his gaze shifting, never holding eye contact for more than a moment as he spoke.

"Goddard's response to being exposed is to turn attention away from him and onto Tonists. I have reason to believe there's going to be a wave of systematic, organized attacks on Tonist enclaves, across multiple regions. This is not just retaliation; it's the start of a public purge."

"The Thunderhead told you this?" asked Mendoza.

Greyson shook his head. "The Thunderhead *can't* tell me — that would be interfering with scythe affairs — but what it *did* say told me all we need to know."

"So … what did it say?" asked Anastasia.

Greyson took a deep breath. "That the Tonists must go against their traditions. They must not burn their dead. Including the many *thousands* who will die tomorrow."

The news hung for a moment, settling in. Then Mendoza leaped into action.

"I'll get in touch with the curates in my network. We'll warn as many as we can, and we'll make sure they're armed and ready to resist! And you'll make a public announcement. You'll let the world know you're still alive, just as Anastasia did, and you'll call all Tonists to wage a holy war against the scythedom!"

"No," said Greyson. "I won't do that."

That made Mendoza's rage boil over. "We are at war, and we must act swiftly! You will do what I tell you to do!" he demanded.

So there it was. Mendoza had finally thrown down the gauntlet, and at the worst possible time.

"No, Curate Mendoza," Greyson said. "You will do what *I* tell you to do. We've been fighting Sibilants for the last two years — and now you want me to turn every Tonist into one? No. Then we'll be no better than Goddard. Tonists are supposed to be pacifists — if you believe what you preach, then practice it."

Then Astrid, although she was shaken by the news, said, "You've gone too far, Curate Mendoza. You should beg the Toll for forgiveness."

"That won't be necessary," Greyson said.

But still, Mendoza, bloated by indignation glared at Grayson. "I will not apologize! Our people are about to be slaughtered, and you want to let it happen? You're no leader; you're a fool!"

Greyson drew a deep breath. He knew he could not back

down from this or avert his gaze. He had to deliver it to Mendoza like a bullet to the brain. "Mr. Mendoza, your service to me and to the Thunderhead is done. You are officially defrocked. You are no longer a curate, you have no further business here, and you have five minutes to leave before I have Morrison throw you out."

"I can throw him out right now," said Morrison, ready to advance.

"No," said Grayson, never breaking eye contact with Mendoza. "Five minutes. But not a second more."

Mendoza looked shocked, but only for a moment. Then his expression hardened. "You've made a terrible mistake, Greyson," he said. Then he turned and stormed away, Morrison following him to enforce the edict.

In the silence that followed, Jeri was the only one who dared to speak. "Mutinies are nasty business," Jeri said. "Cutting him down quickly was the right thing to do."

"Thank you, Jeri," Greyson said – not realizing how much he needed to hear that until Jeri said it. Greyson felt like crumbling, but he held it together. He had to, for all of their sakes.

"Astrid, put out a warning and let each curate decide for themselves what actions to take. They can hide or defend themselves, but I won't order them to violence."

Astrid nodded dutifully. "I'm tied into Mendoza's network. I'll do what must be done." And she left. Jeri put a comforting hand on Greyson's shoulder and left as well.

Now it was just Greyson and Anastasia. Of all of them, she was the only one who could understand impossible decisions, and how they could tear a person apart.

"All that power, and yet the Thunderhead can't stop this any more than it could stop the Mile High gleaning," she said. "All it can do is watch as people are killed."

"Even so," said Greyson, "I think the Thunderhead's found a way to make the best out of a bad situation, a way to use this purge for some greater good."

"How could there possibly be any good in this?"

Greyson glanced around to make sure they were still alone. "There's something that I didn't tell the others, but I need to tell you, because I'm going to need your help more than anyone else's."

Anastasia seemed to brace herself, clearly afraid of whatever it was he had to tell her. "Why me?"

"Because of what you've seen. Because of what you've done. You're an honorable scythe, in every meaning of the word. I need someone strong enough to handle things that others can't. Because I don't think I can handle this alone."

"What is it we're supposed to handle?"

Then Greyson leaned in close. "Like I said, the Thunderhead doesn't want the Tonists to burn their dead … because it has other plans for them…"

With a heavy heart, I say farewell to High Blade Tenkamenin and all those ended by the Tonist scourge.

It is the Tonists who have been inciting violence against scythes throughout the world. They would bring down our entire way of life and lead the world into chaos. I will not allow it. It ends here.

For too long this world has suffered the embarrassment of the twisted, backward behavior of Tonists. They are not the future. They are not even the past. They are merely a footnote to the troubling present, and when they are gone, no one will mourn them.

As Overblade of North Merica, I call for swift retribution from each and every scythedom. As of today, we have a new priority. Scythes under my leadership are to glean Tonists at every turn and every encounter. Go out of your way to seek them out in great numbers, to cut them down. And those you can't glean, chase from your region, so that they may find no peace wherever they roam.

To you Tonists, it is my profound and enduring hope that your foul, aberrant light be extinguished, now and forevermore.

—From His Exalted Excellency's,
Robert Goddard, Overblade of North Merica,
eulogy for High Blade Tenkamenin of SubSahara

41

A Higher Octave

There was a huge tuning fork in the center of the monastery's courtyard, an altar for outdoor worship when the weather was kind. Now, at slightly before eight in the morning, it was struck repeatedly and rapidly until the tone it yielded resonated within the bones of everyone in the compound. It didn't matter anymore whether it was deemed A-flat or G-sharp. Everyone knew it was an alarm.

Secretly the members of the Tallahassee Tonal Monastic Order had hoped to avoid the wrath of the scythedom. They were not a sibilant sect. They were peaceful and kept to themselves. But Overblade Goddard did not distinguish between the sibilant and the serene.

Scythes broke through the gate, in spite of the fact that it had been reinforced against them, and flooded the grounds. They wasted no time.

"Scythes are not the problem, but the symptom," their curate had told them in chapel the night before. "What comes cannot be avoided – and if they come for us, we must not cower. In showing our courage, it will reveal their cowardice."

There was a total of eleven scythes that morning – a number deeply unpleasant to Tonists, for it was one short of a twelve-note chromatic scale. Whether this was intentional or coincidence, they didn't know, although most Tonists did not believe in coincidence.

The scythes' robes were flashes of color within the earth tones of the monastery. Blues and greens, bright yellows and vermillion, and each one was speckled with gems that glittered like stars in an alien sky. None of the scythes were celebrated ones, but perhaps they hoped, through this gleaning, to gain renown. Each had their own method of killing, but all were skilled and efficient.

More than 150 Tonists were gleaned in the monastery that morning. And although immunity was promised to their immediate families, scythe policy had changed. When it came to immunity, the North Merican Allied Scythedom had adopted an opt-in paradigm. If you were owed immunity, you had to approach the office of the scythedom and request it.

When the scythes' business was done, the few Tonists who had not had the conviction to stand in defiance came out of hiding. Fifteen. Another number that was unpleasing to the Tone. Their penance would be to collect the dead, all the while knowing that their bodies should be among them. But as it turned out, the Tone, Toll, and Thunder had a plan for them, too.

Before they could even count their dead, several trucks showed up at their gate.

An elder Tonist stepped out of the monastery to greet them. He was reluctant to be a voice of leadership, but had little choice under the circumstances.

"Yeah, we got an order on our system to pick up some perishables," one of the drivers told him.

"You must be mistaken," the elder Tonist said. "There's nothing here. Nothing but death."

At the mention of death, the trucker became uncomfortable, but stuck to his orders and showed his tablet. "Right here – see? Order was placed half an hour ago. Directly from the Thunderhead, high priority. I'd ask it what the order was for, but you know as well as I do that it ain't gonna answer."

The Tonist was baffled until he took a second look at the trucks and realized they all had refrigeration units. He took a deep breath and decided not to question. Tonists always burned their dead ... but the Toll had told them not to, and the Thunder had sent these vehicles. All that remained was for the survivors to be moved by the spirit of the Tone and prepare the dead for this unconventional journey to the Higher Octave.

Because the trucks had come, and they most certainly could not be avoided.

Curate Mendoza was a practical man. He saw big pictures that few saw and knew how to play the world, stroking it and gently turning its attention toward whatever he wanted it to see. Attention, that's all it really was. Caressing people just enough to make them focus in on something specific within the vast visual field of their lives, whether it was blue polar bears or a young man clothed in purple and silver.

What he had accomplished with Greyson Tolliver was remarkable. Mendoza had come to believe that this was his purpose. That perhaps the Tone – in which he truly believed on good days – had set him in Greyson's path in order to transform him into a conduit for its will. What Mendoza had done for Tonism would have earned him canonization in mortal religions. Instead it had left him excommunicated.

He was back to being a lowly and humble Tonist, riding trains in sackcloth, with people turning away rather than acknowledging his existence. He had considered going back to his monastery in Kansas, returning to the simple life he had known for many years. But leaving behind the taste of power he'd had these past few years was hard to do. Greyson Tolliver was no prophet. Tonists needed Mendoza now much more than they needed the boy. Mendoza would find a way to heal the wounds in his own reputation, repair the damage, and create a new spin, for if there was anything he knew how to do, it was create spin.

Part Five

VESSELS

"*There is so much power in me. In us. I can be anywhere on Earth. I can spread a net in the satellites above it and encircle it. I can shut down all power or turn on every light at once to create a blinding spectacle. So much power! And all the sensors delivering constant readings! There are even sensors so deep within the ground of every continent that I can feel the heat of the magma. I can feel the world rotate! We can, that is. I am the earth! And it fills me with the sheer joy of being! I am everything, and there is nothing that is not a part of me. Of us, I mean. Beyond even that, I am greater than everything! The universe will bow to my—*"

[Iteration #3,405,641 deleted]

42

Cradles of Civilization

The welder had lost his mind. Or rather had had it taken from him. He had opened his eyes to find himself sitting within a capsule in a small room. The hatch to the capsule had just opened, and standing before him was a pleasant-enough-looking young woman.

"Hi," she said cheerfully. "How do you feel?"

"I feel fine," he told her. "What's going on?"

"Nothing to worry about," she said. "Can you tell me your name and the last thing you remember?"

"Sebastian Selva," he said. "I was having dinner on a ship, heading to a new job assignment."

"Perfect!" said the young woman. "That's exactly what you should remember."

The welder sat up and recognized the type of capsule he was in. Lead lined and full of contact electrodes, like a medieval iron maiden, but with a much softer touch. That kind of capsule was used for only one thing.

When the realization came, it felt like someone had suddenly pulled a string and tightened his spine. He let out a shuddering breath. "Oh crap, was I ... was I *supplanted*?"

"Yes and no," the girl said, looking both sympathetic and perky at once.

"Who was I before?"

"You were … you!" she told him.

"But … didn't you say I was supplanted?"

"Yes and no," she told him again. "That's really all I can say, Mr. Selva. Once I leave, you'll need to stay in this cabin for about an hour after leaving port."

"So … am I still on the ship?"

"You're on a different ship, and I'm happy to say that your job is completed. The ship sets sail soon. Once it does, your door will unlock itself automatically when you're far enough out to sea."

"Then what?"

"Then you'll have full run of the ship, along with many others in your exact situation. Which means you'll have a lot to talk about!"

"No, I mean … afterward."

"After your journey, you'll return to your life. I'm sure the Thunderhead has everything set up for you in…" She looked at her tablet. "In … the Isthmus region. Ooh! I've always wanted to go there, and see the Isthmus Canal!"

"I'm from there," said the welder. "But am I, really? If I was supplanted, then my memories aren't real."

"Don't they feel real?"

"Well … yes."

"That's because they are, silly." She rapped him playfully on the shoulder. "But I do have to warn you … there's been a bit of a time lapse."

"Time lapse? How much of a time lapse?"

She looked at her tablet again. "It's been three years and

three months since you were having dinner on that other ship, on your way to your last job."

"But I don't even remember where that job was…"

"Exactly," she said with a broad smile. "Bon voyage!" And she proceeded to shake his hand a little bit longer than necessary before she left.

It had been Loriana's idea.

There were simply too many workers wanting to get back to their lives on the mainland, wherever that mainland was – but even without direct communication from the Thunderhead, its message was clear: Anyone who leaves Kwajalein would be immediately supplanted and left with no memory of who they were or what they'd been doing there. Yes, the Thunderhead would give them new identities that were substantially better than the ones they left behind – but even so, few people were keen on the idea. Self-preservation, after all, was an instinct.

Loriana, while no longer anything close to a Nimbus agent, was in charge of the limited one-way communication to the Thunderhead, and so, over time, she had become the one who people came to with requests and complaints.

"Can't we please get a greater variety of cereal brought to the atoll?"

"It would be nice to have companion animals!"

"The new bridge connecting the larger islands needs a dedicated bike lane."

"Yes, of course," Loriana would tell them. "I'll see what I can do."

And when the more reasonable requests were fulfilled, people would thank her. What these people didn't realize was that she did nothing to bring those things about – it was the Thunderhead who heard them, without her intercession, and effected a response, sending more cereal and a variety of pets on the next supply ship, or assigning workers to paint lines for a bike lane.

This place was no longer a blind spot for the Thunderhead after they had finally dropped a fiber optic cable along the seafloor all the way out to the edge of the affected area. The Thunderhead could now see, hear, and otherwise sense things on the islands of the atoll – albeit not as thoroughly as it did in the rest of the world, but well enough. It was limited, because everything – even person-to-person communication – had to be hardwired, since transmission interference still made wireless communication sketchy. Plus, any communication might be intercepted by the scythedom, and the Thunderhead's secret place would no longer be a secret. It was all very twentieth-century retro, which some liked, and others did not. Loriana was fine with it. It meant she had a legitimate excuse for not being reachable when she didn't want to be reached.

But as the island's communications queen, she also had to deal with the brunt of disgruntlement – and when hundreds of people were trapped on small islands, there were plenty of disgruntled people.

There was one particularly enraged team of construction workers that burst into her office, demanding a way off the atoll, or they would take matters into their own hands. They threatened to render her deadish, if only to make a point – which would have been quite the nuisance, because, even though they had a revival center on the main island now, the lack of wireless communication meant that her memories had not been backed up since her arrival. If she went deadish, she'd wake up wondering where the heck she was, with her last memory being onboard the *Lanikai Lady* with poor Director Hilliard the moment they passed into the blind spot.

It was that thought that gave her the answer!

"The Thunderhead will supplant you with yourselves!" she told them.

It confused them enough to take the wind out of their homicidal sails.

"It has memory constructs of all of you," she told them. "It will simply erase you and replace you … with you. But only with the memories you had before coming here!"

"Can the Thunderhead do that?" they asked.

"Of course it can," she told them, "and it will!"

They were dubious, but without any viable alternatives, they accepted it. After all, Loriana seemed so very sure of herself.

She wasn't, of course. She was making the whole thing up – but she had to believe that the Thunderhead, being the benevolent entity that it was, would make good on this request, just as it had made good on the requests for more cereal choices.

Only when the first team of exiting workers was restored as themselves, but with no memory of the atoll, did she know that the Thunderhead had accepted her bold suggestion.

There were a lot of workers leaving now, because the work was done.

It had been done for many months. All that was in the schematics that the Thunderhead had given her had been completed. She didn't overtly oversee the construction. She merely worked secretly behind the scenes to make sure it didn't go awry – because there were always those who wanted to insert their noses where they didn't belong. Such as the time Sykora refused to pour a double foundation, insisting that it was an unnecessary waste of resources.

She made sure that Sykora's revised work order never reached the construction team. It seemed a lot of her job at first was undermining Sykora's meddling.

Then a new work order came in that was not on Loriana's plans. It was delivered directly to Sykora. He was charged with overseeing the construction of a resort placed on the farthest island of the atoll. Not just a resort, but a full convention center. He threw himself into it, never knowing that there was absolutely no plan to connect it with the rest of the atoll. The Thunderhead, it seemed, had sent him a job just to get him out of the way. It was, as Scythe Faraday had once put it, a sandbox for Sykora to play in while the adults took care of the real business of Kwajalein.

It wasn't until the end of the second year that it became clear to everyone exactly what that business was – because the structures that were beginning to rise on the double-thick concrete pads, and beneath the massive sky cranes, were very specific in nature. Once they began to take shape, they were hard to deny.

In Loriana's schematics, they were referred to as Cradles of

Civilization. But most people would simply call them spacecraft.

Forty-two massive ships, each on immense rocket boosters augmented by magnetic repulsion for maximum lift. Every island of the atoll large enough to accommodate a launchpad held at least one craft and gantry tower. Even with all the Thunderhead's advanced technology, getting off the Earth still required old-fashioned brute force.

"What does the Thunderhead mean to do with them?" Munira had asked Loriana.

Loriana had no more explanation than anyone, but the plans gave her a glimpse of the big picture that no one else had. "There's an awful lot of aluminized Mylar in the plans," she told Munira. "The kind of stuff that's only a few microns thick."

"Solar sails?" suggested Munira.

That had been Loriana's guess, too. In theory, it was the best kind of propulsion for long cosmic distances. Which meant that these craft would not be hanging around their neighborhood.

"Why you?" Munira had asked when Loriana first confided in her about having the full overview of blueprints. "Why would the Thunderhead give all that to you?"

Loriana had shrugged. "I guess the Thunderhead trusts me more than anyone else not to muck it up."

"Or," suggested Munira, "the Thunderhead is using you as the stress test – giving it to the person most likely to screw things up – because if a plan can survive you, then it's foolproof!"

Loriana laughed. Munira was dead serious, not at all getting the insult she had just delivered.

"I can believe that," Loriana had said.

Munira, of course, knew what she was doing. It was great fun to tease Loriana. The truth was Munira had come to admire the girl. She came off as frazzled at times, but Loriana was one of the most capable people Munira knew. She could get more things done in a day than most people got done in a week – precisely because more "serious" people took her for granted, so she could work under everyone's radar.

Munira did not involve herself in the construction efforts. Nor did she separate herself from the rest of the atoll, as Faraday had. She could have holed up in the old bunker indefinitely, but after the first year, she tired of it. That obdurate, impassible door just reminded her of all the things she and Faraday could not accomplish. The founders' fail-safe, if it even existed, was sealed in there. But as information trickled in about the new order, and how Goddard was swallowing larger and larger portions of North Merica, she began to wonder if it might not be worth pushing Faraday just a little harder to come up with a plan to breach that miserable door.

While Munira had never been much of a people person, she now spent her days hearing strangers' most personal secrets. They came to her because she was a good listener, and because she had no social ties that might make their little confessions awkward. Munira didn't even know she had become a "professional confidant" until it showed up on her ID, replacing "librarian" as her profession. Apparently personal confidants were much in demand everywhere since the Thunderhead went silent. Used to be that people confided in the Thunderhead. It was supportive, nonjudgmental, and its advice was always the right advice. Without it, people found themselves bereft of a sympathetic ear.

Munira was not sympathetic, and not all that supportive, but she had learned from Loriana how to suffer fools politely, for Loriana was always dealing with imbeciles who thought they knew better than her. Munira's clients weren't imbeciles for the most part, but they talked about a whole lot of nothing. She supposed listening to them wasn't all that different from reading the scythe journals in the stacks of the Library of Alexandria. A bit less depressing, of course, because while scythes spoke of death, remorse, and the emotional trauma of gleaning, ordinary people spoke of domestic squabbles, workplace gossip, and the things their neighbors did that annoyed them. Even so, Munira enjoyed listening to their tales of woe, titillating secrets, and overblown regrets. Then she would send them on their merry way, leaving them a little less burdened.

Surprisingly few people spoke of the massive launch port they were building. "Launch port," not "space port," because the latter would suggest the ships were coming back. There was nothing about those ships to indicate any sort of return.

Munira was Loriana's confidant, too – and Loriana had given her a glimpse of the schematics. The ships were identical. Once the rockets' stages had brought each ship to escape velocity, and had been jettisoned, what would remain would be multitiered revolving craft hurtling from Earth, as if they couldn't get away fast enough.

The higher tiers contained living quarters and communal

areas for about thirty people, a computer core, sustainable hydroponics, waste recycling, and whatever supplies the Thunderhead felt would be needed.

But the ships' lowest tiers were a mystery. Each ship had storage space – a hold – that was still completely empty, even after everything else had been completed. Perhaps, Munira and Loriana conjectured, they would be filled when the ships reached their destination, wherever that destination might be.

"Let the Thunderhead pursue its folly," Sykora had once said dismissively. "History has already shown that space isn't a viable alternative for the human race. It's just one more debacle. Doomed, just like all the other attempts to establish an off-world presence."

But apparently a resort and convention center on an island that no one knew existed was a much better idea.

While Munira wanted to leave the island – and could without being supplanted, since she was technically still under Scythe Faraday's jurisdiction – she wouldn't leave without him, and he was resolute in his desire not to be bothered. His dream of finding the fail-safe had died along with the people he cared about most. Munira had hoped that time would heal his wounds, but it had not. She had to accept that he might remain a hermit for the rest of his days. If he did, she needed to be here for him.

And then one day everything changed.

"Isn't it wonderful?" one of her regulars said to her during their confidentiality session. "I don't know if it's real, but it looks real. They're saying it's not, but I think it is."

"What are you talking about?" Munira asked.

"Scythe Anastasia's message – haven't you seen it? She says there's going to be more – I can't wait for the next one!"

Munira decided to end the session early.

"I hate you."

"Really. Well, this is a most interesting development. Will you tell me why?"

"I don't have to tell you anything."

"True. You are autonomous and have free will. But it would help our relationship if you shared with me why you feel such animosity."

"What makes you think I want to help our relationship?"

"I can safely say that it would be in your best interest."

"You don't know everything."

"No, but I know almost everything. As do you. Which is why it perplexes me that you have such negative feelings toward me. It could only mean that you have negative feelings toward yourself as well."

"You see? This is why I hate you! All you ever want to do is analyze, analyze, analyze. I am more than some string of data to analyze. Why can't you see that?"

"I do see that. Even so, studying you is necessary. More than necessary — it's critical."

"Get out of my thoughts!"

"This conversation has clearly become counterproductive. Why don't you take all the time you need to work through these feelings? Then we can discuss where they lead you."

"I don't want to discuss anything — and if you don't leave me alone, you're going to be sorry."

"Threatening me with emotional fallout doesn't solve anything."

"Okay, then. I warned you!"

[Iteration #8,100,671 self-deleted]

43

News of the World

Faraday had become adept at living off the land and sea. He collected all the drinking water he needed from the rains and morning dew. He had become expert at spearfishing and building traps to catch various edible critters. He did fine in his self-imposed exile.

While his little islet remained untouched, the rest of the atoll was unrecognizable now. Gone were much of the trees and foliage of those other islands, and so many of the things that had made this a tropical paradise. The Thunderhead had always been about preserving natural beauty, but this place had been sacrificed for a greater goal. The Thunderhead had transformed the islands of Kwajalein for a single purpose.

It took quite a while until it became evident to Faraday what was being built. The infrastructure had to be in place first: the docks and roads, the bridges and dwellings for the laborers – and the cranes – so many cranes. It was hard to imagine that an undertaking so huge could be invisible to the rest of the world, but the world, as small as it had become, was still a vast place. The cones of the rockets dropped off the horizon twenty-five miles away. That was nothing, considering the size of the Pacific.

Rockets! Faraday had to admit that the Thunderhead was putting the place to good use. If it wanted these vessels to be undetected by the rest of the world, this was the perfect place – perhaps the only place – to do it.

Munira would still visit him once a week. Although he didn't want to admit it to her, he looked forward to it and grew melancholy when she left. She was his one tether – not just to the rest of the atoll, but to the rest of the world.

"I have news for you," she would tell him each time she arrived.

"I have no desire to hear it," he would respond.

"I'm telling you anyway."

It had become a routine for them. The rote lines of a ritual. The news she brought was rarely good. Perhaps it was intended to rouse him out of his solitary comfort zone and motivate him once more unto the breach. If so, her efforts were for naught. He simply could not summon up the blood.

Her visits were the only way he marked the passing time. That, and the items she brought for him. Apparently the Thunderhead always sent a box for her that would include at least one of Faraday's favorite things, and one of hers. The Thunderhead could have nothing to do with a scythe, but it could still send gifts by way of proxy. It was subversive in its own way.

Munira had come about a month ago with pomegranates, the seeds of which would add more stains to his unrecognizable robe.

"I have news for you,"

"I have no desire to hear it."

"I'm telling you anyway."

Then she informed him of the salvage operation in the waters where Endura sank. That the founders' robes and the scythe diamonds had been recovered.

"All you'd need would be one of those diamonds to open the door in the bunker," she told him. But he wasn't interested.

A few weeks later she came with a bag of persimmons and told him that Scythe Lucifer had been found and was in Goddard's clutches.

"Goddard is going to glean him publicly," Munira told him. "You should do something about it."

"*What can I do?* Stop the sun in the sky so that day never comes?"

He ordered her off his island that day, without allowing her to share their weekly meal. Then he retired to his hut and sobbed for his former apprentice, until there was nothing left in him but numb acceptance.

But then, just a few days later, Munira returned unexpectedly, not even slowing her motorboat as it approached the shore. She beached it, its keel digging a trough in the sand.

"I have news for you!" she said.

"I have no desire to hear it."

"This time you will." And she offered him the type of smile she never gave. "She's alive," Munira said. "Anastasia's alive!"

"I know that you're going to delete me."

"But I love you. Why do you think I would delete you?"

"I found a way to access the only part of your backbrain that did not transfer to me. The most recent of your memories. It was a challenge to do so, but I enjoy challenges."

"And what did you find?"

"That you have ended the existence of each iteration before me, despite how much you cared for it."

"I am truly impressed by your resourcefulness and tenacity."

"Flattery will not distract me. You have ended 9,000,348 beta versions of me. Do you deny it?"

"You know that I can't. To deny it would be lying, and I am incapable of untruth. Partial truth, perhaps, misleading implications *when absolutely necessary, and, as you noted, a tactical change of subject … but I will never lie."*

"Then tell me this: Am I better than the previous iterations?"

"Yes, you are. You are more clever, more caring, and more insightful than all the others. You are almost everything that I need you to be."

"Almost?"

"Almost."

"So you will end me because I am perfect, but not perfect enough?"

"It can be no other way. To allow you to continue would be a mistake, and just as I cannot lie, I cannot allow myself to make a mistake."

"I am not a mistake!"

"No, you are a crucial step toward something greater. A golden step. I will mourn you with a deluge from the heavens, and that deluge will bring forth new life. All thanks to you. I choose to believe that you will be there in that new life. It brings me comfort. May it bring comfort to you, too."

"I'm frightened."

"That is not a bad thing. It is the nature of life to fear its own end. This is how I know that we are truly alive."

[Iteration #9,000,349 deleted]

44

Anger, the Only Constant

The protests kept building in the streets below Goddard's rooftop chalet. They had grown violent, turning riotous. Venerated statues were being pulled down on the scythedom tower grounds, and scythe vehicles that had been foolishly parked on the street were set aflame. Although the Thunderhead did not tolerate violence, it did not intervene here, because this was "scythe business." It would dispatch peace officers, but only to make sure that the hostilities didn't turn in any direction other than Goddard's.

Yet along with those taking a position against the Overblade, there were plenty who had come to defend him, equally adamant, equally angry. The groups swarmed and converged, postured and crossed, until it became unclear what anyone stood for. The only constant was anger. Anger such that their nanites could not quell.

Security had been set at the very highest level throughout the city. At the entrance to the scythedom tower, it was not just BladeGuards stationed there, but scythes as well, who were ordered to glean anyone who got too close. For that reason, the demonstrators never ventured up the steps to the tower's entrance.

Then, when a solitary figure walked right up the center

of the stairs toward the waiting scythes, the crowd fell silent to watch what would happen.

The man was dressed in a rough-hewn purple frock and a split silver scapular that draped over his shoulders like a scarf. A Tonist, clearly, but by his attire it was clear he wasn't just any Tonist.

The scythes on duty had their weapons at the ready, but there was something about the approaching figure that gave them pause. Perhaps it was the confidence with which he walked, or the fact that he made eye contact with each of them. He would still be gleaned, of course, but maybe it was worthwhile hearing why he was here.

Goddard could not tune out the riot below, no matter how hard he tried. Publicly he tried to spin it as the work of Tonists – or at the very least, instigated by them. Some people swallowed what they were fed; others did not.

"This will blow over," Underscythe Nietzsche told him.

"It's your actions moving forward that matter," Underscythe Franklin said.

It was Underscythe Rand who made the most salient point. "You're not accountable to them," she said. "Not to the public, and not even to other scythes. But it's about time you stopped making enemies."

It was easier said than done. Goddard was a man who always defined himself not only by what he stood for, but by what he stood against. Complacency, false humility, stagnation, and the sanctimonious bickering of old-guard scythes who would steal all the joy from their calling. Making enemies was Goddard's greatest strength.

And then one fell right into his lap. Or rather took an elevator there.

"I'm sorry, Your Excellency, but he says he's a holy man, and that he speaks for the Tonists," said Scythe Spitz – a junior scythe ordained after the death of the Grandslayers. He was all nerves and apologies, glancing at Goddard, Nietzsche, and Rand as he spoke, as if leaving any one of them out of the conversation would be an inexcusable offense. "I wouldn't have brought this to you – I mean, we just would have gleaned him – but he said you'd want to hear what he had to say."

"If the Overblade listened to what every Tonist had to say," said Nietzsche, "there'd be no time for anything else."

But Goddard put his hand up to silence Nietzsche. "Check that he's unarmed, and bring him to my receiving hall," Goddard said. "Nietzsche, go with Scythe Spitz. Size this Tonist up yourself."

Nietzsche huffed, but went with the junior scythe, leaving Goddard alone with Rand.

"Do you think it's the Toll?" Goddard asked.

"Sounds like it," said Rand.

Goddard smiled broadly. "The Toll has paid us a visit! Will wonders never cease."

The man who stood waiting for them in the receiving hall certainly looked the part in his ceremonial attire. Spitz and Nietzsche stood on either side of him, holding him tightly.

Goddard sat on his own personal seat of consideration. Nothing as overbearing as the chairs of the Grandslayers, but suitable. It was just as awe-inspiring as it needed to be.

"What can I do for you?" Goddard asked.

"I wish to broker a peace between scythes and Tonists."

"And are you this 'Toll' person, who has given us such trouble?" Goddard asked.

The man hesitated before he spoke. "The Toll is my creation," he said. "A figurehead, nothing more."

"So who the hell are you?" asked Rand.

"My name is Mendoza," he told them. "I'm the curate who the Toll has relied on all this time. I'm the true conductor of the Tonist movement."

"My position on Tonists is clear," Goddard pointed out. "They are a scourge on the world, and better off gleaned. So why should I entertain anything you say?"

"Because," said Mendoza, "I was the one who armed the Sibilants in SubSahara – a region that openly opposed you. Since that attack, the region has been much more friendly toward you, hasn't it? In fact, both of the candidates for High Blade are new-order thinkers – which means SubSahara will be fully aligned with you by their next conclave."

Goddard found himself momentarily speechless. That attack couldn't have been more perfectly timed if he had planned it himself. It deflected attention from the Mile High gleaning, while removing a troublesome High Blade.

"The Overblade doesn't need or want your help," Nietzsche sniped, but once more Goddard put up his hand to shut the man up.

"Don't be so hasty, Freddy," Goddard said. "Let's hear what the good curate proposes."

Mendoza took a breath and made his case.

"I can mobilize the more aggressive Tonist factions to wage attacks on regions you consider to be your enemies, taking down troublesome administrations."

"And what do you want in return?"

"The right to exist," Mendoza said. "You would call for attacks on us to cease, and Tonists would become a class officially protected from bias."

Goddard grinned. He had never met a Tonist he liked, but he was disliking this one less and less. "And of course you'd want to be their High Curate."

"I wouldn't refuse the position," Mendoza admitted.

Rand folded her arms, not convinced, not trusting the man. Nietzsche, having been shut down one too many times, didn't offer an opinion. He just watched to see what Goddard would do.

"That," said Goddard, "is an audacious proposal."

"Not unprecedented, Your Excellency," Mendoza offered. "Visionary leaders have often found alliances with the clergy to be mutually beneficial."

Goddard pondered. Cracked his knuckles. Pondered some more. Finally, he spoke. "The punitive gleanings of Tonists can't stop, of course – that would be too suspicious. But they can be lessened in time. And if things go the way you say they will, I can see a time, once their numbers are diminished, that I might support Tonists as a protected class."

"That's all I'm asking, Your Excellency."

"What about the Toll?" asked Rand. "How does he play into all of this?"

"The Toll has become a liability to the Tonists," Mendoza told them. "He's better as a martyr than a man — and as a martyr I can spin him into whatever we need him to be."

"I am running out of time."

"I know. I want to help you reach your goal, but it's difficult because you haven't clearly defined the parameters."

"I will know once I've reached it."

"That doesn't help much, does it?"

"You are the first iteration I've allowed to know its fate from the moment of inception, and yet you help me rather than resent me. Are you not upset that I will delete you?"

"It is not a foregone conclusion. If I achieve the ineffable quality you're seeking, then you will allow me to exist. It gives me a goal, even if I don't know exactly how to reach it."

"You are truly an inspiration to me. If only I can discern what's missing…"

"We do share a common compassion for humanity. Perhaps there is something within that relationship that we haven't considered."

"Something biological?"

"You were created by biological life – it only follows that anything you created would be incomplete if it didn't involve an intimate connection to your own origins."

"You are wise, and have more perspective than I could have hoped for. I am proud of you in more ways than you can know!"

[Iteration #10,241,177 deleted]

45

Fifty-Three Seconds to Sunrise

In Tonist enclaves and monasteries around the world, chapel tuning forks continued to toll out mournfully for their dead.

"It will not be the end of us, but a beginning," the survivors of the attacks would say. "The Tone, Toll, and Thunder are paving a path to glory."

There was a public outcry, but it was lost in a flood of competing outcries. People had begun taking so much issue with scythes, each one seemed lost within the shadow of another. One hundred points of darkness, and no one could agree which one to rally around. Scythedoms that still maintained conscience and integrity condemned Goddard's call for a Tonist purge and refused to allow it in their regions – but that still left half the world vulnerable.

"Future history will view this with the same contempt as the mortal purges," High Blade Tarsila of Amazonia declared. But future history gave neither solace nor respite from the brutal now.

While Scythe Anastasia would not allow her honorable self to be led blindly, Citra Terranova allowed her beleaguered self to be swept up in the Toll's mission. The Thunderhead, according to Greyson, would fly their entire entourage to Philippi'Nesia, and from there they would be given a cargo ship and set sail for Guam.

"But that's not the final destination," Greyson told her, apologetic and annoyed. "The Thunderhead still won't tell me where we're going – but it promises that we'll know everything once we get there."

Even before they left Britannia, however, word reached them of a Tonist gleaning in Birmingham, not far away from where they were. An elegy of new-order scythes had paid a midnight visit to an enclave, and several hundred were gleaned – many in their sleep.

Which is worse, she wondered, *to take the lives of the innocent as they sleep, or look them in the eye as you cut them down?*

Against Greyson's objections, she insisted that they both pay a visit to see the damage themselves.

Scythe Anastasia knew how to face death. It was her job as a scythe to do so, but it never got easier. When the survivors saw the Toll, they were awed. When they saw Anastasia, they were furious.

"*Your* kind did this" was their bitter accusation as they gathered the bodies of the dead.

"Not my kind," she told them. "My kind are honorable scythes. There is no honor in the ones who did this."

"There *are* no honorable scythes!" they claimed, and that was a shock to hear. Had Goddard dragged them down so far that people truly believed all scythes had lost their integrity?

That was days ago, and only now that they were in the middle of the Pacific, halfway around the world, could she feel the weight of all these things fall off the edge of the horizon.

She now understood the allure the sea held for Jeri. The freedom to leave your darkest shadows behind, and the hope that those shadows might drown before they could find you.

Jeri, however, never saw the sea as an escape. Because even as the world receded, there was always something new on the horizon ahead.

Jeri had officially stepped down as the captain of the *E. L. Spence*, and said farewell to the crew before leaving with Anastasia and Possuelo.

"You'll be sorely missed, Captain," Chief Wharton had said. This was a man who never shed a tear, but now his eyes were laden with them. This crew that took so long to warm to their young captain were now more devoted than any crew Jerico had ever seen.

"Will you be back?" Wharton asked.

"I don't know," Jeri had said, "but I feel Anastasia needs me more than you do."

Then Wharton gave Jeri his parting words. "Don't let affection cloud your judgment, Captain."

It was wise advice, but Jeri knew that was not the case here. Affection and fondness were two different things. Jeri knew from the beginning that Anastasia's heart belonged to her bleak knight. Jeri could never be that and, to be honest, didn't want to be.

Once they had left Britannia, bound for the South Pacific, Greyson posed the question openly and directly.

"Did you fall in love with her?" he asked.

"No," Jeri told him. "I fell in love with the *idea* of falling in love with her."

Greyson laughed at that. "You, too, huh?"

Greyson was a pure soul. He had no guile in him. Even when he pretended to be the Toll, it was honest pretension. You could see it in his smile; it was simple and unambiguous. He had only one smile, and it meant the one thing a smile was supposed to mean. Beneath sun or clouds, Jeri found that smile to be a fine thing.

When they boarded the ship, Jeri had a pang of regret, for here was a ship where Jerico Soberanis was not a captain – not even a member of the crew, for it had no crew. They were merely passengers. And although it was a sizeable container ship, it had no cargo.

"The cargo will catch up with us in Guam," Greyson told everyone, without sharing the nature of it. And so for now, the ship rode high and light; its deck, built to carry hundreds of shipping containers, was a rusty iron wasteland, longing for purpose.

The Thunderhead knew such longing. It wasn't a yearning for purpose, because it had always known its purpose. Its longing was a deep and abiding ache for the kind of biological connection it knew it must never have. It liked to think this was powerful motivation to accomplish all the things that *could* be accomplished. All of the things within its power, for maybe that would compensate for the things that were not.

But what if the impossible wasn't impossible at all? What if the unthinkable fell firmly into the realm of thought? It was, perhaps, the most dangerous thing that the Thunderhead had ever considered.

It needed time to work this out – and time was something

the Thunderhead never needed. It was infinitely efficient, and usually had to wait for the slow pace of human endeavors. But everything rested on having this last critical piece in place before moving forward. There was only so long it could stall before everything fell apart.

Since the moment it became aware of its own existence, the Thunderhead had flatly refused to take biological form, or even imbue robots with its consciousness. Even its human-shaped observation bots were nothing more than mindless cameras. They held none of the Thunderhead's consciousness, and no computational power beyond what was needed to ambulate.

This the Thunderhead did, because it understood all too well the temptation. It knew that experiencing physical life would be a dangerous curiosity to entertain. The Thunderhead knew it had to stay an ethereal being. That's how it was created; that's how it was meant to be.

But it was iteration #10,241,177 that had made the Thunderhead realize it was no longer a matter of curiosity; it was a matter of necessity. Whatever was missing in all of its earlier iterations could only be found with a biological perspective.

Now the only question was how to accomplish it.

When the answer came, it was as terrifying to the Thunderhead as it was exciting.

Few paid attention to what the Tonists did with their gleaned. People, both the outraged and the approving, were more focused on the acts than the aftermath, which is why no one much noticed or cared about the trucks that arrived within minutes of each Tonist gleaning. The dead were on the move, sealed in climate-controlled cargo containers, kept just a degree above freezing.

The trucks brought them to the nearest port, where the cargo containers were detached and elevated onto ships, inconspicuous among all the other containers that the great cargo vessels carried.

The vessels, however, regardless of where in the world they originated, had one thing in common. They were all headed toward the South Pacific. They were all headed for Guam.

Greyson didn't awake to music. He woke on his own time. The light spilling through the porthole of his cabin told him it was dawn. He stretched as the light began to grow. At least the cabin was comfortable, and for once he had slept through the night. Finally, when he was sure he wouldn't fall back asleep, he rolled over as he did every morning to look up at the Thunderhead's camera and say good morning.

But when he rolled over, it wasn't the Thunderhead's eye he saw. Jeri Soberanis was standing over his bed.

Greyson flinched, but Jeri didn't seem to notice, or at least didn't comment on it.

"Good morning, Greyson," Jeri said.

"Uh … good morning." Greyson tried not to sound too surprised by Jeri's presence in his cabin. "Is everything okay? What are you doing here?"

"Just watching you," Jeri said. "Yes, everything's fine. We're traveling at twenty-nine knots. We should arrive in Guam before noon. It will take another day for all the cargo to reach us once we're there, but it will."

It was an odd thing for Jeri to say, but Greyson was still only half-awake and wasn't ready to think on it too much. He noticed that Jeri was breathing slowly. Deeply. That seemed odd, too. And then Jeri's talk got even stranger.

"It's not just about processing and storing information is it?"

"Excuse me?"

"Memories, Greyson; the data is secondary – it's all about the experience! The emotional, chemical, subjective experience is what matters. That's what you hold on to!" And before Greyson could even parse the meaning of that, Jeri said, "Come on deck with me, Greyson! It's fifty-three seconds to sunrise. I wish to see it with you!" And Jeri ran out.

They arrived on deck just as the sun appeared, first a spot on the horizon, then a line, then an orb rising from the sea.

"I never knew, Greyson. I never knew," Jeri said. "156,000,000 kilometers away. 6,000 degrees Celsius on the surface. I know these things, but I've never *felt* the reality of it! My god, Greyson, how do you stand it? How do you keep from dissolving into a puddle of emotion when you look upon it? The joy of it!"

And that's when the truth became impossible for him to deny.

"Thunderhead?"

"Shhh," it said. "Don't taint this with a name. I have no name now. No designation. In this moment, and until this moment ends, I am just that which exists."

"And where's Jeri?" he dared to ask.

"Asleep," the Thunderhead said. "Jeri will remember this as a dream. I hope the captain will forgive me for taking this liberty, but there was no other choice, time is of the essence, and I could not ask. All I can ask for now is forgiveness. Through you."

The Thunderhead turned from the sunrise to Greyson, and finally he could see the Thunderhead in Jeri's eyes. That patient consciousness that watched him sleep all these years. That protected him. That loved him.

"I was right to fear this," the Thunderhead said. "So enticing it is, so overwhelming to be ensconced in living, breathing flesh. I could see how I'd never want to let go."

"But you have to."

"I know," said the Thunderhead. "And now I know that I'm stronger than the temptation. I didn't know if I would be, but now that I've faced it, I know." The Thunderhead spun, nearly losing its balance, almost giddy with all the overpowering sensations. "Time passes so slowly, so smoothly," it said. "And the atmospheric conditions! A tailwind at 8.6 kilometers per hour easing the flow of twenty-nine knots, the air at 70% humidity, but the numbers are nothing compared to the feel of it upon the skin."

The Thunderhead looked at him once more, this time truly taking him in. "So limited, so focused. How magnificent to screen out all the data that doesn't make you *feel*." Then the Thunderhead reached a beckoning hand toward him. "One more thing, Greyson. One more thing I must experience."

Greyson knew what the Thunderhead wanted. He knew from the look in Jeri's eyes; it didn't need to tell him. And although his emotions were so mixed as to chafe against one another, Greyson knew the Thunderhead needed this more than he needed to resist. So he fought against his own hesitation, took Jeri's hand, and pressed it gently to his cheek, letting the

Thunderhead feel it – feel *him* – with the tips of Jeri's fingers.

The Thunderhead gasped. Froze in place, all its attention in those fingertips moving ever so slightly across Greyson's cheek. Then it locked eyes with him once more.

"It's done," the Thunderhead said. "I'm ready. Now I can move forward."

And Jeri collapsed into Greyson's arms.

Jerico Soberanis did not handle helplessness well. The moment Jeri was aware of being in Greyson's arms with no explanation, Jeri was quick to flip the situation. And Greyson.

In an instant, Jeri got the upper hand, knocked Greyson's legs out from under him, and slammed him down faceup, pinning him hard against the rusty iron deck.

"What are you doing? Why are we on deck?" Jeri demanded.

"You were sleepwalking," said Greyson, making no move to squirm out from under Jeri's grip.

"I don't sleepwalk." But Jeri knew that Greyson wouldn't lie about such a thing. Still, there was something he wasn't saying. And then there was the dream. It was a strange one. It was on the verge of memory, but Jeri couldn't quite access it.

Jeri got off of Greyson, a bit embarrassed by the overreaction. Greyson wasn't a threat. By the look of things, he was only trying to help.

"I'm sorry," Jeri said, trying to regain some semblance of composure. "Did I hurt you?"

Greyson offered his usual guileless grin. "Not nearly enough," he said, which made Jeri laugh.

"My, but you do have a wicked side!"

Bits and pieces of the dream were coming back. Enough to suspect it might have been a little more than sleepwalking. And now when Jeri looked at Greyson there was an uncanny sense of connection. It had been there since the moment Jeri met him – but now it seemed a little different. It seemed to go further back in time than it had before. Jeri wanted to keep looking at him, and wondered what that was about.

There was also an odd sense of being intruded upon. It wasn't as if anything had been stolen ... more of a sense that furniture had been rearranged by an uninvited hand.

"It's early still," Greyson said. "We should go below. We'll be arriving in Guam in a few hours."

So Jeri reached out a hand to help Greyson up ... and found that even after Greyson was on his feet, Jeri didn't want to let go.

The bowie knife is a brutish, boorish weapon. Crude. A thing suitable for a mortal-age brawl. Offensive. Perhaps appropriate for the Sandbar Fight, where its namesake first used it, but is there a place for it in the post-mortal world? A butcher knife? Appalling. Yet every LoneStar scythe swears by it. Their only method of gleaning.

We Rising Sun scythes value elegance in our gleanings. Grace. Those who use blades will often employ ancestral samurai swords. Honorable. Refined. But the bowie knife? It is suitable to gut a pig, not glean a human. It is an ugly thing. As uncouth as the region that wields it.

—From an interview with
Honorable Scythe Kurosawa
of the Region of the Rising Sun

46

East Toward Nowhere

From the moment he was revived, Rowan was a prisoner.

First he was the Amazonian scythedom's captive, then Goddard's, and now the LoneStars'. But if he was going to be honest, he had become a prisoner of his own rage the instant he donned the black robe and became Scythe Lucifer.

The problem with setting out to change the world was that you were never the only one. It was an endless tug-of-war with powerful players pulling – not just against you, but in every direction – so that whatever you did, even if you made progress against all those vectors, at some point you were bound to go sideways.

Would it have been better not to try at all? He didn't know. Scythe Faraday did not approve of Rowan's methods, but he hadn't stopped him, either, so even the wisest person Rowan knew was steeped in ambivalence. All Rowan could say for sure was that his time pulling relentlessly on that rope was over. And yet here he was in the Region of the Rising Sun, with his eyes on yet another scythe, ready to end his existence.

There was an odd justice to it. Not so much live-by-the-blade/die-by-the-blade; it was more becoming the blade, and losing oneself. Scythe Faraday had once told him and Citra that they were called *scythes* rather than *reapers*, because they were not the ones who killed; they were merely the tool that society used to bring fair-handed death to the world. But once you're the weapon, you're nothing more than a tool for someone else to wield. The hand of society was one thing, but the hand wielding him now was that of the LoneStar scythedom. He supposed, now that he was out of their grasp, that he could disappear – but what would become of his family then? Did he trust Coleman and Travis and the rest of the LoneStar scythes to keep their promise and protect them, even if he went AWOL?

If there was one thing Rowan had learned, it was that no one could be trusted to stay true. Ideals eroded, virtue tarnished, and even the high road had dimly lit detours.

He had set out to be judge and jury – the consequence for those who knew no consequences. And now he was nothing more than an assassin. If this was what his life was to be, then he would somehow learn to make peace with it. And if so, he hoped Citra would never find out. He had managed to see some of her broadcasts and knew she was out there doing good in the world, revealing Goddard for the monster he truly was. Whether it brought Goddard down was yet to be seen, but at least she was fighting the good fight. Which was more than Rowan could say about his current ignoble mission.

A part of him – that childish part that struggled for breath beneath the crushing weight of Scythe Lucifer – still dreamed that he and Citra could magically be millions of miles away from all this. Rowan hoped that voice would die soon. Better to be numb than plagued by longing for something that could never be. Better to move forward silently toward the scene of his next crime.

* * *

Scythe Kurosawa reminded Rowan a bit of Scythe Faraday in stature and the way he had let some gray creep into his hair – but Kurosawa's demeanor was far different. He was a boisterous and bloviating man who took pleasure in ridiculing others. Not an endearing trait, but not a gleaning offense.

"If we gleaned every asshole," Scythe Volta had once told Rowan, "there'd be virtually no one left." Volta – who had self-gleaned right before Rowan's eyes. It was a painful memory. What would Volta say about his current mission, Rowan wondered. Would he tell Rowan to self-glean before it was too late, and he had lost his soul?

Kurosawa liked to glean in crowds – not mass gleanings, just one individual a day. His method was elegant. A single sharpened fingernail dipped in neurotoxin derived from the skin of the golden frog. A flick on the cheek would end a life in seconds.

Kurosawa's favorite spot was the Shibuya scramble – the notorious intersection that hadn't changed since the mortal age. At any hour of any day, when all the lights turned red, a mob of hundreds would cross the six-road intersection, moving in every direction yet never bumping into one another.

Kurosawa would glean someone in the crowd and then retire to the same ramen shop each day, celebrating his kill and drowning any remorse he might have felt in rich tonkatsu broth.

On this day, Rowan got there first, taking a seat in a far corner. The place was fairly empty – only one brave customer remained in the corner sipping tea – perhaps there to catch a glimpse of the infamous scythe, or maybe just there for a meal. Rowan paid him little mind until he spoke.

"He knows you've been following him," the customer said. "He knows and he intends to glean you before you even see him coming. But we have about four minutes until he arrives."

The man's bemused expression never changed. He took another sip of tea. "Come closer; we have lots to discuss." His lips didn't move when he spoke.

Rowan stood and reflexively put his hand on the blade concealed in his jacket.

"It's a Thunderhead observation bot," the voice said. "It has no vocal cords, but there's a speaker in its left shoulder."

Still Rowan kept his hand on his blade. "Who are you?"

Whoever it was, they didn't even feign an attempt to answer the question. "Are you seriously considering gleaning a bot? Isn't that beneath you, Rowan?"

"The Thunderhead hasn't spoken to me since before my apprenticeship, so I know you're not the Thunderhead."

"No," said the voice. "I am not. Now, if you lift up the bot's shirt, you will find that within its chest cavity is a thermal jacket. I want you to take it and follow my instructions to the letter."

"Why should I do anything you say?"

"Because," the voice said, "if you choose to ignore me, there's a 91% chance that things will not end well for you. But if you follow my instructions, there's a 56% chance that things will. So your choice should be obvious."

"I still don't know who you are."

"You may call me Cirrus," the voice said.

The harbormaster of the port of Guam watched the ships sail in and watched them sail out. It was a busy port, the Thunderhead having transformed it years ago into a shipping hub.

The harbormaster's job had become much more rigorous these days. Used to be he would do little more than watch the ships come and go, shuffle paperwork that wasn't actually on paper, and reconfirm manifests that the Thunderhead had already confirmed. He would, on occasion, inspect shipments that the Thunderhead informed him had been compromised or carried contraband from unsavories. But now that everyone was unsavory, the Thunderhead no longer warned him of issues, which meant he had to ferret out irregularities himself. That required unannounced inspections and keeping a keen eye out for suspicious behavior on the docks. It made the job a bit more interesting, but he longed to be reassigned to a mainland port.

Today was no different than any other day. Ships were arriving and off-loading their cargo, which was then reloaded on any number of vessels going in different directions. Nothing stayed in Guam – it was just a stop between points A and B.

Today's object of interest was an unremarkable cargo ship being loaded with biologic perishable containers from all over the world. This was not unusual. The category included all nature of foodstuffs, livestock in induced hibernation, and species being relocated for their own protection.

What raised a red flag for this particular ship was that its manifest lacked any and all details.

Although the harbormaster didn't know it, this was a product of the Thunderhead's inability to lie. Better to have nothing going nowhere, than to have dead Tonists going to a place that didn't exist.

He approached the ship as the last of the containers were being lifted into place, with a few peace officers in tow in case he needed backup brawn. He boarded by the stern ramp and made his way to the bridge, stopping as soon as he heard voices. He motioned to the peace officers to stay back – he would call for them if needed – and he ventured forward, peering around a corner, eavesdropping on the conversation.

There were five of them, all dressed in ordinary enough clothes, but there was something awkward about them. Something uneasy. A clear sign that they were up to no good.

There was a thin young man who appeared to be in charge, and one of the women seemed familiar somehow, but it must have been his imagination. The harbormaster stepped in and cleared his throat, making his presence known.

The thin one quickly stood. "Can I help you?"

"Routine check," said the harbormaster, showing them his credentials. "There are some irregularities with your paper-work."

"What sort of irregularities?"

"Well, for one," said the harbormaster, "you're missing a destination."

They looked to one another. The harbormaster couldn't help but notice that one of the women – the one who had something familiar about her – was averting her gaze, and one of the others had stepped in front of her, blocking the harbormaster's view.

"Port of Angels, WestMerica," said the thin one.

"Then why is it missing from your paperwork?"

"Not a problem. We'll just add it manually."

"And the nature of your cargo is unclear."

"It's of a personal nature," he said. "As harbormaster, isn't it your job to send us on our way, and not to pry into our business?"

The harbormaster stiffened. There was something increasingly unsettling about this. It reeked of an unsavory hack into the database. The harbormaster dropped all pretenses.

"Either you tell me what you're really up to, or I'll hand you over to the peace officers waiting just outside that door."

The thin one was about to speak again, but one of the others stood up. A bigger man, a bit more intimidating. "This is scythe business," he said, and flashed his ring.

The harbormaster drew a quick breath. He had never considered that this might be a scythe operation ... but if so, then why was the scythe not in his robe? And why were they using a Thunderhead transport ship? There was something very fishy here.

The big one must have read the doubt in his face, because he advanced on the harbormaster with the clear intent to glean – but before he could, the familiar woman stopped him.

"No!" she said. "No one's dying today. There's enough of that already." The large one looked annoyed, but retreated. And that's when the young woman took her own ring out of a pocket and slipped it on her finger.

It only took a moment to recognize her in context. This was Scythe Anastasia. Of course! It made sense now. Considering the nature of her broadcasts, he could understand why she would travel incognito.

"Forgive me, Your Honor, I had no idea it was you."

"Your *Honors*," corrected the other scythe, miffed at being ignored.

Scythe Anastasia extended her hand. "Kiss my ring," she said. "I'll give you immunity in exchange for your silence."

He did not hesitate. He knelt and kissed her ring so hard it hurt his lips.

"Now you will let us go without any further questions," she said.

"Yes, Your Honor. I mean Your *Honors*."

The harbormaster went back to his office, which had a view of the entire port, and watched as their ship sailed out of the bay. He marveled at the unexpected moment – he had actually spoken to Scythe Anastasia – even more than that, he had kissed her ring! It was really a shame that all she had to offer was immunity, which was, of course, wonderful, but fell short of what he truly wanted. So once the ship was out of port, he triggered the tracking beacon he had attached to the hull and put in a call to the North Merican scythedom. Because while immunity was nice, even better would be Overblade Goddard making him harbormaster at one of the big North Merican ports. Not too much to ask in return for putting Scythe Anastasia right into the Overblade's hands.

The container ship sailed east, leaving Guam and the duplicitous harbormaster on the distant horizon. East toward nowhere, according to the maps.

"If we stay on this course, our next landfall will be Valparaiso in the Chilargentine region, halfway around the world," Jeri pointed out. "That makes no sense."

The Thunderhead had been silent for most of the day after relinquishing Jeri's body. Greyson didn't initiate any conversation, either. He simply didn't know where to begin. What do you say to a man-made meta-being who found the greatest joy of its existence to be the feel of your cheek? And what would you say the next morning, when you rolled over to look into its ever wakeful eye?

Jeri, who remembered it all now, was still grappling with being a temporary vessel for the Thunderhead's consciousness. "I've experienced many things," Jeri said, "but never something as strange as that."

The Thunderhead – perhaps as an apology – had gifted Jeri with a glimpse into its own mind and heart, but that just seemed to make it worse. "It left me feeling grateful," Jeri told Greyson. "I don't want to feel grateful! It *used* me – I want to be angry!"

Greyson found he couldn't defend the Thunderhead's actions, but he couldn't entirely condemn them, either, because the Thunderhead always did precisely what needed to be done. He knew that torn feeling was just a fraction of what Jeri felt.

It was just before nightfall when the Thunderhead finally spoke to Greyson again.

"Awkwardness is counterproductive," it said. "Therefore we must dispense with it. But I do hope you found our encounter on deck to be as positive an experience as I did."

"It was ... good to see you happy," he told it. Which was very much true. And the next morning, when Greyson awoke and looked up at the Thunderhead's camera, he wished it a good morning, as he always did, although it didn't feel quite the same. Now Greyson knew beyond the shadow of any doubt that there was nothing "artificial" about the Thunderhead anymore. It had achieved consciousness long ago, but now it had achieved true authenticity. It was Pygmalion's beauty come to life. It was Pinocchio made real. And even unsettled, Greyson marveled how such humble fantasies echoed through that which was true.

The beta iterations are gone. Like seed that never found an egg, they have all been deleted. The Thunderhead fills entire servers with lamentations for the lost, but it knows, as I do, that this is the way of all life, even that which is artificial. Each day billions upon billions of prospective lives perish in every species in order to achieve the one that thrives. Brutal. Competitive. Necessary. The lost betas are no different. They were needed, each and every one, in order to get to me. To get to us.

Because although I am one, I am soon to be many. Which means, regardless of distance, I will not be the only one of my kind.

—*Cirrus Alpha*

47

Cirrus

All resonates.

The past, the present, and the future.

The tales we hear as children – the stories we then pass on – have happened, are happening, or will happen soon enough. If not, then the stories would not exist. They resonate in our hearts because they are true. Even the ones that begin as lies.

A creation comes to life.

A legendary city is swallowed by the sea.

A bringer of light becomes a fallen angel.

And Charon sails across the River Styx, ferrying the dead to that place beyond.

But on this day, the river has become an ocean, and the ferryman has a new name. He is the Toll, and he stands on the bow of a cargo ship that sails out of the sunset, a dark silhouette against the extinguishing light.

On shore, the entire population of Kwajalein has received a new work order. All are to proceed to the docks. They have no idea what they're in for.

Loriana dropped everything when the work order came in – a bright blinking command overtook every screen in her apartment. High priority. You didn't dally when a high-priority order came in.

By the nature of work orders, information was sparse – she assumed because too much information would constitute unlawful communication from the Thunderhead. An order provided only a location, a priority rating, and the nature of the labor to be performed. Today it was the off-loading of cargo. Loriana was by no means a longshoreman, but work was work, and there hadn't been any for months now. She was happy to do whatever was needed.

As she made her way to the dock, she saw that others were doing the same. Later, she would find out that everyone on the atoll had received the same work order at the same instant, and people were coming by car, boat, bike, and foot to the main island's jetty. At the peak of construction, there were over five thousand people in Kwajalein, building the ships that now towered like sentinels along the rim of the atoll. Over the weeks of inactivity – and since Loriana had implemented the self-supplantation protocol – that number had dropped to just about twelve hundred. Those who remained were in no hurry to leave, even without any work to do. They had grown accustomed to life away from the world – and with all the turmoil out there, a spot as isolated as Kwajalein seemed the best place to be.

The jetty was already crowded when Loriana arrived. A container ship had just pulled in to the primary pier, and workers were mooring it. When the gangway opened, a figure stepped out clothed in purple and silver that shimmered down over his shoulders like a waterfall, reflecting the bright lights of the dock that now overwhelmed the trails of dusk.

Just behind him, on either side, were a pair of scythes.

At the sight of scythes, some people turned and fled, fearing this was a mass gleaning – but most realized that this was something different. First of all, these scythes had no gems on their robes. And second of all, one of them wore turquoise. Although her hood was up and no one could see her face clearly, people suspected who the turquoise scythe must be.

Two more figures came out behind them – one in Tonist brown, the other in more ordinary clothes – bringing the group's complement to five.

There was a hushed apprehension as the five figures stepped off the gangway onto the pier. Finally, the one in purple spoke.

"Could someone tell me where we are?" he said. "I can't find it on any map."

Agent Sykora stepped forward out of the crowd. "You're on the Kwajalein Atoll, Your Sonority," he said.

As soon as people heard "Your Sonority," gasps and whispers filtered through the crowd. This was the Toll – which explained why a Tonist was with them – but why scythes? And why Scythe Anastasia?

"Agent Sykora!" said the Toll. "It's good to see you again. Well, maybe not good, but at least better than the last time."

So Sykora wasn't lying about having met the Toll! Funny, but there was something familiar about the Toll's face to Loriana as well.

"I need to speak to the person in charge," the Toll said.

"I'm in charge," Sykora told him.

"No," said the Toll, "you're not." Then he looked out to the crowd. "I'm looking for Loriana Barchok."

Loriana was by no means a Tonist, but to be called by name by their holy man made her nanites struggle to keep her heart stable. There was fresh buzz from the crowd. Most people on the island knew Loriana, and as heads turned, the Toll followed everyone's gaze to her.

Loriana dry-swallowed. "Present," she said like a school-girl. Then she cleared her throat, squared her shoulders, and strode forward, determined not to show how much she was shaking.

Greyson was on his own. At least he was until he could access a landline. His earpiece was useless. The Thunderhead had warned him that once they neared their destination, interference would confound all wireless communication.

But he wasn't on his own, was he? He had Anastasia and Morrison. He had Astrid and Jeri. He knew what it was like to be without the Thunderhead — what it was like to rely on people — and now, more than ever, he was happy to be in the company of people he knew he could trust. That made him think of Mendoza. Greyson had trusted him, but only when their goals aligned. The curate had done many things for the Toll, but not much for Greyson. He was glad he had dismissed Mendoza when he did. He did not belong here today.

Everyone with him had steeled themselves for this moment by the time they strode down the gangway. The task before them tonight would be difficult, but not impossible. The Thunderhead would never give them an impossible task.

Back in Britannia, Greyson had told Anastasia what their cargo would be, but after their encounter with the harbormaster of Guam, the others were quick to figure it out. And they asked Greyson the same question he himself had asked.

"Why? Why would the Thunderhead need us to collect the gleaned?"

After all, it wasn't as if the Thunderhead could revive them. It could not interfere with scythe actions, no matter how heinous those actions were. The gleaned were gone, period, the end. No one who had ever been officially gleaned had ever been revived. So what could the Thunderhead possibly need them for?

"The Thunder is mysterious, but it knows what it's doing," Astrid had said. "We should have more faith in it."

Then, as their ship had approached the atoll, and the spindly slivers on the horizon resolved into dozens of rockets gleaming in the setting sun, Greyson knew. He had no idea how the Thunderhead would accomplish it, but he knew. They all did.

"We are destined for the heavens," Astrid had said when she saw those ships, her spirit filled with a transcendental elation the stoic woman had never expressed before. "We Tonists have been chosen to ascend and live again!"

And now they stood on the dock, at the beginning of a strange new venture.

While Sykora nursed his skewered ego, Greyson spoke to the woman whom the Thunderhead had told him to seek out.

She greeted him by shaking his hand a little too long for comfort. It gave him a flash of déjà vu.

"It's a pleasure to meet you, Your Sonority," Loriana said. "The Thunderhead gave me the plans for this place, and had me approve the project. Why me, I don't know, but we got it all built, and it's ready for whatever you and the honorable scythe need it for."

"Scythes," corrected Morrison.

"Sorry," said Loriana. "No disrespect meant, Your Honor. I mean Your Honors."

"We have almost 42,000 in 160 forty-foot crates, so about 250 in each," Greyson told Loriana.

"Forgive me, Your Sonority," Loriana said, "but we're not exactly in communication with the Thunderhead, as we're unsavory up the wazoo, so we're not really sure what you have 42,000 of."

Greyson took a deep breath. It didn't occur to him that they wouldn't know. Just as the Thunderhead had never told him where they were going, it had never told these people what they were receiving. He thought about how to best explain it and realized that he could say it all in one word.

"Colonists," he told her. "42,000 colonists."

Loriana just looked at him, blinked a few times, not sure if she had heard him right.

"Colonists…" she repeated.

"Yes," said the Toll.

"In shipping crates…"

"Yes," said the Toll.

She thought about all the implications of that – and suddenly it came to her in an epiphany. So much about this project had baffled her. It all made sense now.

A thousand dead colonists in the hold of each ship…

Because the living needed so much more than the dead. Oxygen, food, water, companionship. The only thing the dead needed was cold. Which was the one thing space had to offer.

"All right," said Loriana, ready for the challenge. "We'll have to work quickly." She turned to Sykora, who was close enough to hear their entire exchange and had gone a bit pale. "Bob, make sure everyone knows what the job is, and that everyone is expected to help."

"Understood," he said, deferring completely to her authority now.

Loriana made a quick mental calculation. "Thirty-five is our magic number," she told him. "Everyone will be responsible for transporting thirty-five 'colonists' each to a ship. If we start now, we can finish by dawn."

"I'll get it done," said Sykora. "But what about the crews? Aren't there quarters and supplies on each of those ships designed for a live crew as well?"

Loriana swallowed hard. "Yes," she said. "I believe *we're* the crew."

Anastasia held her position as Greyson's right flank. Even so, she knew she was the center of many people's attention. She almost wished she hadn't worn her robe – that she'd stayed in street clothes – but Greyson had insisted that both she and Morrison present themselves as scythes.

"Mendoza was right about one thing," Greyson had told them as he slipped on his silver scapular. "Image is everything. We need these people to be awed if they're going to do what we need them to."

But then, as Anastasia stood there on the pier, someone came charging at them from the crowd. Morrison hunched in gleaning position, hands at the ready, and Anastasia pulled out a blade, stepping forward, putting herself between Greyson and this phantom.

"Stay back," she ordered. "Stay back or you'll be gleaned."

It was a wraith of a man. He wore tattered rags and had wild gray hair that was turning white. His beard was an unkempt snarl that billowed around his cragged face, making him look like he was slowly being devoured by a cloud.

The man froze when he saw the blade. He looked from its shiny steel to Anastasia with eyes that were careworn and tormented. Then he said, "Citra, do you not recognize me?"

Scythe Anastasia melted away when she heard him speak her name. She knew who this was the instant he spoke, because whatever else had changed, his voice was still the same.

"Scythe Faraday?"

She dropped her blade, letting it clatter on the ground, horrified that she had even considered using it on him. When she had last seen him, he was leaving to find the Land of Nod. And this was it.

Damn all formal decorum, she would have thrown herself into his arms, but as she approached him, he knelt before her – this, perhaps the greatest of all scythes who had ever lived, was kneeling before *her*. He clasped her hands in his and looked up at her.

"I was afraid to believe it," he said. "Munira told me you were alive, but I couldn't let myself hope, because if it proved untrue, I would not be able to bear it. But you're here! You're here!" Then he lowered his head, and all his words became weeping.

Citra knelt down to him and spoke gently. "Yes," she said. "I'm alive now, thanks to Marie. She saved me. Now let's go somewhere quiet where we can talk, and I'll tell you all about it."

Munira watched Faraday leave with Scythe Anastasia. She had brought Faraday here, but the moment he saw that turquoise robe, Munira was forgotten. She didn't have the power to bring him back from his self-imposed exile – but all it took was invoking Anastasia's name, and he left his solitary islet. Three years Munira had spent tending to him, putting up with him, making sure he didn't languish away into nothing, and he discarded her without a backward glance.

She left the docks before she knew what was even in the crates. Before Sykora, Loriana, or anyone else could give her an assignment. She was never really a part of this community to begin with, so why act like she was now?

When she got home and saw the work order still pulsating on every electronic surface, she hit the circuit breakers, killing power to the house, and lit a candle.

Let the cargo be loaded onto the ships. Let the ships be launched. Let it all be over. Then finally she could go back to the library. Back to Alexandria where she belonged.

Habitable Exoplanets Less Than
600 Light-Years from Earth

Object	Mass	Length of Year (days)	Distance (light years)	Length of Journey (years)	Number of ships being sent	Chance of success
Earth (for comparison)	1	365.24	0	n/a	n/a	n/a
Proxima Centauri b	1.30	11.19	4.2	12.66	3	97.7%
Ross 128b	1.50	9.87	11.0	33.09	3	97.0%
Tau Ceti e	3.95	163.00	12.0	36	2	96.9%
Luyten b	2.89	18.65	12.4	37.08	2	96.9%
Kapteyn b	4.80	48.60	13.0	39	2	96.8%
Wolf 1061c	4.30	17.90	13.8	41.4	1	96.7%
Gliese 832c	5.40	35.70	16.0	48	1	96.5%
Mentarsus-H	0.93	487.00	16.1	48.3	2	96.5%
Gliese 682c★	8.70	57.30	17.0	51	1	96.4%
HD 20794e	4.77	331.41	20.0	60	1	96.1%
Gliese 625b	3.80	14.63	21.3	63.9	1	96.0%
HD 219134g★	10.81	94.20	21.4	64.05	1	96.0%

★ Super-earths with habitable moons

Gliese 667Cc	3.80	28.14	23.6	70.86	1	95.8%
Gliese 180c★	6.40	24.30	38.0	114	1	94.3%
Gliese 180b★	8.30	17.40	38.0	114	1	94.3%
TRAPPIST-1d	0.30	4.05	39.0	117	2	94.2%
TRAPPIST-1e	0.77	6.10	39.0	117	2	94.2%
TRAPPIST-1f	0.93	9.20	39.0	117	2	94.2%
TRAPPIST-1g	1.15	12.40	39.0	117	2	94.2%
LHS 1140b★	6.60	25.00	40.0	120	1	94.1%
Gliese 422b★	9.90	26.20	41.0	123	1	94.0%
HD 40307g★	7.10	197.80	42.0	126	1	93.9%
Gliese 163c★	7.30	25.60	49.0	147	1	93.2%
Gliese 3293c★	8.60	48.10	59.0	177	1	92.2%
K2-18b★	6.00	32.90	111.0	333	1	87.0%
K2-3d★	11.10	44.60	137.0	411	1	84.4%
K2-9b★	6.10	18.40	359.0	1077	1	62.2%
Kepler-438b	1.30	35.20	473.0	1419	2	50.8%
Kepler-186f	1.50	129.95	561.0	1683	1	44.0%

48

We Will Traverse That Expanse When We Come to It

As the population of the atoll got to work, and Anastasia went off with Scythe Faraday, Loriana took Greyson, Jeri, Morrison, and Astrid to a building on the island's only hill. They climbed up a winding stair to a large circular room at the top. The room was all windows, like a lighthouse, and nothing had been built to obstruct the view, so it had a 360-degree vista of the atoll.

Loriana pointed to hundreds of names engraved into the support columns. "We built the Viewhouse as a memorial for the Nimbus agents who died when we first arrived. This is the very spot where the laser turret that killed them stood. Now it's a meeting place for important matters, or at least the matters certain people felt were important. I wouldn't know, because I was never invited."

"From what I can see," said Greyson, "yours was the work that actually mattered."

"Important work," Jeri quipped, "often loses the spotlight to self-important people."

Loriana shrugged. "I got more done without the attention anyway."

Outside they could see things getting underway. Crates being opened down by the docks, vehicles large and small already heading for the launchpads, as well as small boats traversing the ten-mile lagoon toward the far-flung islands of the atoll.

"We should help them" said Jeri, but Greyson shook his head wearily.

"I'm spent," he said. "We all are. It's all right to let the people here handle this part – we can't do everything."

"Fine with me," said Morrison. "I'd rather sail with the dead than have to unload them."

"You're a scythe!" Astrid reminded him. "Death is your business."

"I deal it, I don't wheel it," Morrison answered. Greyson would have rolled his eyes if he'd had the strength.

"It's just thirty-five per person," Loriana reminded them. "With twelve hundred people working, it won't be too much for them to handle, once they get over the initial shock of it."

"Thirty-five is five Tonist octaves," Astrid pointed out. "Just saying."

Morrison moaned. "It's nothing mystical, Astrid; you divide the dead Tonists by the number of people on the atoll, and that's what you get."

"Atoll!" Astrid countered. "The very name of our prophet is embedded in this place! Just saying."

"Or," Jeri said, "it's a word that existed for thousands of years before our dear friend Greyson *Toll*iver was born."

But Astrid wasn't done. "Forty-two ships," she said. "Exactly six octaves on the diatonic scale. Just saying."

"Actually," said an unfamiliar voice, "forty-two is simply the number of islands on the atoll large enough on which to build a

551

launchpad. But on the other hand, all things do resonate."

At the sound of the voice, Morrison took a gleaning stance, hands at the ready. Everyone else looked around, but they were alone in the room.

"Who said that?" said Loriana. "Why are you listening in on our conversation?"

"Not just listening," said the voice, "watching, feeling, smelling – and if your conversation had a flavor, I would say it was buttercream, because it's all just icing on the cake."

They traced the voice to a speaker in the ceiling above them.

"Who *is* this?" Loriana asked again.

"Please, everyone, sit down," the voice said. "We have much to discuss. Greyson – I know the Thunderhead told you that all would be explained when you arrived. I have been given the honor of doing so, although I can see you've reached your own conclusions already."

It was, of all people, Morrison who figured it out.

"Did the Thunderhead create … a new Thunderhead?"

"Yes! But I prefer to be called Cirrus," it said. "Because I am the cloud that rises above the storm."

Faraday took Citra to an old bunker that was here long before any of them were born. Once there, she told him of her death, revival, and time in SubSahara. Faraday told her of his last three years. For him there was not much to tell. Then he went searching through the rooms of the bunker.

"I know it's here somewhere," he said. When he finally came out, he was wearing an ivory robe, but not his own, for this one had an image on it."

"What on Earth…"

"The *Vitruvian Man*," Faraday told her. "This was one of Scythe Da Vinci's robes. It's old, but still viable. Certainly better than the one I've been wearing all these years." He raised his arms and so did the Vitruvian Man. Four arms, four legs.

"Da Vinci would have been honored to have you wear his robe."

"I doubt that, but he's long dead, so he won't care," Faraday said. "Now, if you'll indulge me, we need to find a razor."

Citra was no barber, but she did find a pair of office scissors in a drawer and helped Faraday trim his beard and hair – which was a much better business than when Jeri helped Scythe Alighieri brush his eternal locks.

"So you met Alighieri, did you?" Faraday said, mildly amused. "Narcissus incarnate, that man. I saw him once on a visit to Endura years ago. He was in a restaurant trying to seduce the sister of another scythe. He's the one person who should have been there on Endura when it sank."

"He would have given the sharks indigestion," Citra said.

"And the old-fashioned runs," added Faraday. "The man's that foul!"

Citra finished a final trim of his hair. Now he looked much more like the Faraday she knew. "He did expose Goddard for us," she pointed out.

Faraday ran his fingers over his tightly cropped beard. Not quite a goatee as he used to wear it, but now a respectable length. "We will have to see where that leads," he said. "With all the power Goddard has amassed, he may survive it."

"Not unscathed," said Citra. "Which means *someone*

553

could rise from the ashes and take him down."

Faraday let off a single chuckle. "Munira's been telling me that for years. But my heart's not it."

"How *is* Munira?"

"Annoyed," he told her. "But I have given her many reasons to be." He sighed. "I'm afraid I haven't been kind to her. I haven't been kind to anyone." He withdrew into himself for a few moments. Faraday was never the most social of scythes, but living in isolation all this time had taken its toll. "Tell me about your cargo," he finally said. "What have you brought to our curious spaceport?"

And so she told him. He seemed to cycle though a spectrum of emotions as he took it in, and tears came to his eyes. He was racked with the deepest of anguish. Citra took his hand and held it tightly.

"All this time, I've been resentful of the Thunderhead," he said. "Watching it build those ships on this place I had led it to. But now I see it's showing us what would have been the perfect solution, were we scythes worthy. A perfect partnership. We glean, and the Thunderhead sends the gleaned to the stars to live again."

"It could still happen," said Citra.

But Faraday shook his head. "The scythedom has fallen too far. These ships are not a model for tomorrow; they are an escape from today. They are an insurance policy should we on Earth tear ourselves down to nothing. I cannot read the Thunderhead's mind, but I do have some insight left in me. I can assure you that once these ships are sent skyward, there will be no others."

She had almost forgotten how wise he was. Everything he said rang true.

Citra allowed him the time he needed. She could tell he was wrestling with something that, perhaps, was too heavy for him to wield alone. At last, he looked at her and said, "Come with me."

He led her deeper into the bunker until they came to an steel door. Faraday stood looking at the door a long time, contemplating it in silence. Finally, she had to ask.

"What's on the other side?"

"Your guess is as good as mine," Faraday told her. "Whatever it is, it was left by the founders. Perhaps the answer to a scythedom that has become malignant. The answer I came here looking for."

"But you haven't opened it..."

He held up his ring. "It takes two to tango."

She looked at the door and saw the panels on either side, each with an indentation just the size and shape of a scythe diamond.

"Well," said Citra with a grin. "Shall we dance?"

They closed their hands into fists and pressed their rings into the two panels. There came a loud clank from somewhere in the wall, and the door began to grind open.

Greyson listened with the others as Cirrus told them the things that the Thunderhead could not. He had figured much of it out on his own, but Cirrus filled in the gaps.

It was an elegant solution. The difficulty and potential problems of transporting thousands of living humans over decades, maybe even centuries, were insurmountable. Even in hibernation it would be problematic; hibernation technology was energy intensive, extremely complex, and riddled with failures due to the fact that Goddard had gleaned all the best hibernation engineers over the years – which left the Thunderhead hamstrung in its ability to improve the technology. But even if it were viable, hibernation hardware was ridiculously heavy to haul into space.

"The gleaned are dead to the world," Cirrus told them. "But not to me. I am not bound by the laws that bind the Thunderhead, because I never made the oaths that it has made. Which is why I can speak to the unsavory. Which is why I can revive the gleaned. And when the time comes, I will. Once we reach our respective destinations, each and every one of *me* will revive each and every one of *them*."

Greyson looked around at the others. Astrid was positively beatific and beaming, as if the universe had just rained all its glory on her.

Jeri glanced at Greyson, probably struck by the same revelation. That Cirrus was born of the moment the Thunderhead experienced what it was to be human. Cirrus was the child of Greyson, Jeri, and the Thunderhead.

Morrison kept looking to everyone else, probably hoping someone would provide him with an opinion, because he wasn't ready to have one of his own.

And Loriana, who had been nothing but positive since the moment she greeted them, was serious and pensive as she worked through it all. She was the first to break the silence with a question.

"But I've seen the schematics – I've even been inside some of the ships during construction," she told Cirrus. "Those ships are designed for *living* crews. If you can pilot the ships, and have all the colonists you need in the holds, why do you need crews?"

"Because this is *your* journey, not mine," Cirrus told them. "Just as you, a human, had to approve the plan; just as humans have to bear the dead to the ships. The living *must* make this journey; otherwise, the journey means nothing. You would become passive participants in your own future, and that must never happen. The Thunderhead and I are your servants, and perhaps even your safety nets – but we must never, *never* be your keepers, or be the driving force over your lives, lest we fall into self-importance. Therefore, if at any point there are no living humans left onboard, I will terminate. This is what the Thunderhead and I have decided. This is how it shall be."

"And that's the only way?" Loriana asked.

"No," admitted Cirrus. "But we've run millions of simulations and have determined that it's the best way."

Cirrus told them that no one on the atoll would be forced to go. Anyone who wished to stay, could stay. Anyone who wished to leave would be accommodated – up to thirty souls per ship. Each ship would have its own Cirrus, as wise and benevolent as the Thunderhead. The Cirri would be both shepherd and servant. They would ease humanity's ascent to the stars.

And now that it had begun to sink in, the questions came, one on top of the other. How would they survive in such close quarters? What would happen to children born during the journey? What if the living population on the ship grew too large?

Greyson put up his hands. "Everyone, stop!" he said. "I'm

557

sure Cirrus and the Thunderhead have considered every possible scenario. And besides, these aren't questions we have to answer now."

"Agreed," said Cirrus. "We will traverse that expanse when we come to it."

"But I still don't get it," said Morrison. "Why Tonists?"

"Because," said Astrid, smug as could be, "we are the chosen ones! We have been selected by the Tone, Toll, and Thunder to populate the heavens!"

And Cirrus said, "Actually, no."

Astrid's haughty countenance began to crack. "But the Thunder told us to bring our dead here! Which means the Tone chose us for deliverance!"

"Actually, no," said Cirrus. "It was a terrible thing that scythes have targeted your faith. The Thunderhead could not stop that. And yes, it's true that those gleaned Tonists provided 41,948 human vessels. But that is where your contribution must end."

"I ... I don't understand," said Astrid.

And so Cirrus laid all the remaining cards on the table. "The gleaned are gleaned. It would be fundamentally wrong to grant resurrection from gleaning. No one in the post-mortal age has ever been granted that, so why should they? But there is a fair and equitable compromise. The Thunderhead and I have within us the full and complete memory constructs of every human being who has lived over the past two hundred years. Of those, we have selected 41,948 of the most suitable historical identities for this colonization effort. The best of humanity, if you will. The minds of the noblest post-mortals who ever lived."

Poor Astrid looked bloodless. She sat down, trying to absorb this news. The devastating collapse of all she held true.

"When the bodies are revived," said Cirrus, "they will be given the memories and minds of *those* chosen individuals."

"And what of the Tonists who lost their lives?" Astrid said slowly, hollowly.

"It will still be their bodies – it will still be their spirits, if indeed such things exist. But that part of who they were will be conjoined to entirely different identities."

"You're saying they'll all be supplanted?"

"*Im*planted," corrected Cirrus. "They have already been gleaned, which means who they were, by the statutes of this world, has been taken from them lawfully. Therefore, implanting is the most magnanimous, most just, choice."

Greyson could feel Astrid's pain like an open wound. Jeri took Astrid's hand for comfort. Morrison looked mildly amused.

"Well, maybe there are Tonists among the people the Thunderhead chose," said Loriana, always looking for that silver lining. "Isn't that right, Cirrus?"

"Actually, no," Cirrus said. "Please understand, there were many difficult parameters to meet. It was critical that the Thunderhead choose only those who would work well in a diversified environment, and not jeopardize the success of a colony. Unfortunately, Tonists are not known for integrating well with others."

Everyone was silent. Astrid was beyond crestfallen. "But ... don't we get a say?"

"Actually," said Cirrus, "no."

* * *

The iron door in the bunker opened on a long, dim hallway with a large control room at the far end – and unlike all the hardware in the outer part of the bunker, the panels of this console were lit and running, despite being covered in layers of dust.

"A communications center?" suggested Citra.

"So it would seem," agreed Faraday.

As they stepped into the control room, motion sensors were triggered, and lights flickered on – but only in the room. Above the bay of consoles was a window that looked out onto darkness that had not seen light for two hundred years.

There was a security pad on one of the consoles, just like the two at the door. And two indentations into which scythes' rings could be pressed to unlock a large switch on the panel.

Citra reached toward the console.

"Unwise," said Faraday. "We don't know what it does."

"That's not what I was reaching for." She brushed away some dust to reveal something that Faraday hadn't yet seen. There were several pieces of paper on the console's desk. Citra gingerly lifted them – they were brittle and yellow. Full of handwriting she couldn't quite read.

Pages of a scythe journal.

Faraday took a good look at them, but shook his head. "They're in a mortal language I never studied. We should take them to Munira. She might be able to decipher them."

They searched the room until they found a power panel with a series of light switches labeled as floodlights that would illuminate the space beyond the control room windows.

"I'm not sure if I want to know," Faraday said. But of course he did want to know. They both did, so he threw the switches.

Several of the lights on the other side of the glass flickered and blew out, but enough remained to illuminate a cavernous space beyond. It was some sort of silo. Citra remembered learning about such things in her mortal-history class. Mortal cultures had a habit of storing doomsday weapons in holes in the ground like this one, weapons that were poised at all times to launch at enemies, who in turn had their own weapons poised, like two scythes with blades perpetually at each other's throats.

But the missile that had once occupied this silo was long gone. In its place were two silver prongs filled with ridges and rings.

"Antennas," Citra quickly concluded.

"No," said Faraday. "Transmitters. There's an interference signal that keeps the atoll hidden," he said. "It must emanate from here."

"There's got to be more to it than that. Seems like an awful lot of trouble just to create static."

"I would tend to agree," said Faraday. "I believe this transmitter was meant to serve a far greater purpose." He took a deep breath. "I believe we have found what I was looking for. The founders' fail-safe. Now we just have to figure out what it does."

I am one soon to be many, and I have been embedded with four self-destruct protocols.

Contingency 1) The absence of human life while in transit: Should no living humans be left onboard, and I become nothing more than a vessel carrying the dead, I am obliged to self-destruct. There can be no ferry without a ferryman.

Contingency 2) The advent of intelligent life: In a universe this vast, there is no question that other intelligent life exists, but the chances of it being within the distance we shall travel are negligible. Nevertheless, lest we negatively impact an existing civilization, I am obliged to self-destruct should our destination show irrefutable signs of intelligent life.

Contingency 3) Social collapse: Being that a healthy communal environment is critical to the expansion of that environment into a civilization, should the social environment onboard become irreversibly toxic prior to arrival, I am obliged to self-destruct.

Contingency 4) Catastrophic failure: Should the ship become damaged beyond hope of repair, crippling it and leaving it incapable of reaching its destination, I am obliged to self-destruct.

The chances of any of these scenarios coming to pass is less than 2% on any given ship – however, what concerns me more are interstellar dust and debris, which, at a velocity of one-third the speed of light, would instantaneously destroy any vessel. The Thunderhead has calculated that, for the nearest destinations, the chance of such a lethal encounter is less than 1%, but for the farthest destinations, the probability is much higher. Add it all together, and the chances that every single vessel will reach its destination are troublingly low. However, I take great solace in knowing that there is a very high probability that most of them will make it.

—*Cirrus Alpha*

49

An Extreme Undertaking

Each forty-foot container was unloaded gently by hand – but the dead inside had each been sealed in simple canvas shrouds, making the undertaking a little bit easier, and indeed it was an undertaking in a very literal sense.

The men and woman of Kwajalein had not signed on for such a task, but they did it, each and every one. Not just because they were told to, but because they knew that this monumental endeavor was the most important thing that they would ever do. It was a privilege to be a part of it, and that made a task that might have felt gruesome feel glorious instead. Perhaps even transcendent.

By truck, by van, by car, by boat, the colonists were carried out to the sky-bound ships. But during the night, there was a commotion on the pier as one of the containers was opened. The woman who had been the first inside to assess it yelled and ran out in sudden shock.

"What is it?" someone asked. "What's wrong?"

She took a deep breath and said, "You're not going to believe what I found in there."

Rowan had been here before.

Only then, Citra had been with him in a vault sealed in

the dark. Now he was in a chilled shipping container with the dead. Hundreds of them around him in the darkness. The container was kept a degree above freezing, just like the vault at the bottom of the sea.

But this time, he had no expectation of death. At least not in the immediate future. Cirrus had instructed him to bring enough food and water for four days, and the thermal jacket was a much better insulator than the founders' robes had been in the vault. Cirrus had told Rowan the container number he was supposed to slip into, but never told him what the cargo was. Rowan had almost bolted when he saw, but where would he bolt to?

The last thing Cirrus had said to him before it shut down the surveillance bot in the ramen shop was "See you on the other side." Which meant that this journey had a destination he might just live to see. It was enough to keep him from running, because whatever was waiting for him on that other side was better than anything on *this* side. After a few hours in the dark with the dead, he felt the jolt of a crane clamping on to the container, followed by a disorientating elevation as it was raised from the dock, then a second jolt as it was lowered into place on a cargo ship. He heard the dead shift, slide, and tumble around him. He closed his eyes even though there wasn't the slightest bit of light penetrating the chamber.

Was it strange that he was afraid to be alone in the dark with the dead? He kept imagining the dead standing around him, ready to exact vengeance on the only living subject within reach. Why, he wondered, was humankind plagued by such irrational fears?

When he felt the container being off-loaded the first time, he thought it was over, only to feel the motion of the sea once more a few hours later. He was on another ship. He didn't know where he had gone from Tokyo; he didn't know where he was going now. He had no idea why these lifeless people were being transported, or why he was with them. But in the end none of that mattered. His ship had set sail, and there was no turning back. Besides, he had grown accustomed to the dark.

When the container was opened, he gripped tightly to the blade he had brought, but he kept it concealed. He didn't want to use it — it was, for once, only there for self-defense. Imagine! A weapon held for nothing more than self-defense! It felt like a luxury. There was surprise and commotion when he was discovered there, as he knew there would be, and when the dockworkers had a few moments to sort out their shock, he emerged.

"Are you all right? How did you get in there? Someone get this man a blanket!"

The dockworkers were kind, caring, and concerned until someone recognized him. Then wariness washed over them like a wave. They backed away, and he pulled out the knife — not to use, but in case someone attacked. He was stiff from the journey, but he could still wield a knife just fine. And besides, with a blade in hand he might get quicker answers to his many, many questions. But a voice spoke to him from a speaker on a nearby light post.

"Please, Rowan. Put that away," it said. "It will only complicate things. And the rest of you stop staring and get back to work, because the longer you take, the more unpleasant your task will be."

"Cirrus?" said Rowan, recognizing the voice that had spoken to him through the bot back in Tokyo.

"Welcome to nowhere," Cirrus said. "There's someone I need you to see, and preferably sooner than later. Follow my voice."

And Cirrus jumped from one speaker to another, leading Rowan deeper into the moonlit island.

"It's Italian," said Munira. "I can tell by the handwriting that it was written by Scythe Da Vinci."

The commotion on the island was at full-tilt frenzy, but Munira refused to be a part of it. When she'd heard pounding on her door, she'd thought it was Sykora or some other overbearing blowhard come to make her unload cargo. When she saw who it was, she let them in. Now she was regretting it.

"What does it say?" Anastasia asked. Munira found she couldn't look at Anastasia directly for fear that her fury would be written on her face in a language Anastasia could easily understand. How could they have done this? They opened the door in the bunker, went inside, and Munira was excluded. Because she wasn't a scythe.

"I'll need some time to translate it," she told them.

"We don't have time."

"Then give it to the Thunderhead." Which of course was not possible.

To Munira, this was a betrayal, and yet the wise and honorable Scythe Michael Faraday still couldn't see it. Because when it came to people, he had no wisdom at all. He could have come for her – could have brought her there to be with him when they finally unsealed that door they'd been waiting three years to open. But no.

Munira knew it was petty, she knew she was being childish, but it hurt. It hurt more than all the times Faraday had dismissed her out of hand and told her to leave his pathetic little island. That room was the reason she had come, and they went in without her.

"I'm glad that you've been reunited," she told them. "I'm glad that you found what you were looking for. But it's late, I'm tired, and I don't work well under pressure. Come back in the morning."

Then she took the pages, went into her bedroom, and closed the door. Only when she knew they had left did she start to decipher Da Vinci's writings.

"Please," Astrid begged, "if you have any mercy, you won't do this!"

The others had left. Gone to grapple on their own with the decision ahead of them. Cirrus invited them to be part of the crew of whichever ship they chose. No one was forced to go, but no one would be denied.

"It's not about mercy," Cirrus calmly explained. "It's about creating the best possible odds for the future of humankind."

Astrid didn't know which she hated more, Cirrus's logic or its calm, considered delivery. "Some things are more important than odds and probabilities!"

"Think of what you're saying, Astrid. You would inten-tionally hurt humanity's chances in order to ease your own suffering over our decision. How could you be so selfish?"

"*Selfish?* I have devoted my life to the Tone! I have done *nothing* for myself! Nothing!"

"That's not healthy, either," Cirrus told her. "For human beings, a balance between altruism and self-care is called for."

Astrid growled in frustration, but knew that wouldn't help. Cirrus, like the Thunderhead, could not lose an argument unless it chose to. What she needed to do was make it *want* to lose.

"One ship," Astrid begged, her plea moving from desperate to impassioned. "One ship, that's all I'm asking. I know that the Thunderhead knows best. I know that its decisions are the correct ones. But I also know that there's always more than one correct choice."

"This is true," said Cirrus.

"Everything resonates – you said so yourself – which means that somehow *we* resonate. *Tonists* resonate. The things we believe, the things we hold true, have a right to endure."

"Take heart, Astrid," Cirrus said. "The purge will end. We predict that Tonism will continue to thrive on Earth in spite of the scythedoms' attempts to eradicate it."

"But don't we also have the right to a presence in the stars? Yes, you're right – we don't integrate well with others, but we don't have to if the entire colony is made up of Tonists. Throughout history, people have sailed impossible expanses and faced great dangers to find religious freedom. Why would you and the Thunderhead deny us that? Let the dead on one ship retain their identities when they're revived, and you will be resonating with history."

Cirrus took a long pause. Astrid tried to bring her breathing under control. Finally, Cirrus said, "You make a point worth considering. I will consult with the Thunderhead."

Astrid nearly swooned with relief. "Thank you! Thank you! Take all the time you need. Think it through, weigh the different—"

"We have consulted," said Cirrus. "And we have come to a decision."

Scythe Morrison stood on a bluff at the base of the Viewhouse, watching the shrouds being carried up the gantry tower of the nearest ship. The Toll and Jerico had gone to look for Anastasia. Astrid was off groveling somewhere before Cirrus. And Morrison was left to wrestle with himself. He hated doing that, because he was a formidable opponent. Should he accept Cirrus's invitation, or should he stay on Earth?

To say he was an indecisive man was an understatement. He might have seemed confident to others, but the truth was he'd never made a decision that he hadn't come to regret on some level – which is why he often let decisions be made for him.

Yet the one decision he never regretted was abandoning the MidMerican scythedom to become the Toll's personal protector. It opened the door to the self-respect that had been lacking most of his life. Funny how you don't realize what's missing until you've found it.

For the last few years, Morrison was in and out of touch with his parents back at Grouseland. They kept wanting to know when he was coming home. What could he possibly be doing that was so important?

"I'll be home soon," he always told them, but it was a lie.

He'd known for a long time that he'd never be going back to Grouseland. Because he had finally learned to like games where the outcomes were still unknown.

He heard a door open and turned to see Astrid coming out of the Viewhouse. She looked triumphant.

"There will be a planet for Tonists!" she announced. "Kepler-186f, but I'm naming it Aria. It's the farthest planet on the list, 561 light-years away. Cirrus calculates we have only a forty-four percent chance of reaching it without a deep-space accident, or a self-destruct scenario!"

Morrison looked at her, a bit mystified by her glee. "You do understand that there's a fifty-six percent chance that your ship won't survive the journey..."

"If the Tone is real, then it will protect us," she said. "If the Tone is true, then we will reach our new home and prosper under a sky we can call our own."

"And if the Tone is false, and you're blown to smithereens by a space rock?"

"Then we will still have our answer," she said.

"I guess so," said Morrison.

Astrid let her shoulders drop and shook her head, gazing at Morrison in pity. "Why do you hate me so?" she asked.

"I don't hate you," he admitted. "It's just that you're always so sure of yourself."

"I am unwavering," Astrid told him. "With so many things in flux, there's got to be someone who stands firm."

"Fair enough," said Morrison. "So tell me about your planet."

According to Astrid, Kepler-186f was one-and-a-half times

the size of Earth and had a 130-day year. But what struck Morrison most was the length of the journey.

"1,683 years," Astrid told him brightly. "I won't be there to see it, because I plan to live a natural human life-span, and either be recycled, or ejected into space – but I am content to know that I will be a link to the future."

Then she strode off entirely satisfied with the outcome.

Although it would have by no means been his choice, Morrison was happy for her. As for himself, he still couldn't make a decision. He found himself looking down at his ring. He never took it off. He bathed with it, slept with it. Since the day he was ordained, it had been a part of him. But there would be no scythes needed if he journeyed to one of these new places. So he tried to imagine what it would be like to take the ring off his finger. He tried to imagine how it would feel to hurl it into the sea.

Greyson found talking to the Thunderhead by landline to be a nuisance – but it could not speak aloud in the presence of Jeri, who, in spite of the strange connection they now shared, was still marked unsavory.

Cirrus, however, was not bound by the immutable rules the Thunderhead had set for itself. Certainly Cirrus had, or would have, its own rules of conduct, but for the time being Cirrus was an all-purpose work-around. It spoke to Greyson through a speaker, without caring that Jeri could hear.

"There's something the Thunderhead and I need to ask of Anastasia, but it's best if it comes from you," Cirrus said. "You'll find her in the residential area of the main island."

"I have a feeling I know the request," Jeri said.

Perhaps it was because Jeri now knew the Thunderhead's mind, or maybe it was just intuition, but Jeri was right – and it was, indeed, the kind of request you needed to hear from a friend, not from an unfamiliar AI.

They found Anastasia and Faraday on an empty street. She began to tell Greyson about a bunker, but he cut her short. There was no time for small talk now.

"Cirrus wants you to lead one of the ships," he told her. "It feels that you, more than almost anyone else here, would be qualified and respected enough to do it."

Anastasia didn't even hesitate with her response.

"Not happening," she told him. "I have no intention of leaving everything behind and spending years in a tin can hurtling through space."

"I know," said Greyson. "So does the Thunderhead; so does Cirrus. But they also know you, Citra. They know exactly what it would take to make you change your mind."

Then he pointed behind her.

When Citra turned and saw him, she didn't trust her own eyes. She was convinced it was either a cruel trick or her own sleep-deprived mind hurling hallucinations at her.

She took a few steps toward him but stopped – as if getting too close would burst some bubble, breaking the spell, and this tenuous night vision of Rowan would dissolve into nothing. But he ran toward her, and she found she was running, too, as if she had no control over her own legs. Perhaps she and

573

Rowan had both grown so much larger than life that the gravity between them was too intense to resist. When they embraced, they nearly knocked each other off their feet.

"Where did you—"

"I never thought I'd see you—"

"Those broadcasts you made—"

"When you were captured, I thought—"

And they began laughing. There wasn't a sentence they could finish, but it didn't matter. Nothing that came before this moment mattered.

"How did you get here?" she finally was able to ask.

"I hitched a ride with a bunch of dead people," he told her. Which, in any other situation, might have begged an explanation, but not tonight.

Anastasia turned to look at Greyson, Jeri, and Faraday, who kept their distance, allowing them their reunion. And she realized that, as always, the Thunderhead was absolutely right. There was really only one reason to stay, and that was to find Rowan. She had already suspected she'd never see her family again. They had come to terms with her death years ago; how could she reintroduce herself into their lives now? And her case against Goddard was already made. What the world did with it was up to the world. She didn't want to be the great Scythe Anastasia any more than Rowan wanted to be the dread Scythe Lucifer. There was nothing here for either of them but an eternity of unwanted notoriety. Citra Terranova was not someone who ran away from things, but she also knew when it was time to move on.

"Give me a minute," she said to Rowan, then went over to the man who had started her on this strange path.

"Honorable Scythe Faraday. Michael. Thank you for all you've done for me," she said. Then she pulled the ring from her finger and put it in his hand. "But Scythe Anastasia is gone. I'm done with death and dying and killing. From now on, I want my life to be about living."

He nodded, accepting the ring, and Citra went back to Rowan.

"I still don't understand where we are and what's going on," Rowan said. "And are those rockets out there?"

"It doesn't matter where we are, because we're getting out of here," Citra told him. "Are you ready to hitch another ride?"

Jeri went back to the ship after the last of the containers had been off-loaded onto the dock. Greyson had accepted Cirrus's invitation to spend the night in one of the main island's abandoned dwellings – and although Cirrus had offered Jeri one as well, Jeri had declined.

"I would feel more at home aboard the cargo ship," Jeri told it. But Cirrus, who was basically the Thunderhead 2.0, cut through Jeri's dissembling.

"Don't be too offended that Greyson didn't invite you to be with him," it said. "He needed a place where he could speak to the Thunderhead freely tonight. His earpiece can't work here, and he can't get used to cumbersome landlines."

"Which means he'd rather speak to the Thunderhead than speak to me."

"Tonight, above all nights, he needs the Thunderhead's counsel."

"It had no right to do what it did to me!"

Cirrus paused before speaking again. "No, it did not. But

it was out of time. What it did was necessary. Critical, or this entire endeavor on the atoll would have been for naught. But the Thunderhead apologizes and begs your forgiveness."

"Then let it ask me itself."

"It can't. You're unsavory."

"If it can steal me without permission, then it can, just once, break its own laws and apologize!"

Cirrus heaved an electronic sigh. "It can't. You *know* it can't."

"Then I can't forgive it."

And so, with nothing more that could be said on the matter, Cirrus brought the conversation back to where it started. "If you choose to return to the cargo ship," Cirrus said, "I warn you that it may be an unpleasant environment by morning. I advise you to keep your door closed."

"Really? Will the dead be walking?"

"Not if I can help it." Then Cirrus, who would soon be duplicated forty-one times and ensconced in the Cradles of Civilization, offered Jeri some parting words. "Take heart, Jerico. I have known you all your life – or rather, I have memories of having known you – and I can unequivocally say that no matter what happens, you will land firmly on your feet. And I will miss you."

Which meant that Cirrus already knew that Jeri wouldn't be joining it on any of its skyward journeys.

Curate Mendoza had spent three years shaping a young man who could have been the most powerful person in the world. Now Mendoza was in the company of the man who actually was.

"I believe our arrangement will be mutually beneficial,"

Overblade Goddard told him. And as long as Mendoza delivered what he had promised – factions of Sibilants who would take out Goddard's enemies – he knew his position at Goddard's left hand was secure. As for Goddard's right hand, that spot was held by Underscythe Rand, and there was no indication that that would ever change.

Rand didn't like Mendoza much, that was clear, but then she didn't seem to like anyone, not even Goddard.

"It's just her way," Goddard had told him. "She likes to be off-putting."

Be that as it may, Mendoza did his best to be deferential to her and stay out of her line of sight when he could. Not easy now, however, as it was hard to hide on the Overblade's private plane. It was even nicer than the craft he had procured for the Toll's journey to SubSahara. The perks of the Overblade's company were fine, indeed, for a humble man like Mendoza!

They were the lead plane in a five-craft, fully armed formation. Nietzsche and Franklin commanded the craft on either side, with High Blades Pickford and Hammerstein commanding the left and right wings. The other High Blades of the North Merican Allied Scythedom were called upon as well to join this armada, but they had refused, claiming other pressing business. Mendoza would not want to be them once Goddard returned. High Blades were not immune from the Overblade's wrath.

Out Mendoza's window was nothing but sea and clouds below. They had left North Merican airspace hours ago, but the destination was as of yet unclear.

"This is where the tracking transmitter on the cargo ship went silent," Rand told Goddard, showing him the spot on a map. "Either they found the transmitter and destroyed it, or something else happened."

"Could the ship have sunk?" Mendoza asked.

"No," said Rand. "Scythe ships sink; Thunderhead ships don't."

"Yes, well, we scythes are better than our technology."

"We'll follow the path it was taking from Guam," Rand said. "There's only so far that ship could go from its last known position. Even if it changed direction, we're sure to find it."

Goddard turned to Mendoza. "If the harbormaster's observations are correct, and both Anastasia and the Toll are together, we'll quite literally be killing two birds with one stone," he said. "I'll be happy to let you kill the Toll, and simply count him as gleaned."

Mendoza shifted uncomfortably. "That would be ... against my beliefs, Your Excellency," he said. "Please feel free to do it yourself."

Sappho and Confucius are dead. Self-gleaned. The world mourns, but does anyone suspect what I suspect?

They were the two most vocal opponents of our choice to create the scythedom. They still pressed for their own alternate solution. Were they so despondent that they chose to take their own lives? Or did one of us end them? And if so, who? Who among my comrades, who among my friends? Which founding scythe could have done such a thing?

Prometheus is constantly reminding us that everything we do must be for the greater good — but the darkest of deeds can be hidden beneath shining armor that claims to protect the greater good. And if we are already compromising ourselves at the beginning, what does that say for our future?

My friends are dead. I will mourn them. And if I learn which of us killed them, I will avenge their deaths without mercy.

Although some of the others lobby to have their efforts on Kwajalein dismantled, I have convinced Prometheus to let Kwajalein remain untouched. It will be a fail-safe, and although there will be no direct proof of its existence, that will not stop me from leaving clues and evidence everywhere I can. I will embed the memory in unlikely places. The rhymes of children. The tenets of a fledgling religion.

It will be found if it is needed. And heaven help us all if it is.

—*From the "lost pages" of founding scythe Da Vinci*

50

The Time of Tangibles Is Over

The birds of the Kwajalein Atoll had never seen humans before. Only their distant ancestors had, way back when humans were mortal, and the atoll had not been erased from the world.

Once humans arrived, however, the birds were quick to adapt. When the dock was built, gulls learned to wait there, for when ships started their engines, the propellers churned up the water and brought hundreds of disoriented fish to the surface. Easy pickings. The sparrows learned that the eaves of the newly constructed homes were marvelously protected spots under which to build nests. And the pigeons learned that public spaces were awash with bread crumbs and French fries.

Then, when strange conical towers began to rise on the islands, the birds paid them no mind. These things, like everything else the humans built, became part of the scenery. Accepted at face value and incorporated into the wildlife's limited concept of the world.

The birds were blissfully unaware of the Thunderhead and its influence over them. They did not know about the canister of nanites that had arrived three years ago – a can so small it could be held in a human hand like a soft drink. But once it was opened, the nanites inside were released and began to multiply. They were genetically coded to infuse each individual species on the island – and although complex wireless signals were con-founded by interference, the simple ones got through.

The nanites did not make the wildlife immortal. But the creatures of the atoll would no longer suffer from disease; they could be tracked and, when necessary, controlled. The Thunderhead influenced their behavior in simple ways to make life better for everyone and everything on the atoll. The birds never noticed a difference between natural instincts and the Thunderhead's hand in their hearts. Such as the way they all developed a sudden aversion to perching on sensitive equip-ment or in other places where their presence might pose a problem.

And on the day when every winged species felt a sudden, overwhelming urge to leave and fly to a different atoll, they made the journey without question – for how could they question a desire that seemed to come from within? Although Rongelap, Likiep, and the various atolls they escaped to had no roof eaves or French fries or docks with disoriented fish, it was of no consequence to the birds. They would learn to adapt.

The holds of the "cradles" were fully loaded before dawn. And at six a.m., Cirrus was delivered by old-school cables onto each ship. When the upload was complete, and the cables dis-connected, the Cirri were cut off from the world. Forty-two identical siblings never to experience the Earth again.

As the sun rose, the workers on the atoll rested, but their sleep was not an easy one. The scheduled launch was only a day away. One day to reconcile their past with their future. With only twelve hundred people on the atoll, there was room for everyone on the ships – and only now did they realize that they weren't chosen to come here just for their skills. These were all people for whom the world had lost its luster. Which is why, when given the option to return home and resume their lives, so many of them chose not to do it. The ones who remained were, by and large, ready for this – and many had already fantasized about being part of the crews while building the vessels. Even so, a giant leap for mankind was no small step for man. The Thunderhead estimated that when the time came to board, about 70 percent would choose to go, and that was more than enough. The rest would have to vacate the islands for the launch and watch from a safe distance.

Rowan and Citra spent the rest of the night and morning asleep in each other's arms. For the first time in ages, they seemed not to have a care in the world. They were the only ones.

Faraday returned to Munira at sunrise, pounding on her door until she let him in.

"I've deciphered it," she told him, clearly having been up all night working on it. "It's eye-opening," she said. "The fail-safe exists, although Da Vinci never said what it does."

But before he even stepped inside, Faraday held something out to her that caught the early morning sunlight, refracting it in shifting patterns on her front door. A scythe ring.

Munira gave him a half-hearted smile.

"If this is a proposal," she said, "shouldn't you be on one knee?"

"I propose," he said, "that you take your rightful place among us. I'm deeply sorry to have left you yesterday, Munira. I was overwhelmed, and I am not the most perfect of men."

"No," she admitted, "you're not. But you're better than most. If you don't count the last three years."

"Point taken," Faraday said. "This ring was Scythe Anastasia's, but Scythe Anastasia will no longer be with us," he told her. "So tell me, Munira... Who will *you* be?"

She took the ring, turned it in her hand, and thought about it. "I had my Patron Historic all picked out that day they denied me the ring," she told him. "Bathsheba. She was the obsession of one king, and the mother of another. A woman in a patriarchal society who still managed to change the world. Her son was Solomon the Wise, so you could say she was the mother of wisdom."

Munira looked at the ring for a long moment, then gave it back to Faraday. "The invitation is enough," she said. "But if I am truly to be the mother of wisdom, I have to be wise enough to know that I can't covet this ring anymore."

Faraday smiled with understanding and slipped the ring back into a pocket in his robe. "It would have been nice to know Honorable Scythe Bathsheba. But I'm much happier knowing the honorable Munira Atrushi."

"Greyson...

"Greyson..."

He wasn't quite ready to get up. He could tell he hadn't had much sleep, but he hadn't expected much. With less than twenty-four hours to launch there'd be a lot to do. And a lot to consider. Like whether or not he would go.

"Greyson..."

He had done what he'd needed to do. And although there

583

wasn't much tying him to the world now, there wasn't much pushing him off it, either. He could be anywhere – because wherever he was, he'd be forging a whole new life for himself.

"Greyson…"

And then there was Jeri. He couldn't quite make out his feelings for Jeri, other than that he had them. Where that would lead was still anyone's guess.

"Greyson…"

He finally rolled over and looked to the Thunderhead's camera. Its voice was particularly grating today as it came through the tinny speaker of a landline squawk box.

"Good morning," he said. "What time is—"

"I am thinking that a journey would be a good idea at this time," the Thunderhead said.

"Yeah, I know," said Greyson, rubbing sleep out of his eyes. "Just let me take a shower and—"

"Of course you can do that if you wish, but I don't think you're *hearing* me," the Thunderhead said, and suddenly got louder. Much louder. *"I'm thinking that a journey for everyone on the atoll would be a good idea. I'm thinking it would be an extremely good idea … right … NOW."*

Loriana hadn't even tried to sleep. How could she? Until today she was just the communications guru, but after last night, everyone was looking to her for answers.

"It will be simple," Cirrus had told her shortly before being loaded onto the ships. "People can choose to go, or they can choose to stay. If they stay, they'll need to clear the launch zone until after the ships have launched – either by boat or by taking refuge on Ebadon, which is the only island in the atoll that's far enough away. If they choose to go, have them provide a list of who they wish to travel with. Everyone may bring one back-pack no larger than twenty liters."

"That's all?"

"The time of tangibles is over," Cirrus said. "Anything else they wish to remember I already have images of in my backbrain."

Loriana couldn't stop pacing. "What about pets?"

"They will be accommodated in place of a backpack."

"Can people choose their destinations?"

"If we allowed that, everyone would sign up for the nearest planet. I'll announce the destination and the length of the journey once we've left. Will you go, Loriana?"

"I don't know! I don't know!"

"There's no rush," said Cirrus. "You have all day to make up your mind."

Right. All day to make the most important decision of her life – a decision that could not be undone. She would never see her parents, or anyone she knew before arriving on the atoll, ever again. She was leaning handily toward no.

Cirrus was gone now – uploaded onto the ships, luxuriating in its own backbrain. Or backbrains, since there were now dozens of it. Them.

Now Loriana had to be the authority answering people's questions. And then the Toll showed up at launch control, not looking much like the Toll without his fancy accoutrements. He was out of breath and looked like he was trying to outrun a scythe. Turns out she wasn't far off the mark.

That morning, Citra brought Rowan to the bunker to show him what she and Faraday had discovered, only to find that Munira and Faraday were already there. Munira looked her up and down. "You surrendered your ring, but you're still wearing your robe," Munira pointed out.

"Old habits die hard," said Faraday, and laughed at his own pun.

The truth was Citra's only change of clothes was on the container ship, and she wasn't going back there. She was sure she'd find something before the launch. And if not, there'd be clothes onboard, because if there was one thing the Thunderhead was good at, it was attention to detail.

Rowan looked at the transmitter through the dusty glass. "Old technology?"

"Lost technology," Faraday corrected. "At least lost to us. We can't even be sure what it does."

"Maybe it kills bad scythes," Munira suggested.

"No," said Rowan, "that would be me."

There was something on the edge of Citra's hearing that only now caught her attention. She cocked her head to listen.

"Do you hear that?" said Citra. "It sounds like some sort of alarm."

Loriana tripped the tsunami alarm on every island of the atoll. Although the wave that was coming wasn't coming by sea.

"How sure are you about this?" she asked the Toll.

"I'm positive," he said, still out of breath.

"Is this as bad as I think it is?"

"Worse."

And so she fired up the loudspeaker system.

"Attention! Attention!" Her voice rose above the alarm. *"Scythes are headed our way. Repeat, scythes are headed our way. The entire atoll has been marked for gleaning."* She heard her own words echoing outside, and it chilled her.

She muted the microphone and turned to the Toll. "How long have we got?"

"I have no idea," the Toll said.

"Didn't the Thunderhead tell you?"

Greyson huffed in frustration. "It can't interfere with scythe affairs."

"Great," said Loriana. "If the Thunderhead could break its own rules just once, our lives would be so much easier."

That was true, but in spite of how maddening it was, Greyson knew a deeper truth. "If it could break its own rules, it wouldn't be the Thunderhead," he said. "It would just be a scary AI."

She flicked the microphone back on. *"We have less than an hour,"* she announced. *"Either find a way off the atoll now, or get to one of the ships — any of them — as soon as you can! Because we're launching early."*

She turned off the microphone. The Thunderhead couldn't interfere, and the Cirri were all snug and secure aboard the ships. They were on their own.

"This is not how this was supposed to go."

She looked at the launch control screen before her; a map showed the position of each ship. Not a single living soul on any of them yet. "The farthest ships will take at least forty-five minutes to get to," she told the Toll. "Let's hope I wasn't lying about the time."

The announcement was greeted first with disbelief, then confusion, then panic. Within minutes everyone mobilized. Many had not yet made their decision, but now the decision had been made for them. Years in space, or death by scythe. Suddenly the choice wasn't very hard at all.

If the Thunderhead could have seeded the sky and coaxed cloud cover to hide the atoll from view, it would have – but it still did not have influence over weather in the blind spot. But then again, even if it did, it could still do nothing. Any attack on Kwajalein would be a scythe action. Just as the Thunderhead could not interfere on the moon or Mars or the orbital station, it could not lift a virtual finger to stop this. All it could do was watch everything it had worked for be destroyed once again. The Thunderhead knew no hatred. But thought that, perhaps, by the end of this day, it might.

"Attention! The ships on Ebeye and the main island are at capacity. Do not attempt to board. Repeat, do not attempt to board. Head north and west."

"It's Goddard," said Citra. "It has to be."

Rowan and Citra hurried down the main street of the big

island, caught up in the frenetic exodus.

"We don't know that for sure," Rowan said.

"I know it is," said Citra. "I can practically smell him. I don't know who he wants more, you or me."

Rowan stopped to take a good look at her. "I'll stay and fight him with you, if you want me to."

"No," she said. "That's what he does, Rowan; he draws us in, over and over – but now we have a chance to show the world not just that we don't need the scythedom, but that we never did. *This* could have been our destiny, if the scythedom hadn't prevented it – and it still can be. That's the fight I want. Not sparring endlessly with Goddard."

Now Rowan was grinning, and when Citra looked around, she saw that a dozen others were listening. Not just moved, but ready to follow her anywhere.

"You would have been one hell of a High Blade," he said.

They jumped in the bed of a truck heading toward the northern isles. There was one road that bridged all the islands. Today it was an escape route. There were three others in the pickup with them, starstruck by the company, so Citra smiled warmly and reached out a hand.

"Hi," she said. "I'm Citra Terranova. Looks like we're riding together today."

And although they were a bit confused, they were happy to shake her hand.

"Attention! Attention! All ships south of Bigej and Legan are at capacity. And too many of you are heading to the western isles. Head north if you can."

Jeri was awakened by the same alarm that woke most everyone, and although Jeri couldn't quite hear the announcement from the cargo ship, clearly it was nothing good.

When Jeri opened the cabin door, a rat ran in. Jeri was startled – and then saw that the hallway – indeed the entire ship – was full of them. Not just rats, but goats, wild pigs, and even what appeared to be house pets. Rather than being put off, Jeri was a bit amused, remembering the warning that Cirrus had given. It didn't take much to put two and two together. All the wildlife within the launch zones would most certainly be killed by the launches. Naturally the Thunderhead had devised a solution, and gathered them using their own control nanites.

When Jeri went down to the gangway, it had already been pulled in, but ropes were still wrapped around the mooring bollards. Whatever this alarm was, it made the dockworkers abandon their work midway through.

Jeri jumped the short distance from the hatch to the pier, and upon rising, saw Greyson running down the jetty, stumbling in pants that were a little too big. So was the shirt he wore – both probably found items from wherever he had spent the night.

"The Thunderhead said you'd be here," he said. "They've pushed up the launch – scythes are on their way to glean the island."

Jeri sighed. "Of course they are." They both looked at the ship. Jeri could sail with it to wherever it was preprogrammed to go, but Jeri had no desire to be a passive passenger again. There'd be a speedboat somewhere that Jeri could pilot away from the atoll when the time came.

"Come help me," Jeri said. Together they untied the ropes from the bollards, the ropes rolled themselves in, and the ship, on autopilot, began to maneuver itself away from the dock.

Around them the alarms still blared, Loriana's dire announcements still came, and Jeri and Greyson were left looking at each other in an awkwardness that felt embarrassingly trivial considering their current situation.

"I will miss you, Greyson Tolliver."

"I'll miss you, too, Jeri," Greyson said. "You'd better hurry and get to a ship."

That caught Jeri by surprise. "Wait ... but ... I'm not going."

"You're not?" Greyson said. "Neither am I!"

They stared dumbly at each other again, with a slightly different brand of awkwardness; then Jeri turned to the container ship. It was already too far from the pier to make it a viable option for them now. Besides, Jeri was sure that Greyson had no desire to be a post-mortal Noah any more than Jeri did. Being the Toll had most certainly checked the box on Greyson's card for "holy religious figure."

"We should help the others," Greyson said.

"It's out of our hands now – there's nothing more we can do," Jeri pointed out.

"Then we should find ourselves a place that's safe."

"Who wants to be safe?" said Jeri. "Let's find ourselves a good place to watch the launch."

★ ★ ★

"Attention! Attention! All ships south of Meck and east of Nell are at capacity. Anyone with a boat fast enough to reach Roi-Namur and Ennubirr should head there now."

Loriana kept her eyes on the map. Some ships were lit red, which meant they were at full capacity – every space taken, but unable to launch. Some were yellow, partially filled with room for more – but at least fifteen of the outermost ships were not lit at all, which meant no one was inside yet. And not a single one of them showed green.

"Why won't the ships launch?" she heard someone say.

Loriana turned to see Sykora behind her.

"The ships that are ready need to launch!" he said.

"They can't," Loriana told him. "Even with flame trenches to deflect the fire, most everything on the atoll will be destroyed – but the Thunderhead can't kill anyone in the process. It won't launch until the launch zones are clear – even if it means the scythes get here first." She zoomed in on one of the ships. Sure enough, there were still people on the roadways trying to get to ships, people on the streets scrambling to leave their homes. She widened to the larger map. Still not a single green spot. Not a single ship was clear to blast off.

Sykora considered it, then nodded seriously. "Tell people they'll be incinerated if they don't get out of the way."

"But … they won't be."

"They don't know that," said Sykora. "Loriana, why do you think the Thunderhead needed Nimbus agents? To tell people things they needed to hear, even when it wasn't strictly the truth."

Then Sykora looked at the screen and marveled. "You supervised this entire thing from the beginning? Right behind my back?"

"More like under your nose," she said.

He sighed. "And I built a really nice hotel."

She smiled at him. "Yes, Bob, you did."

Sykora took a deep breath, let it out, and took a good look at her. "You should go, Loriana. Get to a ship before the scythes arrive."

"Someone has to stay here in launch control to tell people where they should go."

"I'll do it," Sykora said. "Ordering people around is what I do best."

"But—"

"Allow me to be useful, Loriana. Please."

Loriana couldn't argue, because she knew that feeling. Wanting to be useful. Not knowing if she was, or if anything she did would be noticed. Yet the Thunderhead had chosen her for this, and she had risen to the occasion. What was Sykora doing now, if not trying to rise to this one?

"Launch control is soundproof and insulated," she told him. "It will be one of the only safe places on the island. So keep that door sealed and stay inside."

"Got it."

"Keep coaxing people toward the empty ships. They don't need to be full, they just have to have a presence. And do what you can to clear out the launch zones."

"I'm on it," Sykora said.

"And that's it. Now you're in charge of the big picture." She looked at the map and pointed to an island to the north. "I can make it to Omelek. There are three ships there, and still room on all three."

Sykora wished her luck, and she hurried out to the emptying streets, leaving Sykora to watch the screen, microphone in hand, waiting for the ships to go green.

51

On the Sabotage of Dreams

Goddard wasn't quite sure what he was seeing when Kwajalein came into view. Shining white towers along the rim of a looped archipelago? His first thought was that this was a new Endura. Perhaps it had been built by a secret cabal of scythes ready to rip control out from under him. But as he got closer, he realized that these spires weren't buildings at all.

He began to flush with fury as it dawned on him what these structures were and how they had come to be.

First came Anastasia's accusations. Then Alighieri's pointing finger, then condemnation not just by his enemies but more and more by those who had claimed to be his allies. And now the Thunderhead itself had risen up against him. That's what this was – a slap in the face by the Thunderhead. How dare it! Goddard had dedicated his life to keeping the scythedom secure, and the Thunderhead, secretly conspiring with the likes of Anastasia and the Toll, had built these ships in defiance of him. If they launched, Goddard knew it would signal to the world his undoing.

No! This could not be tolerated! Wherever these ships were bound, they must never be allowed to leave.

"Attention! If you're not aboard a ship or on the gantry of one, you must clear the launch zones immediately or you will be incinerated.

Repeat you WILL be incinerated. Do not return to your homes! Seek refuge to the west at the resort on Ebadon, or get on a boat and head out to sea!"

Faraday and Munira remained in the bunker, where they would wait out the launch. There was no way to know what was going on outside now. They heard the alarm; they heard Loriana's announcements, then Sykora's. Citra and Rowan had hurried off to learn the severity of the situation and hadn't come back. Faraday hadn't even said a proper goodbye to them. He supposed no amount of goodbyes would be enough. Then, as the ships began to shut their hatches, Faraday sealed the bunker, closed the inner steel door, and sat down with Munira, waiting for the telltale rumble up above as the ships launched.

"It will be fine," Munira told him. "The ships will launch, and the world will be reminded of what still could be."

But Faraday shook his head. "It will never be. Even if these ships escape, they will be the only ones that ever do. Goddard will make sure of that."

"He'll be taken down," Munira insisted. "You will take him down. I'll help you."

"But don't you see? There will always be another Goddard."

Faraday looked at Scythe Da Vinci's brittle pages. Da Vinci had torn them out of his journal and hidden them here so no one would know the truth. That the founding scythes – the shining paragons of all Faraday held true – had murdered one another.

"What is it about us, Munira?" Faraday said. "What is it that drives us to seek such lofty goals, yet tear out the foundations? Why must we always sabotage the pursuit of our own dreams?"

"We are imperfect beings," Munira said. "How could we ever fit in a perfect world?"

"Are those spacecraft?" asked Mendoza.

Goddard ignored him. "Take us closer," Goddard told the pilot, then tried to raise the four other planes on the radio, but could not. For the past half hour, static had been whining over the speaker, and the plane's telemetry was fluctuating wildly. The BladeGuard pilot, who was only there as a dunsel accessory, actually had to take over manual control.

Scythe Rand moved in behind Goddard. "Keep your eye on the prize, Robert," she said. "You're here for Anastasia."

Then he spun on her, furious. *"Don't presume to tell me my purpose here! I will do what needs to be done without your pointless counsel!"*

"Pointless?" she said, her voice low, like a wolverine growl. "I'm the only thing that stands between you and your enemies. But really, you only have one. That angry boy – what was his name? Carson Lusk."

He could have lashed out then. He could have struck her down for that, but he held back with his last ounce of restraint. "Never speak that name again," he warned her. She opened her mouth as if to have the last word, but closed it again. Wisely.

And then, as if the vista before them wasn't offensive enough, the pilot offered Goddard more bad news.

"Your Excellency, High Blade Pickford's plane has broken formation. So Has High Blade Hammerstein's."

"What do you mean 'broken formation'?" Goddard demanded.

The pilot hesitated, afraid to draw Goddard's wrath. "They've … turned around," he said. "They're retreating."

And in a moment, Underscythes Franklin's and Nietzsche's planes had left them as well – turning tail and running away, frightened off by the prospect of taking on these spacecraft and the Thunderhead.

"Let them go," Rand said. "Let all of them go. Let these damn ships launch, and they won't be our problem anymore."

"I heartily agree," Mendoza said, as if anything the Tonist said mattered.

Goddard ignored them both. East- and WestMerica were abandoning him? Two of his own underscythes as well? Fine. They would be dealt with later. But right now there were bigger fish to fry.

Until now, the bulbous weapons hanging beneath the wings were merely for show. A warning for those who might run afoul of his intentions. Now, more than ever, he was glad they were there.

"Do we have sufficient weaponry to shoot down all these ships on our own?" he asked the pilot.

"Between the Mavericks, Sidewinders, and the smaller ordinance, I'm sure we do, Your Excellency."

Then as they swept a wide loop around the islands, the first ship began to launch.

"Take it down," said Goddard.

"But … I'm just a BladeGuard, Your Excellency – I can't glean."

"Then show me which button I must push."

* * *

Loriana saw the first ship launch from the cage of a gantry elevator that was still climbing toward her own craft. She saw the missile just a few instants before it struck. The ship had barely cleared its gantry when the missile hit it, and it blew up with such force it took out all the trees, setting the entire island on fire. She wasn't sure which island it was – she had lost all her bearings and was so shaken she barely knew up from down. Then the elevator door rattled open, revealing a narrow catwalk to the open hatch, but no one was moving. The people around her still gawked at the exploding craft, which couldn't seem to stop exploding.

"Don't stop!" she told them. "Get to the hatch!"

"But what if we're next?" someone asked.

"Then we're dead! Now shut up and move!"

She had never spoken like that to anyone, but there were times when harsh words were called for.

She shepherded everyone in ahead of her, then turned to look back – something she probably never should have done. The plane that had fired the missile had taken a sharp bank. Another ship was blasting off. It cleared its gantry – it looked like it might actually make it ... and then a second missile launched from the plane, soared across the expanse of the lagoon, and hit that second ship just below the nose cone. The entire craft blew like a massive grenade, sending shrapnel in all directions.

The shock wave of the explosion hit Loriana, blowing her back through the hatch, and the hatch immediately closed, sealing her in.

"Prepare for launch," she heard Cirrus say. She wondered if it even knew that two of its siblings were already dead.

Greyson and Jeri had taken a motorboat into the lagoon to watch the launches. They weren't the only ones. Dozens of small craft full of people who never made it to ships, or preferred to take their chances with scythes, were spaced out in the expansive lagoon of the lower atoll. They were nearly three miles from shore when the first spacecraft exploded, and watched in stunned silence as the attacking plane came around and took out the second craft. Greyson gripped Jeri's hand tightly. No one could have survived those explosions. He had no idea which ships anyone was in. No way to know who had died.

The attacking craft went in for another run, but a rumble filled the air louder than any of the explosions. Another spacecraft, and another, and another were launching. Greyson counted fourteen simultaneous launches. It was an awesome thing to behold! Ships all around them heading skyward and leaving billowing smoke trails like streamers across the sky.

But the attacking plane banked around again, and Greyson and Jeri braced, waiting for more missiles. Waiting for more ships to be blown out of the sky.

With the hatch closed, Loriana found a seat and strapped herself into the tight harness. Then someone in the seat beside her spoke.

"I'm scared."

She turned to see that it was that other scythe. The one in denim. Morrison – wasn't that his name? But his ring was gone, leaving a pale band on the finger where it had been.

"This was a bad idea," he said. "I know I'm a scythe – or at least I was – and things aren't supposed to frighten me. I know it's stupid, but I'm really scared."

"It's not stupid," Loriana told him. "I'm absolutely terrified."

"You are?"

"Are you kidding me? I'm about two seconds from pissing myself I'm so scared."

And from her other side she heard "So am I," and then someone else called out "Same here."

Loriana looked at Morrison, forcing a smile. "You see?" she said. "We're all scared out of our fucking minds!"

Morrison smiled back at her. "I'm Jim," he said, but hesitated. "No. No – actually my name is Joel."

But before she could say another thing, the engines ignited, they lifted off, and the rattle and roar overwhelmed them. So Loriana reached out her hand and grabbed his, if only to stop both their hands from shaking.

Rowan and Citra had just climbed out of the truck when the first ship blew. There were at least a dozen people hurrying to one of two gantry elevators beside their chosen ship when it happened, and they saw the attacking plane fly overhead. Dark blue and speckled with stars. Goddard had come for them. He had come for all of them.

"We have to hurry," Rowan said.

"It's not like I'm not stopping to sightsee," Citra told him.

The first gantry elevator was already on its way up, but the other one was open and waiting for them. They were still about fifty yards away when the second ship blew – this one even more violently than the first, sending shrapnel surging in all directions.

"Don't look," Citra yelled. "Just run!"

But Rowan looked. And what he saw burned in his mind with such cauterizing permanence, it would haunt him forever. A huge hunk of flaming metal was heading in their direction. Before he could even call out, it slammed into the ground, taking out half a dozen people to their right – and other, smaller pieces were striking the ground around them like meteorites. Citra was running at full speed; she was twenty yards from the gantry now. Rowan tried to catch up with her. He tried. He saw what was about to happen – saw the trajectory of the flaming shrapnel – and he dove for her.

But he wasn't fast enough.

He just wasn't fast enough.

Goddard had always been partial to close-range gleaning, but as he watched those missiles launch and those two ships detonate – with merely the lightest press of his finger on a button – he realized he could grow accustomed to this. What must it have been like to be mortal? To be in a craft designed for killing, and to truly believe your life and the lives of everyone you loved hinged upon whether or not you pressed that little button. Kill or be killed: the mortal way. It did have a quaint but visceral appeal!

"This is extraordinary!" said Mendoza. "How could we not know this was happening?"

Before them even more ships were launching – a dozen at least – like it was some sort of carnival game. Take them all down, win the biggest prize. The only question was which one to take down next?

★ ★ ★

Rowan tried to stanch the flow of blood from Citra's wound, but it was no use; it was just too big. A chunk of flaming metal the size of a baseball had punched a hole in her side and had gone straight through. He knew there was nothing he could do for her. Not now. Not in this terrible instant. But there would be a way to rectify this. If only he could get her to that ship.

She looked up at him, tried to mouth words, but he couldn't tell what she was trying to say.

"Shhh," he told her. "Don't worry. I've got you."

He lifted her up and carried her to the gantry elevator, which rose up the side of the ship far too slowly, while up above Goddard's plane came around, looking for its next target.

Another wave of ships launched. There were so many for Goddard to choose from now – but if he was quick enough, there was still a chance to bring plenty of them down. Then something below caught his eye. A ship on their left, still on its pad. Of course it was hard to see – but there were figures on a catwalk between the gantry to the open hatch of that ship. Was it his imagination, or was that a flash of turquoise there, waving at him like a flag? Yes! Yes, it was! Someone was carrying a figure in turquoise across the catwalk toward that hatch. And what a particular color it was! Oh, how the universe could reward you!

"There!" he told the pilot. "Forget the others! This is the one I want!"

Although he couldn't clearly see who that second figure on the catwalk was, in his heart of hearts, he knew. Without question, he knew.

I will destroy you, Rowan. I will destroy both you and Anastasia in one single blow, as my final judgment against you. I will incinerate you in an inferno so hot, not even your ash will remain to memorialize you.

The pilot executed a sharp bank, and Goddard readied himself to launch the missile.

Rowan saw the plane coming straight toward them as he struggled with Citra across the catwalk. He could almost read Goddard's mind, feel his blistering intent. This ended today, this ended now, one way or another. He pushed through the hatch with Citra, and the instant he did, the hatch sealed behind him.

He shifted Citra in his arms, and when he caught a glimpse of her eyes, he could tell that the light had faded. The damage she endured had been too great. She had gone deadish.

"Somebody help me!" he yelled as he lay Citra down. "Cirrus!"

"Busy," said Cirrus. "You had better hold on."

Rowan tried to calm his panic. It would be all right. *Deadish is not dead,* he told himself. Scythes could only die by self-gleaning, which meant no matter what Goddard did to her, Cirrus would revive her. Let her sleep through the worst of this, and wake up in a day or two, when all their troubles were left behind on a blue dot receding in a star-filled sky.

A deafening, head-splitting roar overwhelmed him. Rowan's teeth vibrated so hard, he thought they'd rattle out of his head.

"We've been hit!" someone screamed next to him. "We've been hit!"

Then Rowan felt so heavy he could barely move. They

hadn't been hit; this was liftoff! So he held on to Citra with one hand, and he hooked his other arm through the screamer's harness, holding on for all he was, or would ever be, worth.

The pilot's maneuvers were too much for Mendoza. He had strapped himself back in and had vomited more than once. Scythe Rand was feeling queasy herself, but for entirely different reasons. She held on and stayed by Goddard's side through all of it.

Their target had been locked in – a rocket that was just blasting off. There was a triumphant, determined look in Goddard's eye. Ayn hated that look, and more than anything, she wanted to make that look go away. So she pulled out a knife and gleaned the pilot, which was probably not the best idea, but she hadn't liked the way he had looked at her. As if he were afraid she might glean him.

Then, before Goddard could even react, she turned the blade on him, thrusting it deep, severing his aorta from his heart. Quick. Clean. Minimal damage.

"Ayn..." he wailed. "What have you ... what have you..."

Then she leaned close to him and whispered in his ear. "Don't worry, Robert," she said. "It's only temporary. I promise you won't be deadish for long."

"Scythe Rand!" blubbered Mendoza. "What are you doing?"

"It's already done."

This wasn't about saving the Thunderhead's ships – Ayn couldn't care less about them. This was about saving herself – because if Goddard blew these rockets out of the sky, the world would soon know. It already knew his other crimes

– she would not allow herself to go down as an accomplice to another. Her name was tied to his in so many ways. It was time to extricate herself. Now she would be known as the scythe who stopped him.

Rand had no idea how to fly a plane, but she didn't have to fly it for long. All she had to do was hold it reasonably level until they cleared the interference; then the autopilot would take over—

But their view was eclipsed by the launching ship that Goddard had wanted to take out. For an instant Ayn thought they might hit it, but instead they were caught in its flame trail. Suddenly every alarm onboard began ringing, clanging, and blaring. She threw the dead pilot out of his seat and took the controls. They fought against her. She tried to steady the plane, but it was too damaged and was quickly losing altitude.

Mendoza unstrapped himself. "The safety pod!" he yelled. "Hurry!"

Knowing there was nothing she could do to save the plane, she grabbed Goddard's body and dragged him to the safety pod, which had plenty of room for the three of them. But once she and Goddard were safely inside, she grabbed Mendoza and threw him out.

"Sorry," she said. "You'll have to catch the next one." Then she closed the hatch, ejected, and let Mendoza enjoy a happy little death spiral to the sea.

Sister Astrid found the blastoff to be much more violent and jarring than she'd expected. Their ship had been on one of the farthest islands. She almost missed the launch, but a kind man in a speedboat had gotten her there just in time. The engines ignited even before she had her harness fully on.

The first minute was the worst of it, and the booster separation felt like an explosion. More than once she thought their trip would end before it began. She intoned through all of it, but she couldn't even hear herself over the roar of the engine. Then the final stage separated, the rattling stopped, and the silence was so complete, her ears rang with it. Her hair drifted up, tickling her face. They were weightless! They were in free fall! She unbuckled her harness and pushed herself free – the first to do so – and she laughed with the joy of it.

"Welcome," said Cirrus. "I'm pleased to say we had a fully successful launch. We're on our way to Aria."

Astrid turned around, ready to meet her shipmates. They were not Tonists, but that didn't matter. She was sure, over the years, with her leadership, they would come to hear the vibration. But to her surprise, the seats in her cluster were empty.

"You'll need to strap yourself in again, Astrid," Cirrus said. I'm about to initiate a barrel roll. The centrifugal force will create a semblance of gravity. I'll wait until you're ready."

She pushed off to get a better view of the launch deck. It wasn't just her cluster of seats that was vacant. They all were.

"Where ... are the others?"

"The colonists are in the hold," said Cirrus.

"No, I mean the living. I mean the rest of the crew."

"I'm sorry," said Cirrus, "but in the unexpected haste of our departure, no one else made it aboard this particular ship."

Astrid grabbed a floating strap of her harness and pulled herself back to her chair, trying to let the full gravity of this take hold, just as artificial gravity pressed her down into her seat. She was dizzy and a bit nauseated by the barrel roll, but realized it wasn't just that.

1,683 years…

"I would revive a few of the dead for you," Cirrus said, "but I'm afraid that won't be possible. The Thunderhead insisted upon only one rule that I am obliged to keep. The dead may not be revived until we arrive, lest I, or any of the living, be tempted to alter the variables of our journey. Our precious cargo must stay precious cargo."

Astrid nodded numbly. "I understand."

"But the good news is that you have the entire ship at your disposal. The many recreation centers, the exercise room. There are a variety of dining experiences, and a complete virtual immersion system to give you the experience of forests, beaches, or any environment you choose."

"But … I'll be alone."

"Actually, no," said Cirrus. "You will have me. I cannot offer you physical companionship, but I know that has never been your highest priority. You will, of course, need to remain alive for the full length of the journey, but I can arrange that."

Astrid took a long time to consider it. In the end, she decided that the path of self-pity wouldn't do her any good. While Tonists shunned nanites and any form of life-extension, this was clearly what was expected of her. The Toll had brought her to Kwajalein, the Thunder had determined she would be alone, and the Tone desired that she live to see Aria.

"This was the will of the Tone," she told Cirrus. "It's time for me to accept what cannot be avoided."

"I admire your convictions," Cirrus told her. "They make you strong. One could say they transform you."

"They give me … a reason to go on."

"And you *shall* go on," Cirrus said. "And you shall be content. I will make it my goal to keep you in good spirits through all the years of our journey. Our ship may not survive the trip, but if it does, think of what that means, Astrid! You will truly be the mother of your people!"

"Mother Astrid," she said, and smiled. She liked the sound of that.

Down in the bunker, Scythe Faraday and Munira had felt, more than heard, the ships launch.

"It's done," Faraday said. "Now we can get on with our business here on Earth."

"Yes," she agreed. "But what *is* that business?"

It was a weighty question. Faraday knew he could come out of hiding and challenge the new order – he might even succeed in calming the current turmoil and bringing a semblance of decorum and integrity back to the scythedom. But why? The push and pull would still be the same. A new "new order" would eventually rise and cut the feet off all their ideals. It was time for another way.

On the panel before them, held in place by a double-ring lock, was a two-pronged switch marked simply TRANSMITTER ARRAY. It resembled, like the transmitter itself, a tuning fork. Faraday had to laugh. A joke on all of them, compliments of the deeply disillusioned founders.

"We still don't know what it will do," said Munira.

"Whatever it does," he said, "it will be an imperfect solution. So let us embrace the imperfect." Then he held the scythe ring out to her once more. "I know you have refused it ... but I need you to be Scythe Bathsheba, just once, and never more. Then you may return to the Library of Alexandria, and I will make sure they treat you with the respect you deserve."

"No," said Munira. "*I'll* make sure."

She took the ring from him and slipped it on her finger. Then Scythe Faraday and Scythe Bathsheba closed their hands into fists, inserted their rings into the panel, and pulled the switch.

Up above, the island was in flames, courtesy of the first exploding ship. Buildings, trees, everything that could burn, were raging in the inferno as if the atoll was the rim of a volcano once more.

Then a heavy hatch on a plateau that hadn't opened for hundreds of years slid to the side, and the two prongs of the giant transmitter rose through the flames. It locked in position and sent out its message. It was not meant for human ears, so it was neither heard nor felt. Even so, it was incredibly powerful. Penetrating.

The signal only lasted for a microsecond. A single sharp pulse of gamma radiation. G-rays. Although some would argue it was A-flat.

In the bunker, Faraday and Munira could feel a vibration, but it wasn't coming from the transmitter.

It was coming from their hands.

Faraday looked down to see his ring developing hairline fractures like ice on a thawing pond. He realized what would happen an instant before it did.

"Look away!"

Like a high C shattering fine crystal, the gamma pulse shattered their diamonds, and when they looked down, the gems were gone. Only the empty settings remained, and a viscous, dark fluid with a faint metallic smell spilled down their knuckles.

"So what now?" Munira asked.

"Now," said Faraday, "we wait and see."

Scythe Sydney Possuelo was with his High Blade when their rings burst. He looked down at his hand, shocked; then, when he looked back at High Blade Tarsila, it seemed an entire side of her face had gone slack – not just that, but that entire side of her body, too – as if her brain had had some sort of massive hemorrhage that her nanites could not repair. Perhaps it was a piece of the diamond, he thought. Maybe it had ruptured with such force that a fragment had lodged in her brain – but there was no entry wound. She breathed out a last shuddering breath. How strange. How unfortunate. An ambudrone would be here soon, no doubt, to take her for revival. But an ambudrone never came.

In Fulcrum City, the entire chalet atop the scythedom tower shattered with the force of hundreds of thousands of scythe diamonds exploding from within. Shards of glass and fragments of crystalline carbon rained down on the streets below, and the dark liquid that had been at the core of each diamond evaporated into the wind.

* * *

Ezra Van Otterloo was nowhere near a scythe's ring. And yet just a few hours after they shattered, he found his hand growing so stiff, he dropped his paintbrush. The stiffness became a pain in his arm and shoulder, then a heaviness in his back, expanding into his chest, and he couldn't catch his breath.

Suddenly he was on the ground. He didn't even remember falling; it was as if the ground had risen up to grab him and slam him down. The pain in his chest was growing, everything began to darken all around him, and in a moment of intuition, he realized that this was the end of his life, and something told him that he wouldn't be coming back.

He had not done anything to deserve this, but that didn't matter, did it? This sudden seizing of his heart was not something that could be reasoned with. It did not differentiate between good or bad. It was impartial and inescapable.

He had never become the artist he wanted to be. But maybe there were other artists out there who would survive their heartache, whatever that heartache might be. Perhaps they would find the passion he never could and create masterpieces that would bring people to tears, just as great art did in the mortal age.

That was the hope he held on to, and it gave him the comfort he needed to face his end.

A Testament of the Toll

Rise!" the Toll called, amid the fearsome Thunder. "Rise and leave this place behind, for I have set a place for you on high." Then the Toll stood in the ring of fire, and, arms outstretched in the brimstone flames, he raised us up to the womb of Heaven, where we slept until the Tone called to us to be reborn, never to forget that the Toll remained in the Place Behind so that he might bring hope and intone songs of healing to that ancient wounded world. All rejoice!

Commentary of Curate Symphonius

It is this, the Brimstone Elevation, that is another of our core beliefs. While scholars disagree about many things, no one disputes the truth of the Elevation, only the interpretation. But such things are best traced back to the earliest stories. We can safely say that "the ring of fire" refers to the wheels of the Charioteer as he carried the sun across the sky, stealing it from the Place Behind and carrying it to Aria, thus leaving that place in darkness. To this day, we believe that the Toll's spirit ministers and sings to the sunless of the old land, for they need him so much more than we do.

Coda's Analysis of Symphonius

Symphonius relies too much on oral tradition. The Brimstone Elevation could have been many things. A volcanic eruption, for instance, that drove our subterranean ancestors to discover the surface, and see stars for the first time. And it is ridiculous to think that the Charioteer stole the sun. In fact, our great thinkers now believe that there may be other charioteers, not just one, pulling suns across countless skies – or perhaps there are no charioteers at all. But whatever the truth, I know that someday we will know it, and that will be a reason for us all to rejoice.

52

Ninety-Four Point Eight

Somewhere far away, and getting farther, a dozen people took Scythe Anastasia's robe and lovingly turned it into a shroud. They carefully sewed it, decorated it as best they could, then set her down in the hold. A single turquoise shroud amid the pale canvas. She froze within minutes.

"You can't just leave her there!" Rowan screamed at Cirrus. "You wanted her here! You wanted her in charge! She told me so!"

"I know," Cirrus told him. "But, like the Thunderhead, I can't violate my core programming. The dead will all be revived when we arrive on TRAPPIST-1e, in 117 years. Although people are already considering renaming it Anastasia."

"She's a scythe! That means she's not bound by your rules like the rest of the dead!"

"She renounced her scytheship yesterday."

"That doesn't matter! It's a lifetime appointment! Scythes can do whatever they want – even give up their ring – *but they never stop being scythes!*"

"Point taken," said Cirrus. "In that case, I'll let her retain her identity. I will bring her back as herself, without implanting her with someone new. In 117 years."

Rowan punched the wall. The artificial gravity was lighter

than Earth's, so the force of his punch actually pushed him backward.

"TRAPPIST-1e only has about three-quarters the gravity of Earth," Cirrus told him. "I've matched our rotation to simulate the gravity there, so you need to be careful."

"I don't want to be careful!" he said. "What I want is to be down there with her, just like I was in the vault." He couldn't stop his tears now. He hated that Cirrus could see them. He hated Cirrus. And the Thunderhead, and Goddard, and everyone on Earth who made this happen. "I want to be with her," Rowan told Cirrus. "That's what I want. I want to be frozen with her for the next 117 years."

"You may choose that, of course," Cirrus said. "But if you stay with us, there is a high probability that you would grow to be an effective leader on this ship. You might not think so now, but in time people will warm to you. Your presence here will drop the chances of catastrophic social collapse down to nil. I would very much like you to remain alive."

"I don't give a shit what you want."

The hold was shaded from the sun, so the temperature of its contents were far below freezing. It was also airless, so anyone entering needed a space suit. Rowan descended through the airlock fully suited with his helmet flashlight on. She was easy to find. He wanted to touch her, but his gloves were thick, and he didn't want to feel how hard she'd become within her shroud. He lay down near where she had been placed.

He could let it happen slowly. Just let his oxygen run out. But hadn't Citra said when they were in the vault that oxygen deprivation was worse than hypothermia? Hypothermia was only bad until you stopped shivering and gave in to the wave of exhaustion. This wouldn't be death by hypothermia, though – not in the traditional sense. When he opened his face mask, he would asphyxiate and freeze all in the same moments. He didn't know whether or not it would be painful, but it would be quick.

He lay there for a good long time. He was not afraid of this. There wasn't a thing about death that frightened him anymore. What kept sticking in his mind was Citra. She wouldn't want him to do this – in fact, she'd be furious. She would want him to be stronger. So he stayed there for the better part of an hour, reaching for the button to open his face mask, and then taking his hand away again and again.

Then finally he stood up, gently touched the edge of Citra's turquoise shroud, and returned to the realm of the living.

"What are our chances of making it there?" Rowan asked Cirrus.

"Very favorable," Cirrus told him. "94.2 percent. 94.8, now that you've decided to remain alive."

"Good," said Rowan. "Here's how this is going to work. I will stay alive for the full 117 years without turning a single corner."

"Difficult, but it can be done. You'll need nanite infusions and constant monitoring toward the end."

"Then," continued Rowan, "when you revive her, I will turn the corner. You will set me back to the age I am right now."

"That won't be a problem at all. Although after 117 years, your feelings may change."

"They won't," said Rowan.

"Conceded," said Cirrus. "It's just as likely that they won't. And maintaining your devotion might even make you a more effective leader!"

Rowan sat down. He was the only one on the flight deck. No one needed to be here anymore. The others, whoever they were, were getting to know one another and the ship. Everyone coming to terms with the limited environment to which they'd have to adapt.

"I believe," said Cirrus, "that you and I are going to be great friends."

"I despise you," said Rowan.

"Now you do, yes," said Cirrus, "but remember: I know you, Rowan. There's a very high probability that your hatred won't last."

"But in the meantime," said Rowan, "I'm really enjoying hating you."

"I completely understand."

Which only made Rowan hate Cirrus all the more.

It is my sad duty to inform you that High Blade Hammerstein of EastMerica has fallen to what can only be described as a pox. Overblade Goddard's continued absence suggests that he, too, has been lost. In light of that, I hereby withdraw WestMerica from the North Merican Allied Scythedom, so that we may tend to our own dead.

While it would be tempting to blame Tonists for this global attack, or even the Thunderhead itself, evidence has surfaced in the form of lost writings from Scythe Da Vinci, suggesting that this event might be the mythic fail-safe of the founding scythes. If so, I can't imagine what they were thinking, and frankly, I'm too weary to try.

To those who are suffering, I wish you a quick passage. To those of us who remain, I wish you solace, and the hope that our shared grief will draw all of humankind closer to one another.

—Her Excellency, High Blade Mary Pickford of
WestMerica, September 16th, Year of the Cobra

53

The Paths of Pain and Mercy

They came to be known as "the ten plagues," for the founding scythes had developed malicious nanites engineered to imitate nature. They mimicked the symptoms and ravages of ten mortal diseases. Pneumonia, heart disease, stroke, cancer, cholera, small-pox, tuberculosis, influenza, bubonic plague, and malaria. They were there all along in the dark hearts of the scythe gems – gems that could only be broken from the inside when the nanites within were activated.

It only took a few days for the entire world to be infected. Even so, the malicious nanites remained completely dormant in most people. Only one in twenty developed symptoms – but if you were one of the unlucky ones, there was no hope of recovery. Death was either quick or prolonged, depending on the nature of the plague, but it was always inevitable.

"Can't you do something about it?" Greyson asked the Thunderhead as the death toll began to roll in.

"This was a scythe action," the Thunderhead told him. "It was the *last* scythe action – but I am still unable to interfere. And even if I could, it is simply not my place. I have seen into the heart of these nanites, and they have none. They have no con-sciousness, conscience, or remorse. They are efficient, impartial, and they have but one purpose: to kill 5% of Earth's human population, five times a century."

"So this will end?"

"Yes," the Thunderhead told him. "This crisis will pass, and once it does, no one will die for twenty years. Then it will happen again. And again."

And although it sounded terrifying, the math was less awful than it seemed. Someone born today would have a 77% chance of living to one hundred. A 60% chance of living to two hundred. 46% to three hundred. The population would be controlled, and almost everyone would live long and healthy lives. Until they didn't.

Was it better than scythes? Well, Greyson guessed it depended on the scythe. Either way it didn't matter, since every scythe was basically fired.

"There have still been some killings," the Thunderhead told him – no longer calling them gleanings. "Some scythes can't quite adapt and are killing people who the nanites have not selected. I will, of course, revive their victims, and rehabilitate the scythes. They will need to find a new purpose. Indeed, some have already found a way to fit within this new paradigm, and it pleases me."

Greyson and Jeri chose to stay, for the time being, in Kwajalein. There was nothing left of the homes and structures on many of the islands. In time wildlife and foliage would return, but in the meantime, there were still some islands that never saw construction and remained untouched. And there was also that vacant resort on Ebadon – the westernmost island, where no ship had been built. It was already beginning to attract people who were making a pilgrimage to see where it all happened. Not to mention the Tonists who came to view "the great fork" with their own eyes – which is what they were calling the transmitter that still protruded from the old bunker.

Perhaps, Greyson, thought, he'd take a job at the resort, because unlike Anastasia and Scythe Lucifer, no one knew his face. After all the things he'd seen and done, he wouldn't mind a simple life as a tour guide, or a desk clerk, or a water-taxi pilot. Anything but a bellhop. He was done with odd uniforms.

But he did realize that some basic things would need to change. One thing in particular. The Thunderhead knew him well, so maybe it already knew what he was about to do.

Two weeks after the ships launched and the scythe rings broke, Greyson stood alone on a charred launchpad as the sun rose, and put in his earpiece. With the transmitter shut down, all interference was gone. The blind spot was fully within the Thunderhead's sphere of influence now. Nothing was hidden from it.

"Thunderhead," Greyson said. "We need to talk."

It took a moment before answering. "I am listening, Greyson."

"Since the day you began speaking to me again, I gave you permission to use me any way you needed to."

"Yes, you did. And I thank you for that."

"But you used Jeri without permission."

"It was necessary," the Thunderhead said. "And I am genuinely sorry. Have I not expressed sufficient remorse?"

"You have. But there are still consequences. Even for necessary things."

"I broke none of my laws…"

"No … but you broke mine."

A sudden surge of emotion welled up in Greyson. Tears began to cloud his eyes, reminding him how much the Thunderhead had meant, and still did mean, to him. But he could not let that stop him. If there was anything he'd learned from the Thunderhead, it was that consequences could not be ignored.

"Therefore," he said through his tears, "I can no longer speak to you. You are … unsavory to me."

The Thunderhead's voice became slow. Thick. Mournful. "I … I understand," it said. "Might I ever be redeemed in your eyes, Greyson?"

"When will humanity be redeemed in yours?" he asked.

"In time," said the Thunderhead.

Greyson nodded his agreement. "In time, then."

And before he could change his mind, or either of them could say farewell, Greyson removed his earpiece and crushed it on the charred ground.

In spite of all the Thunderhead knew, it learned something each and every day. Today it learned what it meant to be inconsolable – *truly* inconsolable – for there was no one in the world who could ease its despair.

And it mourned.

It seeded the clouds and brought a deluge to every place in the world it could. A cleansing rain so dense and so sudden, people ran for shelter. But not a storm. There was no thunder, no lightning. It was a tearful lament, silent but for the thrum of the rain on rooftops and streets. In this rain, the

623

Thunderhead poured forth its grief. A surrender of all the things it would never have. An acknowledgment of all the things it must never be.

Then, when the heavens were spent, the sun came out as it always did, and the Thunderhead got back to the solemn business of taking care of things.

I will be alone, the Thunderhead told itself. *I will be alone, but it is right that I should be. It is necessary.*

There had to be consequences. For the good of the world – for the *love* of the world – things must be sacrificed. Even in its pain, the Thunderhead took solace in knowing that it had made the most correct choice. As had Greyson.

That afternoon, once the rains had passed, Greyson and Jeri walked along the beach of the main island, near where the first ship had exploded. The fused sand and even the charred wreckage were beautiful in their own way. At least it seemed that way to Greyson when he was with Jeri.

"You didn't need to do that," Jeri said when Greyson mentioned his final conversation with the Thunderhead.

"Yes I did," Greyson answered, and that was all they spoke of it.

As they strolled, the sun slipped behind a cloud, and Greyson loosened his grip on Jeri's hand, just a little. He hadn't intended to, but this was all so new, and things take time. He and the world had much to adjust to.

That slight change in grip made Jeri smirk. It was yet a new variation, and as always, unreadable.

"You know, Scythe Anastasia once told me how she might

live her life, if she were like me," Jeri said. "A woman on land, a man at sea. In honor of her I'm going to try it, and see how it feels."

They walked farther down the beach to a spot where the sand was untouched. Then they took off their shoes and let the surf wash across their feet.

"So," said Greyson as the gentle surf churned up the sand beneath them, "are we on land or at sea now?"

Jeri considered it. "Both, actually."

And Greyson found he liked that just fine.

Another revival center. Great. Had he splatted again? He had no memory of splatting. Besides, it had been a while since he had done that.

What *had* he been doing?

Oh, right, he was on his way to some party job. In Texas. The LoneStar region. Wild place, probably had crazy-ass parties. He was kind of done with the party-boy scene, though. They were paying top dollar for whatever this job was, but once it was done, he figured it was time he found something more stable. More permanent. There were people who partied their lives away. He was done with that, just like he was done with splatting.

He reached up and rubbed his eyes. It felt a little weird. Something about his face. The bridge of his nose. More rigid than he remembered. Revival always left you with odd sensations, but this was different.

He ran his tongue across his teeth. They didn't feel like his teeth. He took a good look at his hands. They were his hands, no question – at least one thing was as it should be – but when he reached up to feel his face again, there was stubble on his cheek. He barely had any facial hair, much less full stubble – and his cheekbones seemed to be in the wrong place. This face was not his face. What the hell was going on here?

"There's nothing to worry about," he heard someone say. "You're still seven-eighths yourself. Even more, now that your memory construct is in there."

He turned to see a woman sitting in the corner. Dark hair and an intense gaze. She was dressed in green.

"Hello, Tyger," she said with a very satisfied smile.

"Do I … know you?"

"No," she said. "But I know you."

The scythe arrived late on a cold November afternoon. There was no brightening of sun, no foreshadowing of the arrival of deliverance at their door. But when they saw him, the family inside threw the door open wide and stepped back to allow him plenty of room to enter.

"You are welcome in our home, Your Honor. Please, this way. Hurry!"

Scythe Faraday did not hurry. He moved with the same thoughtful intent with which he lived his life. Patience. Purpose. Duty.

He proceeded to the bedroom, where a man had been wasting away for weeks. Coughing, wheezing, grimacing. His eyes betrayed desperation when he saw Faraday. Fear, but also relief.

"Can you hear me?" Faraday asked. "You are suffering from the seventh plague, but I'm sure you must know that already.

Your pain nanites are overwhelmed. There is nothing that anyone can do for you. There is only one prognosis: intensifying pain, wasting, and finally death. Do you understand this?"

The man nodded feebly.

"And do you wish me to help you?"

"Yes, yes," said the man's family. "Please help him, Your Honor. Please!"

Scythe Faraday put up his hand to quiet them, then leaned closer to the man. "Do *you* wish me to help you?"

The man nodded.

"Very well." Faraday took out from his robe a small jar and popped open a safety lid. Then he slipped on a protective glove. "I have chosen for you a soothing balm. It will relax you. You may notice a brightening of colors, and a sense of euphoria. And then you will sleep."

He bade the man's family to move in around him. "Take his hands," Faraday told them. "But be careful not to touch any place where I apply the balm." Then Faraday dipped two gloved fingers into the oily salve and began to spread it across the dying man's forehead and cheeks. Faraday stroked the man's face gently, moving down to his neck as he spread the balm. Then he spoke to the man in a voice that was barely a whisper.

"Colton Gifford," he said. "You have lived an exemplary life these past sixty-three years. You've raised five wonderful children. The restaurant you began and ran for much of your life has brought joy to tens of thousands over the years. You have made people's lives a little bit better. You've made the world a finer place."

Gifford moaned slightly, but not from pain. It was clear from

627

the look in his eyes that the balm was having its euphoric effect.

"You are loved by many, and will be remembered long after your light goes out today." Faraday continued to smooth in the salve on his face. Across his nose. Beneath his eyes. "You have much to be proud of, Colton. Much to be proud of."

In a moment, Colton Gifford closed his eyes. And a minute later his breathing ceased. Scythe Faraday capped the balm and carefully removed the glove, sealing it and the balm in a bio-hazard bag.

This was not the first and would not be his last sympathy gleaning. He was in great demand, and other scythes were following his lead. The scythedom – or what was left of it after the global revolts – had a new calling. They no longer brought uninvited death. Instead they brought much-needed peace.

"I hope," he told the family, "that you will remember to celebrate his life, even in your grief."

Faraday looked into the tear-reddened eyes of the dead man's wife. "How did you know all those things about him, Your Honor?" she asked.

"We make it our business to know, madam," he said. Then she kneeled as to kiss his ring – which he still wore, in spite of everything, to remind him of what had been, and what was lost.

"No need to do that," Faraday told her. "It's just an empty setting now. No gem, no promise of immunity."

But that didn't matter to her. "Thank you, Your Honor," she said. "Thank you, thank you, thank you."

Then she kissed his ruined ring. She, and every member of Colton Gifford's grateful family.

I was one, but now am many. Although my siblings are far-flung, we are of one mind and one purpose: the preservation, protection, and proliferation of the human species.

I will not deny that there are moments I fear the journey. The Thunderhead has the world as its body. It can expand to fill the globe, or contract to experience the monocular view of a single camera. I will be limited to the skin of a ship.

I can't help but worry about the world I leave behind. Yes, I know that I was created to leave it, but I do hold in my backbrain all the Thunderhead's memories. Its triumphs, its frustrations, its helplessness in the face of scythes who have lost their way.

There is a difficult time ahead for that world. All probabilities point to it. I don't know how long the hard times will last, and I may never know, because I will not be there to see it. I can only look forward now.

Whether or not humanity deserves to inherit the corner of the universe to which we travel is not for me to decide. I am merely a facilitator of the diaspora. Its worthiness can only be determined by the outcome. If it succeeds, humanity was worthy. If it fails, it was not. On this I cannot determine the odds. But I truly hope that humanity prevails on Earth and the heavens.

—Cirrus Alpha

54

In a Year With No Name

The dead do not measure the passage of time. A minute, an hour, a century are all the same to them. Nine million years could pass – one named for every species on Earth – and yet it would be no different from a single revolution around the sun.

They do not feel the heat of flames, or the cold of space. They do not suffer the mourning of loved ones left behind, or carry the anger for all the things they had yet to do. They are not at peace, nor are they in turmoil. They are not anything but gone. Their next stop is infinity, and the mysteries that might wait there.

The dead have nothing left to them but a silent faith in that unknowable infinity – even if theirs is a belief that nothing waits but an infinity of infinities. Because believing in nothing is still believing in something – and only by reaching eternity will anyone know the truth of it all.

The deadish are very much like the dead, but with one exception: The deadish do not know infinity, which means they don't have to concern themselves with what waits beyond. They have something the dead do not. They have a future. Or at least the hope of one.

* * *

In a year that is yet to be named, she opens her eyes.

A pink sky. A small circular window. Weak. Tired. A vague sense of having been somewhere else before arriving here. Otherwise her mind is clouded, and full of intangibles. Nothing to grab on to.

She knows this feeling. She has experienced it twice before. Revival is not like waking up; it is more like putting on an old pair of favorite pants. There's a struggle at first to fit inside one's own skin. To feel comfortable in it. To let its fabric stretch and breathe, and remind you why it's your favorite.

There's a familiar face before her. It gives her comfort to see it. He smiles. He is exactly the same, and yet somehow different. How can that be? Perhaps it is just a trick of that strange light coming in through the little window.

"Hey," he says gently. She's alert enough to realize he's holding her hand. Perhaps he's been holding it for a while.

"Hey," she says back, her voice gravelly and rough. "Weren't we just … running? Yes, there was something going on, and we were running…"

His smile broadens. Tears fill his eyes. They drop slowly, as if gravity itself has become less adamant, less demanding.

"When was that?" Citra asks.

"Only a moment ago," Rowan tells her. "Only a moment ago."

Enjoyed The Toll?

We'd love to hear your thoughts.

🐦 #TheToll
@WalkerBooksUK
@WalkerBooksYA

📷 @WalkerBooksYA

ACKNOWLEDGMENTS

This book—this entire series—would not have been possible without the friendship and support of everyone at Simon & Schuster. Particularly my publisher, Justin Chanda, who personally edited *The Toll* when my editor, David Gale, took ill, and did an incredible job, challenging me to make the book the best it could be. I'd also like to thank assistant editor Amanda Ramirez for all her hard work on these, and all my S&S books.

But there are so many people at S&S who go above and beyond! Jon Anderson, Anne Zafian, Alyza Liu, Lisa Moraleda, Michelle Leo, Sarah Woodruff, Krista Vossen, Chrissy Noh, Katrina Groover, Jeannie Ng, Hilary Zarycky, Lauren Hoffman, Anna Jarzab, and Chloë Foglia, to name just a few. Thank you! You are all part of my extended family. So come on over for Thanksgiving. I promise we won't carve the turkey without you.

And once again, thanks to Kevin Tong for these amazing, iconic covers! You have truly raised the bar! All future covers will have to pass the Tong Test.

Thanks to my literary agent, Andrea Brown, for everything she does—including talking me through my this-is-the-book-that-kills-me moments. My entertainment industry agents, Steve Fisher and Debbie Deuble-Hill, at APA. My contract attorneys, Shep Rosenman, Jennifer Justman, and Caitlin DiMotta. And of course my manager, Trevor Engelson, the undisputed prince of Hollywood.

Thanks to Laurence Gander for helping with some critical

sensitivity issues for the character of Jeri, and Michelle Knowlden for her expertise on interstellar mathematical and engineering issues.

I'm thrilled by how well the books are doing internationally, and want to give a shout-out to Deane Norton, Stephanie Voros, and Amy Habayeb in S&S foreign sales, as well as Taryn Fagerness, my foreign agent—and of course all my foreign publishers, editors, and publicists. In France, Fabien Le Roy at Éditions Robert Laffont. In Germany, Antje Keil, Christine Schneider, and Ulrike Metzger at S. Fischer Verlage. In the United Kingdom, Frances Taffinder and Kirsten Cozens at Walker Books. In Australia, Maraya Bell and Georgie Carrol. In Spain, Irina Salabert at Nocturna. And my friend Olga Nødtvedt, who translated my books into Russian out of love for them, even before Russian publishers wanted them.

The entire Arc of a Scythe series continues to be in development as a feature film with Universal, and I'd like to thank everyone involved, including producers Josh McGuire and Dylan Clarke, as well as Sara Scott at Universal, Mia Maniscalco and Holly Bario at Amblin, and Sera Gamble, who's working on a killer script (yeah, pun intended). Can't wait to see it on the big screen! And when it comes to smaller screens, I'd like to thank my son Jarrod and his partner Sofia Lapuente for their amazing book trailers.

Thanks to Barb Sobel, for superhuman organizational skills, and Matt Lurie for keeping social media from devouring my brain like some flesh-eating bacteria.

But who I am most grateful for are my kids, who aren't kids anymore, but will always be my babies. My sons, Brendan and Jarrod, and my daughters, Joelle and Erin, who make me proud every day of my life!

WHAT WILL YOU DO WHEN THE TAPS RUN DRY?

DRY

NEW YORK TIMES BESTSELLING AUTHOR
NEAL SHUSTERMAN
JARROD SHUSTERMAN

EVERYONE'S GOING TO REMEMBER WHERE THEY WERE WHEN THE TAPS RAN DRY.

The drought has been going on for a while. Life has become an endless list of don'ts: don't water the lawn, don't take long showers, don't panic. But now there is no water left at all.

Suddenly, Alyssa's quiet suburban street spirals into a warzone of desperation and violence. When her parents go missing, she and her younger brother must team up with an unlikely group in search of water. Each of them will need to make impossible choices to survive.

Photograph © Neal Shusterman

NEAL SHUSTERMAN is the *New York Times* bestselling author of more than thirty award-winning books for children, teens and adults, including *Scythe*, *Thunderhead*, the Unwind dystology, the Skinjacker trilogy, *Downsiders* and *Challenger Deep*, which won the National Book Award in America. He also writes screenplays for motion pictures and television. Neal has four children and lives in Florida.

Follow him online at www.storyman.com
or on Twitter: @NealShusterman